'I think in England it often rains "cats and dogs", but I wonder how surprised you British people would be if one day it started to rain £5 notes. This is what nearly happened during the war. Hitler and Himmler planned to pour English money all over your country from aeroplanes. £5, £10 and £20 notes would have floated down all over the larger towns and villages. Millions and millions of them. And I was ordered to make all these notes – every one had to be perfect, just like the real ones. Just think what it would have done to your people. It would have created a beautiful chaos. The value of the British pound would have dropped to nothing, and soldiers and workers would have found their pay packets valueless. It would have had such a terrible psychological effect. It would have corrupted your whole nation. Imagine men and women fighting to pick up all those millions of pounds. Then they would all stop work and start spending them before the Government could stop them. Of course it never happened. But I made all the money and it was stored in safes in Berlin. Hitler wanted to use it as a secret weapon just before he invaded England. Then everyone would have been so confused with money that everything would come to a standstill. But there was a last-minute hitch . . .'

Alfred Naujocks,
from *The Man Who Started the War*
by Gunther Peis

PRIVATE SCHULZ
Jack Pulman

Novelised by
Martin Noble

NEW ENGLISH LIBRARY/TIMES MIRROR

A New English Library Original Publication, 1981
Copyright © 1981 by Jack Pulman
Novelisation Copyright © 1981 by Martin Noble

First NEL paperback edition 1981

NEL Books are published by
New English Library Limited,
Barnard's Inn, Holborn,
London EC1N 2JR.
Printed and bound in Great Britain by
Collins, Glasgow

450 04335 5

Disclaimer

This is a work of fiction. Though it is based on the true story as told to Peter Eton by John Otto Rasch about his involvement in Operation Bernhard and other activities by the SS during the Second World War, and many of the characters and situations in the story are based on real people and incidents, it is in all other respects fictional, and any resemblance to living people is purely coincidental.

In particular, the authors and publishers would like to point out the following:

1 The resemblance between the character and background of Alfred Neuheim and Alfred Naujocks is intentional, though obvious fictional licence has been taken.

2 Ephraim Solokoff is a pseudonym for Solomon Smolianov, one of the chief forgers who worked on Operation Bernhard, and whose whereabouts since the war are unknown.

3 The various references to the prison in Hamburg are purely fictional.

4 All references to Frederick Schwend are supported by documentary evidence.

5 The various references to the activities of the British police and Intelligence agents during and after the war are fictional, though based on a true incident.

6 According to Rasch the canister was buried near Maidstone. References to people and places around the area of Brenzett are therefore again fictional.

7 The names of the two British agents kidnapped by Naujocks at Venlo, and the actual way in which the kidnapping took place, have been changed, though again this is based on a true incident.

8 The major output of Operation Bernhard is still, to the authors' knowledge, buried in Lake Toplitz.

Prologue

'Come in, young man, don't be shy.'

He threaded himself through the dangling beaded curtain at the threshold of the booth. Inside, it was a magic emporium, reeking of mystery and incense. Behind a table covered with silver lace sat a lady with long painted nails and crimson lipstick, her cheeks stained with rouge and her eyes, like crystal balls, fixing him in their penetrating stare from beneath hooded eyelids. His grandmother would not have approved.

'I can see that you're not shy at all,' said the lady, waving him to a chair opposite her. He was pinned to her eyes. 'You're quite an intelligent young man, aren't you?'

He nodded.

'And a little bit crafty. Yes, I would say there's quite a lot of craft in you. You are one for schemes, young man. Great schemes and great dreams. Let me see your hand.' He held it out and she stroked the palm with her long, long nails. It tickled.

'Your head line is strong,' she intoned. She pointed to a line that ran parallel to the first line and swerved off at a crazy tangent. 'That is your heart line. You are a man with a great heart, but wayward. You are a hunter, a man for the chase, and you must beware of letting your imagination run away with you. You will discover many means but you will forget that there are also many ends. Be warned of letting too few ends justify too many means.' She stared at him again and he nodded, in a trance. 'But I see that you are kind – and that is a saving grace, for if your purposes are the right ones –'

She left the sentence hanging, leaving him to wonder what the right purposes could be. The lady seemed to be in

7

a trance herself: she was still stroking his palm with her nails. Beneath the rouge she seemed to blush.

'Shuffle these and take a card,' she said in a voice as dark as the booth, handing him a tarot pack. He did so.

'The Searcher – as I thought: you will search long and hard, but do not forget that the Searcher sits on a patch of diamonds.'

Automatically he looked under the chair. The lady was now opening a huge black tome.

'When were you born, my dear?'

'21 March 1909,' he replied. She gasped.

'The cusp,' she said. 'Pisces and Aries: you sit between the two greatest stools in the heavenly bodies and you must take care not to fall through the middle.'

He moved uneasily in his chair.

'I am the Alpha and the Omega,' she chanted, 'the beginning and the end.... You, young man, are destined for something immense and extraordinary, yet deep and hidden. In you is a potential for a future the like of which the world has never known ... I will now look into the crystal.'

She gazed long and hard into the crystal and a puzzled look crept across her face.

'That's ... that's extraordinary!'

'What is it? What do you see?' he asked.

Instead of replying she got up from her chair and switched on a light. The booth instantly looked more like a junk room than a magic emporium. There was a half-eaten sandwich and a bottle of beer on the floor.

She stared once more at the crystal ball.

'It's still there!' she gasped.

'What is?' he said, leaning forward to look for himself.

A look of pure greed had leapt into her eyes. She gazed at him as though he were the rest of her sandwich.

'Money,' she murmured. 'I see money. Money surrounds you wherever I look.'

8

1

There was talk of war in the intellectuals' wing these days but Schulz wasn't interested. As far as he was concerned, all war was treason to the self, in which subject he had an intense personal interest. It was not simply a question of cowardice, though it was true that people in authority had always frightened him – not a good start in life for a German and certainly not much help to him in prison. It was more that Schulz regarded the human race as utterly, hopelessly mad, and from an early age this had caused a certain healthy cynicism to breed in him like an antibiotic. In a bolder man this might have developed into arrogance. But the fact of the matter was that Gerhardt Otto Schulz genuinely didn't like to hurt other people's feelings, besides which he had decided it would be prudent not to make known his own until the time was ripe.

Time ripened erratically with Schulz, like a distorted clock in a Dali landscape. As a result he tended to oscillate between long periods of extreme caution and sudden bursts of genius as he swung manically close to his own particular sun on an elliptical orbit through life. He had, as a child, been made uncomfortably aware of this tendency and had developed, as a protection against its most harmful side effects, a habitual meekness of manner – which some construed as slyness – behind which his brain peeped out at the world like a pre-electronics pocket calculator. Most of the time it was quietly content to add up and subtract but at peak hours it would speed up dramatically, dividing and multiplying like an amoeba that had struck lucky, until some automatic fuse within him shut off the whole thing before it exploded.

On this trembling day in late March 1939 Schulz and his brain were more in danger of implosion, such was his apprehension of imminent collision with a destructive comet.

The comet in question was Herr Untermeyer, governor of Hamburg prison, down the corridor of which Schulz was being marched for his pre-discharge sermon. The stench of skilly and carbolic and the cocktail of metal polish and urine turned his stomach, which had already been prodded mercilessly by the podgy finger of the head warder, Beck, as though he were trying to poke one of his rusty keys into a particularly intransigent lock.

'Step! Step! Keep in step!' bellowed Beck, giving Schulz an extra hard dig as they reached the governor's office. 'Wait for the Governor!' he added, as if Schulz was an obedient but affectionate spaniel who couldn't wait to drown Herr Untermeyer in passionate licks.

It was the practice for Beck to brief Herr Untermeyer in advance, hand him the departing prisoner's dossier and remind him of the prisoner's good points, so that the governor had them at his fingertips when the prisoner was ushered into his presence. Schulz had already seen the Welfare Man who, with childlike innocence, had formulated his standard diagnosis for all criminal tendencies.

'Misunderstood,' said the Welfare Man. Schulz would have given him gold for it.

On the other side of the office door he could hear Beck singing his praises.

'Complete fraud,' he heard. 'Thorough bad hat.'

Behind him the cell doors began to clang as they brought the skilly round on a trolley. Schulz didn't have any clear idea of what was happening in the outside world, and he wasn't entirely looking forward to finding out. It wasn't that he was suffering from jail fever, the sort that old lags like his friend Ephraim Solokoff, the Jewish-Russian forger, had. That kind had been in so long they were frightened to see real trees. It was that the real world out there was three years worse, if that were possible. The general conversation in the prison canteen didn't concern itself much with politics, but in the intellectuals' wing the whisper was going through that you had to be a Party man to sell an honest match in the street. Schulz, who had a university education of sorts, might have put this more aptly, but he had to admit

10

that the message was loud and clear. With his record, it was likely that he would find it difficult to make a start again and it was therefore all the more important that he made a correct impression on Herr Untermeyer.

Presently Beck returned, looking inflamed and frustrated.

'Right – next!' he bawled. Schulz looked round as though he were at the head of a queue, but there was only one of him.

'You!' barked Beck. 'Are you blind? Step forward!'

In fact Schulz was a little short-sighted and for that reason he wore steel-rimmed spectacles which lent him a slightly owlish appearance, though some called it crafty. He adjusted them, his hair and his uniform and stepped forward.

'Stand before the Governor!'

The door opened and Schulz found himself staring at a bottle of Schnapps in a bookcase, noticing *Mein Kampf* prominently displayed beside it and a photograph of the Fuhrer on the wall behind, with a gold eagle above. Herr Untermeyer stood framed in the middle, a stern looking man with a close-cropped iron-grey head. Schulz found himself trembling.

'So you are leaving us, Schulz?' he said in a kindly tone. Schulz had been misinformed.

'Yes, Herr Untermeyer,' he said, standing stiff and erect on the carpet in front of him.

'This was your second term in prison.'

'Yes, sir.'

'The first for defrauding an old lady of her life savings.'

'I prefer to think, Herr Untermeyer,' Schulz replied with some dignity, 'that I invested them badly. I was young and inexperienced.'

Herr Untermeyer nodded slowly, not wholly convinced. 'And this time it was also for fraud. You raised money, life savings in some cases, to form a company that was supposed to make gold from iron oxide and quartz by heating them in an electric furnace – a chemical impossibility.'

'It wasn't considered so at the time, Herr Untermeyer. I think I can truthfully say that our company was the first

11

to prove, beyond a shadow of a doubt, that it simply couldn't be done!'

'I shall never understand how normally sane people allow themselves to be fooled so easily,' Herr Untermeyer sighed. 'Well, I hope you've learned your lesson. A man of your education and abilities should amount to something, not spend his life in prison.'

That was precisely Schulz's intention – but he was actually thinking along rather different lines.

'The Welfare Officer has a high opinion of your intelligence, Schulz. His opinion is that you are often misunderstood. And I see that you have a gift for languages that has never been utilized.'

'Ah yes, sir. That was my English grandmother.'

'English, French, it says here ... Serbo-Croat? And some Dutch too,' the governor said, squinting at the form sheet.

'In the diamond business in a small way. Amsterdam.' Schulz was wondering where all this was leading.

'Then there is every hope you may be of some use to the Fatherland, Schulz?' It was posed more as a question than a statement.

Nothing was further from Schulz's mind. Not only was he frightened of people in authority, but he had never believed in the Fatherland. Of course, looking back later, he realized that every German of his age had said this, but in his case it was genuine.

'Knowing how hard it is for a man leaving prison to find work,' Herr Untermeyer continued, 'I have arranged a post for you with a most civic-minded employer, a most patriotic man, Herr Krauss of Krauss Underwear. He is short of staff due to conscription and will give you employment. Let us hope that peace will prevail and that you will make good there.'

In the prison garden, early daffodils stood in file at precisely measured distances like sentries, not a petal out of place. Here was Germany of the old order, thought Schulz, correct to the last detail, the last measured lump of soil.

Even the breeze came through the courtyard at a precise right angle and it could almost be heard marking time.

'One off,' Beck said to the gate officer. '*Herr* Schulz.'

Beck smiled his crooked razor-slashed smile, showing stumps of teeth like lumps of brown sugar dotted in his gums. He'd replaced his cap and now the visor bisected his face and his eyes glistened.

'You'll be back,' he said.

Malevolence flooded every vein of his rheumy eyes like watered red ink.

'Thanks, Beck,' said Schulz.

He was still trembling as he went through the gate and the sweet smell of the air did not calm him. He had been ejected on to the streets like an unwanted pfennig from a slot machine. Perhaps at that moment he had an inkling that he had just finished being an almost-free man.

2

'The clouds of war are gathering,' Schulz muttered to himself behind his morning paper, 'and this time there's going to be an unholy smash-up. No more peace conferences. This time, everybody's going to fight. The point is, what can I do about it?'

What Schulz really meant was, 'What can I do to get out of it?'

'I think there's going to be a war this time, Herr Schulz,' his landlady said as she put down his morning cup of ersatz coffee, 'and, personally, I would welcome it. It will clear the air.'

'It will certainly do that,' Schultz agreed, turning to the situations-vacant column. 'It may clear a lot of other things too.'

'It's what we've all been waiting for,' she went on, 'and to tell you the truth I'll be glad to get it over with. It's like that operation I had done last year. It wasn't nearly as bad having it done as thinking about it.'

Schulz tried not to think about it. The thought of Frau Nusbaum's hysterectomy held no pleasure for him, but it seemed to give her endless satisfaction for she went on :

' "Now, don't worry, Frau Nusbaum," that young doctor said, "I'm removing the nursery not the playroom".' She smiled coyly at Schulz whose eyes flicked dutifully up over the top of his paper. 'Herr Nusbaum would have approved of that. Herr Nusbaum had such a sense of humour. He was quite noted for it. What a pity you never met him.'

Schulz smiled weakly. Herr Nusbaum's image stood on the mantelpiece. If the eyes had ever twinkled they didn't now.

'Playroom!' She laughed what she imagined to be her high, tinkling laugh and no doubt thought of as a thousand tiny silver bells. 'Playroom,' she repeated. 'What a thing to say!'

'Anyway,' said Schulz as he always did, 'I'm sure you feel better for it.'

'Well, of course,' Frau Nusbaum replied. 'Wouldn't you? And anyway,' she added, 'it does remove a lot of problems. After all, even at my age – well, you never can tell.'

Schulz said nothing. He couldn't afford to offend Frau Nusbaum. Times had been difficult since he came out of prison. His room was very cheap and comfortable and there were little things on the side that he appreciated. One of the little things on the side that he did not appreciate was Frau Nusbaum's playroom which he felt obliged to enter every Saturday night. It was excessively roomy. He felt that his presence went almost unnoticed and that vast barn of a place would have accommodated Herr Nusbaum as well without seeming overcrowded. If the truth were known, he would have preferred the smaller attic room at the back but when he once tentatively approached her on this subject she had been shocked and replied, firmly, that that had belonged exclusively to Herr Nusbaum and she could not think of its use by a mere guest.

Fortunately, he was expected in only on Saturday nights after they had both consumed several bottles of dark brown beer, purchased by Frau Nusbaum as her small treat: a ritual, she explained, initiated by her husband which she was now happy to carry on with Herr Schulz. What pleasure she derived from these little Saturday night escapades Schulz couldn't imagine. If it meant so little to him what on earth could it mean to her? Yet as each Saturday night approached her eyes sparkled more brightly, the laughter tinkled more bells, her soft, quivering flesh would somehow contrive to brush against him as they passed on the stairs or in the kitchen, and by four o'clock on a Saturday afternoon she was locked in the bathroom singing gaily and splashing water and he knew in his sinking heart that the playroom was being thoroughly done out again.

'And what will you do when war breaks out, Herr Schulz? You're not too old to fight.'

Schultz had been thinking much the same. He has escaped the carnage of the first insanity by the skin of his milk teeth and was hoping to do the same with the second. But it was now touch and go. He was thirty, and while he knew he wouldn't be the first to go, if it lasted long enough, which he was certain it would, the war would catch up with him.

'I'm ready to do whatever the country and the Fuhrer require of me,' said Schulz imperturbably, reciting the standard formula of the sane in these circumstances.

'I'm glad to see you're not one of those rushing for reserved occupations,' Frau Nusbaum observed. 'We had a lot of those in the last war, though Jews mainly, and a very hard time we gave them, I can tell you. I simply cannot be doing with people who use every trick to dodge their duty to the government.'

'But wasn't it the government who reserved them for essential work?'

'Well, that may be,' replied Frau Nusbaum, 'but that doesn't make it any better. A man should be prepared to fight for his country whatever the government says, just as a woman is prepared to bear children. Will you join up straight away?'

'I think,' said Schulz, 'we must avoid clogging up the

15

machinery. Too many people of my age rushing to join the army would create bottlenecks, you know.' He lifted his head aggressively. 'We have a patriotic duty to avoid bottlenecks in time of war.'

'That's true,' Frau Nusbaum agreed, rather impressed. 'Still, I suppose it won't be long before you receive the call. Mind you, Herr Schulz, I should miss you. The playroom will seem – empty.'

Impulsively, she stretched out a plump little hand and covered his. The jellied touch of that soft white flesh produced – as always – an intense urge to tear himself away, which – as always – he resisted. It was not entirely out of self-interest. He hated to wound anyone's feelings, even Frau Nusbaum's. So, instead, he patted the jelly with his free hand and gently slid his other hand from beneath hers.

'Ah, well,' she sighed, 'perhaps it will all be over in a few weeks and you won't need to go.'

Perhaps it will, perhaps it won't, thought Schulz, *but I can't afford to take chances.* Frau Nusbaum rose to get on with her morning work while Schulz quickly scanned the situations vacant. Some situations were clearly going to be reserved, they always were. What was certain was that selling ladies' underwear would merit scant consideration.

That the world was mad Schulz had no doubt. His whole life experience proved it. Having been born a few years before the First World War he had been old enough to follow the sequence of lunatic events that came after. They were the first to suggest to Schulz that there were several screws loose in the human head. Schulz laughed out loud whenever he thought of them.

That great cataclysm had ended with fifty million dead and the victors had promptly demanded that Germany pay for the war damage. This was called reparations. Germany's economy, however, had been smashed to smithereens. How could it make war reparations when it had nothing to make them with?

16

Solemnly, the victors provided the losers with money to restart their economy and pay the reparations. The losers then worked very hard to pay off this immense debt. Millions of tons of goods began flowing out of the country and the victors were delighted. But not for long.

The German workers who had been paid to make them, now had virtually no goods left in the country to spend their wages on. Naturally, the price of what was left began to rise and went on rising until their money bought nothing at all. The value of the mark was annihilated. Once more the economy lay shattered, and victor and loser gaped at each other across the ruins brought about in the great inflation of 1923.

The victors began again. They lent the losers more money, this time to stabilize the mark and get the economy going again in order to send more goods to the victors to pay not only for the war damage but also, now, for the further huge sums of money they had lent the losers to stabilize the mark. It was insane, but not yet as insane as what was to follow.

The losers restarted their economy once more, but as soon as the goods began flowing off the assembly lines and on to the ships bound for the ports of the victors, the victors began to complain bitterly that these goods were hurting their economies by depressing their home markets and creating unemployment.

Many conferences were called to solve this problem but by the time the victors had worked out how best to receive these goods with the smallest damage to themselves, everyone was producing so many goods that the victors decided they were better off without them. This, of course, threw even more people out of work, not only in Germany but everywhere else. When the victors finally admitted defeat and decided that the losers need pay no more war reparations, the losers complained bitterly about it and added one more injustice to their collection.

Thus Schulz was under no illusions about the sort of world he lived in. The problem was to survive in it. Judging quickly that the key to survival was money and in that case

17

he had better understand it properly, he had entered a university on leaving school and acquired a sound knowledge of finance, though he was compelled to leave after two years through lack of it.

The years that followed were very hard for Schulz, as they were for millions of others. He had had no proper training but by the time he went to prison for the first time, in 1931, he had gained a qualification that would impress Untermeyer and Beck and which would eventually precipitate him into the most amazing events of his life.

He had acquired this knowledge by an accident of birth and through an exceptionally good ear. His grandmother had been English, a governess who had settled and married in Germany in the 1870s. At the age of sixteen, he had been sent to stay with relatives in Kent where he also went to school. He never forgot that time. The village girls were extraordinarily free compared with their German cousins. Schulz was, by nature, shy and not overly attractive in appearance but because he was foreign, and therefore different, the girls were more generous than he had a right to expect. He remained forever grateful for the way and the frequency with which they brought him out and brought him on. He returned home to all intents and purposes English, too English for his grandmother who must have imagined England, when she sent him, to be in the same high, moral climate she had left it in.

After being compelled to leave university, Schulz had been unemployed for some time. Then, in 1928, he had taken a post offered by a wealthy family, the head of whom was a Dutch-Jewish banker. He was engaged to teach the children German and English. He hoped, in the meantime, to learn something of the world of banking. Closeness to money always warmed him.

After two years in Amsterdam, the family had moved to Zurich and later to Zagreb where Schulz stayed with them for another year or so. In Amsterdam he acquired fluency in Dutch, in Zurich he acquired a great knowledge of the street names, and in Zagreb a fluency in Serbo-Croat. All this time Schulz lived a life of comparative luxury, acquiring not only a knowledge of the finer things in life but a taste for them. But all this would end when the world economy turned round in one more circle and fell over again.

Schulz returned to Germany late in 1930 where, instead of millions being out of work because of too much money, as they had been during the great inflation, they were now out of work because of too little. *There is something crazy about this system,* Schulz remembered thinking. *The working man cannot win.*

Early in 1931 he found work as a messenger in a small printing firm and had taken lodgings with a middle-aged widow who, like Frau Nusbaum, had become very affectionate. She had a fair amount of money saved and Schulz spent hours explaining to her what a fine printer he was and how, with her money and his skill, they could set themselves up in business. Neither was he backward in pressing her hand often while he spoke.

He had borrowed a little money to buy machinery, refusing to take more than the deposit and taking her with him to select it. Instead, however, of paying the deposit on the machinery, he had used it to set up a delinquent youth he had met at the labour exchange in a small office as a solicitor.

The youth, having been a solicitor's clerk, knew something of the law of conveyancing, and when Schulz found the premises he wanted to buy, or told the widow he wanted to buy, the youth represented with some skill both parties to the transaction, the widow and the mythical owner.

By an extraordinary coincidence the widow met, at the house of a relative, the real owner of the empty premises who declared himself totally ignorant of any such impending sale. Investigations followed and, unfortunately for Schulz, the widow was persuaded to allow the negotiations to proceed to their completion. At the very moment that the large sum of money passed from the lady's hands into that of the delinquent youth, a police officer stepped into the room and arrested both him and Schulz. The widow burst into tears.

The court had been severe. It was a wicked and despicable thing to deceive a widow in that way. Such confidence tricks struck at the roots of German society, destroying people's faith in one another and leading, in the end, to anarchy. Schulz did not dispute this, yet it seemed small, as confidence tricks went, compared with the one that had been played on him during the great inflation, when a little inheritance from his father had been wiped out overnight. He could never work out where it had gone or who had it.

When Schulz emerged from prison for the first time in January 1933 something catastrophic seemed to have happened to Germany. The nation seemed divided into two armed camps, reflected in frequent clashes on the streets, public marches and public demonstrations. Adolf Hitler, a little man in a light brown trench coat and a lock of hair that fell across his forehead, had become Reich Chancellor. Before he went into prison, Schulz had seen his photograph staring out from the pages of newspapers, heard his voice from time to time on the wireless, but had taken little interest in him. Now, next to the ageing idiot Hindenburg, he had become the most important man in the country.

Everywhere the talk was of the Fuhrer and Germany and of dedicating oneself unselfishly to the state. This worried Schulz. The capacity of the human race periodically to commit acts of unselfishness was one of the forms its madness often took. It seemed to break out from time to time, like the flu, and Schultz didn't like it. A man acting in his own self-interest was unlikely to do much damage to the fabric of human society. He was apt to be limited, after all, by the dedication of everyone else to *his* own self-interest. The trouble with this craze for unselfishness was that people tended to forget where their own self-interest lay. Schultz was uncomfortably aware from his reading of history that people were capable of acting more ruthlessly in the unselfish pursuit of a public interest than ever they were in pursuit of their own – and it scared the hell out of him.

His second term of imprisonment was not for such an absurd crime as Herr Untermeyer, the governor, had made it sound.

20

In Hamburg Schulz had met a chemical engineer, Albrecht, who had developed a theory of harmonic chemistry and a mathematics to measure the supposed related vibrations of the elements. As a result he believed that gold could be made economically from iron oxide and quartz by heating them in an electric furnace at very high temperatures. Schulz understood nothing of the mathematics and was certain it was all nonsense, but Albrecht was a brilliant and well-known chemist. What was not so generally well known was that he was unsound of mind. Schulz had sized that up at the first meeting.

For a number of years now, people had been trying to make gold in various scientific ways since there was a world shortage, and Schulz saw the possibility, in the current climate of insanity, of making a lot of money for himself and clearing out of the country.

He formed a company with Albrecht and raised enough money to buy some rudimentary equipment. Albrecht's first experiment was a total failure which certainly did not surprise Schulz, who had expected nothing less. The object of the experiment for Schulz was to find a way of ensuring that a particle of gold was found in the crucible when it was withdrawn from the furnace during the public demonstration that was to be arranged for prospective shareholders.

This he did. The demonstration was a success and money began flowing into the company, several leading Party officials, including Dr Ley, the Labour minister, contributing heavily. Unfortunately, just as Schulz had accumulated sufficient funds in a bank account in Switzerland, Albrecht went completely mad and had to be locked up. Investigations were carried out and questions raised as to how particles of gold had ever found their way into the crucibles, since experiments carried out with Schulz in custody were never as successful as when he was at large. In 1936 he was sentenced to four years hard labour in the Hamburg jail.

In March 1939 he emerged.

Schulz folded the newspaper down several times to frame an

21

advertisement that had caught his eye. His heart beat a little faster. It was for postal censorship and required a knowledge of at least four languages. Now that was heartening. A job in postal censorship could be made to order for him. The German bureaucracy was vast, a honeycomb of tiny offices where a man might live out his life unmolested and untroubled.

An endless game could be played. Simple laws could be found to be defective until they had been sufficiently complicated. Complicated laws could be found to be unworkable until they had been simplified. Simplifications involved complication, and complication created new posts for those needed to deal with the complexities created by the defects of the new simplifications. It was never-ending. Jobs spawned jobs.

Schulz was as aware of this as any other German and felt immensely encouraged by it. Not having to leave for the office for another ten or fifteen minutes, he went up to his room, took out paper and pen and wrote a letter applying for the post. He sealed it carefully and posted it on the way to work.

3

Schulz heard nothing for several weeks. His anxiety grew with the passing of time and the increasing frequency with which the Fuhrer referred to his eastern neighbour, Poland. It cropped up ominously, every time he opened his mouth, and to be mentioned by the Fuhrer, even in passing, meant that a subject had to be viewed with as much apprehension as an invitation to a drink with the Borgias. Now Hitler had pulled another ace from his pack – an agreement with his most implacable enemy, Russia. There was no end to the somersaults this man could turn. He mesmerized everyone. They stared, stupified, as he somersaulted nearer and nearer, each somersault higher than the last, until he landed perfectly upright on his two feet in front of them and with his hands clamped firmly around their throats. There was no mistaking it. Poland was for the chop and, this time, Britain and France would fight. About that there was no doubt in anyone's mind, except, curiously enough, the Fuhrer's. He firmly believed they wouldn't. His intuition told him so.

Still, this only added to Schulz's anxiety for if the collection of lethal lunatics now running the country actually thought the democracies *would* fight, it might have given them pause. As it was, the war was now certain and Schulz's desperation increased with each passing day. Finally, two days before the Fuhrer ordered his troops to march, a small buff envelope landed on the clean woolly mat in Frau Nusbaum's hall. She brought it up in a state of some excitement.

'Is it your calling-up papers, I wonder?' she asked.

Schulz's heart missed a beat. It was more than possible. He tore open the envelope with shaking hands and read the letter inside. It was short and to the point. He was to call at the address given above at 10.30 the following morning and bring all relevant documentation with him. He was to ask for a Herr Ditzer. The signature underneath was undecipherable.

'They want to see me in connection with a job in the postal service,' said Schulz.

'Why, Herr Schulz, surely a man of your standing wouldn't want to become a postman?'

'It has nothing to do with delivering mail,' Schulz answered testily. 'It's in postal censorship.'

'But doing what?' asked Frau Nusbaum.

'That I am not at liberty to say,' Schulz replied with a touch of importance. 'Censorship, after all, must begin at home.'

It required only a short detour on his way to work. The address was on the east side of Hamburg, a district he knew quite well, and it didn't take him long to find it – a grey,

23

four-storey building with offices on each floor leading o
the stone staircase and a rickety old lift that trundled u
and down in its own good time or not at all as the fanc
took it.

Schulz opened the first door he found on the ground floc
corridor and went inside. There were row after row of desk
one behind the other. Behind each sat a man, pen in han
head bent over forms of buff and pink and white, som
bound in ledgers, others lying loosely on the desk. As h
entered they all stopped working and looked up at him, pe
held poised as if ready to resume writing the instant h
turned round and went out again. No one spoke. No one g
up to come and see him.

He cleared his throat and said, 'I'm looking for He
Ditzer.'

No one moved. There was an air of sullen surprise that h
should have spoken at all.

'Do you know where I can find Herr Ditzer?' he repeatec
but the question trailed off into a thick tangle of silenc
followed by the resumption of nib-scratching as the eyes lo
all interest in him and returned to their desks. Schu
flushed.

'I would like to see Herr Ditzer,' he shouted sharply. '
there no one here with any manners at all?'

Once more the pens stopped scratching and the eyes fixe
themselves on him. In the new silence, a grey-haired ma
rose from his desk at the rear of the large room and cam
slowly towards him, a look of reproof on his face.

'There is no Herr Ditzer here,' he said.

'Then you might have said so before,' Schulz replied. 'D
you imagine people ask these questions because they'v
nothing better to do?'

'You didn't address yourself to anyone in particular,' th
man replied, 'and it seems to me very bad manners to ent
a room and address us all as if we had no individuality.'

'I'm not here to be lectured on manners,' said Schul
shifting his case of samples to the other hand. 'I'm her
to see Herr Ditzer and I'm a busy man. Please tell me wher
I can find him.'

'I have no idea where you can find him,' the man explained patiently, 'since I do not know the gentleman. For all I know he may be in South America.'

'This *is* the post office I suppose?' Schulz asked with a touch of acidity.

'No, this is Main Drainage,' answered the man, 'the post office is next door. You have come in at the wrong entrance.'

Schulz cursed under his breath, turned on his heel and walked out, rather rudely, he reflected afterwards, since the mistake was obviously his. Yet his mistake, which was, after all, a simple human error, had been compounded by their wooden indifference. *What is it about our national character*, he reflected as he left the building and found his way to the next, *that elevates precision and attention to detail to the level of a national obsession? We lack balance*, he added to himself as he pushed open the door of the first office, *we definitely lack balance*.

The chief clerk, or so Schulz presumed him to be, came out of a smaller office into the large one and took the letter. He studied it for so long that Schulz began to get nervous once again.

'This is the post office?' he asked with a short laugh. 'I went next door by mistake.'

'Yes, yes,' the man answered rather impatiently, 'this is the post office.' He studied Schulz for a while, thoughtfully. Then he seemed to make up his mind. 'Wait here,' he said and, taking the letter with him, he went out through the door Schulz had come in by. Schulz remained standing there. The minutes dragged by. He looked round the room which held nothing of interest for him. A few clerks went about their business paying him no regard. He wondered if he should sit down but since no one asked him he decided against it. Finally, a phone rang on one of the desks and a clerk picked it up. He listened for a while and then hung up. He looked at Schulz.

'Please go to room 403,' he said. 'It's on the fourth floor. Take the lift but do remember to shut the gate after you.'

Up on the fourth floor, Schulz knocked on the door of

room 403 and heard a voice say, 'Come in.' Inside, the room was bare. There were no cupboards or shelves or carpet. Only a desk with a chair behind it in which sat the man who had taken his letter downstairs.

'I don't understand,' Schulz said. 'Are you Herr Ditzer, then?'

'That's no concern of yours,' the man answered. 'You're not here to ask questions.'

'But why was Herr Ditzer mentioned in the letter?' asked Schulz.

'I'll say only this,' the man replied, 'and then there will be no need to refer to it again. You may look upon "Herr Ditzer" as a code which is meaningful to me but not to you. It's a matter of security. These are grave times and we can't be too careful. It wouldn't do for anyone to walk in here and know instantly who he was talking to. I'm sure you will appreciate that. I may be Herr Ditzer or I may not be. Herr Ditzer may exist or he may not. It's of no consequence.'

Schulz said nothing. If this was to be the way things were to be carried out in the future it was not for him to criticize them. Not openly at any rate. It all seemed rather foolish but he also realized that, in time of war, precautions had to be taken.

'So you want to be in postal censorship?' the man asked rather gravely, studying Schulz's application as if Schulz had applied to enter a monastery and had not fully considered all the implications. 'Is there any reason for this?'

'Well,' said Schulz, 'I want to serve my country in the best way I can. I speak several languages fluently. It seemed to me I could be very useful here.'

The man nodded, pulling at his lower lip for a moment, a movement Schulz decided was sympathetic.

'Well, of course, we shall need all the help we can get from our citizens,' he replied. 'I see you speak Serbo-Croat. That could be a distinct advantage.' He didn't say why.

There was a short silence while he again studied Schulz's application.

'I see you are thirty?'

Schulz nodded.

'You look older. Perhaps that is the result of your prison sentence.'

Schulz blinked. It seemed that a prison record was not necessarily a disadvantage in the new Reich.

'I've always been mature looking,' he said, 'even as a child.'

'Are you a member of the Party?'

'No,' said Schulz.

'Have you ever applied?'

'No.'

'That in itself is no bar.' He shrugged. 'It may even, at this stage, be construed by some as an advantage. Too many people of doubtful character have jumped on the bandwagon these last few years. I remember when times were hard, when to be a member of the Party was to invite contempt and derision. Now of course everyone wants to belong. But everyone *can't* belong!' He brought the flat of his hand down sharply on the desk with a sound like a pistol crack.

There was a further silence. Schulz felt slightly uncomfortable. He had expected a different sort of interview and wasn't sure how to deal with this. Something, however, in his letter of application was absorbing his interviewer's attention. He picked it up, holding it at the side between thumb and forefinger and brought his grey bullet head closer to it, as if he were trying to smell it. Perhaps this was the first time he had seen the letter, for there was no evidence that this man was the author of the illegible signature on the letter Schulz had received.

'I see you are a traveller in ladies' underwear?' he said, slowly raising his eyes to Schulz who felt the usual twitch in his stomach when the subject of his profession came up.

He swallowed hard and nodded.

'Ladies?' the man asked, giving the word slight emphasis as if to make sure there could be no misunderstanding.

Schulz nodded again.

The man stared at him and Schulz laughed nervously, and was about to make his usual joke about travelling in ladies' underwear but said nothing instead.

27

'What sort of underwear?' the man asked, gazing at him intently.

'What sort?' Schulz repeated.

'Yes. Describe it.'

Schulz laughed again. 'Well,' he said, 'it's woollen, mainly, but some silk.'

'Woollen mainly but some silk,' the man repeated slowly, giving the words a soft emphasis as if quite taken with the description and about to note it down carefully. 'I suppose you supply all kinds?'

Oh Christ, thought Schulz, *he's looking for a handout for his wife. People always seemed to think they were entitled to them. Well, I've got a caseful and if it oils the wheels a little, why not?* He smiled brightly at the man and nodded.

'Oh, yes, all kinds,' he answered. 'Slips and panties, brassières and negligées and such like.' He only just managed to suppress a wink. This at least would put them on more equal terms. 'We import the silk ones from France.'

'And lace, I suppose, on the edges?'

'Lace trimmings, of course,' Schulz laughed. 'What would these things be without the lace trimmings?'

The man stared at him a while, then took out a handkerchief, cleanly laundered and folded, which he flipped open from a corner, put his hand beneath the centre, lifted to his nose and blew loudly, his eyes all the while on Schulz. He carefully folded the handkerchief and put it away again.

'Tell me, Herr Schulz,' he said, leaning forward, 'why do you think it is that women's underwear is made of such softer material than men's? I'm thinking of the silk, especially, though even in the case of wool, a woman's ... panties – yes, I won't flinch from using that word – a woman's panties are softer and more pleasant to the touch. I am wearing silk underwear myself, at this very moment, but there is no comparison with the things they produce for women. Why is it, Herr Schulz? You're in the trade – a professional, one might say – and must have given this some thought?'

Schulz stared at him, dumbfounded. He had never given it any thought.

'Is it,' the man went on, 'that they think men are insensitive, coarse creatures who wouldn't know the difference? I assure you that would be a very wrong assumption. Yet it's a very depressing experience for a man to go out looking for underwear that he would be proud and excited to present next to his naked body in the privacy of his bedroom.'

Schulz nodded and coughed sympathetically.

'I don't want you to get the impression, Herr Schulz, that I am one of those people who derive a curious and unhealthy pleasure from putting on women's clothes. I have nothing but contempt for such people. If the truth were known there are far too many of them in our Party – I tell you this in strictest confidence, of course – and at the highest levels too.'

There was a long silence. Schulz cleared his throat and started to say, 'Well, now ...,' a sound that startled him so much that he failed to proceed with it, though he was relieved to find he still had his voice. The man had ceased to lean forward and was now leaning back, gazing at Schulz anxiously as if waiting for some kind of oracle from the horse's mouth.

Finally the man stood up and walked slowly over to the window and stood gazing out.

'Is there anything else you'd like to ask me?' Schulz asked hesitantly.

The man turned and allowed his gaze to rest lightly on him for a moment and then turned away.

'There's nothing I can think of,' he answered. 'You must take a form and fill it out – three forms to be exact.'

'Of course,' Schulz murmured. He hesitated a moment, then went on: 'Do you think it might be successful?'

'Oh yes, I hope so, yes. I'm sure it will – in some form or another – yes.' There was another silence, then he said, 'I would deem it a great personal favour if you would allow me to examine your merchandise.'

Schulz sighed. He got up and lifted his case on to the desk. He snapped the locks open, but paused as he was about to lift the lid when the man intervened by raising a hand slightly in a restraining gesture.

'Would you consider it a grave impertinence if I examined them in private?'

Schulz thought for a moment. 'Would you like to keep them,' he said.

'Ah, that's too kind, I never thought – I never expected ...' He seemed slightly overcome. He took his handkerchief out and blew his nose again. 'I shall keep them in a night safe at the bank. They will be safer there than at home ...' He trailed off, clearly feeling he need say no more.

Schulz removed the samples from the case and placed them on the desk, closing the lid again. He looked at the man and wondered if he should sit down, but the man had turned away once more towards the window and stood gazing out as if Schulz's presence and even the memory of it had already faded from his mind. There seemed no further point in staying. What would happen to his application Schulz had no idea. Perhaps it would go through normal channels. Perhaps his tacit collusion in the fantasies of a silk fetishist would help. Perhaps not.

He picked up the three forms the man had pushed towards him, and left the office, closing the door, but catching, before he did so, a momentary glimpse of his interrogator moving towards the object of his affection, his hands outstretched in greedy anticipation as if, when he reached them, he might plunge his whole, parched being into their cool, reviving waters.

All that day, while at work, Schulz thought about the interview, turning it over and over in his mind, trying to recall what he had said and what he had not said. But the more he tried to grasp it the more the experience slipped away. He had no calls to make that day outside the office and therefore attended to an accumulation of paper-work. He had not mentioned to his employer that he had applied for another post, and he wasn't looking forward to doing so. Herr Krauss was in one of his familiar rages and this time it was fortunately turned against Herr Sturmer, the man from the Ministry of Supply. There was nothing of the bureaucrat about Sturmer. If 'Herr Ditzer' had given Schulz a foretaste of the more introspective government official, Sturmer was, in complete contrast, a man who would have looked more at home on a racecourse.

'Eighty marks a gross for underpants? What are you trying to do, ruin me?' Krauss was screaming. His eyes were pale blue and sad, as though he had already been ruined by the ladies' undergarment trade. Now there was a pink flush to his fat little cheeks.

'Herr Krauss, there's a war on,' said Sturmer. He was sweating profusely as though he were wondering if he'd backed the wrong horse.

'Am I supposed to pay for it on my own? You've taken half my staff for the army. Don't you think I know there's a war on?'

'See here, Herr Krauss,' said Sturmer, 'the Ministry has calculated that the price gives a reasonable profit. The Ministry is very sympathetic to the problems of the manufacturing industry.'

'Eighty marks a gross is *not* sympathetic! At eighty marks a gross I'd be better off in the army! In fact I've a good mind to *join* the army! Let somebody provide *me* with underpants at eighty marks a gross!'

Sturmer was busy gathering his papers. 'I'll talk to my superiors,' he said.

Krauss wouldn't let it go. He was concerned about quality. 'In a week they'd be full of holes, Herr Sturmer,' he said. His lenses were quite steamed up by this time.

Sturmer stopped at the office door. 'If I could get eighty-one and a half would that be acceptable?'

Krauss, thinking that he'd driven a patriotic wedge into his bargaining position, decided to make an appeal on behalf of the war effort.

'What impression would the British get if they take our boys prisoners wearing underpants full of holes? Have you thought of that?'

Sturmer started to walk out.

'Eighty-one and a half would be acceptable,' said Krauss, accompanying him to the outside door.

'Leave it to me, Herr Krauss,' said Sturmer. 'I hope to get back to you in a few days. They say the war will be over by Christmas ...'

His parting remark failed to convince Schulz. Intermittently through the rest of the day he examined the situations column.

When he returned home that evening Frau Nusbaum was waiting for him in a state of great excitement. A telegram had arrived. She waved it at him as she hurried along the hall towards him. It arrived only half an hour ago or she would surely have telephoned him at the office. What could it be? A telegram was so unusual. Herr Schulz had no relatives who might be ill or dying so she was quite sure it had to be something important. Her state of excitement was such that he wondered how she had restrained herself from opening it.

The telegram was terse. It merely ordered him to report to the Brandenburg Barracks in Duisberg not later than four o'clock on the afternoon of 31 August. It was signed – Ditzer.

Schulz stared at the telegram. Could they be short of staff? Had he made such a vivid impression that they wanted to grab him before some other department? Duisberg! thought Schulz. It was miles away. Today was 30 August.

He sat down and calculated. He wasn't mentally prepared for such an upheaval but the important thing was that he had achieved the first object of his programme for surviving the holocaust to come. Somewhere in Duisberg, a small niche was waiting for him where he might sleep out the chill winter of war and emerge into the sunlight when it was over, one way or another.

Frau Nusbaum, however, wept when she read the telegram. She had not seriously contemplated his departure. She had not imagined the war could so swiftly touch their lives or break their little friendship she said. Why, it had not even begun yet and here he was making ready for departure to a strange city. She could not accept it.

She paused abruptly, looking at him, a soft, moist smile upon her face. Schulz shuddered inwardly. Thank God, he thought, taking out his watch to look at the time, thank God today is Wednesday.

'Do you know what I shall do, Herr Schulz? It has just entered my mind to do it.' She came and stood in front of him, looking down into his eyes for she was taller than he and considerably wider. She placed the fat palm of each fat little hand on his lapels and spoke softly. 'Do you realize – oh, I'm sure you do, you naughty man – you will not be here on Saturday? I shall break my rules, Herr Schulz. Today must be counted exceptional. I know you would not dare to ask, but – yes, this once, you shall have the keys to the playroom on a Wednesday.'

Schulz sighed inwardly.

'And,' she went on, 'as a special treat I think we may even entertain the idea of opening the attic.'

4

Schulz went to the office before taking the early morning train to Duisberg. Krauss had not calmed down since his negotiations with Herr Sturmer from the Ministry of Supply.

'Eighty marks a gross, what does he take me for? If you can't make a profit in wartime, you might as well blow your brains out!'

'The war could be over by Christmas, Herr Krauss,' said Schulz as cheerfully as he could make it sound.

'Jesus Christ,' snapped Krauss, 'what are you trying to do, depress me even more? I've got contracts here for a hundred thousand pairs of army underpants! Where will I get orders like that in peace time?'

'I only thought –' Schulz began.

'You've no right to go around raising people's hopes!

There's a new law about that! That's called "endangering the defensive power of the German people". Some idiot was shot for it the other day.'

'Sorry, Herr Krauss. Er, there's something –' but Krauss hadn't finished.

'Over by Christmas! That's the most depressing thing I've heard all week. What's the matter with everyone? Nobody wants to fight! The damned Poles collapsed in three weeks! Draft an ad for the papers. If I don't get more labour I'll never meet those contracts on time.'

Once more Schulz took the plunge. 'I'm leaving, Herr Krauss.'

'You're what?' Krauss looked like an elderly greying baby who was about to lose his dummy.

'Leaving.'

'But you've only been here a month!'

'The telegram came yesterday afternoon. I've got a job in Postal Security. I've to report there this afternoon.'

Krauss looked as if his own underpants were pinching him. He jammed his spectacles higher up his nose and bore down on Schulz, his breath coming in hot patriotic little gasps.

'You selfish little sod! You don't give a damn about me, do you? You don't give a damn how I meet that contract or whether I attract the penalty clauses for failing to deliver on time?'

'The country comes first, Herr Krauss,' said Schulz stiffly.

'To hell with the country! How am I to produce underpants if everyone keeps joining the army?'

'I am going into Postal Censorship, Herr Krauss. You see, I happen to speak five languages and –'

'You self-absorbed little swine!'

'Come, Herr Krauss ...'

'You've found yourself a nice little number, haven't you? You want to sit the war out in some safe little office and just read about it in other people's letters. I should have known better than to employ an ex-jail bird. You needn't think I'm taken in by you, Schulz. I am perfectly aware that what you've done is nothing more than a cowardly

34

device to protect yourself from induction into the armed forces where you might just possibly run the risk of being killed in action. You've just spoiled my morning and left me with a very nasty taste in my mouth and all I can say is that you can do as you damn well like. Go and be a bloody postman. I hope the British drop a bomb on the building and blow it to bits! If I were running the country I'd have you shot. Now get out of my office and I hope to God I never set eyes on you again.'

Duisberg was bathed in the afternoon sun of a summer drawing to its close. Schulz found the barracks and was directed to a large building in the centre of a courtyard. Inside, the place was swarming with SS men, which was quite unexpected.

I've come to the wrong building again, thought Schulz. He turned round and went outside to check the address. No question about it, the address was right. He went back inside and stopped a clerk on his way across the hall.

'Excuse me. Er – Herr Ditzer ... ?'

'Go down to the basement,' the clerk said. 'It's the room at the far end of the corridor.'

Ah, thought Schulz, *this is different from that affair in Hamburg. People here seem to know what they are about.*

In the room at the end of the corridor a middle-aged, grey-haired lady in the uniform of the SS sat at a desk working.

'To see Herr Ditzer,' said Schulz.

'Name?'

'Herr Schulz.'

'Herr Schulz.' She opened one of the drawers of a filing cabinet and fingered rapidly through the files, finally pulling one out and opening it.

'Gerhardt Otto Schulz,' she said, pronouncing the end of her search.

Schulz nodded.

'Come with me.'

She led the way out of the room and back along the

corridor. She walked with a heavy, rhythmic tread. Schulz had almost to run now and then to keep up with her. She opened a door and stood aside for him to enter.

There were half a dozen other men in the room sitting on chairs in total silence. Things were now going in the way Schulz would have expected.

He did not, however, expect a uniformed SS officer to step smartly in through the other door and to stand staring at them all with a glittering hostility.

'Stand up,' he said in a high-pitched, and, Schulz thought, slightly hysterical voice. 'Stand up when an officer enters the room!'

They stood, rather embarrassed, making an effort to look as if they were standing to attention without actually doing so. This seemed to mollify the officer for he said, in a somewhat lower key, 'Sit down.'

They sat down again and waited. The situation was beginning to puzzle Schulz. For one thing he could find no connection between the interview he had had in Hamburg and this SS officer who stood before him. Was it possible that postal censorship had been taken over by the SS? He really had to find out. He half rose from his chair, his hand automatically lifting itself in a long-forgotten, infantile gesture to attract attention, but froze midway as the officer suddenly turned and peered at him.

'You,' he barked, 'come with me.'

Schulz was now beginning to tremble. He followed the officer down a corridor into a room identical to the previous one. The officer was talking to another man in plain clothes. Both were eyeing Schulz as they conversed and were examining a file on which he suddenly saw his name printed. They seemed to be arguing. Finally they nodded to each other and the plain-clothes man approached him.

Schulz decided it was time he took some initiative. 'What sort of kit do I need for postal censorship?' he asked.

The man didn't appear to have heard him. 'You're in the army now,' he said blandly. 'You're a Hippo, an Auxiliary Army policeman.'

* * *

Some men do not belong in uniform. Schulz was one of them. There was something ludicrous about it, a touch of the clown. He did not have the face for the peaked cap. They tried first to straighten the uniform on Schulz and then, in mounting frustration, to straighten Schulz inside the uniform, but no pleasing effect could be achieved either way. In the end they gave up.

Schulz hated being shouted at. He marched, when he marched, with a kind of co-ordination, but the wrong arm always seemed to swing in time to the wrong leg. Martial music made his hair stand on end. He seemed to be alone in his uneasiness. The men he was now with were all, unlike Schulz, bursting with enthusiasm. It was as if the war had given them the chance to make up for all that had gone wrong in their lives previously. They were the awkward squad, but it was an eager awkward squad. When one man had trouble with his teeth he had them all out rather than be invalided out of the army. The teeth went for the Father-land.

At the end of their induction they were given bright yellow shoulder flashes to sew on to their tunics, with labels that said, *Geheime Feldpolizei*, Secret Field Police.

One day about six weeks after Schulz had arrived at Duis-berg, he decided to voice his anxieties to the platoon leader, who happened to be the little jeweller who had had all his teeth removed. Within an hour Schulz was in a truck with two guards, being escorted to Dusseldorf.

There he was taken to a room that looked peculiarly like a cell but they did not lock the door. Down the corri-dor he could hear someone in authority raving in a speech that echoed through the whole building.

'Don't forget we are fighting against bitter enemies who do us immense harm and damage. It is our duty to fight them with every available weapon.'

So the war has really started, thought Schulz. Atrocities had obviously been committed. He wished he had read the newspapers that day. But as he carried on listening he began to realize that the voice was not referring to the British. The SS were raving about the Gestapo.

Presently an officer entered the room. The fact that he had come to see Schulz and Schulz had not been ordered to see him was a good sign, but he then announced that he was an interrogating officer. He began to talk about some slighting reference to the road signs the SA secret head-quarters that Schulz had made. Schulz protested that he was being treated as if he were responsible for the first of the bomb plots against the Fuhrer. When two crop-haired thugs appeared in the room to assist the interrogator, he realized he was.

The first thing they did was to tear off the *Geheime Feld-polizei* flashes from the shoulders of his roomy tunic. It was almost like a court martial and Schulz was made to feel as though he had let down not only the regiment but the whole Fatherland. The flashes came off quite easily due to the fact that Schulz had sewn them on himself, and one of the SS men, anticipating difficulty, heaved with unnecessary force and ripped so hard that he brought his hand down and hurt it on the edge of the table.

'I'm extremely sorry, *mein herr*,' mumbled Schulz. 'My needlework has never been exemplary.'

The interrogator, who Schulz later found out had been a primary school teacher sacked for indecency, grew very angry at this apology which he obviously took to be a deliberate impertinence. It soon became clear to Schulz that he thought he had unearthed a master spy. He backed away from Schulz.

'I can seen at once you're very dangerous,' he said.

In one respect Schulz was fortunate. This particular inter-rogator was a novice who believed that everything in front of him was a masterpiece of deception. Being an ex-school-master, he liked to mark pieces of paper and when Schulz was unable to give him the answer he wanted, he would set Schulz exercises, giving him reams of paper to write down every detail about his life, over and over again, and in particular, facts concerning the stories Schulz had told about his foreign contacts. For days he was kept busy filling up pieces of paper and at the end of each day the interrogator would read his classwork and then say, 'Not good enough, Schulz,' after correcting the punctuation.

Then one day another interrogator came in and asked Schulz about his prison life and why he had described it as a home away from home. It finally turned out that he'd been at the same prison himself. After that, things were a lot easier for Schulz. But since they had stripped him of his shoulder flashes, he was now hanging about the building like a janitor.

At first he had been told he would soon be receiving his billeting orders, but no billet came. After a few days he began to make himself useful to the SS clerks who had difficulty in filing all the forms that were flooding the building and he was allowed to use the canteen. Schulz was beginning to have the feeling that every lucky soldier knows, of being forgotten about, a lost digit in the pile. He learned to make himself invisible, making sure that he was never seen in the corridors on the way to the canteen without a file in his hand.

Nobody bothered him. He wasn't molested. The food was so good in the canteen that he was almost becoming afraid that if he went out he wouldn't be allowed back in. He did not, of course, go anywhere near the prisoners' cells at the rear of the building, and he tried to look as officious as possible, a vital cog in the machinery at the centre of the war effort. In short, he kept a low profile.

One day when he walked into the canteen he found it had been cleared of tables, and rows of chairs had been arranged to face the counter. Three or four dozen obviously new entries were sitting at attention in total silence. An SS NCO half-escorted, half-pushed Schulz into an empty place in the front row where he felt disagreeably conspicuous amongst all the yellow-flashed shoulders.

A door opened and an SS officer entered. 'Stand up,' he said.

Schulz recognized the high-pitched, hysterical voice that

had greeted him on his arrival at Duisberg.

'Attention!'

By now the drill was familiar.

'You are now probationary members of the Schutz-staffeln. Or, to be more precise, of the Intelligence wing of the Schutzstaffeln, the Sicherheitsdienst.' The voice was clear, clipped, like a precocious adolescent's. He stood surveying them, a short lock of blond hair falling across his brow, his eyes a piercing blue.

Schulz sank back in his chair, stupified. He considered asking to be excused as this lecture had nothing to do with him, but that might only draw attention to himself.

'I am Major Schellenberg,' the officer went on. 'It's my duty to welcome you into the SS. I intend to make short work of it so you needn't think that any words of mine are sincerely meant because they're not.'

A muscle twitched rapidly at the corner of his mouth as he gazed round at them, a movement Schulz was not foolish enough to mistake for a smile.

'I've got no time for people like you. It's a disgrace and an abomination that we have to accept you into our ranks. Where were you in those grim dark days when our Party was crying out for men? When our Leader was alone but for the few, a handful of brave and loyal helpers?'

In prison, thought Schulz nostalgically.

'And now, when we are about to achieve our greatest rewards, when all the hard work is behind us, you come crawling out of the woodwork to pick up the crumbs. Well, don't think I'm taken in by it. I know you and by thunder you'll know me!'

Schulz felt as though he were going to be sick.

'You're here because of the pressing needs of war and that's all. Fortunately, the war will be over by Christmas so your days are strictly numbered. Make the most of them. See that every waking moment of your lives you show yourselves worthy of the high honour that has been conferred on you. But remember this. The SS is an elite body of men and women of true Nordic type, whose children are intended as the future rulers of Germany. This you may never aspire to. The standards set are too high. However, let me say this – if you cannot conform, physically, to that Nordic ideal which Reichfuhrer-SS Himmler has laid down, you can at least be truly Nordic in spirit. And, by God, if you can't, we have camps where we can show you how. Stand up!'

Everyone shot to his feet, freezing solid, a group hewn out of solid rock.

'Raise your right hands and say after me – "I swear to you, Adolf Hitler, as Fuhrer and Reichchancellor, loyalty and bravery. I owe to you, and to those you have named to command me, obedience unto death, so help me God".'

Dazed and nauseous, Schulz repeated the oath with everyone else. His voice shook, earning, he thought, a brief if grim nod of satisfaction from Schellenberg.

Once again Schulz donned a new uniform; once again it had as little chance of fitting him as he had of fitting it. He was told to bundle up his last uniform with his civilian clothes which he had brought with him and report to the administrative office on the ground floor. A woman took his bundle, put it into a bag and wrote a reference number on it. She then consulted a list. There was no sign of Schulz's name. Schulz was just beginning to feel that he had been let off the hook once more when an SS officer appeared as if from nowhere, smiling at him.

'What is your expertise, my man?'

'Underwear,' said Schulz, 'ladies' and gents'.'

Immediately the place erupted into bedlam, with the woman in administration being blamed for not having Schulz's papers, inner security for letting Schulz in, outer security for not kicking him out. Accusations and counter-accusations flew over Schulz's head as though he were a net in a demented game of tennis. Someone suddenly remembered that he was still there and he was packed off to the second floor, to a room with a name on the door that would change his life.

5

If Adolf Hitler, as Fuhrer of the Third Reich, could be considered the head of a deranged but highly efficient piece of machinery that resembled, for the purposes of the metaphor only, a human shape, his left arm was Heinrich Himmler who ran the SS with a bureaucratic fervour never before known in human history. Himmler's forearm was known as the RSHA or Reich Security Administration. The fist of this sinister limb was Reinhardt Heydrich, who ran the SD or Sicherheitsdienst, the Security Service. And if its thumb was Heinrich Muller who ran the Gestapo, or Secret Police, as Dept IV of the RSHA, it also had a crooked little finger. The nail of this crooked little finger was Heinz Jost who ran Dept VI, the foreign intelligence. But the nail was a long one and it had a nasty little point. The point was called Neuheim.

Captain Neuheim ran Dept VIB of the RSHA, a section that specialized entirely in devious practices of one kind or another. Whether Neuheim had the sheer brainpower necessary for such deviousness, there was no doubting his enthusiasm, nor his physical qualifications. Some might have said he would have done better in the state machine's right arm, or even as its big toe.

Alfred Helmuth Neuheim was born on 2 September 1911 in Kiel where he early distinguished himself as a boxer and dockside hoodlum. He soon discovered in the early thirties that there was more power and glory to be gained – and just as much blood and money – in working for the Nazi cause.

This suited him down to the ground where his victims usually stayed. Neuheim had nothing particularly against communists or Jews except his fists or a knife, but was quite reconciled to eliminating them if that was what the Nazi doctrine required of him.

He soon became known as the scourge of the communists, who had put a price on his head. He had been ambushed more than a dozen times, his body covered with the scars of bullet wounds and knife thrusts, his nose broken with an iron bar, and he had lost the use of one eye which was now covered by a sinister looking patch, adding to the impression that he made on people that he was only half there. The half that was there, however, was volatile, dangerous and liable to pounce on anything that the half that wasn't couldn't, and call it his. He had, inevitably, come to the notice of Reinhardt Heydrich at a crucial stage in Heydrich's career, and when Heydrich became Head of the SD he took Neuheim with him as his right-hand man and occasional confidant.

Neuheim was a fanatic: essentially a man of action who would nevertheless prove useful in a department specializing in the production of false documents, agents' radio sets and miniature cameras, which only needed a nominal head to make sure that the technicians didn't slacken. Heydrich's judgement was absolutely right, Neuheim had the department running brilliantly, primarily because he delegated everything and then struck the fear of God in his delegates.

Thus, Neuheim could be freed for more original capers. It was here that Heydrich made a mistake. Originality was not one of Neuheim's strong points. He demanded perfection of others and was critical in the extreme, but when he himself was required to handle a delicate operation from its planning stage he seemed to go into a kind of internal frenzy, which he would turn immediately on whichever delegate was closest to hand. He was, however, blind to this particular shortcoming, a blindness aggravated by several years in which he had got away with it without attracting any comment, since it was a common feature of those who rose in the SS hierarchy.

His years in the SS had civilized Neuheim to a degree. His pugilism was now less physical and more mental – and thus more formidable than ever. His uniform was always immaculate. He also had a compulsive hatred of waste and dirt.

Since Neuheim implicity believed that anyone who was not above him on the SS ladder came into that category, he regarded most of the human race as sewage, though he had learnt that some sewage could be profitably recycled since he hated waste even more than he hated dirt. The safe in his inner office was already a miniature museum of war booty, even though the war had only been going for two months.

Schulz had been assigned downstairs to a corporal named Schumacher, a moonfaced little man who, though the same age as Schulz, was already showing signs of middle-aged spread, and who had been staring at Schulz almost as though he found him an attractive morsel. Schumacher had taken a critical scrutiny of his uniform and, after negotiating with the stores clerk, had provided Schulz with the requisite trimmings of the SS, the badges and the flashes and emblems of the black-terror brigade.

When Schulz and Schumacher arrived on the second floor, the corporal left him standing in the corridor while he investigated the possibilities of useful employment. Minutes later, he was back, looking disgruntled.

'All they need around here is typists. Most of them are women, though, and I prefer men, don't you?'

Schulz shook his head and said, 'Yes.'

'I don't suppose you can type?' said Schumacher, looking at him doubtfully.

Schulz nodded and said, 'No.'

'Good,' said Schumacher. 'Then you'll be useful. They could do with a male typist.' Schumacher, like all corporals, knew the advantage of having a minion.

He escorted Schulz to an office on which the name: 'SS Captain Neuheim, Dept VIB' was painted in black and gold, colours for which, Schulz noted, the SS seemed to have an inordinate fondness. When they stepped into Neuheim's outer office, however, it was immediately obvious they had arrived at the wrong moment. Inside a *blitzkrieg* was in progress.

'Scum! Traitors! You're a disgrace to the German Army and we'll have you shot for this! Take those uniforms off, you're not fit to wear them!'

Neuheim was furious. In front of him, looking pale and badly shaken, stood two General Staff officers, who began slowly and awkwardly to unbuckle their tunics and belts. They were soon down to their underpants.

'A nice little game, you've been playing, haven't you?' Neuheim screamed as he paced up and down, dwarfing everyone in the room. 'You thought we didn't know about it, didn't you?' He wheeled round on them. 'Do you think we're idiots?'

Outside Neuheim's inner sanctum, Schulz could make out the highly-polished boots of the officers from his low vantage point, crouched against a radiator underneath the window. Next to him Schumacher had slid behind a desk and was doodling on a pile of forms, as though he had heard Neuheim's outbursts a thousand times before.

'We've been following every move you've made,' Neuheim was saying. 'Your contact, Muller, was picked up a week ago and confessed everything! Your little plot to assassinate the Fuhrer and make peace with the British' (Neuheim spat out the word 'British' as though he had discovered a cockroach in his caviare) 'is known to us! And to the Fuhrer!'

At that moment a portly, fleshy-looking captain, whose name Schulz later discovered was Kube, and who had been standing behind Neuheim, passed by the half-open door. Schulz caught a glimpse of the Staff officers' underpants and wondered idly if they were the brand manufactured by Herr Krauss.

'And don't think we don't know there's more behind you! The whole higher command of the army is riddled with traitors! The army's not worthy of the Fuhrer's trust! We'll clean it out, out!'

To Schulz's ears, untutored in the subtle nuances of SS hysteria, the voice could well have belonged to the Fuhrer himself. The significance of what was being said escaped him for the time being but he did manage to catch a glimpse of the owner of the voice in the form of a black patch on a deadly white face, scarred down one cheek, a cigarette holder clenched menacingly between his teeth, as Neuheim passed by the half-open door, Schumacher at once busied himself with the pencil. Then the switchboard buzzed and Schumacher put through the call. SS Captain Kube picked up the phone on Neuheim's desk.

'Yes, *Oberstgruppenfuhrer*, he's here, just a minute.'

His voice was less hysterical, but more deadly than Neuheim's. It oozed jovial charm. He covered the mouthpiece and turned to Neuheim.

'Heydrich.'

Neuheim took the phone.

'My dear Reinhardt . . .' said Neuheim, his voice instantly transformed from high rage into low wheedling. 'Yes, I've got them both here. They're supposed to meet the two British officers tomorrow morning in a café at Wilma – that's just across the Dutch border.'

A silence followed. Heydrich was obviously in the driver's seat.

'Of course, Reinhardt,' Neuheim continued. 'Don't worry. I'll have those Britishers in Berlin by tomorrow night. Goodbye.'

Schumacher swivelled his eyes from the files of paper on his desk and looked down at Schulz, smiling a secret smile. Schulz stared back at him blankly. Apparently everything in the outer office came to a halt when Neuheim performed a cross-examination.

'Have you met those British officers before?' he began again.

'No,' said one of the underpanted officers.

'But they're waiting for you? To bring the peace proposals?'

'Yes.'

'What are their names?'

There was no reply. Neuheim slapped him across the face, but he still did not answer.

'Colonel Clyde Withers and Major Harrison Smith!' Neuheim shouted. 'I know their names! They both work for the British Secret Service! How are you to identify yourselves?'

There was a long pause. Then the first officer spoke again.

'By a phrase.'

'And what exactly is the phrase?' Neuheim's voice had become very gentle, simmering with sarcasm.

' "The war could be over by Christmas", Captain.'

Presently the General Staff officers were led out, still in their underpants. There was a lift at the back of Neuheim's office and Schulz, watching the guards carrying the tunics which they had removed, realized that they would be going through the pockets in the lift. It seemed to Schulz as if the whole war had been enacted in miniature in that first meeting with Neuheim.

'My dear Neuheim, Holland is a neutral country,' Schulz could hear Kube saying in his treacle-smooth voice. 'How does he suggest we do it without creating a diplomatic incident?'

'Oh, let the diplomats worry about the incidents,' replied Neuheim, closing the door to his inner office. Schulz could only hear their muffled voices now, as Schumacher stood up and stretched himself.

'Well, Schulz,' he said. 'You've come at a good moment.'

'A good moment?'

'It's always a good moment when Neuheim has something on the go. It keeps his mind away from the office.'

Schulz wished there was some way he could back out, but he had heard the soft thump of a blackjack as the guards had taken the two officers out of the lift and he felt a chill go down his spine as it occurred to him that nobody walked out of the back door of the SS building.

He remained squatting against the radiator and looked at

47

Schumacher for instructions. Presently the buzzer went inside the inner office and Schumacher jumped and disappeared after it. A few moments later he stuck his head out of the door and beckoned Schulz to come in. Neuheim, Schulz later discovered, liked everyone to report to him once a day. This was Schulz's moment to report, and first impressions with Neuheim were important.

'What the hell is that?' said Neuheim, as Schulz appeared before him. In a uniform that was several sizes too large for him, Schulz looked bizarre and ridiculous.

'Private Gerhardt Otto Schulz reporting for duty, *Herr Hauptsturmfuhrer*,' said Schumacher. 'Schulz is your new private and confidential clerk.'

Schulz flapped one of the sail-like sleeves in a salute.

'Heil Hitler!' he said. It seemed a reasonable thing to say. Schumacher's announcement was as much news to Schulz as it was to Neuheim but there was very little he could do about it, now that he was staring directly into that meaty nose. Above it the black patch glistened while his good eye screwed itself up like an enraged marble. Neuheim had a dangerous quality about him, Schulz felt it instantly. There was no doubting that he was a powerhouse of energy.

'Is this some kind of a joke?' Neuheim said finally.

Schumacher, who had been almost soporific only five minutes earlier, was now almost manic, like an advocate before a judge who was about to disappear down a moving staircase.

'Certainly not, sir! Private Schulz has been drafted here. All the documents arrived this morning.'

If Schulz was ever going to say anything, now was the time.

'There may have been some mistake, Herr Captain,' he interjected. 'I had an interview for Postal Censorship. This isn't Postal Censorship.'

'Postal Censorship?' barked Neuheim. 'Of course it isn't Postal Censorship – what is he babbling about?'

Schumacher's voice became low and confidential. 'From time to time,' he said, 'suitable applicants are passed on to us from Postal Censorship, Herr Captain. Private Schulz has had a technical education and speaks five languages fluently.'

As far as Schulz was concerned the first part of this was a complete fabrication, but he couldn't help being impressed by the sheer conviction with which Schumacher spoke. He never hesitated and every word came out with the absolute ring of truth. And, as Schulz was to learn, you could never hesitate with Neuheim. He only responded to an immediate stimulus, like a well-trained dog. Schumacher seemed to have him tamed.

'Including English?' Captain Kube had emerged from behind a filing cabinet.

'Including English, Serbo-Croat, Dutch, Danish and Romanian,' Schumacher reeled off, determined to prove that it was impossible for Schulz to have entered the SS building by mistake. 'He also has a prison record, Herr Captain.'

Kube looked impressed. 'What for?'

'Fraud, *mein Herr*,' said Schumacher deferentially as if this were the cherry on the cake.

'Fraud?' said Kube. 'He could be useful, Neuheim.'

Schulz was getting desperate by now. 'But it's all wrong, sir. I shouldn't be here at all. I'm supposed ...'

'Shut up, damn you,' snarled Neuheim, 'or I'll have you shot! Who do you think you are? *We* decide who comes into the SS and who leaves! Get him out of here and for God's sake get him a tailor!'

'Yes, sir,' Schumacher said.

'Just a minute,' said Neuheim, changing his mind. 'Speaks English, and Dutch, you say?'

'Yes, Herr Captain.'

'I'll take him with me,' said Neuheim. 'Get him a suit of clothes, a false passport and some traveller's cheques. I want him ready to leave for the Dutch border tonight.'

6

Life, thought Schulz as he was being marched down again to the clothing store, is something you pay for on hire purchase. Except that you keep paying the interest, without the chance of getting hold of the goods until you've repaid the loan, which you never do because the interest rate keeps going up. And what was the good of paying interest when the things you paid interest on kept being taken away from you? It was like a series of confidence tricks.

You no sooner get used to the nice warm comfort of the womb than you're pushed out into the cold, bleak world. Then, having spent the first years of your life adjusting to the freedom it can offer you and just when you're getting to enjoy the idea of playing in the woods for the rest of your life, someone comes along and sits you at a desk in a dusty classroom. Then, when you are beginning to appreciate the value of education and are thinking of becoming a perpetual student, they throw you out into the street to fend for yourself.

And then, just in case you're thinking of reneging on the agreement, they give you a quick peek at the goods. In Schulz's case the quick peek had been given to him during his stay with the Jewish banker, and it had been snatched away as if to say: Not so fast, you'll have to work for it first. And so it went on, from cradle to grave. Perhaps thought Schulz, the only premises that were not false ones were the type they locked you up in. At least prisons offered either no hope at all or the tangible reward of getting out.

At this moment Schulz genuinely wished that someone would explain to him the meaning of such confidence tricks. How was it possible that, by answering a small advertisement for a nice quiet position in Postal Censorship, he had earned himself a trip with Captain Neuheim into enemy territory? Neuheim was without doubt an unstable

50

human being, thought Schulz. He looked as though he had
cut throats for a living. And yet he had chosen Schulz of all
people to accompany him on some reckless espionage trip
which would most likely end Schulz's admittedly miserable
life that very night. It just didn't add up.

'Plain-clothes now?' the storeman said, breaking into
Schulz's morbid thoughts like a church organ after a congregation's silent prayer.

'Confidential clerk to Captain Neuheim,' Schumacher
said, smiling proudly. By this time he had definitely decided
that Schulz was his own personal creation.

'Counter-espionage, eh?' the clerk said.

Schulz's eyes fell morosely on the newly deposited uniforms of the two General Staff officers. It seemed they
didn't waste much time in the SS.

'Right,' said Schumacher cheerfully, when they'd kitted
Schulz up again. 'Now the armoury.'

'Armoury?'

'Small-arms job this. Feel inside the pocket of that raincoat. Specially strengthened.'

'Strengthened?'

'To carry the gun. They think of everything in the SS.'

'But look here –'

'He'll explain on the way. Just listen to everything he
tells you, and forget it as soon as he's said it and play it by
ear.'

'But I don't know anything about espionage!' Schulz
wanted to cry.

'You'll learn.'

'Or small arms.'

'Oh, don't worry. Just do what he does when he does it.'

When Schulz was issued with a pistol his first fear was
that it would go off in his hand.

'Now that is a danger,' Schumacher agreed, 'Especially if
you've got it cocked when he's driving. I should make sure
the safety catch is on when you're in the car with him if I
were you. Very dangerous, that is.'

'What is?'

'His driving. Now then, let's have a look at you. Suit's a

51

better fit, the hat'll do, shoes okay, tie very sombre, good
You'll do. Just remember, never contradict him and appear
to do what he does. He's the leader, right? And I should
keep myself on the side of his good eye if there's any fire-
works. Oh, and there's just one more thing. When you get
in the car with him, it might be a help if you kept your eye
on the main road from time to time. He tends to get carried
away when he's got something on his mind, if you know
what I mean? I'd better put you in the car now in case he
changes his mind. When he comes, take your hands out of
your pockets and rush to open the door for him. And don't
let the ironmongery show – he's very hot on that.'

'The ironmongery?'

'The gun, you fool. What do you think you're going to, a
picnic?'

'Will I be on my own?'

'No, it's all been planned by the Captain. We'll have half
the department there. Now just remember the password.
What is it?'

'Password?'

' "The war could be over by Christmas". Haven't you
heard that treasonable saying before?'

'Well, yes.'

'Don't forget it then. And make no remarks about his
driving whatever you do. Just act normal, in short.'

Neuheim's driving would have endangered life in the middle
of the Sahara Desert. He hunched himself over the wheel as
if trying to bend it towards him; a cigarette holder was
wedged, as ever, between his teeth; his single eye scanned,
not the road ahead, but the verge. He appeared not to see
traffic lanes other than his own and when he overtook any
vehicle he had a habit of leaning away and looking under it
as he passed as if suspecting enemy agents or foreign bodies
lurking there. This meant that he virtually ignored on-
coming traffic, expecting, despite the fact that both he and
Schulz were in plain clothes, that all drivers would know
who was approaching and react with proper respect. This

wasn't, of course, the case.

Schulz clung to the grab rail in the seat beside him, wishing he could climb up it and make his escape. They were heading for the Dutch border and Schulz had decided that the best way to deal with Neuheim was to deliberately exaggerate his own appearance of naïveté. If he came across as an idiot there was a chance that Neuheim would have no hesitation in dispensing with his services. It had not escaped his notice that Schumacher had taken great pains to avoid the expedition and Schulz had been packed into the car with Neuheim as if he were the Captain's own personal and private sandwich lunch.

Schulz had heard rumours from Schumacher and others on the second floor that Neuheim was zealously looking for ways to implicate as many army officers as he could in gross cowardice. He wanted bodies, as the phrase went. Schulz had begun to worry about this and was wondering about his own precise use to Neuheim when the Captain, who had been driving at breakneck speed with a look of fiendish anticipation on his face, took his eyes off the road once again.

'Not far now,' he spat at Schulz. 'You look a bit green?'

'It's nothing, sir,' said Schulz. 'It's just that I've never kidnapped two British officers before.'

'We'll have them stuffed in the boot of the car before they can say "knife".'

'Knife, Herr Captain?'

'Knife.'

Schulz pondered this as they drove in silence. It seemed an odd thing for anyone to want to say. He couldn't help but take an interest in the situation, however. There were, to Schulz's mind, certain problems involved in getting people over the border, Holland being neutral at that time. What Schulz didn't appreciate was that access to Holland was easy: Germans living near the Dutch frontier were still allowed to cross over to shop in neighbouring Dutch towns.

'How do we get the car back across the border, sir? The guards are sure to open the boot.'

Neuheim's good eye gleamed. A lorry had had the impertinence to be in front of him. Another, coming in the opposite direction, veered towards the centre of the road. Neuheim put his foot down and seemed to ignore both.

'Cunning and dash!' he said. 'You're in counter-espionage now, you should be able to work that out for yourself!'

'Yes, sir . . .'

The lorries approached, congealed, divided. Neuheim went through them like paste in a sandwich and did not even notice.

'Well?' said Neuheim.

'Er . . .' Schulz remembered Schumacher's practice of giving Neuheim an answer straight away. 'Would the "cunning" be in approaching the barrier as if we were going to stop, and the "dash" be in putting our foot down just as we got to it, sir?'

Neuheim stared at Schulz for an entire minute during which time Schulz registered out of the corner of his eye a fleet of cars, lorries and a bicycle swerving to avoid crashing into them. The cyclist came off his bike and landed in a patch of grassy verge.

'By God, you're sharp!' said Neuheim at last. Schulz sighed with relief as he returned his eye to the road. 'You've read my mind exactly.'

'Yes, sir,' Schulz nodded.

There was a pause.

'Of course, the guards will open fire?' Schulz added.

Neuheim, who had never once taken his foot off the accelerator since they had started, now seemed to be polishing the sole of his shoe, and the needle was nearly off the speedometer. Through the window all that could be seen was a blur of smoke. There was an acrid smell of burning rubber.

'Naturally,' he grinned. 'But we shan't be going as slowly as this, I can tell you.'

He negotiated the next bend as if it were the combined staffs of the British and German armies. However, when they reached the frontier, having handed the briefcase full of false documents to Schulz, he slowed down. When the

Dutch immigration officer handed them back their passports, Neuheim spoke like an old Lutheran pastor.

'Thank you, you're too kind. And now we drive off through your beautiful country. Long live Queen Wilelmina! Good morning to you.'

The heavy-handedness of this flattery didn't seem to rouse any suspicion and two sentries lifted the barrier. They drove through the usual no-man's-land for about three hundred yards and at the end of it a café appeared, with a large car-park fronting it. Schulz suddenly realized he hadn't eaten for hours and the smells coming from the Café Backus invaded his nostrils in great waves. His stomach began to rumble uneasily as he savoured the aroma of garlic and wine, fried steak and tomatoes ...

'Confound it!' Neuheim rasped in his ear. 'Intelligence told us the café would be virtually empty at this time of the morning.'

Schulz followed Neuheim's gaze and saw that a tourist coach had drawn slowly to a halt. A party of monks on their way to Germany were alighting and entering the café.

'Just monks, sir,' said Schulz, hoping this would mitigate Neuheim's growing anger.

'I can see that, you idiot,' Neuheim hissed. 'Oh well,' he added, eyeing Schulz, 'you know what to do?'

Schulz had very little idea what to do but nodded nervously. He had however remembered the recognition phrase. And of course there would also be other SS men planted around the place.

Neuheim drove the car off the road and on to the forecourt. As they approached the café Schulz observed a long file of the monks forming a queue to go to the toilet. There seemed to be a regiment of them, all red-cheeked and plump, their hands patiently folded. Schulz wondered if they might be agents. As they passed them, Schulz could see the two British officers sitting at a table, quietly talking. Two hatchet-faced men dressed as labourers at another table near the wall, covertly watching the British officers, were obviously SS.

In fact, thought Schulz, the whole set-up was obvious.

Although the British officers were in mufti they could no[t] have looked more British with their highly polished brogu[e] shoes and their quiet tweeds. Schulz remembered seein[g] identical types during his stay in England, coming out [of] Harrods with their white riding macs and thornproof[s] straight-backed and military despite the autumn shade[s.] One of them even smoked a briar pipe and Schulz kne[w] that it would be from Dunhill. Even as he looked, the office[r] brought out a tobacco pouch in striped regimental colour[s.] The hatchet-faced cover men seated nearby gave visib[le] gleams of recognition below their ill-fitting workmen's ca[ps] as Neuheim entered.

It was all so obvious, thought Schulz again. All exce[pt] the file of monks waiting as though for confession. Then [it] dawned on him that they were absolutely silent, like a ro[w] of toby jugs. Neuheim had reminded Schulz of the passwor[d] in a whisper as they entered the café and Schulz had alread[y] been briefed about the false names they were to adopt. H[e] went up to the squarer and straighter of the two Englis[h] men, the sort of man, thought Schulz, you might expect [to] see as president of the village cricket team. He stood [up] politely as Schulz approached.

'Good morning?' Schulz said. It was half-statement, ha[lf] question.

'Morning,' said the Englishman.

' "I hear the war could be over by Christmas"?' It w[as] half-question, half-statement.

'So do we,' the Englishman answered. 'How do you d[o.] Glad you could make it. Sit down and have a drink.' H[e] pointed to the thinner officer who was older and greyer, h[is] severe nose set like a cutting instrument in an even seve[rer] face. 'I'm Harrison Smith, he's Withers.'

Neuheim, who was standing behind Schulz, clicked h[is] heels in a passable imitation of the General Staff office[r] whom he had so recently eliminated.

'Colonel Goertler,' said Schulz, also clicking his hee[ls] though not so efficiently. 'This is Major General Steiner.[']

Neuheim came forward and the second British office[r] Colonel Withers, stood up. They all shook hands as thoug[h]

56

they were judges in a dog show. Behind them the undercover man intensified his studied indifference. Even the monks were beginning to look at them.

Neuheim, Schulz and the British officers sat down and Harrison Smith gave a polite smile. 'Did you have a good journey?' he asked. 'We had a beautiful drive. The weather's been really lovely, hasn't it? What are you drinking, if it's not too early?'

Neuheim had changed his expression. 'Right now, Major,' he said in menacing, heavily accented English, 'my revolver is trained on your stomach beneath the table. My colleague here has his trained on Colonel Withers.'

Schulz jammed a hand in his pocket just in time.

'Behind you are two SS men, also with guns in their pockets. I must ask you not to make any sudden movements.'

There was silence. Smith and Withers looked at Neuheim and Schulz as if they had committed some very grave breach of manners, then turned to look at the SS men who patted their bulging pockets and grinned evilly. Harrison Smith gave Withers a pained glance.

'I see. We've been had, Clyde,' he said. 'They're not Steiner and Goertler after all.'

'Correct,' said Neuheim. '*Gorregt!* Steiner and Goertler are under arrest. My orders are to take you back to Germany for interrogation.'

Withers gave him an insolent look, as if to an impudent ticket collector. 'And how do you propose to do that, ol' boy?'

'In my car,' said Neuheim drily. 'You'll both fit very snugly into the boot.'

'And what,' said Withers icily, 'if we choose not to go? This is Holland, you fool, you can't go shooting people here.'

'Excuse me, Colonel Withers,' Schulz said nervously, 'but *he* can, I promise you.'

Neuheim ignored him. 'It's my intention to take you both back, Colonel, or leave you here dead,' he snarled.

Schulz began to feel that the gun in his pocket was somehow vulgar, like showing one's braces at a funeral.

'But my dear chap, how will you get us through customs?' asked Withers. 'You can hardly declare us?'

'In one minute,' Neuheim said, 'you will stand up slowly and proceed towards the door.'

To Harrison Smith this whole interlude had presented itself as a chess problem, a matter of academic interest. 'Mmm,' he said, making no sign of any movement at all. 'Look here, let's look at this thing from our point of view. I'm not being awkward, you understand, but I take it none of us wants to get killed yet? The war's only just begun.'

'Quite,' said Withers.

'I think it's you who are about to get killed, Major, no one else,' said Neuheim.

'Let him finish, ol' boy,' said Withers.

'Thank you, Clyde,' said Smith, pausing for maximum effect or perhaps because he had not intended to continue. 'The question Withers and I have to ask ourselves as Intelligence officers, is this,' he said finally. 'What's the point of our going quietly with you now, to avoid a lot of nasty bloodshed *here*, just to have you blowing everybody's brains out when they try to open the car at the border?'

Schulz didn't like the way Neuheim was eyeing Smith.

'That won't actually happen, Major Smith. Our plan is to approach the barrier cautiously and then make a dash for it.' This was Schulz's first major speech in Counter-Intelligence and both Smith and Withers looked at him aghast.

'A *dash* for it?' said Smith.

'Afraid of a little rifle fire, Major?' Neuheim sounded rather smug, Schulz thought.

'Not rifle fire, old boy, no. It's *that* I'm afraid of.'

He gave a nod at the larger of the two café windows. Through the flyblown curtain they could make out a light tank trundling soundlessly up the road, its tracks glistening as it made its way towards the barrier.

'Didn't your Intelligence tell you that the Dutch had moved an armoured division up here?' It was Withers who sounded smug now. 'That thing's always up and down the road now. I've no desire to be in the boot of your car when they put one of those shells up its arse. Sorry, it's just not on, I'm afraid. We'll take our chances here.'

They had obviously reached a kind of stalemate. Neuheim glared furiously at Withers as though he were a new kind of insect that had miraculously found the power to hit back. By this time Schulz was sweating profusely. The next moment his fears were proved justified.

'I'm not so easily trifled with, Major,' said Neuheim quietly. 'I'm taking you back alive or leaving you here dead. The choice is yours.'

Schulz could feel a nervous twitch coming on. If Neuheim started shooting he was as likely to shoot him as the British. The still-patient file of monks was still queuing for the toilet. Obviously they must have taken a vow of silence. Suddenly he had an idea. The British had a very simple objection. They just didn't want to be shot at by the Dutch and had decided that Neuheim was crazy enough to provoke everybody into firing.

Neuheim rose from the table. 'Stand up,' he hissed.

The British officers didn't move.

'I shall count to three,' said Neuheim. Schulz heard a grunt from the other table. The SS men were preparing themselves for the orders-to-kill – probably the only thing they understood, he thought

'... and then we'll shoot you both,' Neuheim was saying, 'and blast our way back across the border. One ...'

Smith turned to Schulz. 'Is he acquainted with the rules of the Geneva Convention?' he said and began rummaging in his pockets. 'I've got a booklet here ...'

Schulz's idea related to the monks and to their waiting coach outside in the forecourt. Who would shoot a monk? he thought.

'Keep your hands still!' Neuheim was saying. 'Two!' He nodded across at the other SS men. One of them strolled across to the counter to cover the proprietor. Clearly Neuheim had meant what he said.

'Could I make a suggestion?' said Schulz.

'No point, ol' man,' said Smith. 'We'll all be blown to

smithereens in that car anyway – you included.'

'That's just what I'm trying to avoid,' said Schulz. 'I think I have a way out that will suit all parties.'

Neuheim was looking at Schulz now as if he'd changed sex.

'In that case, hadn't he better retract that number "two"?' said Withers. 'It's sort of – hanging in the air a bit.'

'Get on with it, then,' snapped Neuheim.

'I take it, sir,' said Schulz to Smith, 'that you're prepared to come quietly with us provided we've got a sporting chance of getting you back in one piece?'

'Well,' Smith said, 'I agree – in the circumstances, and seeing that we're outnumbered – we'd have no choice. We've rather buggered this thing up, you know, Clyde.'

'We've been sold down the river, Harrison. Or is it "up"?'

'Down, I think,' said Smith. 'But we're not getting into that car, with a tank on the prowl, I can tell you that,' he added for Schulz's benefit.

'I'm sure it won't be necessary,' said Schulz, giving Neuheim, who was still staring at him, a heavy wink. 'The war will not be over by Christmas for the monks,' he added, but Neuheim was by now beginning to question the value of first impressions. The man he had hired that morning was clearly an idiot and would have been more usefully employed in postal censorship.

'The situation calls for a foursome in the lavatory, Captain,' Schulz added, hoping that that would prod him.

'The lavatory?' Neuheim repeated, mystified.

'Nobody is going to fire tank shells into a bus full of monks,' Schulz replied.

A smile began to creep along Neuheim's face. The penny had dropped.

'Would you bring them along, sir? We'll have to hurry,' said Schulz. Unaccountably he seemed to have taken charge of the situation.

Withers and Smith had also understood. They rose quite willingly and followed Schulz, Neuheim and the two SS officers tailing behind them.

*   *   *
60

The coach-horn had been blowing impatiently for the last of the monks to return. There was still a queue of two of the monks waiting outside the lavatory. When Schulz and his party halted in front of them they smiled at Schulz and Schulz smiled back at them. But the monks started to get slightly puzzled when Schulz made no movement to go inside. He seemed to be waiting for something.

They heard the sound of water flushing. Shortly the lavatory door opened and two more monks emerged. Quickly, Schulz bundled all four into the lavatory, while Neuheim and one of the SS men pushed the British officers in after them, slamming the door.

By this time Neuheim had convinced himself that it was his idea and had begun to overlord the proceedings. There was a little diversion when it was discovered that one of the monks was wearing female underwear (again Schulz wondered whether the fame of Krauss's brand had spread to Holland) but there was no time to go into it. Whether or not the monks were German or Dutch was never discovered: throughout the operation they remained as silent as the grave.

Back in the café the proprietor stared open-mouthed at the remaining SS man who started to approach him with a Luger aimed at the centre of his chest.

Outside, the coach was still waiting, the driver still tooting his horn impatiently. Even the passengers were now getting restless and the driver was just about to get down to hurry the stragglers when the four monks who had been holding them up appeared through the emergency exit-doors of the café Backus. They hurried with heads down and cowls hanging over their faces to the coach, boarding it in twos. If any of the monks noticed that the second couple to board the coach were now armed with Lugers they said, as was their custom, nothing. The door was quickly closed and the coach drove back towards the border.

At the barrier the coach drew to a halt while the immigration officer inspected the documents handed to him by the driver. A customs officer gave a cursory look along the coach, the documents were handed back, the barrier raised and the coach moved forward to the German barrier where it stopped once more. This time four monks alighted. The coach reversed rapidly and sped back towards Holland.

'I didn't know you had it in you, Schulz,' said Schumacher, doodling as usual on a pile of forms in Neuheim's outer office. 'If I had been in your position I would have left it to Neuheim.'

If I had left it to Neuheim, Schulz reflected, *I would probably be dead by now.*

The news of Operation Wilma, as it was now being called, had quickly spread through Dept VIB. Heydrich had congratulated his old friend and passed the news on to the Fuhrer. As a result Neuheim had received a special commendation from Adolf Hitler who had promoted him to Major and personally awarded him the Knights Order of the Iron Cross for bravery and initiative. Specifically for having masterminded the daring removal of two British officers from under the noses of the Dutch. Only Schumacher knew that this was in fact Schulz's doing.

In the wake of the event Schulz had felt an odd sense of anti-climax. It was not that he necessarily enjoyed being in the heat of the action. Indeed if it had not been for Neuheim's monotonous count up to three and his fingers itching to press the trigger, Schulz would have never dreamt of taking any initiative at all. But he was so sure in that moment that Neuheim intended to shoot them all, including Schulz, if only because there was nothing else that he could think of doing, that Schulz had been forced to act out of a pure and simple instinct for self-preservation.

No, Schulz was feeling anti-climactic because during those golden minutes when he was in neutral territory it had occurred to him that he was in an excellent position to disappear forever from the Fatherland and put as much distance between himself and Neuheim as possible before the Captain involved him in any more of his crazy ideas. But in the end he had only done his duty, he thought sadly.

'I was only doing my duty,' said Schulz.

'Well, your appointment to SS Counter-Intelligence is confirmed,' Schumacher said. 'And Neuheim has asked for you to be seconded to him permanently.'

Schulz could not have felt more despondent.

7

Throughout his life Schulz had had the unswerving conviction that Fate had singled him out as a special case. The trouble was that Fate, having singled him out, kept losing track of him, either out of absent-mindedness or wilful sadism. It was as though he had been given sealed orders at birth for a secret mission – and had then found it impossible to open them, without getting his fingers stuck in the glue. It was as though he had been cast adrift in a stormy sea: the higher a wave scooped him, the lower he sank in its trough; sometimes he felt that he had been slowly drowning since he set sail. It was not as though he had begun on the oar-bench. He had been planted in the crow's nest and could see things more clearly than others, though sometimes he saw them too quickly and this tended to hold things up. He had been equipped with a higher-than-average intelligence and education but these things only made people like Neuheim defensive and then people like Neuheim would try to hide the fact by attacking him.

Schulz had always been afraid of being attacked. When he was afraid he trembled. Worse, he had a nervous twitch that started in his stomach and stayed there, though neither the twitch nor the tremble could be seen. It was as if something had gone wrong with the inside of a cuckoo clock, as Neuheim quickly spotted.

'We have the clock,' Neuheim unkindly told him, 'but the hands do not even tell the time and when the moment is ripe for the bird to pop, a dumb silence is the only result.'

Schulz made Neuheim very defensive and with very good reason. Neuheim in his turn spent the first few weeks in which Schulz worked for him abusing Schulz and the missing cuckoo and then carried on doing so for the rest of the war. But it seemed as though they were already bound together by mutual distrust and intrigue. Schulz-and-Neuheim, Neuheim-and-Schulz, their names began to be mentioned in one breath: they were becoming the Laurel and Hardy of Counter-Intelligence. Whatever Neuheim liked Schulz had to lump.

Schulz had now been attached to the Dusseldorf Intelligence HQ for nearly six weeks. Admittedly three of those weeks had been spent loitering around the canteen, but since he had been seconded to Captain, now Major Neuheim his anxiety had increased dramatically. It was not as if he spent every waking moment in close proximity to Neuheim. Sometimes hours would go by in which he and Schumacher would sit, often in silence, in Neuheim's outer office, Schumacher doodling, Schulz pondering.

Sometimes Schulz would be trying to decipher some illegible piece of scrawl that Neuheim had thrown at him – it was Neuheim's task to produce an endless flow of counter-espionage ideas that would meet with the approval of his masters, when a rasping cough would announce the fact that Neuheim had been silently surveying Schulz in bemused wonder for whole minutes. Schulz assumed that Neuheim had been holding his breath because otherwise he would have been sure to have smelt the garlic and Schnapps.

The truth was that Neuheim was intrigued by Schulz and at the same time horrified that such a weakling had somehow found his way into *his* office. Yet, with very little effort on his part, Schulz had made himself indispensable, not because of his secretarial skills – Neuheim had fired dozens of better typists, male and female – but because he made such an intelligent doormat.

When you thought about it, then, and Schulz thought about it constantly, it was easy to see how Neuheim had been unconsciously waiting for someone like Schulz to act as those missing parts of his grey cells for a very long time.

If things went wrong Neuheim could blame Schulz; if they went right then Neuheim would receive the credit due to him by virtue of his natural superiority. What was more difficult to see was why Schulz allowed such a situation to develop.

Schulz was reminded of an incident in his childhood when one night he had seen a rabbit literally mesmerized by the headlights of a car. Neuheim mesmerized him. He could no more openly abuse or disobey the major than he could avoid feeling queasy every time that black eye-patch glanced in his direction. Perhaps, he thought disconsolately, this was the fate he had been singled out for.

Coinciding with the constant mental tension of working for a man who had a screw loose, Schulz had been suffering the torments of a sexual frustration which grew in intensity as the days wore on. The tantalizing glimpses he was afforded of the blonde frauleins who decorated the second floor did nothing to relieve this.

Neuheim himself seemed to take a vicious pleasure in titillating Schulz by leaving the door to his inner office half open when some urgent dictation needed to be done by one or other of the frauleins. Each time, Neuheim had contrived to arrange the typist's chair so that Schulz could not fail to get a view of legs which crossed and uncrossed at regular intervals. The sight of those legs, the sound of silk sliding against silk like the tide going in and out, and the smell of perfume began to drive Schulz into a cold sweat. Neuheim would invariably close the door after a quarter of an hour of this torture as though, having allowed Schulz as it were to get a sniff of the *hors d'oeuvres*, he could safely leave the rest to his victim's by-now frenzied imagination – an imagination stoked up every now and again by the muted sound of giggling and once even a gasp, whether of triumph or horror Schulz could not decide.

Schumacher always managed to make himself scarce at these times – perhaps, thought Schulz, he had his own fish to fry – but for Schulz there was no way out.

* * *

A few weeks after he had been deposited on Neuheim – and vice versa – Schulz was leafing through a folder of memoranda that had been passed to Neuheim from Heydrich. A loose sheet fell out and Schulz found himself perusing a list of what appeared to be the most frequented dens and red-light districts of Berlin. By now Schulz recognized Heydrich's handwriting and was amazed to discover that the Gestapo chief not only had a consummate knowledge of individual brothels but an insatiable interest in the most trivial gossip of their inmates. He had even devised an elaborate scoring system, taking into account such factors as the quality of the clientele, the nature of the perverted practices to be found therein and, most intriguing of all, the number and names of General Staff officers who were known to visit each brothel.

Schulz was baffled. Why should the Head of Security concern himself with such matters in a time of war? If the army wanted to enjoy itself that was its business. Of course Schulz knew that Heydrich, like Neuheim, was keen to find evidence of treason amongst army officers. From the very beginnings in the thirties, the army had not approved of the SS which they considered a private army of hoodlums. They had been reluctant even to give the SS any training and when they did it was at first limited to small arms. The SS men had then got into brawls with their instructors, calling them *monockeltraeger*, or monocle-wearers, knocking over statues of the beloved Kaiser and generally abusing the stiff-necked officers of the *Kriegsakademie*. It had only been recently that the SS had managed to attain its present executive powers over the army.

But what use could this information be put to? Schulz passed the list to Schumacher who merely yawned. At that moment Neuheim stepped out of his office, scowling.

'Is anything the matter, Herr Major?' said Schulz. 'Is anything on your mind?'

'You are the matter, Schulz ... and nothing is in your mind,' Neuheim paused and glared at him.

Neuheim was looking so furious that Schulz decided not to laugh.

'These yellow-bellied army types make me want to puke,' commented Neuheim as though providing Schulz with a clue to a crossword puzzle.

'They are depraved scum and should all be taken out and shot,' he went on, warming to his theme.

This seemed to Schulz an odd thing to say considering the evidence of Neuheim's own predilection but it gave him an idea.

'I don't suppose the *Oberstgruppenfuhrer* could utilize his great knowledge of the army's habits, Herr Major?' he suggested.

'What are you talking about?'

'I'm referring, sir, to *Oberstgruppenfuhrer* Heydrich.'

'Heydrich? What about him?'

'Well, I was wondering, sir . . .' Schulz was trying to think of a way of phrasing it that would reflect maximum credit on the SS and not blemish the personal honour of Neuheim's boss. 'It is well known, Herr Major, that the *Oberstgruppen-fuhrer* has a consummate knowledge of the army's sexual weaknesses.' Schulz was not sure whether it was so well-known, but boldness, as Schumacher had shown him, was best with Neuheim. 'The problem is, Herr Major, that the Fuhrer requires proof. It is a well-known fact, sir, that the way to catch people off their guard is when they are under the stimulus of great sexual excitement.'

Neuheim grunted.

'Now if it were possible to overhear the confidences of these army personnel at such times, Herr Major, well . . .' Schulz trailed off. Neuheim looked as though he were going to explode.

'Don't be so bloody ridiculous,' he barked. 'It's not only the most stupid idea I've ever heard but it's not possible, it wouldn't work. The Fuhrer is not a man to stoop to such methods, Schulz, and if you value your position here I suggest you shut up and pay more attention to your shorthand which is *slipshod*!'

With which Neuheim stormed into his office and slammed the door.

* * *

But the seed had been planted and an hour later Neuheim phoned Heydrich. Heydrich was appalled and slammed the phone down. An hour after that he rang Neuheim back. The Fuhrer, it seemed, was extremely interested in Heydrich's highly original idea and had ordered its immediate implementation. Neuheim earned himself a special tribute from the Fuhrer for having offered his services in performing the arduous task of monitoring the conversations. The listening device to be employed was a tape-recorder which used steel to capture sound magnetically. The Fuhrer had been very interested in this scientific invention and realized that this would be an excellent opportunity to put it to a glorious use.

Because Dept VIB was a technical division of Intelligence, Neuheim's department was to be moved to the Delbruckstrasse in Berlin. Heydrich had ordered a comfortable hotel to be rented through an intermediary and to be luxuriously appointed as a cat-house. It was the job of Schulz, Schumacher and other SD personnel and Gestapo technicians to instal the microphones. Soon even intimate corners of bars – and of course bedrooms – were bristling with bugs. The tape recorders were installed in the cellars of the building. Neuheim had chosen to take personal command of the recruitment of the girls who were said to have been selected not only for their beauty and charm, but for their intelligence, culture, knowledge of languages and patriotism. Whether or not Neuheim was capable of judging any of these qualities, it was surprisingly easy to cream off, as it were, volunteers not only from the demi-monde but from the best society who were apparently only too eager to serve the Fatherland.

The Salon Kitty was soon to be frequented by a select clientele, among whom were foreign diplomats to whom well-meaning friends did not fail to give the address. Heydrich himself made frequent personal inspections of the Salon, but always insisted that the microphones be disconnected while he was there.

If Schulz had fathered the scheme, its progenitor was either a well-kept secret or had become instantly forgotten.

To all intents and purposes Heydrich had given it a virgin birth and delivered it to Neuheim for adoption with the blessings of the Fuhrer, the godfather. Neuheim however was not a man to be lumbered with babies and was only too happy to pass it down the line to Schulz for the dirty business of attending it, washing its nappies and feeding it, while Heydrich and Neuheim, like proud parents, sat back and watched its progress.

It was Schulz's fortune to be given the job for which Neuheim had earned his special tribute in advance: that of monitoring the conversations in the bedrooms and bars. Neuheim told Schulz that he had been awarded the appointment for his help in Operation Wilma. Schulz was delighted. At last, he thought, the months of sexual hunger would be satiated in an orgy of secret liaisons with fellow employees, both during and outside work hours....

Schulz had been at the Salon Kitty for a fortnight and had not been near a bedroom. His place was in the basement boiler-room where the listening apparatus had been installed. His task was twofold: to man the tape recorders that would provide proof of treason in an undeniable form; and to write down, independently of what was captured on tape – since the machines were always breaking down – every scrap of sound that floated down to the boiler-room via the pipes through which the microphone cables led. He did not know which job he hated more: the boiler-room was already like an oven and the machines themselves were constantly having to be switched off to avoid overheating. As if that were not enough, Schulz, jammed against the pipes, sweating from the heat of the cumbersome headphones and the tape recorders which had to be oiled continuously to lubricate their revolving drums (making them even more inefficient), had now to listen in on conversations which were either erotic in the extreme, making his experience in Neuheim's office seems positively relaxing in comparison, or deadly tedious.

The girls were well aware that they were being monitored

and would sometimes stretch out a performance, to Schulz's anguish, for hours on end. Schulz's shorthand was not particularly good – in that respect Neuheim had been correct – and there were nights when his wrists would seize up from writing. Not only did he have to transcribe every grunt and sigh – which might, Neuheim maintained, conceal a treasonable intent – but everything had to be timed, and forms with two columns, one for the girl and one for the visitor, had to be filled in. Schulz soon discovered that other people had been employed just to watch the monitors and check that they kept on the job throughout their shift.

It was like being continually tickled with a feather and not being allowed to laugh. To add to Schulz's torment he was obliged to listen to the dance music which was played in the main salon, and which alternated between rousing and sugary, blasting through his headphones and making it impossible to make out what was being said. Needless to say, at the end of a shift Schulz was a nervous wreck.

The only thing that made the job remotely bearable for him was Fraulein Freyer. Not that Fraulein Freyer had promised Schulz anything by word or gesture, but there was so eloquent a promise in her eyes and in her sinuous walk that had Schulz been a banker he would have been only too happy to accept it as collateral for a billion marks – in pre-inflation currency. Schulz, though, was a practically penniless private and Fraulein Freyer was very conscious of rank. So he would go home and have a cold shower.

But the promise of Fraulein Freyer's walk and dreamy eyes would not leave Schulz. She had other talents too that Schulz was one of the few people to know about, because of his privileged position. Fraulein Freyer performed with remarkable subtlety at her end of the microphone, as if she wished Schulz to understand exactly what it was that he would never have a chance of possessing. Of course, Schulz had become a recipient of those fruits before he had set eyes on her, such was the unfortunate nature of his task, but they were fruits which it was impossible for him to devour.

The first time he saw her was a week after he had begun his tour of duty as *aureur* at the Salon Kitty. He had gone upstairs, trying to look invisible, to find some salve for a burn he had contracted from touching a hot-water pipe. She was leading a general downstairs after what Schulz happened to know had been an exhausting hour. The general was obviously puffed out and still highly stimulated. Fraulein Freyer looked as cool as a glacier, making her even more desirable to Schulz who was developing an aversion to heat. She was wearing a green off-the-shoulder dress which, like a silken skin, tightly hugged her incredible body. Schulz just stared.

The general was buttoning up his jacket, missing a button or two, and Fraulein Freyer was helping him as they paused on the bottom step. The general whispered something to her, nibbling at her ear lobe at the same time. She shook her head, seeming to emerge in a froth of blonde hair like a swimmer breaking water after a dive and just said, 'Next time!'

Those two words haunted Schulz. What had the general asked her to do? What she had already done with him during the previous hour had, as far as Schulz's education stretched, scaled the heights and plummeted the depths of what it was humanly possible for two people to achieve within the confines of a bedroom.

During the weeks to follow, as the winter of 1939 set in, Fraulein Freyer became Schulz's obsession. When he saw her she was ice-cream, delicious and glacial; when he heard her through the headphones she was lemon meringue, hot and provocative – and a little perverse. Finally Schulz plucked up the courage to introduce himself one evening, after she had melted an ambassador with a suggestion that had set Schulz's mind reeling.

'Good evening, Fraulein Freyer, I'm Gerhardt Schulz,' he said, his stomach turning to jelly.

She stared at him as though he were a beetle.

'I work downstairs,' said Schulz sheepishly.

'Well,' she replied, 'and what grave secrets did our master spy overhear tonight?'

Schulz was floored. He had not expected such familiarity and disdain.

'Oh, nothing much,' he said. 'Just the usual sort of thing, you know,' he mumbled, aware as he said it that they both knew what they both knew.

'What do you expect to hear from a whore's bedroom? Counter-espionage?' she said.

Schulz was shocked. Somehow he could not reconcile the vision in front of him with the experienced sexual practitioner he knew her to be.

'I was wondering, Fraulein Freyer, if maybe, perhaps, one night, when things were slack, if you and I . . . ?'

She laughed. The sound was like syrup and it rippled down Schulz's intestines.

'I doubt whether you could afford me, Schulz,' she said, smiling and murmuring the words so suggestively that he began to speculate madly about the heavenly delights that money would purchase. 'Besides,' she added, 'I can't do it with anyone below the rank of major.'

She gave him another infuriatingly provocative smile and disappeared, leaving Schulz dry-throated and aching with desire.

It was probably true. Schulz had heard it said of Fraulein Freyer that she came from a wealthy, aristocratic family and that she was doing it purely for the Fatherland. Of course they didn't know what Schulz knew and the knowledge drove him crazy.

After that however, Fraulein Freyer would occasionally visit Schulz in the basement, perhaps to taunt him with her unpickable fruits.

'I can get hold of some real coffee,' Schulz said one night, feeling rather sordid even as he said it. 'Good coffee beans if you want to know.'

Fraulein Freyer merely smiled.

'I've got a cupboard full of coffee,' she said, caressing a chair with her exquisite fingers.

Schulz groaned.

'Are they mad, the British?' Neuheim screamed, bursting into the office one morning in a fury.

He dumped a pile of paper on Schulz's desk.

'They're bombing us with leaflets! They dropped five million pieces of paper on the Ruhr last night! Paper!'

'That's typical of the British, sir,' said Schulz, pandering to one of Neuheim's pet hatreds. 'They're the worst litter louts in Europe. I can remember filth everywhere when I was there.'

This was quite untrue. England had impressed Schulz as a green and pleasant land, and a clean one.

When Schulz spoke to Neuheim now he had developed the habit of speaking to his nose, as if it were a person in its own right. Schulz talked to it as to a subnormal nose that had lost its reason in a traffic accident. Schulz prayed that one day Neuheim would actually have one and that only his nose would walk away.

'They surely don't expect the German people to read them?' said Neuheim.

'Oh, no, sir,' said Schulz. 'They're just hoping to make our cities as filthy as their own.'

Neuheim considered this. He seemed very impressed. He took his nose back into his inner office where Kube was lurking. He, too, had been promoted to Major.

The switchboard buzzed and Schumacher put the call through to Kube.

'Heydrich's on the line,' Kube said. 'He's in a fury over those leaflets. He wants to know if he should advise Goering to drop our own leaflets on London. I've put the call through to you, Neuheim.'

Neuheim opened his mouth to curse Kube, when the phone rang on his desk. He stared at it desperately, letting it ring.

'Well, what do you think?' he hissed at Kube. 'Would the British read them if we dropped them? Is it worth it?'

Kube shrugged. The phone kept ringing.

Schulz decided that someone ought to answer the phone and he might as well do so. He walked into Neuheim's office and picked up the phone.

'Major Neuheim's office?'

A sound like a rattlesnake hissed in Schulz's ear.

'*Oberstgruppenführer* Heydrich, sir,' he said to Neuheim.

Neuheim cursed under his breath. Considering they were supposed to be friends it seemed a peculiarly unequal relationship. He covered the mouthpiece and his eye registered the closest thing to panic Schulz had ever seen in it.

'You've lived in Britain,' he said, pointing his nose at Schulz. 'Do you think the British would read our leaflets if we dropped them over there? London, say?'

Schulz was still standing at attention. 'I doubt if they'd even notice, sir. There's too much rubbish lying about in the streets already.'

As so often recently Neuheim stared at Schulz, almost mesmerized with fascination. He slowly uncovered the mouthpiece: it was hissing again.

'My dear Reinhardt,' he simpered, 'what can I do for you?'

There was a long pause during which Neuheim arranged his features in a variety of grimaces which were all distant cousins of a smile.

'Yes,' he finally said. 'Kube and I were just discussing them.'

Another pause followed in which Neuheim locked his eye on to Schulz.

'Well, in my opinion,' he said winsomely into the phone, 'dropping leaflets on the British would be a waste of time. Their streets are so filthy they wouldn't even notice them.'

He listened apprehensively for a few moments and then chuckled, pleased.

'Thank you, Reinhardt. Of course we'll think of something,' Neuheim said and put down the phone.

Kube let out a huge sigh of relief. 'Thank you, Alfred,' he said and hurried out of the room.

Neuheim was looking at Schulz curiously.

'You're a clever little fellow, aren't you? Got it up here,' he muttered, tapping his forehead. 'Some of our SS types think it's enough to be fair-haired and blue-eyed but if that were so where would the Fuhrer be, eh?'

'Not in the SS, sir,' said Schulz dutifully.

'Exactly,' said Neuheim. 'Well, that's Himmler's problem,

not mine. Mine is what to do about these damned leaflets ...'

He was looking at Schulz again.

'May I make a suggestion, Herr Major?' Schulz was getting rather tired of the leaflets.

'Well?'

'We put out a statement over the radio to London. We thank the British for their contribution to the German war effort and inform them that the leaflets have been swept up, repulped and turned into toilet rolls.'

Neuheim was now staring at Schulz in open admiration. He turned to Schumacher.

'Get me Dr Goebbels on the phone.'

8

Several days later, on his way to the Salon Kitty for the late-night shift, Schulz was himself caught up in an air raid, probably one of the very first of the war. He was badly shaken. The street was dark and empty and the low throbbing of planes and the dull crump of anti-aircraft fire suddenly increased in volume, until the air over the Ruhr was thick with the roar of RAF planes and the cracking of anti-aircraft guns. Searchlights groped the sky above him and red tracer bullets chased each other dementedly.

Schulz could hear the patter of falling shrapnel and hastily he put on his steel helmet and made a run for it. But he was too late. All hell seemed to be let loose around and above him and suddenly there was a tremendous juddering as a local battery opened up. He flung himself down by a doorway and waited for it all to end, covering his helmet with his hands, impotently.

A moment later a shower of paper fluttered gently down upon him, swirling in the wind. The noise of the planes receded, the guns went quiet. He picked himself up, feeling rather foolish, and noticed the paper lying around him like a sudden snowfall. Fumbling in his pocket for a torch he switched it on, focusing the beam on a sheet of paper. He stared at it incredulously.

'*Clothing* coupons?' he muttered. 'They *are* mad.'

He stuffed some of them into his pocket and walked on to the Salon Kitty.

Fraulein Freyer was still sitting on the lap of an embassy secretary. His lips were nuzzling her cleavage and her arms were around his neck so that she was able to glance at her watch. It was 11.50 p.m. She was very tired – it had been a hard day and her imagination was almost exhausted, which was unusual for Fraulein Freyer.

The door bell rang.

'I'll be back in a minute, *liebling*,' she smiled at her client who seemed to be in a stupor.

It was Schulz.

'You're late,' she said. 'Schumacher's downstairs waiting to be relieved.'

She was about to return to her client whom she was eager to pack home to his bed, when Schulz stopped her.

'Fraulein Freyer,' he said, 'please let me talk to you.'

'Not now, Schulz,' she replied. 'I'm tired. I haven't been on my feet all day. What do you want, anyway? You know I can't do it with anyone below the rank of major.'

'I've got something I think you'd like,' said Schulz.

She sighed. 'Which means I've got something you'd like. I've told you before . . .'

'Would you take clothing coupons?' said Schulz, staring at a nipple which had managed to escape the flimsy clutches of her brassière. A woman like Fraulein Freyer always seemed to need clothes . . .

'Clothing coupons?' she laughed. 'Don't be ridiculous!'

She turned to go but paused. 'How many have you got?' Greed was creeping into her eyes.

'About fifty sheets,' said Schulz, greed creeping into his eyes.

'Fifty sheets!' She gave a little screech and pressed herself up against Schulz as sensuously as a cat demanding to be fed.

Schulz trembled. Her skin was like the touch of a warm peach.

'Ssshh!' he whispered. 'Come down to the basement.'

Fraulein Freyer's block was about to be removed.

In her tastefully furnished boudoir, the embassy secretary had nodded off blissfully.

Schulz had forgotten about Schumacher who was sitting in the boiler-room, squirming beneath the headphones. Sweat beaded his moustache.

'Where have you been?' he scowled as Schulz led Fraulein Freyer between the pipes.

'I got caught up in an air raid,' said Schulz, silently giving thanks to the British for bestowing their bounties on him.

'I didn't hear any air raid,' said Schumacher, ignoring Fraulein Freyer. Schulz wondered whether he might be homosexual.

'I'm not surprised,' he said, nodding at the headphones.

'Why don't you go and take a cold shower,' Fraulein Freyer purred. For a moment Schulz feared she was giving him the brush-off yet again, but from her glance he realized it was Schumacher to whom she was talking.

'I hate this job,' he said, nodding grumpily at her. 'It's such a waste of time.'

As soon as he'd gone, Schulz pulled the wad of clothing coupons from his pocket. Fraulein Freyer opened her little silver bag and took out a pair of thick-rimmed glasses which she only wore when she was not entertaining. She put them on and began to examine the coupons while Schulz tentatively pressed his lips to her shoulders, her earlobes, her breasts. He was soon lost in passion while Fraulein Freyer ignored him totally. She might have been a librarian examining the date of an overdue book.

'Where did you get them?'

Schulz was too engrossed in his work to hear her.

'Schulz,' she repeated, 'where did you get these?'

'Black market,' he muttered, switching to her other breast.

'They're forged,' she said.

'What?' Schulz's voice was muffled.

Fraulein Freyer pushed him away and straightened her blouse. 'I said they're forged.'

Schulz snatched the coupons and held them up to the light.

'And pretty crudely forged,' she said. 'Did you seriously think I could be bought with forged clothing coupons?'

Schulz bit his lip. In the light the printing on the coupons looked terrible, as if it had been done on a child's rubber printing block. It could not have been cruder.

'What about genuine ones?' he said.

'Actually, I prefer foreign currency,' said Fraulein Freyer, removing her spectacles and returning them to her silver bag, briskly, businesslike. 'Now, if you could get hold of Swiss francs or British banknotes . . .'

'British banknotes?' Schulz laughed, incredulous. 'But we're at war with the British!'

Fraulein Freyer shrugged.

'Anyway,' added Schulz, feeling a little peeved, 'I can't get foreign currency.'

'No, but I can, and do. And I have tucked it away against the day –' She hesitated.

Schulz laughed. 'You think Germany could lose the war?' he said.

'I don't think anything – a woman has to hedge her bets.' For a moment Schulz saw that she was being completely honest with him. But then he remembered the talk of Fraulein Freyer's patriotism.

'I'm beginning to have doubts about your war aims, Fraulein Freyer,' he said, gently teasing.

She studied him seriously for a moment. 'Listen, my friend,' she said. 'My aims are very simple. One is to survive the war, the other is to do well out of it – which, as far as I can see, is no more than the leaders of our beloved Party hope to do in their own different ways.'

'I should be careful who you talk to,' laughed Schulz,

trying to make light of her words. But she had struck a raw nerve in him.

'I am,' she said. 'And I only talk to you because I know that your war aims are no different from mine.'

She smiled at him a moment longer, turned and left, her walk as sinuous as ever, her words ringing in Schulz's ears.

Strange, thought Schulz, that such a seductive creature should turn out to be a kindred soul. If only she could be one or the other. But both – it's impossible.

Disconsolately he sat down at the seat that Schumacher had vacated and flipped a switch.

'Wait a minute, Walter,' came a girl's voice, 'don't be so rough! You'll tear them. Here, let me take them off ... There, how's that?'

'Oh, Inge ...' groaned a voice that Schulz presumed was Walter's.

He flipped another switch.

'Oh, Gretchen ...' another voice groaned.

He flipped again.

'Oh, Hilda ...'

'Oh Christ!' said Schulz, switching them all off, utterly frustrated.

The forged clothing coupons caused a major row at counter-espionage headquarters. It went on for weeks with Herr Fritsch, the Deputy Minister for Economics, opposing Neuheim's plan to retaliate with their own forgeries. Finally, the two arms of the Reich were seen to be at complete loggerheads and one day the order went out for a meeting at the Reich Chancellery where the main points of the opposing arguments were to be put before the Fuhrer himself.

Neuheim and Kube were to be there, together with aides from both departments. At the last minute Schumacher and Schulz were detailed to accompany their chiefs to take notes.

This was the first time that Schulz had met Adolf Hitler, or at least his back, which he presented to the assembled company throughout the meeting. Schulz and Schumacher sat behind their SS bosses, Schulz himself almost hidden in a recess where he crouched like a spaniel at Neuheim's feet. The Fuhrer was paradoxically a small and oddly timid figure, with a mild, almost gentle voice. Schulz was far more frightened of Neuheim than of Hitler, though possibly if the Fuhrer had turned round even once this might not have been the case. He appeared to be preoccupied, however, with an architect's model of a magnificent city centre. This seemed to annoy Fritsch somewhat. Like all the bankers that Schulz had ever met, outside prison that is, he was a man who went by the book and he began by trying to give Neuheim and Kube an economics lesson.

Neuheim was not going to have this and quickly lost his temper.

'We insist on retaliation!' he screamed as though hoping to impress the Fuhrer as an eligible understudy. 'Counter-Espionage will not stand by and see the German economy undermined by the dropping of forged clothing coupons! This is total war and we *must retaliate*!'

Fritsch adjusted his pince-nez and regarded the coupons. 'But they're such bad forgeries, Neuheim. Look at them.'

'They'll get better unless we retaliate,' Neuheim replied, again trying to catch Hitler's attention by gesticulating at him. The Fuhrer coughed slightly and everyone froze.

'Shouldn't we do *something*, Fritsch?' Hitler said mildly.

'Fuhrer,' replied Fritsch, 'in Dr Funk's opinion – and in mine – it would be a misuse of resources to put men to work forging clothing coupons. Frankly, I consider it childish.'

'The British disagree with you,' Neuheim snapped.

'The British are indulging their national passion for games,' said Fritsch calmly. 'And besides, it has obviously escaped the notice of SS Counter-Espionage that clothing is not yet rationed in Britain.'

'Neuheim, you've not done your homework,' said Hitler, wagging a finger at Neuheim without turning, as though he had eyes at the back of his head. For all Schulz knew he had. Neuheim was obviously in a spot now and he tried to bluff his way out of it.

'Food is rationed, isn't it? We can drop forged ration books!'

Neuheim was finding it very difficult to remain in his seat for more than seconds at a time and every little speech he made was accompanied by a series of bows and waves. Now he sat and folded his arms as though he had clinched the argument. The Economics faction thought otherwise. They rolled their eyes in disbelief at this blatant example of his ignorance. Even Hitler turned slightly and looked at Fritsch.

'Fuhrer, this discussion is becoming childish,' Fritsch said on cue. 'The British are not short of food and won't be until the U-boat war gets fully under way. Apart from which,' he added, glaring at Neuheim, 'it is the intention of the Ministry of Economics to fight this war according to the rules of the Geneva Convention.'

'What has that got to do with it?' said Kube. This was the first time that Schulz had ever heard Kube say anything at all that was even remotely to do with the war, even though it was only as the feed for which Fritsch had obviously been hoping. He could now deliver his punch line.

'Nowhere in those rules,' said Fritsch, 'does it allow for the barbarous destruction of a nation's economy by the dropping of forged ration books! In my opinion, it could easily constitute a war crime.'

'Then the British have already committed one!' said Kube, doubling his score.

'Exactly!' said Fritsch. 'And those responsible for it will answer in the courts after the war.'

'Are you insane at the Ministry?' Neuheim was beginning to feel left out of the conversation. 'Do you think anyone cares about the courts? We're at war!'

'There are rules of war, Neuheim,' said Fritsch as if talking to a five-year-old who had been handed a loaded revolver, 'and while Dr Funk is Head of the Ministry of Economics those rules will be adhered to.'

'Fuhrer,' said Neuheim, standing up again, 'I appeal to you.'

'He's right, Neuheim,' said Hitler quietly. 'What will the dropping of forged ration books accomplish if the British aren't yet short of food?'

'We can drop other things!' said Neuheim. He was getting excited again.

Hitler sighed. 'Such as what?' he said.

'Anything that will disrupt the British war effort!' said Neuheim, pounding on the table. 'We'll drop forged driving licences, savings certificates, and fake university degrees! We'll drop stocks and shares and forged identity cards and Post Office Savings Bank books! Medical certificates that keep you out of the army ...'

Neuheim was almost purple with excitement by now but unfortunately he'd dried up. Schulz saw the chance he'd been waiting for ever since his conversation with Fraulein Freyer.

'And British banknotes,' he whispered in Neuheim's ear.

'And British banknotes!' screamed Neuheim. 'We'll forge everything! Every new document they invent we'll forge! We have the capacity! We can destroy their power to organize anything!'

At the mention of banknotes, Fritsch had slowly risen to his feet, shaking with fury.

'Bank notes? *British* banknotes? *Never*, while Dr Funk is alive, will British banknotes be forged! Never!'

'Why not?' said Neuheim.

'You are despicable, Neuheim! Despicable!' Frisch was now as demonstrative as Neuheim had been earlier. 'Killing is one thing. That is inevitable in time of war. In the heat of battle an army may even burn a church, sometimes with a congregation in it – though that would be deeply regrettable. But when you attack the integrity of the British pound and encourage others to do the same with the German mark, you strike at the very heart, the very roots of European law and order. Never will we permit it, never!'

There was a short pause while everyone around the table digested the awesome implications of Fritsch's outburst. Hitler broke the silence.

'Come, Fritsch, there's no need to get so upset.'

'My Fuhrer, forgive me,' said Fritsch, practically sobbing, 'but I remember 1923 and the misery of that inflation. And I feel compelled to say that if such a monstrous proposal were

82

accepted you would have Dr Funk's resignation in the morning.'

Another silence ensued while everyone now considered the dire implications of Dr Funk's resignation. Dr Funk, Schulz learned later, was incapacitated with the piles. Perhaps at the mention of his name or perhaps because he hated these rows, Hitler sighed. Then he brightened as he remembered something.

'Did you hear Goebbels on the radio last night, Fritsch?' said the Fuhrer. 'On the subject of the leaflets the British dropped?'

'I was working late last night,' said Fritsch sulkily.

'Oh,' Hitler was evidently disappointed. There was a pause, then he added brightly, 'He was wonderful. He thanked the British for their contribution to the German war effort and said the leaflets had been swept up, repulped and turned into toilet rolls.' He laughed. 'Joseph! Sometimes, you know – so clever.'

Nobody laughed.

Hitler sighed and returned to the business at hand. 'Well,' he went on, 'if the Ministry of Economics objects, you must think of something else, Neuheim.'

This pleased Fritsch who immediately got up from the table, saying, 'Thank you, Fuhrer. Good day, Fuhrer. *Heil Hitler!*' and left the room, which was an obvious cue for the meeting to be adjourned.

'*Heil Hitler!*' said everyone while Hitler raised his arm briefly in salute. Papers were gathered and people started to leave. But Hitler beckoned Neuheim to one side while the rest of the SS contingent waited. The Fuhrer trusted the SS and opened up only when the Ministry people were out of the room.

'Oh, Neuheim,' he said to Neuheim's nose, 'you haven't seen the model of the new Linz I'm going to build after the war. Come and look at it.'

Neuheim, who had been sulking since Hitler's last remark to him, now went dutifully to the model and they bent over it. Schulz waited near the door.

'I like your idea, Neuheim,' the Fuhrer said, 'about the

banknotes. Of course, I couldn't say so, not in front of Fritsch.'

Neuheim brightened immediately. 'I understand, my Fuhrer,' he said obsequiously.

'Bankers are all so stuffy,' Hitler continued. 'All they see is keeping the economy stable, but I have to see everything.' He spread his arms around him to encompass the world.

Neuheim nodded gravely. 'And you do see everything, Fuhrer.'

'Yes,' said Hitler, ignoring him, 'all my life people have been telling me, "You can't do this and you can't do that".' He raised his voice sharply. 'But I say to them, "Remember Dr Heinkel and the bumble bee".'

'Bumble bee, Fuhrer?' Neuheim was completely lost.

'Bumble bee! I am assured by Dr Heinkel that according to the laws of aerodynamics the bumble bee cannot fly. It has something to do with the ratio of its wing span to its weight. But the bumble bee, Neuheim, ignorant of this scientific fact, *does* fly! And so I say to people, "Yes, sometimes it's better to be a bumble bee than it is to be Dr Heinkel".'

'I'll remember that story, Fuhrer, for the rest of my life.' Neuheim was genuinely impressed.

'It's not only innocence that protects itself, Neuheim, but ignorance, too. That has been my experience. Now, can it be done, this forging of British banknotes?'

'I'm certain of it!' said Neuheim.

Hitler nodded. 'Well, do me a report, Neuheim – but not a word to the Ministry of Economics. The whole operation must be kept top secret. Between me and my little SS, eh?'

'Yes, Fuhrer. Heil Hitler!'

Hitler, who had addressed Neuheim's nose throughout this little chat, saluted briefly, turned and walked out of the room. Neuheim quickly went up to Schulz.

'We're going to break the Bank of England, Schulz,' he hissed savagely. 'We're going to forge millions of English banknotes and then inject them, like a dose of 'flu, into the British economy.' He laughed maliciously. 'The Bank of England will shortly be running a high temperature.'

Schulz was already thinking of Fraulein Freyer's un-achieved breasts. 'I'll get to work on it right away, sir,' he said, delighted.

'You?' Neuheim laughed disdainfully. 'This is no job for an amateur, you fool! We need professionals! I shall hand the whole thing over to the technical section of the SS. They've had a vast experience of forging everything.'

Schulz wondered if Neuheim realized that technically he was part of the technical division and in any case knew as much about forgery as anyone in the SS. However, he said nothing.

In the car going back to the Delbruckstrasse Schulz thought about Hitler's story of the bumble bee. If, as Hitler said, the bumble bee flew against all the known laws of science then surely there must be hope that Fraulein Freyer could break rank.

9

Even though Neuheim had called Schulz an amateur, he summoned him to his office the next morning and asked if he had had any fresh thoughts on the subject of forging British banknotes, a subject, Neuheim added, about which he had been thinking seriously for some time. Schulz replied off the top of his head, since the only fresh thoughts he was having were about Fraulein Freyer. As the top of Schulz's head just about reached Neuheim's ears, however, this did not seem to worry the Major.

'Well, sir,' said Schulz. 'The obvious thing is to scatter them as widely as possible. Some would be handed in, but probably most of them would be spent or banked.'

Neuheim nodded, impressed.

'So if there were enough of them,' Schulz continued, see-ing he was on the right track, 'the banking system could be undermined. It could be a real secret weapon, sir. We could flood the world with them, shake confidence in the pound and put paid to the British for good.'

'I like it, Schulz. Very clever,' said Neuheim, scratching his nose – a sign, Schulz knew, of deep thought. 'Why don't you develop the scheme, just between ourselves, Schulz? Write me a report, put down your thoughts, eh? You know, you could make your mark in this war, Schulz.'

All Schulz wanted was for the war not to make its mark on him, but he nodded respectfully. Then another thought occurred to him.

'Imported British undies, sir, have always outsold German ones and –'

Neuheim swore deafeningly. 'If you want to avoid immediate transfer to front line infantry duties you will at once set about preparing in detail a draft plan for the immaculate forging of Bank of England notes. And it had better work.'

'You mean find out how the right paper and inks can be produced, how the best plates can be made, work out the right numbering – all that sort of thing, sir?'

'Exactly what I was going to say, Schulz. Now get going.'

Schulz got going. During the next two weeks he slaved away at the report which was by no means easy. Since he had been co-opted into working night shifts in the boiler-room he had been so exhausted during the day that it was hard for him to keep his eyes open. Schumacher did not help matters either. He had recently taken to humming out of tune in the office and every time Schulz looked up, Schumacher would be gazing at him. Schulz was now convinced that Schumacher was homosexual.

Finally Schulz handed in his report. For several days he heard nothing. Subsequently he discovered that Neuheim gave the report to one blonde secretary for redrafting, had it retyped by another and then, without reading it, signed it and sent it to Hitler. The Fuhrer liked it and confirmed that Neuheim should expand his Special Operations unit to cope with the manufacture of the counterfeit notes, awarding Neuheim another Iron Cross and promoting him to Colonel. Schulz was, however, confirmed in the rank of Senior Private, which gave him some comfort, since it was one step nearer to becoming a major.

The fact that Neuheim had not read Schulz's report soon became obvious, to Schulz at least, when, in the following week, he launched what became known as Operation Andreas. Neuheim had decided that the best way to begin was by flushing out the Security Service, which had a special department which dealt with secret-service forgeries. The head of this section was a Captain Ohm, a slight, bespectacled officer who made the mistake of being condescending towards the new colonel. Schulz accompanied Neuheim, carrying the *Geheime Reichssache* file which Neuheim had opened.

'It can't be done, Colonel Neuheim,' said Ohm, shaking his head.

'What do you mean, it can't be done?' Neuheim snarled.

Ohm shrugged. 'It can't be done. Oh, it can be *done* – but not properly. The forgeries would be spotted in no time.'

'Why?' said Neuheim.

'The paper for one thing,' said Ohm. 'You can't get it. Since about 1750 it's been supplied to the Bank of England from their paper mills. No one has ever succeeded in getting any of it out.'

'Then we'll make our own,' said Neuheim impatiently.

'We can't. We've shredded it and pulped it and analysed it. We've destroyed a thousand pounds in British five-pound notes doing it. No one can identify where the paper comes from or how it's made. It's a linen of some sort, probably from their colonies in Asia, but that's all we can tell you.'

Neuheim stared at Ohm. 'Are you telling me that what I've promised the Fuhrer would be done, can't be done?' he said very slowly.

Ohm laughed. 'What can't be done can't be done, Herr Colonel. With all our technical resources we don't know how to do it – not properly.'

Schulz wanted to warn Ohm that the look on Neuheim's face indicated imminent danger.

'Have you never heard of the bumble bee, Herr Captain, and how it manages to fly?'

'No,' said Ohm.

'It flies, damn you, because it doesn't know *how not to*!'

'With due respect to you, Herr Colonel,' said Ohm stiffly, 'and to the bumble bee, my department has a vast experience in forging everything. Now, if it were roubles for instance –'

'I DON'T WANT ROUBLES!' Neuheim screamed.

'Or Japanese yen,' Ohm went on bravely, 'or a complete dossier on Marshal Tukshevsky which we supplied to Stalin in 1937, implicating his commander-in-chief in negotiations with the Third Reich –'

'All right, all right, you've had your successes!' said Neuheim. 'But you can't forge British five-pound notes, *that's* what you're telling me!'

'Yes, Herr Colonel, that is what we are telling you. That is our opinion after considerable research.'

Neuheim maintained a furious silence for the rest of the day, making telephone calls on his private line which only seemed to confirm what Ohm had said. Schulz had kept out of his way, busying himself with files, but eventually he was obliged to enter Neuheim's office for a stamp.

'You fool!' Neuheim blasted at him. 'I should never have listened to you in the first place!'

Schulz didn't know what to say. There was a kind of primeval helplessness in Neuheim at that moment, as though he were a madman caged inside a private zoo whose very bars were constructed out of madness. Schulz decided to adopt a confidential tone.

'Excuse me, sir – Captain Ohm may be very brilliant in some ways but ...' he paused. Now was his chance either to steer Neuheim towards success or plunge them both into ruin. 'If you'd allow me to take this over as I suggested in the first place, I think I can get a little further than Captain Ohm.'

'He *says* it can't be done,' Neuheim snarled.

'Oh, come, sir.' said Schulz, realizing that what Neuheim really needed at that moment was a psychiatric nurse. 'We mustn't accept defeat so easily. Remember – sometimes it's better to be a bumble bee than it is to be Dr Heinkel or even Captain Ohm.'

'What are you trying to say, Schulz?'

'It may be, sir, that he hasn't got hold of the best men.'

'What other men are there?'

'Well, forgery, sir, is a specialized business,' explained Schulz, 'and the people who are good at it don't advertise themselves. They lie low.'

'Who are they? Where are they?'

'Well, they'll take a bit of finding, Herr Colonel,' said Schulz.

He had suddenly had a vision of whiling away the war in faraway places on an endless search. Unfortunately Neuheim had by now grasped his original point.

'Prison!' he shouted. 'Of course, you're a jail bird!'

It now appeared that Neuheim had deliberately selected Schulz to be his confidential clerk because of his prison record. He bellowed for Schumacher and soon Schulz was issued with a briefcase full of passes, requisitions, and a letter instructing the prison authorities to render him every aid and facility in carrying out his 'essential war work for the High Command of the security forces of the SS', all signed by Colonel Alfred Neuheim.

'... and to render him every aid and facility in carrying out his essential war work for the High Command of the security forces of the SS ...' read Herr Untermeyer. He handed the letter back to Beck.

'What can the SS want here?' said Untermeyer. 'You'd better ask him to come in.'

Schulz walked through into Untermeyer's office, deposited his case on one chair and sat down on another.

Untermeyer stared in disbelief. Beck was dumbfounded.

'Schulz!'

'Yes, Governor,' said Schulz calmly.

The immaculate SS uniform only added to Untermeyer's confusion.

'But I – I thought you were with Krauss of Krauss Under-

wear!' he protested. 'That's what they said in Resettlement.'
He had aged since their last encounter as if Schulz was not
the only representative of the new elite who had paid him a
visit.

'Never mind that now,' said Schulz. 'You have a prisoner
here – Ephraim Solokoff?'

'Solokoff? Ah, yes – the Jew. He's working just down the
corridor.'

'Bring him in here,' said Schulz.

Untermeyer flipped a switch on his intercom.

'Fetch Solokoff to my office at once,' he said then, switching off the intercom, 'He's to be transferred to a camp, I suppose?' he went on, staring at Schulz's SS insignia with a
kind of respectful suspicion. 'Very natural. Much more
suitable. What else can I do for you?'

'You can clear out of the office while I interrogate him.
I don't wish to be disturbed,' said Schulz.

'Of course, of course,' said Untermeyer, eyeing his valuables nervously. 'Please make yourself at home.' He hurried
out of the room closing the door gently behind him.

Immediately Schulz went to Untermeyer's cupboard and
took out a bottle of Schnapps and two glasses. *That's one
thing that hasn't changed*, he thought. As he was pouring
himself a glass a middle-aged man with a shock of wild
white hair was admitted into the office by a guard. The
forger obviously did not recognize Schulz : he was shaking
as though the death brigade had come to remove him to the
mortuary. Prison had aged him beyond his years and his
fear looked as though it would round him off.

'Hello, Solly,' said Schulz, raising his glass.

Solokoff peered at him with keen eyes.

'Gerhardt?' he asked, faltering.

Schulz nodded.

'Gerhardt Schulz?'

Again Schulz nodded and smiled.

Solokov unexpectedly burst into tears. Schulz went over
and put his hands on Solokoff's shoulders.

'Now, now, Solly,' he said, comforting him.

'I thought ...' Solokoff stopped crying and looked incredulously at Schulz. 'What are you doing in that uniform?'

'It's a long story, don't worry about it. Sit down. Schnapps?'

Solokoff sat down, still dazed. 'Schnapps? Are you crazy? That's the Governor's liquor!'

'He told me to make myself at home,' said Schulz. 'It's amazing the effect this uniform has on people. Here, drink it down.'

Solokoff stared at the glass for a moment before swallowing it in a gulp. He shuddered and held it out for a refill. Schulz noticed that Solly's hands had quickly recovered from the trembling. They were strong and supple.

'How's prison life these days?' enquired Schulz who was not really very interested in prison life, though he was fond of Solly.

'It's good,' Solly replied. 'The staff – they're a good bunch. I've no complaints. In fact, I live in fear I'll get transferred out – you understand?'

Schulz understood: he remembered the fear of seeing the trees. 'You've got another five years here?'

'Please God,' said Solly.

Schulz decided that it was time for business. He opened his briefcase, took out a large, white, English five-pound note, and spread it on the desk in front of Solokoff.

'Have you ever forged one of these, Solly?'

'An English fiver?' Solly was shaking his head. 'I don't think it can be done.'

Schulz winced – this was going to be difficult. 'Don't say that. I'm relying on you.'

'On me? Why?' Solly stared at Schulz and started to get up. 'What are you – crazy or something? I'm in here doing a stretch for counterfeiting and you're talking to me in the Governor's office about forging fivers! Don't you realize, Gerhardt, I'm scared stiff that they might let me out at all? Why do you think I'm on my best behaviour?'

'Calm down, Solly, calm down,' said Schulz, pouring him another glass of Schnapps. Solly sat down again and Schulz now leaned forward, speaking in a quiet, measured tone: 'I have official clearance from the highest authority to start forging English five-pound notes. Millions of them.'

Solly stared at him aghast. Schulz laughed softly. 'They're all a bit mad outside, Solly,' he said.

'The highest authority?'

'The very highest.'

'And they've put you in charge?'

Schulz nodded.

'They *must* be mad!'

Schulz laughed again and poured some more Schnapps. 'I need your advice,' he said. 'The technical section of the SS say that it can't be done. They say it's impossible to get the paper.'

Solly nodded. 'They're right,' he said. 'Nobody's ever succeeded in getting hold of any.'

'Did you ever find out what it was and where it comes from?'

'Sure, I found out,' said Solly. 'I worked on it, once, with a Czech chemist called Kapper, back in the twenties. We destroyed so many real notes finding out, we ran out of money.'

'What did you discover?' Schulz was beginning to make notes which he knew Neuheim would want to see.

'It's made from a special linen they import from India.'

'India ...' Schulz thought about it. 'That would be difficult.'

'You don't need to go to India,' Solly went on. 'We found out there's a place in Turkey that produces an identical linen. But, listen, Gerhardt, forget it. It's too difficult, I know. And believe me, I've forged every major currency in Europe in my time.'

'What are the other problems?' Schulz ignored him.

'There's the ink.' Solly was now pacing about the room like an advocate trying to convince Untermeyer's bookshelves that he had a watertight case. 'We never succeeded in breaking down the dyes. Look at that water-mark.' He held the note up to the light and Schulz peered at it with him. 'Look at the folds in the gown of Britannia and the number of curlicues. It's so easy to miss just one. Do you know how they put that water-mark into the pulp?'

'How?'

'It's pressed in with a wire mesh that's got to be accurate to five-tenths of a millimetre. And then when you've made the plates, you face your biggest problem of all – the figures and dates of the series. They have to coincide exactly. Otherwise they'll be spotted.' Solly shook his head. 'I'm telling you, my friend, it costs a lot of money to make money. I wouldn't be here if it didn't.'

Now Schulz was pacing the room.

'I can get all the resources I want,' he said, 'which you never could. I can get the co-operation of printing works, chemical works, paper mills. Anything I want I can have. All my life I've waited for an opportunity like this. I've got the chance of making a fortune and I don't intend to let it slip.'

Outside the window Schulz could see the geraniums, standing in neat regimental order as the daffodils had been when he had left the prison. Solly did not seem to have grasped that what had begun as a bizarre idea had now become government business.

'Well, good luck to you,' said Solly. 'I've told you all I know.' He stood up. 'Listen, Gerhardt, put in a good word for me, eh? I'd like to finish my term here. It's a good prison, the people are decent. If I get transferred to a camp –'

Schulz placed his hands on Solly's shoulders again. 'I need more than your advice, Solly,' he said. 'I want you to take charge of the operation.'

'Me? But I'm in prison!'

'I'll get you out,' said Schulz. 'This is essential war work, Solly, you'll be working for the government.'

'The government? But I'm a crook!'

'So are they! The only difference between them and us is that they're all homicidal maniacs.'

It was all too much for Solly: he sat down again, dazed.

Schulz opened one of the drawers in Untermeyer's desk and took out two cigars, handing one to Solly who bit the end off thoughtfully.

'What do you say?' said Schulz.

'I'm scared, Gerhardt. I tell you frankly, I'm afraid to leave this place, I feel safe here.'

Seeing that Solly was even too scared to light the cigar, Schulz lit it for him.

'Listen, old friend,' he said. 'We're going to make millions and millions of five-pound notes and drop them over England. If we siphon off a few hundred thousand, who's going to notice? But they've got to be perfect. If they are, they'll buy your passage out of Germany, Solly, and me a villa in Spain and all the women I've ever dreamed of.' Bertha Freyer would be enough for a start. 'We'll be rich. The war's a windfall for us.'

'And a graveyard for a lot of others,' said Solly.

Schulz lit a cigar for himself. 'But what can you do? When the lunatics take over the asylum it's every man for himself.'

There was a silence. The prison suddenly seemed a very sane place.

'All right, what can I lose?' said Solly, lifting his glass. 'It's business as usual, then?'

'Business as usual.'

They clinked glasses and Schulz leant back, puffing luxuriously on his cigar and putting his feet on the desk.

'Put your feet up, Solly,' he said. 'Pour yourself another drink. Get used to it. We're going to be rich, richer than you ever dreamed of.'

On his way out Schulz thanked Herr Untermeyer for the cigars. The Governor did not seem to understand.

'Krauss of Krauss Underwear,' he was still murmuring.

Still, thought Schulz, as he drove back to Berlin, if the cigars were all that Untermeyer lost in this war he would be an extremely lucky man.

10

When a top begins to spin crazily, the very crookedness of its wobble seems to make it spin faster before it eventually collapses.

Schulz could never pin down the precise moment when the top had begun to spin. It was not his offhand remark to Neuheim at the Reichchancellery about forging banknotes; he had only said that because he had been daydreaming at the time that Bertha Freyer would forget that he was a poor kindred soul and treat him like a rich client. But he would never have met her had it not been for Heydrich's list – which he would never have read had he not applied for a job in postal security ... *It may be an endless chain of causes and effects stretching back far beyond my birth, probably,* thought Schulz, *to the dawn of man.* All he knew was that from the moment he acquired the services of Solly Solokoff the top had started to spin him off his feet and hurtle him into madness.

Once the full machinery of the SS had been harnessed to Operation Andreas it seemed that there was nothing that could not be done. It was Heydrich who powered the machinery. A suggestion from Schulz became an order from Neuheim, but Heydrich turned it into a law. Heydrich was Himmler's left-hand man and was sometimes merely known as 'C'. He had that essential flair of a top Party man – he was no man's friend, not even his own. It was said that when Himmler spoke, it was with his own voice, but the words were Heydrich's. What was never said – because it was never found out – was that when Neuheim spoke, in a parody of all the top Nazi brass, the words were Schulz's.

As for Schulz, the realization that each one of his ideas, no matter how silly or trivial, was being put into action the moment it landed in Neuheim's ear or in his in-tray, may have gone to his head. He could not help becoming enthused by the sheer dynamism of the Reich, but, more than that, the idea of forging on such a massive scale became an obsession. In any case he was determined that, come what may, he would have enough fivers stashed away by the end of the war to keep him in luxury for the rest of his life.

With Solly's help, Schulz began by combing the jails and concentration camps for men whose skills had made them legendary in the underworld. Solly knew them all – and he handpicked every one.

On his return Schulz presented Neuheim with his report. He had never seen the colonel so ecstatic, practically slobbering like a dog over the details. Schulz wondered about this. Neuheim had hardly expressed any gratitude for the preliminary plan which had earned him his promotion to colonel. Schumacher had told Schulz the true story of Neuheim's promotion at the first available moment, watching Schulz's face closely to gauge his reaction. Frankly Schulz could not have cared less what games his chief was playing as long as Operation Andreas went ahead. What interested him more was a hint that Schumacher dropped about Captain Ohm. It seemed that the SS's own forging department, run by Ohm, was under surveillance from Heinrich Muller's Gestapo. Muller, it was rumoured, had argued to Heydrich that forgery posed a threat to Reich security and demanded that Neuheim look somewhere else for people to do his dirty work for him.

It was well known that a private war was being fought between the SS and the Gestapo. What was curious was how Schumacher got his information. Schulz wondered whether he might be having a liaison with some top-ranking SS official. It would make sense, because Schumacher seemed to know something that Neuheim didn't: either Captain Ohm genuinely didn't believe the forgery was possible or he had been ordered to say so by, possibly, Heydrich. Schulz had heard rumours that Heydrich was homosexual and it was not beyond the bounds of reason that it was Heydrich who had informed Schumacher. Schulz decided he would have to tackle Schumacher about all this. Anyway, it explained Neuheim's drooling over his notes: he could now go to the

Fuhrer and show that he could make his bumble bee fly without the aid of the SS technicians. It was all very curious and wonderful.

After Neuheim had got over his first attack of euphoria, he leapt into action.

'Turkey?' he said. 'They have linen for the paper in Turkey, do they?'

'Yes, Herr Colonel. According to my informant.' Schulz was beginning to act the part of a secret agent.

'Get it!' Neuheim bawled at Schumacher.

'Paper – Turkey.' Schumacher scribbled on his note pad.

'A Czech chemist called Kapper, eh?'

'Yes, Herr Colonel.'

'Get him, find him, bring anybody in who knows him!'

'Chemist – Czech, Kapper and associates,' Schumacher wrote busily.

'What's this about serial numbers?'

'According to my informant, we could make the most perfect notes but unless we get a run of serial numbers that corresponds to the British system of numbering, any banker could detect the forgery, Herr Colonel.'

'Ah,' said Neuheim, who had not really understood a word. 'Well, that is not beyond the powers of the German counters.'

Counters? ... accountants ... he means mathematicians! thought Schulz.

'See that it's done.'

'Serial numbers to be attended to,' Schumacher wrote.

'But the most important thing, Herr Colonel, is that I be allowed to assemble a team of top forgers. We'll need banking experts too, engravers, skilled metal and dye workers, and photographers of course.'

'Get them,' said Neuheim, and Schumacher wrote it all down.

'And of course we'll have to bear in mind that it's top secret. We will and they will, Herr Colonel,' said Schulz.

'Right then,' said Neuheim. 'You'll set up your factory in one of the camps.'

Schulz had been afraid of this but since many experts in

forgery happened to be Jewish and were already in the camps it did not seem to make much difference. Although he had never seen a concentration camp, however, he remembered Solokoff's preference for the Hamburg prison where the diet, he often said, was like that of a five-star hotel compared to that of the camps.

'Our men will have to work hard, Herr Colonel, and they'll have to be treated well,' Schulz hazarded.

'Yes, yes,' said Neuheim, who could already see the notes rolling off the presses and another decoration from the Fuhrer. 'See to it. Assemble them. Pick the very best and I will come down and address them.'

'Very good, sir.'

'Remember one thing, though, Schulz,' he added, his good eye gleaming in its bloodshot socket as a positive thought was spiked on to his mind. 'You're a thief and you're dealing with thieves ...' His voice trailed off meaningfully, then rose: 'But above you, there's me, and I shall miss nothing, not a note that might go astray! Understand?'

'Yes sir,' said Schulz. Would this be a good moment to ask if he were going to be relieved of his eavesdropping duties?

'By the way, from now on, I expect you to resume your listening at the Salon Kitty. We don't want you getting above yourself, Schulz.'

'Ordinary duties to continue,' Schumacher wrote.

'You'll be sorry you started all this,' Schumacher told Schulz later, 'What if they don't make good enough notes? What if they make them and the British find out they're forgeries straight away? What is Himmler going to say to Heydrich and Heydrich to Neuheim, and Neuheim to you? You're in too deep, Schulz.'

'How's Fraulein Freyer?' said Schulz, changing the subject.

Schumacher stared at Schulz. 'How should I know?'

Schulz was now positive that Schumacher was homosexual.

The first Christmas of the war had come and gone. By now

Schulz had assembled in Barracks 19 of Sachsenhausen camp the most brilliant team of forgers ever to be put together under one roof.

Sachsenhausen was enormous. A permanent barracks, its seventy-odd buildings housed 40,000 prisoners who either worked in the prison stone-breaking or were sent out as forced labour to the nearby complex of Heinkel aircraft factories. The prison was run by a staff of 3000 Deathshead SS men with a reputation for frightening brutality and callousness. By contrast Barracks 19, situated in the centre of the camp, was a comparative haven of peace and sanity. It was fenced off, cleared of inmates and the forgers moved in. The gas chambers, however, were left, and it was in one of them that Colonel Neuheim had gathered them for his opening address. They were a motley crew of cropped-headed prisoners, all in the regulation striped camp uniforms, sitting listening to Neuheim's words with a mixture of hostility and open-mouthed incredulity.

Neuheim was his usual light-hearted self.

'... and you needn't think that the Party in any way condones your disgusting profession just because it intends to profit from it,' he was saying. 'On the contrary, it abominates it! However, in war time every resource, however unpleasant, must be used, and you may look upon yourselves as sewage being recycled into the national war effort.'

The men looked rather disgruntled, even chastened by this unfair description of their skills. Neuheim did not seem to notice and in any case it would not have bothered him.

'Naturally, I want you to put your hearts and souls into this work for your country,' he continued relentlessly. 'I want you to work with as much skill and artistry as if you were producing the notes for yourselves.' His tone changed to one of menace. 'Do not, however, come to regard any of them as yours. *Oberschutze* Schulz, here, has devised a foolproof system of accounting that will mean certain death for anyone who so much as thinks of it.'

Schulz nodded in grave and solemn agreement, avoiding Solly's covert look.

Neuheim continued on a more cheerful note: 'Rations

will be good, as good as those outside. You'll be allowed newspapers, a radio, a cigarette ration. If things go well, I shall even permit the playing of ping-pong matches with the guards – who are very keen on ping-pong. And now, go to it with a will. Forge for the Fuhrer! Give him another weapon in the fight against England!'

Schulz applauded loudly and vigorously and after a moment the prisoners joined in politely. Neuheim nodded, satisfied.

On the way to Neuheim's car, Schulz fell into step with him.

'Anything you need, just ask for it,' said Neuheim in remarkably good humour.

'I don't need anything, sir – except, of course, the date and number series of the banknotes. You said you could provide those.'

'Don't worry about that,' said Neuheim breezily. 'We've got an agent working on it.' As he stepped into his car, he turned to Schulz and added, darkly, 'This had better work. I've given my word to the Fuhrer.'

'You can rely on it, sir,' said Schulz, giving him a '*Heil*' Neuheim stared at him for a moment and then nodded grimly.

'There is one other thing, sir,' said Schulz through the closed car window.

'What is it now?' said Neuheim winding down the window impatiently.

'The Salon Kitty, sir – do I have to, Herr Colonel? There's never anything of value to report.'

'Patience is everything in espionage, Schulz,' said Neuheim briskly. 'The night you *don't* listen in on those bedrooms is the night some weak-minded fool lets fall vital information. Just be sure you're there to record it.'

Neuheim closed the window, signalled to his driver and drove off. Schulz cursed.

'He must be mad!'

A deep bronchial laugh came from an almost toothless

head. Becker, a grizzled old counterfeiter, was standing at one end of a table in one of the larger of Barracks 19's huts which Schulz, Schumacher and other Dept VIB men had hastily converted into an office-common room. There was also a ping-pong table and a locked drinks cupboard which some of Solly's top men – whom Schulz had convened there for a briefing – were eyeing longingly.

Becker was referring to Colonel Neuheim. Since Schulz *knew* that Neuheim was mad, he decided to ignore this and get down to business.

'You can go,' he said to the two SS guards, who had not yet adjusted to the idea that these were no ordinary prisoners. They mooched out of the hut and Schulz turned to the others.

'Let's sit down,' he said and after chairs had been pulled round the table with a great deal of muttering and wisecracks, Schulz began.

'Well, you heard what Colonel Neuheim said? We're here to produce a great many of these.' He took out a crisp five-pound note and held it up for all to see. 'Or, rather, perfect copies of it.'

'Perfect,' said Becker who seemed to like exercising his bronchial tubes.

'Good enough to fool even the Bank of England.'

'Solly says you're a friend so I'll be frank,' wheezed Becker. 'I'm not complaining, you understand. I'd rather be here playing ping-pong with the guards than having them kick my head in somewhere else. So whatever you want to do I'll do. No arguments, nothing. Only – what you're asking can't be done. For a start, you've got a paper problem.'

'It's been solved,' said Schulz wearily.

'You ordered a couple of reams, maybe, from the Bank of England?' Again the deep bronchial laugh.

'Solly partly solved it some years ago,' said Schulz. 'He found a high-quality linen in Turkey that exactly matches the linen the Bank uses. And a paper mill in Stettin has worked out the formula for making the paper up.'

'With the water mark impressed?'

'*With* the water mark impressed,' said Solly. 'It'll start

arriving shortly.'

'As for the ink,' Schulz interposed quickly, 'the dyes are being analysed by a chemical works in Stuttgart. They're already very close to an answer.'

Becker looked impressed.

'All right,' he said. 'But what about the numbering? The date of issue, the cashier's signature, the serial number? If you're just printing a few and intend to skip the country pretty quick, it doesn't matter. But you're talking of thousands.'

'Hundreds of thousands,' said Solly.

'Thousands of thousands,' said Schulz.

'Then how will you find the correct numbering system?'

'It'll be done,' said Schulz, 'that's all I can tell you.' *There it goes again*, he thought, *the numbering*. But he did not show his concern.

'All the technical problems will be solved, I promise you,' he said, looking around at the extraordinary group of technicians, and wondering. 'The rest is up to you.'

'Well, if you buy governments bonds at $87\frac{1}{2}$ ... which is where they stand now ... and you hold them for three years ... when they'll be redeemed ... then at a rate of 3% – my God, that feels good – well, you'll make $31\frac{1}{2}$ marks which is nearly 22·5%, a very good return on your – don't stop – in ... *vest* ... ment!'

Heinrich Bodelschwingh, Professor of Mathematics at the University of Berlin, was deeply engaged in extra-curricular studies at the Salon Kitty and at that very moment had achieved a gratifying breakthrough.

'You can do all that in your head?' murmured Fraulein Freyer into his ear. The professor's percentage rates were increasing rhythmically and dramatically.

'Yes, my little one,' he gasped, 'but I didn't come here to ... practise my ... ar*ith*metic!'

'I wish I were as clever as you, Professor,' crooned Fraulein Freyer, squeezing a muscle that caused Bodelschwingh to squeak with the exquisite pleasure.

'You don't have to be.' The professor was finding it difficult to concentrate. 'And if I looked like you,' he puffed, 'I wouldn't ... have to be ... EITHER! ...'

Fraulein Freyer ran a crimson fingernail down his back. 'Do you think I should buy, then?'

'Why not?' groaned Bodelschwingh in blissful agony. 'You can't lose ... It's a safe ... INVESTMENT!' he screamed in joy as his life savings were securely invested in Fraulein Freyer.

Schulz was doodling on a pad – a habit he had caught off Schumacher – a replica of a five-pound note. This made him think of Bertha Freyer and suddenly, remembering why he was down in the basement, he flicked on her switch.

'Do you think the war will be over soon?' Her voice had a honeyed, contented note that Schulz recognized as her post-coital purr. He bit his lip.

'By the end of the summer it will all be over.'

Schulz correctly identified the voice as that of the plump, balding, jolly little professor who was now one of Bertha Freyer's regulars. Bodelschwingh had never seen Schulz who was becoming rather clever at making himself invisible.

'Oh, they said it would be over by Christmas,' breathed Bertha.

'No, my little apple, it could never have been over by Christmas.'

Smug bastard, thought Schulz.

Upstairs, Fraulein Freyer was slowly dressing. Deliciously slowly, thought Bodelschwingh, who found the sight of her divine legs disappearing into sheer black stockings and suspenders peculiarly arousing, as though a simple mathematical problem were being deliberately complicated to add to the pleasure of its solution.

'How can you be so sure?' she said, noticing his fresh excitement and lengthening the process of straightening her stockings.

'I'm in a position to know,' said Bodelschwingh, glassy-eyed. 'I hear all sorts of things.'

'A position to know! How intriguing! Are you engaged in secret work?' The brassière that she had been fastening slipped to the floor revealing her perfect geometry once more to the delighted professor.

'Oh, my little Fraulein Freyer,' he squealed, running his hands over her. In a paroxysm of desire he pulled her hard up against him and she allowed him one more lingering kiss. Then she prodded him playfully with her finger.

'Are you?' she repeated, prodding him again. 'Engaged in secret work? I think you're a spy.'

The professor giggled in contentment.

'You are,' said Fraulein Freyer. 'Admit it!'

She pushed him back on to the bed and tickled him furiously.

'You're a spy, you're a spy, admit it! You're a spy!'

'No, no, don't!' screamed Bodelschwingh, laughing hysterically. 'Fraulein Freyer, please – I admit it! Yes, yes, I'm a spy, I'm a spy, I'm a spy!'

He collapsed on the floor in uncontrollable laughter, clutching himself everywhere as a protection against her probing, teasing fingers. Finally Fraulein Freyer stopped tickling him, satisfied with his admission, and draped herself seductively over him.

'I always knew you weren't just a professor of mathematics, you naughty, naughty boy!' she said and he giggled again. 'What sort of work do you do? Tell me.' Bodelschwingh spluttered. 'What are you laughing at?'

'You,' he said, pointing his podgy finger at her.

'Me?' she laughed. 'Why? Tell me?'

Bodelschwingh was now shaking with mirth. 'Because you're the prettiest, sexiest, most seductive and clumsiest spy I've ever seen.'

The smile froze on her face. 'What do you mean?' she whispered, sitting up.

'Oh, Fraulein Freyer, come back to bed!' he said, fumbling at her body.

She slapped his fingers. 'Tell me what you mean!'

He laughed again. 'My dear Fraulein Freyer, you're priceless.'

'How?'

'*You* know that I work in the code-breaking department of military intelligence. *You* know – because Colonel Neuheim knows. And Colonel Neuheim is such an ass that he thinks a man has only to get on top of you and he'll tell you everything you want to know.'

Fraulein Freyer was a little put out. 'That's not true!' she said, slipping on her kimono.

'My dear,' Bodelschwingh giggled, 'I even know he's got this place bugged. Do the SS really think we're such fools in military intelligence? Look.'

He went over to a little ventilator grill on the wall and blew a long, wet raspberry into it.

Schulz yanked the phones off his head and stared furiously at them as the raspberry continued for a long, rude, raucous minute.

'I even know there's a little man in the basement,' the professor's voice screeched through the headphones, 'sitting there with pencil poised and hoping to hear some tale that Neuheim can go running to the Fuhrer with. Little man in the basement – go home!'

Schulz threw down his pencil in disgust.

'I suppose everybody knows,' said Fraulein Freyer sulkily, sitting on the bed.

'I don't know if everybody knows,' Bodelschwingh laughed. 'But *we* know. You can tell Neuheim from me that the electrician who wired the place up for him was working for us.'

11

Schulz should have reported immediately to Colonel Neuheim that the spies were being spied on, but he decided to keep it to himself – and Fraulein Freyer – for the moment.

Within a week Barracks 19 had been transformed into a miniature replica of the British Royal Mint. Three large screens had been erected in the main workshop on which the enlarged images of five-pound notes were projected, each one showing all the markings in minute detail. In front of them sat three engravers, copying the notes with great care on to paper, while in another room Becker, who was proving to be a real artist, operated a photo-engraving machine. Parcels of fine white paper soon began to arrive, complete with watermark and every sheet and watermark was inspected by Solly before he let it pass. A printing machine had been installed; the sheets of paper were hand-cut to size; and in another department a group of forgers would test the ink and copy the elaborate curves surrounding the words BANK OF ENGLAND. Then there were the engravers, also working under Solly's supervision.

There were about twenty counterfeiters altogether, organized into teams with leaders elected by themselves, and on the day Neuheim came for his second inspection, they were all hard at work.

Neuheim still regarded Barracks 19, not unnaturally, as his own little empire. This was nothing new for the SS who had long made a practice of appropriating small business schemes of their own. Building firms, clothing and shoe factories, even a firm for making mineral water, were part of Himmler's empire, this last because he was anxious that alcohol should not undermine the sadistic strength of his manpower. Barracks 19, however, was something rather different, and Neuheim was quite out of his depth – which was shallow at the best of times. By this time Schulz was something of an expert himself on the technical aspects, having been trained by two masters: Solly and Becker.

'We're using a photo-engraving process to produce the plates,' he announced as they walked into a room where Becker and one or two others were operating the equipment. 'That's the machine that does it.'

'How does it work?' asked Neuheim, who was becoming progressively more ignorant as the scheme developed.

'We photograph the notes, Herr Colonel, and develop the negatives on glass plates covered with an emulsion of silver salts. Then we transfer the negatives on the glass plates to the metal plates. In other words, the metal plates become the prints.'

'Why couldn't the technical section of the SS have done that?' asked Neuheim. 'It sounds easy enough.'

Schulz knew why not but decided not to remind Neuheim at this late stage of Ohm's part in this. Instead he would blind the colonel with science.

'It's not that simple, sir. You see, there's no emulsion known that will duplicate the exact depth of lines or their shading.'

A nostril flickered. But comprehension remained a mirage. 'I see,' he said. There was a pause, then: 'Why not?'

'It's the silver particles in the emulsion. They're of an irregular size and shape so they produce lines that look jagged and irregular under a magnifying glass.'

'And the Bank of England are likely to do that?'

'Use a magnifying glass?' Schulz laughed. 'Oh, yes, sir, they're a very suspicious lot. Sooner or later they'd get the feeling there were more five-pound notes in circulation than there ought to be.'

'I see,' said Neuheim. There was another pause. 'Why should they?'

'Well, more will be coming back, on average, into the tills,' said Schulz patiently. He had not quite appreciated the extent of Neuheim's intellectual difficulties. 'However,' he added, 'if we've done our job well, they'd put it all down to an increase in the volume of trade and the velocity of circulation of money.'

Neuheim stared at him irritably. 'Why they didn't put you in the Ministry of Economics I'll never know,' he snapped, as they walked on to the next hut.

'I'm very happy here, sir,' said Schulz. 'I never realized what opportunities there were in counter-espionage.'

'Opportunities?' Neuheim raised an eyebrow.

'For serving Germany and the Fuhrer, Herr Colonel.'

The main hut was a hive of concentrated activity.

'And how do we get over this little problem of jagged lines and magnifying glasses?' Neuheim asked.

'This is where Solokoff and his team of engravers come in,' replied Schulz. 'They get to work on the plates, retouching them with their tools. You'd never believe the transformation they can work on them. Would you like to see the paper, Herr Colonel? It's wonderful.'

He led Neuheim over to where Solly was examining a batch of paper, comparing a sheet with a new five-pound note. Neuheim snatched them unceremoniously out of Solly's hands and held them both up to the light.

'Amazing!' he said. 'The watermark's perfect.'

He handed them back to Solly who glanced briefly once more at the sheet of paper and then screwed it up and threw it away. Neuheim looked taken aback.

'Some of the sheets come out better than others, Herr Colonel,' said Schulz hurriedly. 'Solokoff's selecting only the best.'

Neuheim had obviously had enough. 'Well, you seem to have everything under control,' he said.

'Yes, sir, except, of course, the serial numbers. The whole operation depends on that.'

'You'll get those, don't worry. Our agent in London has reported that he's made a contact inside the printing works of the Bank of England. I have every confidence that the relevant issue will be in our hands shortly. Keep it up! And remember,' he added, addressing the company at large, 'wrecking the British economy is worth a brigade of tanks to the Fuhrer – and to me. Remember that!'

He strode off to his car.

'What did he want?' said Solly.

'Just making sure that everything's on schedule,' Schulz replied.

'Everything's on schedule except him. Where are the serial numbers?'

'They'll be here, don't worry. Our agent in London is working on it. How soon will you get a good first sample, Soly?'

'That depends. Why?'

'I want to keep him happy,' said Schulz. 'I want to keep everyone happy. I don't want them suddenly losing interest.'

'Have you thought what's going to happen to all of us when we finish our work here? No one's going to work faster than he needs to.'

'Solly, the most important thing is to *prove* that it can be done. *Then* they'll commit themselves to mass production, and *then* you can take as long as you like.'

But the next day, in Neuheim's office, calamity crashed around Schulz.

'You fools! You blundering idiots!' Neuheim was screaming at a very pale-faced Captain Ohm. 'Is that section of yours good for nothing at all?'

In the outer office Schulz stopped typing and heard it all.

'No!' Neuheim exploded again. 'It could only happen to you! And that section of yours! You've ruined everything, do you know that? Everything!'

'We can try again,' said Ohm, standing stiffly to attention while Neuheim paced furiously around him like a stormy sea attacking a lighthouse.

'It will take *weeks* to get an agent into the position that man was in! And for all I know the Bank of England has already been alerted to what we're doing. The alarm bells may already be ringing!'

'It's unfortunate but ...'

'Unfortunate?' Neuheim snarled. 'Unfortunate? Your whole section's unfortunate! First you tell me it's impossible to forge English five-pound notes, then when I show you *how*, you lose the one man who could have made it all possible!'

The door to Neuheim's office opened and Schulz was standing there, as white as a ghost. Neuheim glared at him.

'Our chief agent in London, if you please, has been caught,' he screamed at Schulz, as though his clerk was somehow in collusion with Ohm. 'And do you know why? Because these fools,' he pointed at Ohm, 'forged his papers beautifully, and their printers printed them beautifully – except, where they should have printed an "I" in his name, they printed a "J" – an old German habit that nobody spoted except an *English policeman*!'

Neuheim was so enraged at this final ignomity that he looked as though he were having a heart attack. Schulz's legs had gone weak at the knees and he had to clutch at the door to prevent himself from falling as he saw the imminent collapse of his dreams.

'Is there no one else?' he said hoarsely.

'No one!' cried Neuheim. 'We've got no one in the position that agent was in! You can wrap up the whole operation and send everyone back where he came from.'

A stunned silence followed. Finally Ohm cleared his throat.

'Couldn't we invent the serial numbers?' he suggested tentatively. 'It might work for a while.'

Neuheim turned on him savagely. '*You* could invent them, and I daresay *would*! Doubtless you'd also print the chief cashier's signature on the note with a "J" instead of an "I", but you'd be the only one FOOL ENOUGH TO TRY AND SPEND IT!'

Ohm pulled himself up to his full height. 'Well, Herr Colonel,' he said, 'I've made my report and now I'll leave. I must, however, formally protest at being spoken to in this way in front of a subordinate.'

'Oh, formally protest all you like, what do I care?' Neuheim growled. 'You've wrecked a major operation with your bungling!'

'The technical section did point out that the scheme was impossible in the first place,' Ohm replied tightly. 'However, one cannot argue with a closed mind. Perhaps in future you'll listen to our advice instead of the advice of a –' he looked at Schulz '– a jumped-up clerk.' He turned and walked out.

Neuheim glared at Schulz. The thrust of Ohm's parting words had gone home.

'There must be something we can do,' said Schulz nervously.

'You get down to those barracks and wind that operation up and then STAY OUT OF MY SIGHT!' Neuheim roared.

'But we can't give up so easily!' Schulz pleaded. 'There must be a way! We should –'

'Should what?'

'Well – remember the bumble bee, at least? And Dr Heinkel?'

'Are you mocking me?'

'Certainly not, sir!'

'Then what do you suggest we do – put a phone call through to the Bank of England asking them what serial numbers they've issued over the last twenty years? Don't you understand? There's no way of getting serial numbers except by having access to the Bank's files. We don't have access any more! And to manufacture notes on the scale *we* propose without the serial numbers is a waste of time and resources! Now then GET ON WITH IT!'

Schulz swallowed his anger.

'Yes sir,' he said.

For a long time Schulz sat at his desk turning it over and over in his mind. He thought of the Brighton astrologer who had seen him surrounded by money. He remembered the Dutch-Jewish banker who had told him he would never make a banker. He pictured Herr Krauss, ekeing his sweaty living out of underwear. And Bertha Freyer, in her green off-the-shoulder dress, removing her spectacles and saying, 'Now if you could get hold of British banknotes;' and her voice coming through the headphones whispering 'I only talk to you because I know that your war aims are no different from mine . . .'

*   *   *

111

Neuheim stared out of his office window at the grey February sky over the Delbruckstrasse. How could he have been so stupid as to have been taken in by the half-baked ideas of a wheedling little postal clerk who should have been thrown into the front line where, with any luck, he would have been blown to pieces by a hand-grenade? He should have known that that pompous creep, Ohm, would bungle the whole thing and leave it to some filthy little Sherlock Holmes to detect what anyone with any brains or eyes could see at a glance.

He turned and gazed at the framed photograph of Adolf Hitler pinning the Iron Cross on his chest. 'It's not only innocence that protects itself, Neuheim, but ignorance too ...' those had been the Fuhrer's words. Yes, the Fuhrer understood. He, like Neuheim, was surrounded by ignorant incompetents. Now he, Neuheim, would have to explain that Operation Andreas could not be carried on. No doubt the Fuhrer would throw Dr Heinkel at him. Well, a man of the Fuhrer's spiritual stature was entitled to. For Schulz to quote the Fuhrer's words was an abomination and a travesty. He had a good mind to punish him. Perhaps he could get Schulz to prepare a few alternative scenarios for retaliation against the British. Of course he and Heydrich would need to make the decisions ...

Suddenly the door opened and Schulz walked in, with a look of desperate defiance on his face.

'Excuse me, sir,' he said, 'but – do we have any genuine five-pound notes in the office?'

Neuheim swore deafeningly.

'There's someone to see you, Heinrich.' Frau Bodelschwingh, dressed in hat and coat ready for church, presented a formidable picture of German matriarchy in all its handsome severity.

'On a Sunday morning, *mein lieb*?'

The professor was busy writing a letter at his study desk. If only his wife wasn't always so punctilious, he thought, and sighed.

'He says it's important.' The expression on Frau Bodel-schwingh's face clearly indicated that nothing could be so important that it could hold up her departure for church.

'Is it one of my students?' asked Bodelschwingh, reaching for his blotter.

'No. He's – in the SS,' she said disdainfully.

At the mention of 'SS' Bodelschwingh looked up and frowned. 'Did he say what he wanted?'

'Only that he wanted a word with you in private.'

'Well, show him in. I won't keep you long, *mein lieb*.' He picked up an envelope and licked it.

'I hope not, Heinrich.' Disapproval permanently surrounded Frau Bodelschwingh like barbed wire.

'Will you come through, please?' the professor heard her saying and a moment later a rather insignificant looking SS man entered.

'My husband can't give you long,' said Frau Bodel-schwingh haughtily. 'We're on our way to mass.' She swept out.

Schulz smiled cheerfully at the puzzled professor.

'Who are you?' he said, standing up.

'*Oberschutze* Gerhardt Schulz, Herr Professor – SS Intelligence. We're in the same business, I believe, but – we work for different firms.'

'Different firms?' Bodelschwingh laughed. 'I don't know what you're talking about – different firms?'

He slowly removed his spectacles and polished them, staring carefully all the while at Schulz. 'I should be careful what you say if I were you,' he added. 'What do you want?'

'May I sit down?' said Schulz, looking round Bodel-schwingh's book-lined study. When there was no reply he sat down anyway. 'I need your help,' he said amiably.

'You have a personal problem?'

'Well, it's personal in a way, but,' Schulz added brightly, 'it's for our country too, Herr Professor.'

'I help my country in my own way.' There was a pause while the professor replaced his glasses. 'I see you're only a private in the SS,' he went on. 'Why should I help you, anyway?'

113

Schulz sighed.

'Everybody's so obsessed with rank, I don't understand it – actually I'm a senior private and, well, I work for Colonel Neuheim.'

'Neuheim?' said Bodelschwingh cautiously. 'I've met him socially once or twice. Why didn't he come himself?'

'It's a delicate matter, and I believe our departments aren't on the very best of terms.'

Bodelschwingh stared at Schulz through his thick lenses, trying to make up his mind about him. 'I've no idea what you're talking about, young man,' he said finally. 'My department is the Faculty of Mathematics at the University of Berlin. Excuse me, you'll have to go,' he said, rising and walking towards the door. 'We're on our way to mass.'

'You blow a very good raspberry, Herr Professor,' said Schulz calmly, and lit himself a cigarette. Bodelschwingh, who had just opened the door, immediately closed it again and turned. He had sagged a little, like a deflated football. 'I know,' continued Schulz, 'because I was on the receiving end of it the other night at the Salon Kitty.'

The professor smiled at Schulz glassily and shrugged his shoulders.

'Are you ready, Heinrich?' came the imperious voice of Frau Bodelschwingh.

'My dear,' the professor called jovially, 'something's come up that's important. Why don't you go on? I'll join you later.'

'Really, Heinrich, on a Sunday . . .'

The front door slammed. Bodelschwingh looked nervously at Schulz. 'Are you threatening me?'

Schulz thought about this. 'Yes,' he replied eventually.

'Then I must tell you that I consider your threats to be empty ones!'

'You mean that Frau Bodelschwingh knows you visit the Salon Kitty?'

'No,' replied Bodelschwingh, 'but Neuheim would never dare disclose such information for the simple reason that no one would ever use his salon again.'

'Well, that's true,' Schulz laughed. 'He wouldn't. But I would.'

Bodelschwingh stared at him, and pulled from his pocket a large polka-dotted handkerchief with which he wiped his sweaty palms and brow.

'Are you a moralist or something?'

His tone implied that there were all kinds of crackpots at large these days. Schulz agreed.

'I shall never use that place again! Never!' said the professor, blowing his nose.

'Oh, don't say that, sir,' said Schulz. 'I should hate to be the cause of depriving you of so much innocent pleasure.'

'I love my wife, you understand?' said Bodelschwingh vehemently. 'I respect her!'

'Of course, Professor.'

'It's just that Fraulein Freyer – she's so ... so ...'

'Ah, Fraulein Freyer,' said Schulz. If only he could have explained to Bodelschwingh that he had her interests at heart too. 'I do sympathise, sir. I share your feelings entirely. Why don't you sit down and hear what I have to say? I promise you it won't be nearly as painful as you think.'

'I warn you,' said the professor as he sat down reluctantly, 'you'll get no money out of me!'

'Why, sir, it's not your money I want!' Schulz laughed. 'I wouldn't stoop to blackmailing you for your money. There's no profit in that – not on a professor's pay.'

'What *do* you want, then?' Bodelschwingh was now very confused.

'Your brains, sir. And knowing there's no love lost between military intelligence and the SS, I could think of no other way of persuading you to lend them to me.'

'I don't follow you.'

Schulz smiled cheerfully and reassuringly and took from his pocket a five-pound note, placing it on the little table between them.

'And now I have to tell *you* a little secret that will, unfortunately, place me entirely in your hands.' He laughed. 'I hope you wouldn't think of abusing that position?'

'That's hardly likely, is it, since *you* have a little secret that puts *me* entirely in yours!'

'My word, Professor, it really is a pleasure to do business with you, your mind is so quick. I thought exactly the same as I said it. Well, there you are – I've given us both a weapon to defend ourselves with. I couldn't be fairer than that, could I?'

'You haven't given me anything yet,' said Bodelschwingh grimly.

'Well, here it is: Counter-Espionage – *my* firm, that is, not yours – wishes to go into the business of manufacturing English five-pound notes.'

'Counterfeiting?' The professor's eyes bulged with disbelief, behind the pebble lenses.

'Yes – some people call it that. And due to my exceptional business experience I have been put in charge of the operation. Our object is to undermine the British economy.'

'Are you serious?'

'Oh yes. Unfortunately, the whole operation is about to founder on the rock of a single intractable problem – we have failed to get the right serial numbers to duplicate.'

Bodelschwingh seemed to relax a little. 'Well, I'm not surprised,' he laughed. 'They're a closely guarded secret. It's a clever idea but I can't help you.'

'I think you can,' said Schulz and pointed at the note. Herr Professor, that serial number – it's not chosen at random, is it?'

'Oh no.'

'The Bank of England must do the same as any other national bank. It must issue serial numbers according to a precise system, otherwise it would never know where it was.'

'Well, what of it?' Bodelschwingh was beginning to get impatient.

'Well sir – isn't it really just a sort of code? I mean, if you know the system, you know the code. You know where it begins and where it ends. Now, surely, it would be less difficult for a man like you then to break down an enemy code? And you're doing that every day.'

Bodelschwingh was now scrutinizing Schulz as if he himself were an enemy code. He picked up the note and examined it.

'I don't know,' he said, scratching his head, 'I've never thought about it before. It's an interesting problem.'

Schulz was delighted. 'I *knew* it would fascinate you, sir! I knew it would be in your line of country! There are some people who just love problem-solving, and I judged you rightly for one.'

'It would be more like a cipher than a code,' the professor mused thoughtfully.

'I leave that entirely to you, sir.'

'Obviously they must have a numbering system. The date, the signature and the figures must run in series – but there'll be breaks. Then the letters – yes, that's a complication. How would they do it?' He paused. 'I'll talk to our own bank. I imagine the principles on which they issue notes and their numbering systems can't be very much different from any other. That, at least, will put me, so to speak, inside the head of the issuing authority. The code *makers*.'

Schulz beamed. 'Now why didn't I think of that?' he said.

'Of course,' Bodelschwingh added, 'from then on, it's partly luck – stumbling on a meaningful sequence and so on.' He sat thinking for a moment and then looked at Schulz. 'To break a cipher you need three things – first, a high degree of intelligence; second, endless patience; and third, innumerable variation to play with. How many of these notes have you got?'

Schulz pulled a bundle out of his pocket. 'Would four hundred do?' he asked.

'Well, I think so. It's a start,' replied the professor, looking rapidly through them. 'May I keep these?'

'Of course.'

'I'll take good care of them. What's this?' Schulz was handing him a pencil and a sheet of paper.

'The receipt, sir, just sign it at the bottom. I'm sorry to trouble you with it. It's not that I don't trust you, it's just that Colonel Neuheim doesn't entirely trust *me*. He's never said as much, of course, but I usually know what he's thinking.'

117

'You're a very clever man,' said Bodelschwingh, as he signed the receipt and handed it back. 'In my opinion you're wasted in the SS.'

'Oh, no, sir, no!' Schulz laughed. 'I'm hoping to do very well.' He looked at his watch and rose. 'And now, I really think you ought to be getting to church, sir. We mustn't keep Frau Bodelschwingh waiting too long.'

'Yes, yes, of course,' said the professor, hurriedly rising. 'I'll start work this evening.'

They shook hands.

'Well, if you would – it is urgent,' said Schulz and smiled. 'I think you and I understand that it must take priority over anything else.'

'Absolutely!' agreed the professor as he put on his coat.

At the door Schulz paused. 'Oh, and – not a word of this to anyone,' he said.

'I understand.'

'That's very important.'

'Of course,' said Bodelschwingh, now looking at *his* watch.

'You're a Catholic, sir, aren't you?'

'Yes,' said the professor, slightly taken aback.

'Go to confession regularly, I suppose.'

'What of it?'

'Do be careful what you say, sir,' said Schulz. 'You just never know *who* you're talking to these days. Thank Frau Bodelschwingh for receiving me so warmly.'

12

As the weeks went by, Schulz found himself fighting a desperate rearguard action against Neuheim, who was becoming increasingly impatient and was again ready to scrap the whole thing. Just as, in England, Chamberlain was saying that by not attacking during the winter of 1939–40, the Fuhrer had 'missed the bus', so it was being said in and outside Dept VIB that Neuheim had missed the bus in his phoney-war retaliation.

Professor Bodelschwingh now spent most of his time at his desk, surrounded by sheets of paper covered with rows and rows of serial numbers. He had stopped going to the Salon Kitty, but as the solution of the numbering problem had now become an obsession with him, it more than compensated for the lack of Fraulein Freyer, for the time being at least.

The crunch came on 9 April 1940, when Hitler invaded Denmark and landed in Norway. By May he was thrusting into the Low Countries and France. The war in the West had begun.

Schulz read about it in the *Berliner Zeitung*. 'BEF FALLS BACK ON DUNKIRK' read the headline and below, in smaller letters, '3 FRENCH ARMIES DESTROYED'.

'I have the distinct impression, Solly, that time is running out,' he said, shaking his head more in sorrow than in anger. They were sitting in the common room of Barracks 19 and their conversation was punctuated by martial music and hourly bulletins from the radio. From the other end of the hut two of the SS guards were playing ping-pong with two of the inmates. Work on Operation Andreas had virtually ground to a halt.

'For whom?' said Solly, who had been reading the paper over Schulz's shoulder.

'For us. We're going too fast. The war could be over quicker than we thought. Who'll want our forged fivers then?'

'No news from our professor?' said Solly, already knowing the answer. Schulz shook his head. 'I thought you were a bit optimistic.'

Schulz stared mournfully around the room. The ping-pong ball sounded like a funeral knell in his jaded ears.

'All this beautiful equipment,' he sighed, 'all these highly skilled men – what a criminal waste! We'll never have a chance like this again. They've given us a glimpse of Paradise, Solly – but the swine may not let us in.' He clenched his fists bitterly.

'Paradise?' said Solly, shrugging. 'I'm not bothered. It doesn't worry me, you understand? What really worries me is if they'll let me back into prison. I really like that place in Hamburg.'

'I've let you down, Solly,' Schulz nodded miserably. 'We've *got* to get those serial numbers.' He crashed his fist down on the table and at that moment the phone rang. 'Neuheim, what do you bet? Wondering why the hell I'm not back in the office.'

But it was Professor Bodelschwingh.

'... I'm sorry to hear that ... Really? ... Can it be cured?'

Bodelschwingh was going into tedious detail about a minor plumbing problem from which his wife suffered. Finally he came to the point. The numbers.

'Yes, yes, I'm sorry,' said the professor. That's what I was calling you about. Listen – fascinating! Absolutely a most fascinating exercise! I think I've done it. I think I've solved the whole problem ... Are you there?'

Schulz swallowed hard. 'Yes, yes, I'm here. Did you say "solved it"?'

'Yes! Really, you know, you're a clever chap.' Bodelschwingh giggled. 'I think I'm a clever chap, too. I've broken new ground. I've even invented a machine, a code-breaking machine. It could win the war for us. Let me tell you how it works –'

'Herr Professor –' Schulz interrupted impatiently.

'You see, ciphers, unlike codes, are systematic substitutions –'

'Herr Professor, I beg you!' Schulz was now shouting down the phone. 'Not over the phone, are you mad?'

'Oh, my God, what am I doing? You're right! You see, I'm so excited –'

'Yes, yes, I understand,' said Schulz. 'But we must remain calm at all times – icy calm!'

His hand was shaking so violently that he spilled his cigarettes all over the floor. 'Calm, Herr Professor,' he went on. 'Iron self-control is expected of us. Now, you say you think you've solved the problem of the serial numbers?'

'Yes, yes, I do,' sang Bodelschwingh. 'Tell me, have you

got a five-pound note there?' He giggled again. 'A genuine one, of course.'

'A five-pound note? Yes.' said Schulz, trying to sound calm. He turned to Solly. 'Fetch one of the notes.'

Solly returned with two or three.

'What do you want me to do, Herr Professor?' said Schulz.

'Well, if I'm right,' came the professor's excited voice, 'I should be able to forecast the upper and lower limits of the serial number on the note you are holding if you give me the date of issue.'

'I see. Wait a minute.'

Schulz spread the note out in front of him. 'This one is dated 10 July 1936, Herr Professor,' he said.

'10 July 1936,' repeated the professor. 'Yes, yes, just a minute . . .' Schulz heard the sound of papers rustling on the other end of the line. 'It should be signed K. O. Peppiatt and the serial number should lie . . . between AU 65002 and AU 65501.'

Schulz stared open-mouthed. 'That's right!' he shouted into the phone. 'This one's AU 65389 and it's signed "Peppiatt".'

'I knew it, I knew it!' squealed Bodelschwingh. 'Have you got another one there?'

'Another note? Yes, here's one. The date of issue is – 17 August 1938.'

'Just a minute . . .' Again Schulz heard the sound of rustling papers. 'Ah – here it is: signature, K. O. Peppiatt again and the serial numbers should be between TK 38754 and TK 38986.'

'The serial number is TK 38766.' There was awe now in Schulz's voice. 'Herr Professor, you're absolutely right!' Everyone had stopped what they were doing. Even the ping-pong players had put down their bats and had gathered round the telephone.

'We've done it,' cried Schulz. 'We've broken the numbering system used by the Bank of England. We're in business! Gentlemen, we really are, at last, in business!'

* * *

In less than a week the notes were rolling off the presses. Neuheim was suddenly a regular visitor to Barracks 19, filling his briefcase with stacks of notes.

By this time the idea that the whole of England should be blanketed with thousands of forged notes had slipped into the background. From the time it had been appreciated how difficult it was to manufacture the notes, the idea had changed subtly and now they were aiming at producing notes to be surreptitiously put into circulation : notes raining out of the English sky would have probably led to the white fiver being withdrawn from circulation altogether. The order had come from the top, presumably because the Fuhrer did not want Dr Funk at the Ministry of Economics to hand in his resignation.

Meanwhile Schulz had plans of his own. The administrator of the Barracks 19 money factory had become a little intoxicated with power. He had never had so much of it in his life. Police chiefs all over Germany were reporting directly to him. After forms had been sent out appealing for forgers, the telephone had rarely stopped ringing.

'My colleague is dealing with this matter,' Schumacher would say and Schulz would find himself laying down the law to a provincial police chief who was terrified of upsetting the SS.

'Who is that?' he would bark. 'Hamburg? Well, come along, Hamburg, what have you got for me? I want a real record, I'm looking for top forgers and engravers, don't bother me with anything less.'

When Neuheim was out of the office Schulz was literally in command : Schumacher either went by the book or absented himself completely. His disappearances were still a constant mystery to Schulz, but he had little time to investigate the corporal's private life. Perhaps, he conjectured, this was happening all over Germany – frightened little men like himself being thrown into uniforms until there was a conspiracy of idiots, people in uniform ceasing to be human beings and only the uniform doing the talking. Everything impossible was now becoming possible and the crazier an idea sounded the more likely it was to succeed.

Of course Schulz was still obliged to report twice weekly to the Salon Kitty, preparing the reports for the file which was then stamped and dated for Neuheim's return from the front line where he was following the victorious armies as they rolled west. And the absurd incongruity of Schulz's double life was taking its toll on him. He began losing sleep, dreaming about what he could do with the money and Bertha Freyer.

By the time Bodelschwingh had solved the numbers problem and the notes started to be printed, Schulz's frustration had reached a kind of masochistic peak where he was ready to risk all to put himself out of his misery.

One night in early May, when the warm scents of summer cruelly insinuated themselves into his distraught mind like the advances of a gentle rapist, he was sitting in the basement, plugged in, as always, to Fraulein Freyer's bedroom. That particular evening she had been entertaining an elderly general with a white thatch of hair like cigarette ash who only seemed to want to talk. Specifically he wanted advice on how to handle his daughter who was showing signs of being like any other normal healthy young fraulein. It was, in fact, such a domestic evening that Schulz had begun to grow sentimental, which only added a romantic haze to his lust.

Actually Schulz had become even more sentimental earlier in the week when, with Neuheim, Kube and Schumacher absent from the office, he had formed an instant rapport with Neuheim's safe keys and had gone home with a bulging satchel.

Fraulein Freyer was already bidding the general goodnight when Schulz snapped off the microphone switches and the listening tags so that they would not whistle as they occasionally did. He walked through the main salon which, as usual, was impregnated with the aroma of sex, the sounds of sweet music and laughter drifting casually through the air, and the occasional popping of a champagne cork. In Schulz's hands were a tray with a glass of milk. A man with a glass of milk and a tray caused no trouble, he had long ago discovered. When he got to the top of the stairs, he

123

dodged into a corner as the general left, clicking his heels with a stiff 'Goodnight, Fraulein!'

She was dressed in white, probably, Schulz decided, to accentuate her girlishness. The general may have been losing one daughter but he was gaining another. She looked adorable.

'Why, Gerhardt, you've brought me some milk, how sweet of you,' she said and turned to go.

'I wanted a word with you.'

She stretched languidly, allowing Schulz to dream ...

'Oh, not now,' she yawned. 'I'm tired – I've only just got up.'

Schulz knew this was not true but he let her indulge in her innocent jokes. Again she turned to go.

'Bertha –'

'You're not going to offer me forged clothing coupons again?'

'Of course not!' said Schulz, offended. 'What do you take me for?'

'I'm not sure. Anyway, I've told you I can't –'

'What about British banknotes?'

She stopped and turned to him. Again, the gleam. 'Where would you get British banknotes?'

She was standing very close to him. Schulz could now see that the flimsy white cotton, far from being a confirmation dress, was utterly profane in its coy indecency.

'Never mind,' he swallowed. 'Would you take them?'

She paused. 'Are they genuine?' she whispered.

'Well, of course,' he said. 'What do you think, I've got a printing press of my own?'

She considered this for a few seconds.

'All right,' she nodded, 'let's see them.'

'Not here,' said Schulz, excitement welling in his throat and groin. 'Let's go up to your room.'

'Well – show me?'

Schulz looked at the divan. There was a half-bottle of champagne still in the ice bucket, a few biscuits and a jar of caviar. The general knew how to entertain his surrogate daughter.

'Couldn't we do this in a more civilized way?' he suggested, licking his lips. 'Can't we have a drink first.'

'Gerhardt, I think it would be more civilized to show me the money first,' she said. 'You could just be having me on.'

'You're so mercenary.'

Fraulein Freyer nodded sympathetically. 'I know,' she said. 'And you're so idealistic. Could I see the notes?'

Schulz pulled a bulging wallet from his pocket, grumbling as he did so. 'It wouldn't hurt you to acquire a few ideals, Bertha.'

'I'm saving up for them,' she replied sweetly. 'That's why I have to be so mercenary.'

Schulz extracted a sheaf of crisp white notes and handed them to her. She looked at him for a long while, then stood up and went to her dressing table, opening a drawer. She pulled out a cash box, inserted a key which she had taken out of her purse, opened the cash box, fished inside and took out another five-pound note. Then she put on her thick-rimmed spectacles as she had done previously and compared her note with one of Schulz's, putting it close to her ear and rustling it, smiling as she listened to the crackle. Then she did the same with each of Schulz's notes.

Schulz watched her, fascinated. If she could apply such wonderful finesse to the sexual act, he thought, the next few hours were going to be pure heaven. But she seemed to be taking such an inordinately long time to satisfy her doubts that Schulz began to worry.

'Good God,' he said, 'you don't seriously think they're forged, do you?'

'I can't afford to take a chance,' she said. She now seemed to be stroking her cheeks with them.

'Don't you trust anyone?'

'No.'

'Not even me?'

'Especially not even you. Especially not even anyone.'

She now produced a magnifying glass from the drawer and started to examine each note under it, comparing it with the

125

note she had taken from the cash box.

'What are you looking for?' said Schulz, burning with curiosity.

She did not look up or reply immediately.

'The wavy lines show up jagged and uneven on a forgery,' she said presently, still absorbed. 'It's got something to do with the crystals they use in the photo-engraving process.'

'Wherever did you find that out?'

'It's in my survival kit,' she said, looking up at him. 'All sorts of tips.' Again she rustled the notes. 'These seem genuine. I'll need another *one*.'

'*Another?*' said Schulz, alarmed. 'Christ, what rate of exchange are you using?' He produced another note with a hand that was now beginning to tremble. 'The pound's pretty strong, you know.'

'If I ever need to change these notes it will have to be on the black market and they'll be subject to a discount.'

'Where did you get the other five-pound note?' said Schulz with a trace of suspicion.

'From a client – why?'

'May I see it?'

She hesitated, then handed him the note. Schulz held it up to the light, crackled it like she had, pressed it against his cheek, peered at the signature and smelt it.

Fraulein Freyer drew close to him and he could sense her alarm. Finally he laughed.

'What are you laughing at?' she said.

'Nothing.'

'It's not forged is it?'

'Oh, no! Certainly not,' he said and, smiling, handed it back to her. 'It's as genuine as the ones I gave you.'

She returned the note to her cash box and removed her glasses.

'Tell me,' said Schulz, 'why are you so keen on British banknotes. What's wrong with German marks?'

In reply, Fraulein Freyer took his hand and gazed at him for a moment, before leading him to the divan. She took out a silver cigarette case and from it produced a cigarette. Schulz lit it for her. Her eyes were suddenly clouded.

126

'My mother died when I was two,' she began. 'My father died when I was fifteen. He left me 10,000 marks – his life savings. It was to be my little nest-egg – for when I got married. After all, I was an orphan, I had nothing. Well, that was 1923 ...' Schulz knew what was coming next. 'One day I got a letter from the bank where he'd kept his savings all those years,' Fraulein Freyer went on, chanting almost, as if it were a story which she had repeated to herself every night since. 'The letter said they could no longer look after the savings and they were returning his 10,000 marks herewith. Actually, they enclosed a million-mark note because they couldn't find anything smaller. The stamp on the envelope cost five million. It was crazy: crazy figures, crazy money. Nothing made sense. And somehow I never regained my faith in the mark after that.'

Schulz understood exactly. They were both children of a bankrupt era. His own father had died in 1922 leaving fifty thousand marks, the fruit of a life's work and his frugality. By the time Schulz had received his inheritance in the autumn of 1923 it had been enough for a box of matches. At that moment if Fraulein Freyer had wanted apples he would have bought her an orchard. And he could only see one way in which their individual interests could be combined to their mutual advantage.

'Why don't you marry me?' he whispered, intensely serious, and gripping her hand so hard that it hurt. She gently relieved the pressure.

'You?' she laughed, and shrugged. 'What for?'

'I'd like to take you away from all this,' he said, unable to come up with a more original reply, doubly so because he meant it.

'But I don't want to leave it.'

'I'll make you a promise, Bertha. Marry me, and one day you'll be rich, rich beyond your wildest dreams.'

'And how will that come about?' she said lightly.

Schulz took a breath. 'I'm involved in a scheme in which I shall literally make millions.'

'Millions?'

'Yes.'

Her face seemed to relax. She smiled and stood up, but did not release his hand, drawing him up towards her. Over her shoulder Schulz could see the bedroom beckoning like an oasis. She knew what he was looking at, what was in his mind, and kept on smiling. Schulz began to breathe more quickly.

'*Korporal* Millions?' she teased.

'I mean it,' he said.

There was a hint of sadness in her eyes as she pulled him towards the dressing table where she ran her free hand over the batch of notes he had given her.

'You keep the millions,' she said softly. 'I'm happy with these.'

She broke free of his grip and put the notes in her cash box and locked it.

Schulz was suddenly irritated.

'You're just a peasant, Bertha; you can't see beyond the next crop.'

'Can't I?'

'No!'

'And what, Gerhardt, would that crop be?'

She let her hair, which had been piled up on her head, fall around her shoulders.

'Wild dreams!' said Schulz. 'I don't think you ever have any.' His heart was beginning to race.

'Probably not,' she said and began to unbutton her dress. 'But if I did, I don't think you'd be in them.' She let the dress fall. 'The trouble is we're both out of the same Berlin gutter, Gerhardt.' She stepped out of her dress and began to remove her brassière. 'I deserve something better than you, and, to be fair,' she pressed her breasts against him, 'you deserve something better than me.'

Schulz could hardly think, hardly speak. 'I've waited a long time for this, Bertha,' he mumbled hoarsely. She lifted her knee and nudged it against his thighs.

He ran his trembling hands over her breasts and shoulders and down the small of her back towards her buttocks. She sighed softly and mumbled something indistinguishable in his ear, gently stroking his erection through the coarse material of his uniform. He began to unbutton his trousers with one hand and, with the other, felt her buttocks stiffen.

Fraulein Freyer's buttocks stiffened because the door had suddenly burst open and the boots and uniform of two field policemen were apparent in the periphery of her line of vision.

'You're under arrest!' shouted one of the policemen. 'Fall in outside! Move!'

Fraulein Freyer screamed. Schulz let go of her firm little buttocks as though they were hot potatoes, which later he reflected fondly was a very apt description of those magnificent parts of her anatomy.

13

'I'm amazed! Did you really think you'd get away with it? Do you know the maximum penalty for embezzling funds in wartime is death by shooting?'

Neuheim was almost grinning with malice. At least, thought Schulz, he had not been shot. Detection, trial, sentence and execution in one day would come later in the war. As it was, he had been bundled off to the same cell that he had been in earlier. This time he was stripped of his clothes – and also of his rank, and was back to private. There was no interrogation, and no food either. No light or heat. He had shivered in the darkness until Neuheim had eventually appeared. Schulz would have preferred to remain shivering in the darkness. However he was beginning to catch 'flu.

'So the cuckoo had fouled its nest?' Neuheim said grimly. 'How do you like your medicine?'

'I'd be much happier serving the Reich, sir,' said Schulz, standing stiffly and nakedly to attention. Neuheim grunted, impressed by Schulz's patriotism.

'May I ask, sir, how you discovered the notes were missing?'

'By installing my own system of bookkeeping, that's how. Does that surprise you?'

Nothing about Neuheim surprised Schulz.

'It may also surprise you to know that I have a master switch which enables me to listen to any conversation in the Salon Kitty, at any time, in the comfort of my office. I can, of course, control whether the microphones are switched on or off. Does *that* surprise you?'

'No sir,' Schulz finally replied. 'On reflection, it – hurts more than it surprises.'

Neuheim nodded darkly. 'Yes,' he said. 'And so would a bullet in the eye – just remember that. Sit down.'

Schulz looked round. There wasn't a chair so he sat on the floor, looking up at Neuheim's glinting eye patch. Immediately he started to cough. Neuheim waited for the fit to subside.

'So,' he said, 'at last you're beginning to catch a little bit of the war fever. I'm glad to hear it,' he said unkindly.

Fortunately Schulz was too weak to reply.

'Well, Schulz, you're lucky. I've just come from the Fuhrer. He's seen the notes we've produced and is delighted with my whole operation. In fact, he's given me his personal commendation and promotion.'

'Congratulations, sir,' spluttered Schulz between coughs.

'He now wishes to have them tested. You are being let off lightly, Schulz, I hope I don't need to remind you. I am sending you to Switzerland at the Reich's expense.'

Schulz could not believe his ears but once again a fit of coughing prevented him from replying.

'You will be given a passport, £195 of genuine British currency and one forged five-pound note. Enjoy yourself. Don't come back till you've spent the lot. Which you will do in one week, Schulz, if you value your life.'

Was this some kind of macabre joke? Schulz wondered. Was he being tempted with paradise to make the hell that was being prepared for him even more loathesome?

'May I ask, Herr Col – Brigadier, why I am being treated so leniently?'

'You may ask, Schulz. But if I were you I would not look

a gift horse in the mouth.'

Schulz was seized by another coughing fit. Between coughs he heard Neuheim saying, 'I will, however, say just this, Schulz. You are being given one – just one – chance to make amends for your dishonesty and to serve your country. You will be in Switzerland for seven days and seven days only. And if on your return you dare to go anywhere near Fraulein Freyer I will personally make sure you are instantly dispatched to the front line from which, have no fear, YOU WILL NEVER RETURN!'

Schulz was almost more shaken by Neuheim's parting words, than he had been by the experience of the previous week. It seemed inconceivable to him that Neuheim's warning him off Bertha could have been purely out of altruism to protect her long-departed virtue. The only conclusion he could reach was that Neuheim had some kind of vested interest. The thought of Neuheim vesting his interest in Bertha Freyer was somehow revolting, even though the fact that countless other high-ranking officers had done likewise now merely caused in him a habitual dull ache of remorse.

So Schulz took the train to Switzerland, a mixture of euphoria and deep depression circulating through his mind like a poisoned cocktail. The £200 cheered him slightly, of course, and he was already counting the ways in which the money could be spent.

'It'll be interesting to see how easily the phoney one goes,' Neuheim had said. 'Swiss banks are short of foreign currency – that's why we're giving you British fivers, you'll get more francs for your money.'

As the train sped south towards Leipzig, in between uncontrollable bouts of coughing Schulz enjoyed his first taste of luxury for many, many months.

'Get me the Basel police, at once, Schumacher!' Neuheim barked.

'At once, Herr Brigadier!' Schumacher replied, getting

busy on the switchboard. He yawned: there had been precious little sleep for him the previous evening ...

Neuheim yawned. He had had precious little sleep the previous night. That amazing little fraulein at the Kitty, what a body – and what an imagination! He chuckled. It was wonderful what a few of those crisp, white, forged British banknotes could do for a woman's imagination. Schulz may have been a sneaking, dishonest little thief with no backbone or allegiance to the Fuhrer and the Fatherland, but he did have good taste in women. Fortunately it would be Schulz's only taste of Fraulein Freyer, he would make damn sure of that. She seemed to have such boundless energy ...

'Your call, Herr Brigadier,' Schumacher buzzed him.

'Basel police? SS-Brigadier Alfred Neuheim here, Berlin. We believe a man named Gerhardt Schulz is travelling to Switzerland on a false passport. You can expect him to arrive on the night train from Berlin tomorrow morning ... Yes, he's posing as a Swiss businessman ... ladies' underwear ... I said, LADIES' UNDERWEAR! ... That's right ... not at all, I hope you get your man.'

Neuheim slammed down the phone and looked at his watch. There'd just be time if he hurried.

'Schumacher, tell Kube I won't be in the office for the rest of the afternoon. I have a high-level meeting to attend.'

'Very good, Herr Brigadier.'

Neuheim opened his safe and extracted two five-pound notes, smiling as he looked forward to those high-level breasts and those firm little buttocks, just like hot potatoes.

Schumacher yawned.

Schulz had been dozing fitfully as the night train travelled on through Nuremberg and headed for the Swiss frontier.

He felt as though he were suffering from battle fatigue. This was curious considering that, apart from the *Wilma* incident which could conceivably be called fieldwork, he had never been anywhere near a battle. But he had read about the Fuhrer's fondness for *blitzkrieg* and now liked to think that serving under Neuheim was as traumatic an experience as any that could be expected by the front-line troops in France or Holland.

'Excuse me, may I see your passport, Herr . . . ?'

A spindly little official in a uniform that Schulz assumed to be that of the Swiss immigration office was eyeing him beadily.

'Schulz,' he answered hastily and, for some reason, guiltily, though, when he later thought about it, quite unnecessarily so.

'Ah! . . . mmmm. Herr Schulz, I would be most obliged if you would come with me, I have some questions to ask you,' said the official, who then waited patiently while Schulz nervously reached for his brief-case and stood up.

'I think you will find that my passport is in order,' he said. 'I am a Zurich businessman, a traveller in ladies' underwear. I was on my way back.'

'We shall see, "Herr Schulz", we shall see,' said the official, emphasizing his name with mock severity. 'In Switzerland we do things properly, as you no doubt well know, "Herr Schulz".'

In the end Schulz's Swiss holiday lasted five days, four of them spent in jail. He was deposited in a Basel prison cell while his passport was examined microscopically in Berne. It was then pronounced genuine and, much to his surprise, he was released, with apologies for their having treated a Swiss citizen so badly. The information they had been given, he was told, was obviously malicious. Schulz, who had guessed only too well the source of that information, agreed heartily. In high spirits he made his way to Zurich, where he headed straight for the bank and presented the exchange bureau with a sealed envelope which he knew contained a letter of introduction and the British currency.

He was promptly arrested again and held in a dingy jail with no explanation or interrogation. The letter, which had, of course, been written by Neuheim, declared, to whom it may concern, that there was a possibility that the notes were forged. After another two days, during which the notes were sent to London for investigation, Schulz was again released, London having confirmed that the notes were absolutely genuine.

Schulz decided he had had enough of Swiss hospitality and returned to Berlin furious and wanting to kill someone. Instead he decided to visit Fraulein Freyer.

This time Schulz took no chances. He arrived at the Salon Kitty in the early afternoon when, he surmised, business would be at its slackest, and went straight up to Bertha's room.

She came to the door in a negligée. She had obviously only just woken up. The poignant sound of a violin came from a radio in her bedroom.

'Gerhardt!' she gasped in astonishment, 'but I thought you were –'

'SSShh!' he whispered, putting a finger to his lips.

He went straight to her small basin, ran the hot water tap and wetted a tablet of pink freesia-scented soap. Bertha stared at him in curiosity, her imagination racing. He smiled mysteriously at her and took the soap over to the ventilator grill and pushed it down on top of the hidden microphone, where it miraculously stayed. If Neuheim could control the microphone, then, Schulz had decided, he would have to make sure that the live microphone could only pick up soap.

'Gerhardt –' Fraulein Freyer whispered tenderly.

'I've got them, Bertha, two hundred of them!' he said excitedly, wiping his hands and drawing her towards him almost in one movement. 'Two hundred pounds – a present from the SS.'

'But Gerhardt –' she said softly.

'Not a word,' he said, pressing his hand over her mouth and kissing her furiously.

'Gerhardt –' she began again and now he could see that she was getting as excited as he was. She was gazing in the direction of the bedroom and a look of urgent passion had come over her face.

134

'In a minute, *liebling*. First, I want to tell you that as far as I am concerned the SS can go to hell, and that includes that evil, slimy, treacherous bastard, Neuheim *and* his boss Heydrich, who's just a homosexual pig who –'

'Gerhardt!' she screamed and pointed silently at the bedroom door which was now opening to reveal the full regalia of the SS and, inside it, the tall, blue-eyed, blond and speechless form of SS-Oberstgruppenfuhrer Reinhardt Heydrich, who held in one hand his beloved violin.

'You are luckier than you deserve!' Brigadier Neuheim spat into Schulz's face, depositing on his eyelid a drop of saliva which made it difficult for Schulz to see.

'Heydrich was all for having you shot on the spot. That would of course have given me the greatest of pleasure. At the very least you should have been courtmartialled and sent off to the front line. However . . .'

Neuheim paused and walked over to the window where he stood gazing at the sky long enough for Schulz to wipe the saliva away with the back of his sleeve.

'However,' Neuheim swung round and glared at him with his one eye, 'the Fuhrer is very pleased with the way the forgery went through undetected, and were it not for that . . .' He trailed off, letting the rest hang on the air like a monstrous threat. 'As you know, this scheme of mine, this little brain-child, is very close to my heart.'

Again he paused and his features rearranged themselves into a contorted smirk.

'For that reason, I pleaded for leniency in your case. Of course, there is now no question of promoting you to *Oberschutze*. A senior private is a man with a basic sense of decency and honour which, naturally, you could not be expected to have.'

'Yes, Herr Brigadier,' said Schulz, agreeing for the first time.

'But a private has his uses, Schulz, so do not be completely disheartened. Which brings me to the point.'

Schulz wondered if there was any point in anything at all.

135

'The Fuhrer has now agreed, to mass-produce the notes,' – a flicker of brightness passed across Schulz's hitherto impassive face – 'if, and only if,' continued Neuheim, 'we can successfully place in circulation in England two million pounds-worth of them.'

Neuheim was now looking at Schulz like a tarantula at its prey; he had become appetising.

'Place them in circulation, sir?' Schulz was quickly calculating whether the conditions in English prisons might be better than those in the Swiss.

'Yes. And I've decided that you're the man to do it. We are going to drop the notes by plane.'

Schulz paused while he tried to work this out. Then: 'I don't understand, sir. I thought the plans to drop the notes by plane had been abandoned.'

'They have, in a manner of speaking. We're going to drop you with them.'

Schulz paled. His hand moved involuntarily to his throat. 'Drop me with them?'

'Yes.'

'You mean – jump out of an aeroplane?'

'Yes,' snapped Neuheim impatiently. 'Well, don't look so glum about it, they give you a parachute before you jump!'

'But why? Why can't we just scatter them by plane?'

'Don't be obtuse, Schulz. As you well know the Ministry of Economics are violently opposed to the idea. If we were just to scatter the notes they would soon get to know about it. We've been through this hundreds of times. Our plan has always been that we'll inject them secretly through the British bloodstream.'

'You mean *I* will?'

'Yes. All you've got to do is to spend the money unobtrusively and, if you can, get back to Germany. Others will then follow.'

'Surely this is work for an agent, sir.'

'Exactly.'

Schulz tried again. 'How do you spend two million pounds unobtrusively?'

'I've thought about that,' said Neuheim who seemed to be

in a very good mood now. 'In the first place, we have friends in England. They're businessmen and they'll help. Secondly, there are many ways of spending money without attracting attention. On the black market, for instance, and in gambling halls. You can buy property and businesses – we'll put you in touch with solicitors. You could even invest in the British film industry – that's money right down the drain.'

There was now a dreamy contentment in Neuheim's face as though he was at last engineering an idea of his own. Schulz thought about it all: there was definitely something wrong.

'Why me, sir?' he said at last.

'Think, Schulz!' Neuheim bawled, making Schulz jump. 'One, you have the languages – your English is, I understand, perfect; two, you have such a dull, unmemorable face that you make an ideal candidate; and three ...'

'Yes, sir?'

'If you don't you will be shot or sent to the Russian front, which amounts to the same thing.'

Schulz considered this and had to admit that it was logical. 'And what happens if I'm caught?'

'Well ...' Neuheim hesitated. 'As an enemy agent you could, in theory, be shot.'

'And in practice?'

'In practice ...' He paused. 'You could also be shot. But, then, you *will* be shot if you stay here so you won't actually be worse off.' His face brightened at this comforting suggestion and immediately darkened again. 'I would have thought you would have welcomed the opportunity.'

'No, sir. Oddly enough, I don't. In fact, to be perfectly frank, I don't want to go.'

Neuheim adjusted his black patch and stared at him. 'What do you mean "don't want to go"?'

'I don't know any other way of putting it, sir – I just don't want to go. This is a job for a volunteer and I am volunteering not to go.'

* * *

137

Actually, Schulz had only imagined the last part of his conversation with Neuheim, when he later upbraided himself with what he should have said. What he had really said was: 'This is a job for a volunteer...'

Neuheim had then said: 'Quite right.' And Schumacher had said, 'Well done.' It was only *after* that that Schulz remembered that the English had just shot the previous German agent in the Tower of London. By that time Schumacher had been instructed to kit him out for the mission. This was the task for Captain Ohm's department and after the fiasco of the serial numbers, Schulz was dreading the prospect of being fitted out like Sir Walter Raleigh, or Lord Nelson, or Benjamin Disraeli.

In the event what they decided on was almost as bad.

Captain Ohm had acquired a pair of plus-fours, a particularly English garment, he said, with thick woollen socks and green garters. With this was included a bowler hat. Over the whole costume Schulz was to wear a flying suit with a hood and, on his feet, a pair of stout brogue shoes which had been discovered in a shop in a small street in the Charlottenburg district, quite near the Delbruckstrasse. When Solly saw the brogues on a brief visit to Barracks 19 he roared with laughter.

'You look ridiculous, Gerhardt!' he said. 'Please God I never forget the sight of you in those shoes. They're unfakeable.'

Schulz was not amused. He was rather sensitive about his physical appearance and was beginning to think he would look like a keeper of a miniature golf course. And by the end of that week, which was also the end of May 1940, he felt as if he had been processed through a jam factory.

'What's that?' he asked a storeman, pointing at the bowler.

'Captain Ohm has called it a top priority,' the storeman replied.

Even his underpants were of the thick woollen kind that steelworkers wore and around his neck was an old school tie, believed to have belonged to an Old Etonian who had defected to the Nazi cause in the mid-thirties. Ohm seemed

138

to have used the novels of P. G. Wodehouse as his prime reference source.

'One thing,' said Schumacher who held one of the dozens of lists, all of them headed with Schulz's name with 'Priority' stamped across them.

'What?' said the storeman.

'He must have his cyanide capsule.'

'Here we are,' said the storeman. 'You counter-espionage boys think of everything.'

'Don't use it unless you have to,' said Schumacher.

One of Captain Ohm's technicians explained about the explosive device fitted to the metal canister which was to contain the money. It had a small, evil-looking lever which Schulz was instructed how to set when he buried the canister.

Schulz was also to undergo a crash course in parachute jumping at a sports club in North Berlin. Unfortunately, there was very little time, Neuheim having been anxious to launch the trial run as soon as possible, having given his word to the Fuhrer. On the day Schulz attended the sports club it was closed for repairs. However, the parachute trainer was only too happy to explain the theory of jumping, which he did for two hours, with the aid of a blackboard and chalk and frequent references to the theory of human aerodynamics and the use of terms like 'drag', 'air flow velocity' and 'opening shock'.

'The magnitude of the drag force,' he explained, 'is dependent on the square of the velocity of descent, the magnitude of the projected area of the parachute and the specific gravity of the air.'

Schulz did not quite follow this but he did remember that he was supposed to open the parachute by means of a ripcord and he noted this as a very valuable piece of advice.

He was then taken to the Department of Foreign Maps where further sealed instructions were awaiting him. Nobody had given much thought to what happened if he lost the canister, but he was provided with an English garden spade to enable him to bury it.

The flight was due to be launched at 4.00 a.m. on Sunday, 2 June 1940. Neuheim came to the aerodrome to see him off, as did Captain Ohm and Schumacher. Out on the tarmac a lonely Heinkel bomber was warming up its engines. Neuheim was almost maternal in his anxiety but Schulz was under no illusion that Neuheim had come to say a fond goodbye to him – his concern was all for the two million pounds – his little brain-child.

'You've got your identity card and your ration book?' he said, staring at Schulz's flying suit with a look of outraged wonder. Schulz nodded glumly. He was wondering if Neuheim could possibly be going to tip off the English that here was a man suspected of carrying forged notes. Then he remembered that Neuheim's hatred for the English exceeded even his apparent need to manipulate him and he relaxed. A ground staffman was loading the aluminium canister on board. Neuheim pointed to it.

'Don't forget, if anyone finds it and tries to open it . . .' He threw up his hands to demonstrate the effect. Schulz nodded again.

'Have you got your cyanide capsule?'

'Yes, sir.'

'Don't use it unless you have to.'

Schulz had now been told this by every member of the technical section as though they had been instructed to programme his subconscious by repetition.

'That's good advice, sir,' he said. 'Thank you.'

'Well, good luck!' said Neuheim, offering Schulz his hand. 'For Germany and the Fuhrer!' He laughed and slapped him on the back with absurd bonhomie. 'The way the war's going in France we'll be in England before you spend half that money!'

Ohm handed Schulz the bowler hat, which he took and stuffed down the front of his flying suit, and then zipped himself up.

'I'd give anything to be in your shoes when you spend the first note,' said Ohm. 'Imagine it!'

'Are you quite sure they're still wearing plus-fours in England now?' Neuheim said quietly to Ohm, out of Schulz's hearing.

'Pretty sure, sir.' said Ohm.

140

Schulz climbed into the belly of the plane clutching his briefcase and the bomb doors closed. As the engines began to roar and the Heinkel taxied towards the take-off point, it suddenly occurred to him that today was a Sunday and all the shops in England would be closed. This was the pretext he had been trying to conjure up throughout the past twenty-four hours for calling the whole thing off.

But it was already too late.

14

They took off in the moonlight.

Schulz, huddled against the side of the aircraft and wearing an oxygen mask, could see the boyish faces of the Heinkel's crew gazing at him with awe. He was, he realized, a glamorous figure in their eyes; a secret agent on an unknown mission, maybe to abduct the two daughters of King George for all they knew. To be a German secret agent at this time was, arguably, to have reached a pinnacle of prestige at the most prestigious time in Germany's glorious history. Schulz, on the other hand, felt more like a seaside entertainer in an English Punch and Judy show. By what weird alchemy, he wondered, as the Heinkel flew diagonally across the Belgian coastline towards the English Channel, had he been transmuted from a salesman in ladies' underwear to a secret agent loaded with forged fivers? And what Dread Hand was posting him, like an envelope without a stamp – or even an address – into the door or Germany's deadliest enemy?

By this time he had opened the sealed envelopes and was as briefed as he was ever likely to be about his mission. The flight would take a mere thirty minutes. He was to drop just before dawn. His destination: the heart of the flat, green Kent countryside where he had lived fifteen years earlier. This gave him a certain nostalgic sense of coming home. His contact was to be a Mr Melfort who lived in Kent, but who was, in fact, a German agent, planted long before the war. Schulz had been given passwords and map references. With Melfort's help, he was to get the money into rapid circulation and then make his way back to Germany as best he could. The map on which he had to mark the location of the canister was printed on waterproof silk which, when folded, compressed to almost nothing. It was hidden in a secret compartment in the hollowed-out heel of his stout English shoes. It, like the hollowed-out heel, was obviously the work of dedicated experts. The pocket money was in the briefcase, together with some English bookmakers' slips and even a note of the current date. The efficiency with which the technical division had set to work on the scheme impressed Schulz, but he could not forget the agent who had been shot in the Tower. In his present insecure mood he was not prepared to trust anyone, even the wireless operator when he handed Schulz a Thermos flask of coffee.

'Not for me, thank you,' Schulz said.

'We'll be there soon, sir,' said the wireless operator deferentially.

Schulz changed his mind and took a gulp, noting wrily that it was, as ever, ersatz. He dozed for a few minutes.

The next thing he knew he was being awoken by the dispatcher who shouted in his ear that they were about to descend. Schulz was cold, hungry, frightened and extremely sleepy. The sound of the engine changed.

The dispatcher strapped the spade to Schulz's chest, testing the harness of the parachute to which he also attached the canister. Then he removed his oxygen mask and Schulz followed suit.

'We're nearly there,' said the dispatcher. 'How do you feel?'

'How would you feel?' said Schulz.

The dispatcher taken aback lapsed into silence. Suddenly the engine cut out. The dispatcher hooked up Schulz's life line, opening the jump door. Schulz looked him in the eyes. Perhaps he would be the last German that Schulz would ever see again: a young man without a doubt in the world. They had not encountered a single fighter nor any evidence of flak.

'Get ready!' the dispatcher shouted.

Schulz nodded dully.

'Go! Go! Go!' the dispatcher was shouting at him. The captain had emerged from the cockpit and Schulz noticed the Luger on his belt.

He jumped.

He felt the rush of cold night air hit him in the throat and chest. He coughed as he fell, over and over into the blackness, phrases like 'air velocity' drifting inconsequentially through his mind. He remembered to pull the ripcord: nothing happened. Nothing happened for what seemed like an eternity and then there was a jerk and the parachute opened and he was hanging with the canister in the middle of nowhere. He could see nothing, so he shut his eyes and waited, as the sound of the Heinkel's engine started again and it made its disinterested way back to the Fatherland.

For some reason the idea of the bowler hat, tied to him by special straps designed by Captain Ohm's engineering geniuses, comforted him. Who would shoot a man with a bowler hat in England on a Sunday morning in June? He told himself confidently.

He landed like a leaf, just before the dawn broke, in a field near which there was a stream with a culvert and a small wood. The drop was perfect.

He lay on his back for a long, blissful time. Even though it was dark, Schulz could see the shadowy outlines of trees nearby and smell the peculiar sweet-grass smell that brought memories of England flooding back to him. His arrival had disturbed the birds but soon they were silent again. In that pre-dawn stillness he felt like Adam must have felt in the Garden of Eden, devoid of a past, utterly content. With the moist grass underneath him and hardly a sound except for the trickle of the nearby stream he was suddenly glad that he had no firearms of any kind: indeed there was nothing dangerous about him at all, although, of course, there was the explosive in the canister's self-destructing device.

From being paralysed with terror before the drop, Schulz was now so comfortable he was reluctant to move, and in this state of complete relaxation he fell asleep.

When he at last opened his eyes and looked at his watch, he discovered he had slept for nearly three hours. It was 7.15 a.m., but still perfectly quiet and still.

He got to his feet and took the harness off; detached the canister and gathered the billowing folds of the parachute. There was a good trade in Germany in silk for the production of ladies' underwear, but he decided not to risk entertaining any thoughts in that direction. Instead, he would follow instructions and bury it.

It was nearly eight o'clock by the time he had rolled up the webbing and had dug a sizeable hole near the culvert. The soil was chalky and easy to shift, but he used the parachute as a protective sheet, in order not to disturb the ground too much, taking care to lay the bowler and briefcase carefully to one side. He had become almost fond of them, as though they were mantelpiece ornaments.

Fortunately the metal spade did not hit a single stone and it was not Schulz but the early morning light that woke the birds to life again. By that time he had safely buried the parachute, the flying suit and the canister, filled in the hole and relaid the turf which he had taken care to remove in one large slab. Before burying the canister he had opened it and removed several wads of five-pound notes which he packed into his briefcase.

Now, as he sat in his plus-fours with bowler planted firmly on his head, he took the map out of his heel and waited for the dawn to grow lighter so that he could take a bearing on a distant church tower to establish his position.

When it was finally light enough he took a cross-bearing on the squat tower and a large hillock with some kind of water tank on top of it – he had been told to look for two such landmarks – and then replaced the map in its hiding place in his heel, together with a little sketch of the copse.

There was a country lane nearby and the church tower

a few miles away marked the village of Brenzett. He stood up, dusting himself down, cleaned his hands and shoes in the stream, gave the replaced turf a final tap and looked at his watch. It was now nearly ten o'clock. He picked up his briefcase and strolled towards the hedge. He kept his eyes open for a farm : if he were stopped, he had planned to say that he was from the Ministry of Agriculture, but there was not a house in sight. It was perfect.

Some poppies were growing by the roadside and Schulz picked one, putting it into his buttonhole. He now looked like some romanticized picture of an English gentleman out of *Punch* or the *Tatler*. He stared up into the blue sky and, even as he did so, the perfect calm of an English Sunday morning was broken by the whine of aircraft engines. Schulz could not restrain himself from ducking as a squadron of Spitfires roared overhead in close formation. They were probably bound for France, he thought. In this quiet place it was difficult to imagine what was going on in Europe, although he had heard that the French roads were jammed with refugees. As he began to stroll towards the distant village, he imagined the dive bombers, whose scream-sirens were the Fuhrer's own idea and fitted at his direct command, swooping out of the French skies and creating untold destruction and havoc. Now, however, the war and Germany seemed like a bad dream and if he felt anything at all it was a sense of having miraculously escaped all the madness.

Suddenly Schulz froze. He had just remembered that he had forgotten to set the lever on the destructive device inside the canister. Now anyone could open it without risk. Neuheim's instructions had been quite categorical. If the British were to get word of the amount of forged fivers buried there, there would be no question of the economy being subtly ruined.

Pull yourself together, Schulz thought, *you're beginning to think like Heydrich. What the hell does it matter?* If his motto was survival at all costs, he was at least free of the stamp of jackboots. As soon as he had made his contact, he could return for the money and simply disappear. On the other hand he had made such a good job of burying the canister that it would be a shame to disturb it now. Better to spend the money he already had and count himself lucky that he had not been shot or sent to join the Russian campaign. In the end he decided to wait until the time came for a decision. It was too nice a day to worry about it.

The village was further away than he had originally thought and the road kept winding, first towards it and then away, meandering wildly like a drunk. The sun was now beating down, the birds were in full song, and Schulz, in his tweeds, plus-fours and bowler, soon began to sweat with the unaccustomed effort of walking. He cursed Captain Ohm and his ill-informed ideas of seasonal English wear and was trying to practise not thinking in German when he heard the crunch of a bicycle on gravel around the next bend.

At first he saw a cloth-capped head bent over an old bicycle, as the man pedalled laboriously towards him. Probably a poacher, Schulz thought, noting a brace of rabbits over the crossbar. He was wearing moleskin trousers, and the jacket and waistcoat of a threadbare suit which was several sizes too small for him. He was in his fifties, with a walrus moustache on his wind-burnt face which seemed to come alive when he saw Schulz. He gawked at the bowler hat in amazement.

'Good morning!' said Schulz cheerfully, 'Lovely day,' and raised his bowler.

The cyclist grunted, touched his cap and rode away at speed, saying nothing. Schulz decided that his bowler hat lent him an air of authority and certainly it seemed to put the fear of God into poachers.

He was delighted at his first success and as he strode on he practised saying 'Good morning' to himself. He was now in such a magnanimous mood that he even ignored the sound of more fighters streaking across the sky above his head. He breathed deeply, inhaling the fresh morning air, and noted happily that his cough seemed to have vanished for good.

'So far two hundred and sixty thousand men have been evacuated from the beachhead which is still holding. It is estimated that a further eighty thousand are still waiting ...'

The landlord of the Fox and Grapes lowered the *Sunday Express* to listen to the latest radio bulletin.

'Hundreds of small boats have responded to the Royal Navy's call to make the journey backwards and forwards across the Channel. Thousands of soldiers in small groups have been brought back to the Channel ports in this way. Fierce fighting is going on around the rim of the perimeter outside Dunkirk, but so far the perimeter has been held. Along the Somme, the French High Command reports ...'

He switched the radio off in disgust and returned to his *Sunday Express*, shaking his head sourly at the headlines.

'We've been caught napping again,' he said and belched. He was a big, red-faced, burly man, whose lack of confidence in his own political leaders was only matched by his instinctive distrust of foreigners.

'This country never wakes up till somebody gives it a bashing,' said his wife, who was mopping the floor.

He studied the paper again. 'It says here that the Fuhrer's directing the German army personally from the front. Why don't *our* generals go to the front?'

'How can they? Their wheelchairs get stuck in the mud. Are you going to stand there all morning reading that paper? It'll be opening time in an hour.'

'I've got to see how the war's going!'

'I can tell you how it's going – down the drain where this pub'll go if you don't get on with cleaning it.'

Having delivered her warning broadside she picked up her weaponry of mop, carpet-beater and broom and turned to go out to the back of the pub, but paused as she heard footsteps in the doorway.

'Good morning?'

The landlord looked up, puzzled, wondering if he had left the radio on. The voice was just like one of those BBC men. Then puzzlement changed to astonishment. Standing in front of him with a broad beam on his face was a man wearing plus-fours with green garters, a bowler hat and an old school tie. On his feet he had some kind of brogue shoes and on his face a pair of steel-rimmed spectacles. He was carrying a briefcase. It was one of the most bizarre and extraordinary sights the landlord had ever seen.

'Good morning, sir,' he replied politely.

'Lovely morning!' Again the plummy accent.

'Yes, I suppose it is,' the landlord nodded. 'What can I do for you, sir?' he said carefully.

The man raised his bowler. 'Whisky and Soda, please.'

Schulz moved towards the counter and deposited his briefcase on it. The publican was staring at him blankly. For the first time Schulz wondered if anything was wrong. He seemed to be the only customer in the pub which still smelled of stale tobacco smoke and the previous night's beer. Behind the florid publican was a large, blowsy-looking woman with a scarf over her hair whom Schulz assumed to be his wife. They were both now staring at him. The landlord turned and fixed his eyes on the clock on the wall with a heavy significance that escaped Schulz, who followed his gaze. The woman was looking too. The hands on the clock pointed to 10.50.

'It's ten to eleven,' the landlord finally said, as though something dreadful was going to happen at eleven o'clock. Maybe a bombing raid, Schulz thought, and then realized that was absurd.

'We don't serve liquor until twelve o'clock, sir.'

His wife nodded, outraged, as though Schulz had said something about the King of England's German ancestry.

'Oh, really?' Schulz laughed, slightly nervous now. 'I always thought it was ten-thirty.'

'No, sir,' said the landlord slowly, as though instructing a six-year-old child. 'That's weekdays, sir. This is Sunday.'

The woman nodded, her curlers glistening like the barrels of machine-guns shining in a spiky hedge.

'Yes, yes, of course,' said Schulz, covering up his embarrassment with an affectation of irritability. 'I know it's Sunday.' *Why hadn't Captain Ohm remembered such an elementary thing?* he thought. The English licensing laws were the laughing stock of Europe. He could now see that the landlord was weighing him up and he laughed again, carelessly.

148

'I never go into pubs as a rule,' he added.

'I can see that, sir,' replied the landlord without taking his eyes of Schulz for a second. 'If you did, you know you wouldn't get no Scotch either. There's a war on. You've heard about that, I suppose?'

'Oh, yes,' said Schulz, removing his bowler hat which he decided was not likely to impress this particular local. 'I've heard about that.' The woman was looking at his hair as if she thought there might be something sinister lurking inside it. Schulz was beginning to sweat, holding the briefcase and the bowler hat in one hand as if they didn't belong to him. 'I'll have a cup of coffee, then,' he said.

Immediately he knew he had committed another cardinal blunder. The landlord exchanged suspicious looks with his wife.

'Oh, don't bother,' Schulz said hurriedly. 'I haven't really got time, anyway.'

But the landlord was now coming towards him and taking his arm. 'No! no! No bother, sir,' he said. 'A cup of coffee, is it? You sit there, sir. Ethel'll have you fixed up with a cup of coffee in no time, won't you, Ethel? No time at all, sir. Have you seen this morning's paper, sir? We're taking a terrible beating over there ...'

Schulz could see that Ethel's jaw had dropped but she moved towards the door while the landlord continued gushing over Schulz as though they were short of customers.

'We're taking a terrible beating over there. I only hope we get our boys off those beaches and back home. Never mind their equipment, just get them back home, that's what I say. Don't you agree, sir?'

He thrust the *Sunday Express* into Schulz's hand and disappeared into the back of the pub, jerking his head to his wife to follow him. Schulz sat pondering the situation for a moment. It was clear that the publican was suspicious and that anything he might now say would only compound his suspicions.

'Make yourself at home, sir. Coffee won't be a jiff!' the landlord called out from the kitchen. Schulz pretended to read the paper and began to look around the pub, noticing

149

little details like the fact that the doors had been propped open by a barrel, and that in front of the bar there was a pile of dustpans and cleaning cloths. The place was obviously open for business. Schulz became aware of the publican's low voice just beyond the kitchen door and he got up, moving cautiously around the counter to hear what was being said ...

'... Well, I don't know,' whispered the landlord. 'There's something odd about him. I think you should come over and take a look. ... Well, he came in here – quarter to eleven it was, and asked for Scotch. And when I told him he couldn't have any, he asked for a cup of coffee! ... *Coffee*, in a pub!' He listened to the voice on the other end of the line and then went on: 'Well, I suppose he may be a Norwegian or a Dane, but he's got up like an Englishman and the papers are always telling us to be on our guard against spies ... No, I'll keep him here, don't you worry ... Ethel's making him a cup of coffee. I'll go out and chat to him. You get over here as soon as you can.'

The landlord quietly put down the receiver and walked back into the bar. It was empty.

Schulz had taken his leave through the rear exit between the pub and the lounge bar where the lavatories were. Fortunately the door was unlocked and opened silently, so he hoped the landlord might think he had left by the front door. He made straight for the far side of the village, which was still practically deserted. Then he noticed, to his horror, that there was a police block down one road, which he carefully avoided. What was also strange was that there did not seem to be any signposts which, from his previous visit to England, had been as common as roses were in English gardens. Across another road he could see that wires had been laid, as if, he thought, to stop parachute landings. And everywhere there were crudely cemented pillboxes.

He was now beginning to curse the bowler and decided to ditch it as soon as possible. There was an incinerator burning in a back garden but he hurried on, not knowing whether or not a burning bowler would smell. Burning a bowler hat in England, he decided, was probably as grave a sin as asking for coffee in a pub. Presently the houses thinned out a little and he came to a small bridge with a tow-path underneath. He ducked down beside it so that he could not be observed; then he knelt down on the briefcase and leaned over, tipping the brim of the bowler into the water so that it gradually filled. When the water lipped over the rim, he gave it a push, and it sank, gurgling slightly, and vanished from view.

Further down the tow-path was a small warehouse and, beside it, a telephone kiosk. It was time to ring his contact.

'Hello? ... Melfort here.'

The speaker was a tall, thin, handsome man in his early forties, who in his red plush velvet dressing-gown presented a stark contrast to his two visitors. They wore belted raincoats, and sat rather stiffly in armchairs, magazines on their laps. They had been there since dawn.

'Mr Gerald Melfort?' came Schulz's voice at the other end of the line.

'That's right,' said Melfort in a rich cut-glass voice that spoke of port and Havanas, like the one he was gently puffing. 'Who is that?' he added casually.

'"They call me Whitey but that's only a nickname. Have you ever had a nickname?"' recited Schulz carefully.

There was a pause. Melfort turned slowly and signalled to one of the raincoats to pick up the extension phone.

'"Have you ever had a nickname?"' Schulz was repeating anxiously.

'"At school I was sometimes known as Pinky".' Melfort now recited in turn, in a voice that purred like George Sanders. 'When did you arrive?'

'Last night,' said Schulz. 'Were you told I was coming?'

Melfort cleared his throat. 'Yes, some days ago.'

'I can't tell you how glad I am to hear a friendly voice,' said Schulz.

There was a slight click as the extension was lifted.

Schulz picked up the sound immediately.

'Are you alone?' he asked nervously.

'Yes, yes, quite alone,' said Melfort, sounding relaxed and reassuring. 'Where are you?'

'Just north of Brenzett. I'm on a tow-path near a bridge, not far from a pub called the Fox and Grapes.'

'I know it,' Melfort nodded into the phone.

'I think I did something foolish in the pub. I asked for a coffee. I think they got suspicious.'

'Yes, that was foolish,' Melfort replied calmly. 'Pubs don't serve coffee; you ought to have known that. They should have told you. Never mind. Look, if you walk on a few hundred yards, you'll come to another bridge. Follow the road north to a bus stop. In about ten minutes a green bus will come along. Get on it and go to the end of the run. There's a small hotel there called the White Swan. Meet me in the bar there, all right?'

'The White Swan – right,' said Schulz.

'How will I recognize you?' said Melfort.

Schulz thought for a moment. 'I'm wearing a red poppy in my buttonhole. What about you?'

Melfort looked at a vase of flowers on the table in front of him.

'I'll be wearing a white daisy,' he said. 'I'll see you there in half an hour.' As an afterthought, he added, softly, 'Long live the Fuhrer.'

'Yes,' said Schulz thoughtfully. 'Long live the Fuhrer.'

Melfort hung up the phone and took a daisy from the vase, putting it in his buttonhole.

'Another one in the bag,' grinned his fellow-listener and took the daisy out of Melfort's buttonhole, shaking his head. 'Let *us* keep the advantage, sir.'

Schulz stood in the phone booth, feeling decidedly unsettled. There was something not quite right about Melfort's timing: too many pauses – and then there was that click. From his experience in the Salon Kitty, he had gathered enough about surveillance to know that either the call was being monitored or that there was someone listening with Melfort on another extension.

Some children were waiting outside. Schulz picked up his briefcase and left the kiosk, feeling their eyes on his plus-fours. At the end of the road was a large poster on a wall, warning of the danger of incendiary fires. 'Keep a bucket handy,' it read. 'Be safe not sorry.' Schulz stared at it.

Be safe not sorry.

Slowly, he took the poppy out of his buttonhole and slipped it into his pocket. Then, clutching his briefcase firmly, he walked off towards the next bridge. As he reached it he was dismayed to notice his bowler hat had caught up with him, bobbing merrily in the water. Resigned, he pulled it out: it smelt slightly, but apart from that and the fact that it was soaking wet, it was still resolutely – triumphantly – as much of a bowler hat as it had ever been.

15

'He's a spy, Sam, a German spy!' The landlord was growing even redder than normal in his excitement. 'I knew it as soon as he came in.'

Sam Maynard, Brenzett's village bobby, was gravely taking notes as if he had stepped out of Toy Town. Ethel was standing next to her husband to give him moral support.

'Well,' said Maynard, 'we'll see about that. We mustn't prejudge the issue. He could be a harmless foreigner, you know.'

'You mean a Pole or a Czech or something?' asked the landlord. This was obviously just as bad in his eyes.

'I haven't yet met a Pole who didn't know what time an English pub opened,' said Ethel, as though Poles were her bread and butter. 'If you ask me, they all learn that at school.'

The constable ignored this. 'Can you give me a description of this – er – spy?' he said.

'Rather short!' said the publican.

'Rather tall!' said his wife simultaneously.

They turned and glared at each other.

'Medium or heavy build?' asked Maynard resignedly.

'Medium ...' said the publican.

'Heavy ...' said his wife simultaneously.

Maynard sighed. Clearly these were not going to be the most reliable of witnesses.

'Well, can you remember what he was wearing?'

'Plus-fours and a bowler hat!' they replied in unison.

Maynard looked pleased. 'Well, there doesn't seem to be much doubt about that.' He closed his notebook. 'They'll get a message out to all points. Thanks, Ethel.'

'You're welcome, Sam,' she said, picking up her carpet beater to renew her attack on foreign bodies.

'News ain't good, Jack,' said the policeman, once they were outside the pub. A squadron of fighters had just zoomed overhead.

'No,' said the landlord. 'We could have Jerry here in a few weeks. Still, you look out for that spy! I reckon they'll be dropping a lot of them right now, just to add to the confusion. The sooner they flood the Marshes the better, I say.'

Schulz had been waiting for over twenty minutes and was just about to start walking when he saw a green bus in the distance, slowly moving up the road towards him. It was steadily catching up with a cyclist who seemed to be stationary. The bus soon overtook the cyclist and eventually reached the bus stop. An old lady with a Pekinese dog was taking her time and Schulz, who liked helping old ladies off buses, especially when he was in a hurry in an enemy country, decided to be helpful.

He picked up the Pekinese which promptly bit his wrist. The old lady began to fuss – more over the dog than the wrist – and as Schultz was trying to extricate himself from both the old lady and the dog he saw that the cyclist had not been stationary, but was pedalling furiously and was rapidly approaching the bus. He was also dressed as a policeman.

154

The combination of the two facts was not one that encouraged Schulz to linger. With his active help the old lady and the dog finally achieved separation from the bus, which slowly began to move off.

'Wait! Wait a minute! Excuse me, sir! Can I have a word with you? Wait!' the policeman was yelling.

Schulz pretended that he was the last person in the world the policeman could be addressing and slunk down in the rear of the bus. There was only one other passenger, a drab little woman who was hardly likely to invite the attention of anyone, let alone a policeman. This passenger was now staring at Schulz, rather like the publican had, and even the conductor was joining in, after waving back at PC Maynard in his friendliest manner and pressing the bell. In the distance Schulz could still see the policeman cycling furiously but he finally seemed to give up the chase, removing his helmet to wipe his brow.

Now that Schulz was seeing where they were going he didn't like seeing where they were going. The bus was returning via the Fox and Grapes and as they passed the pub, Schulz could see the landlord and his wife standing outside, talking excitedly to a small crowd. By the way the publicans were gesticulating it was clear to Schulz that they were trying to describe something. The landlord had his hand lowered to a height of three feet from the ground as though describing a midget, and his wife was raising her palms above her head, as though it were a monster. Schulz then realized that they were describing him and he burrowed himself into the back seat of the bus.

'Swan,' he said to the conductor, who was looking at him most oddly. Fortunately at that moment the sound of aircraft could be heard once more and the Spitfire returned, flying low in the same formation as before. The conductor quickly pocketed Schulz's money, handed him change and a ticket and turned to the woman passenger.

'We could have Jerry here in a few weeks.'

'I most sincerely hope not!' said Schulz in his best English. The two of them stared at him in consternation.

'Manners!' the passenger said to the conductor who nod-

155

ded in agreement. 'The sooner they flood the Marshes the better.'

Schulz noted this last remark with alarm – thinking of the canister buried not far from Walland Marsh. But it was clear that he had committed yet another cardinal blunder and he decided to keep his mouth shut. The woman was now talking about Dunkirk and how her nephew had come home laden with brandy and how she tried to make him hand it in to the police. Her tone implied that it would have been better if he had come home with half a leg.

The marketplace was already crowded with people coming out of church. Schulz jumped off the bus almost before it had stopped, hoping for a quick reconnoitre of the hotel doorway. He could see a number of people loitering at the bus stop. Any one of them could have been Melfort – or a British counter-intelligence agent for that matter. Over the hotel entrance there were geraniums in flowerpots and hanging baskets, and under it a man wearing a plain belted raincoat who glanced at Schulz in a way that was now becoming familiar to him. The man seemed to be scrutinizing everyone entering the hotel but appeared to take no interest in Schulz, who walked on through the lobby into the bar to look for a man with a white daisy in his buttonhole.

Barnes had been waiting outside the Swan for half an hour and there was still no sign of the German agent wearing a poppy in his buttonhole. He finally grew tired of standing there and turned back into the hotel lobby. As he entered the bar, he brushed past the absurd looking character in plus-fours and a wet bowler hat who had walked in a minute before. Barnes edged his way through the bar crowd, consisting of a heavy sprinkling of HM Forces – both men and women – plus the usual lunchtime regulars. Presently he made out Melfort drinking a gin and tonic at the bar. Next to him was Barnes's assistant, also dressed in a plain belted raincoat, sipping uncomfortably at a pint of Guinness, and taking great pains to appear as if he were on his own.

'He didn't get off the bus,' Barnes muttered to Melfort

as his assistant handed him a pint of bitter.

'Blast!' said Melfort.

'Do you think he smelt a rat?'

'I don't think so,' said Melfort, looking round the bar at the noisy milling throng. 'Perhaps he did get off the bus. Perhaps he just took off his poppy to give himself time to size up the situation a little. Perhaps,' he went on, looking round even more closely, 'he's here *now*, looking for *me*?'

All three of them, struck by that unusual thought, stared at the faces around the bar. Barnes turned to Melfort, his brow contracted in a puzzled frown.

'But if he's looking for *you*,' he said, 'he's looking for a man with a white daisy in his buttonhole.'

Melfort nodded. 'True,' he said, 'but then, he's not going to find me, is he?'

'No,' said Barnes. 'But then, if *he* can't find *you*, and *you* can't find *him*, how are you ever going to meet?'

Melfort nodded again. The thought had already occurred to him. He felt that he ought to have been asking Barnes that very thing.

'I think I should have left the white daisy in my button-hole,' he said, finally reaching the obvious conclusion.

Barnes nodded slowly. 'Yes, I think you should. It never occurred to me he'd take the poppy out of his own.' He paused. 'If he has, of course.'

'Should I – put the daisy back, do you think?'

'Well,' said Barnes, downing his bitter and taking out a pipe which he proceeded to light slowly and deliberately while Melfort waited for a decision, 'there are two arguments against that, sir.' He drew at his pipe and billows of blue smoke shrouded the air between them. 'In the first place, it gives *him* the advantage and he may have already spotted you talking to us. That could scare him off.' He puffed some more. 'And secondly we didn't bring the daisy with us.'

Melfort nodded slowly and sighed. Barnes's arguments were all sound and valid but led nowhere. Like his pipe they just clouded the issue.

'Well,' he said at length, 'let's wait a while. I'm sure he'll make himself known. I'm his only contact in this country. He *needs* me. He's either just being cautious or he's already missed that bus.'

Melfort got up and sauntered casually to an unoccupied table and sat down, while Barnes and his assistant ostentatiously turned their backs. A bizarre looking man, wearing steel-rimmed glasses and plus-fours with an old school tie, clutching a briefcase and a damp looking bowler hat in one hand and a Scotch and soda in the other, sat down opposite him. He noticed that everyone in the bar was laughing at this odd little chap and he couldn't blame them.

Melfort continued to cast his eyes around the room: he was beginning to lose a little of his suavity.

Schulz carefully placed his briefcase and bowler on the floor beside him and sipped his Scotch, his gaze falling for an instant on the man sitting opposite, who was tall and thin with a pencil-line moustache and a debonair appearance. There was, however, no white daisy in his buttonhole. Suddenly it occurred to Schulz that it might be possible that his contact, like himself, had removed his flower. *Why should he do that?* he wondered, fingering the poppy in his pocket.

Finally, and surreptitiously, he pulled it out and looked at it. He could not shed an uneasy feeling that had begun when he rang Melfort and heard that click. He remembered the Café Backus at Wilma and the gullibility of Harrison Smith and Withers. It was such an old trick. For a moment Schulz wondered whether Neuheim had tipped off a double agent to manoeuvre him into being captured, once having ensured that his little brainchild had found itself a nursery in the slow death of the British economy, with Melfort's help of course. But in his heart Schulz liked to think that Neuheim needed him. Why else had he engineered Schulz's reprieve from disgrace and death on at least two occasions? If Schulz had been the rabbit mesmerized in Neuheim's headlights, then, conversely, he was also the rabbit who continually popped out of Neuheim's conjuror's hat, the puppet that pulled the string of his puppeteer.

Thus reassured to a certain degree, Schulz reminded himself that it was still better to be safe than sorry and slipped the poppy back into his pocket. As he did so, the man sitting opposite him, who had been nervously twiddling his left foot, accidentally kicked over Schulz's briefcase.

'So sorry,' said the man and stooped to retrieve it.

'Thank you,' said Schulz and smiled amicably. He was pleased to discover here a fine example of British manners at their very best and this gave him an idea. He waited till he had caught the man's eye again. Then he leaned towards him confidentially.

'Could you – keep an eye on that for me?' he said, indicating the briefcase.

'Of course,' said the man politely.

At least it was in trustworthy hands, Schulz thought, as he got up and walked to the bar. The man continued to sit there, watching the door and scanning faces.

'MR MELFORT? Is there a Mr Melfort here?' called the hotel porter.

Melfort, lost in reverie, looked up, startled. 'Yes?' he said.

'Telephone, sir! At the desk!'

Melfort looked across at Barnes who nodded approval. He turned to go but suddenly remembered the briefcase. There was now a white-haired military looking gentleman in the seat that the odd little fellow had just vacated. The old man was deep in conversation with someone on the next table.

'Excuse me,' Melfort said. The old man turned to him. 'Would you mind keeping an eye on that?' He pointed to the briefcase. 'I shan't be long.'

'Certainly, certainly,' said the old gentleman, only too happy to be of service, but immediately absorbed once more in conversation.

* * *

159

Schulz stood in the telephone kiosk in one corner of the hotel lobby, anxiously waiting to see who was going to answer the phone on the desk. To his astonishment it was the man who had been sitting opposite him. Could the porter have got the name wrong?

'Hello? Melfort here.'

No, thought Schulz, *it's him all right.*

'I'm sorry,' he said, 'the bus didn't stop.'

'Blast!' said Melfort.

'I'm waiting for the next one,' said Schulz. 'How long will it be?'

'About twenty minutes. I'm glad you phoned. I was beginning to wonder what had happened to you.'

'Don't worry. I'll be there.'

Schulz put down the receiver, watching Melfort do likewise and then return to the bar. He slowly came out of the booth and stood thinking for a moment. Of course, it was comforting to know that the distinguished looking man was his contact but he had to be certain. He followed Melfort back into the bar.

'He missed the bus,' Melfort whispered to Barnes.

'But he's coming?' said Barnes anxiously.

'Yes. He'll be on the next one.'

'Well, at least he's not here.' Barnes grinned. 'I thought for one moment he'd got a step ahead of us. Time for another pint, then. Same again?'

Schulz, standing two feet away, heard everything. The two raincoated men were so obviously policemen of one kind or another, and it was equally obvious that this so-called British contact had been turned and was now in fact, a British agent. He tried to stop himself from trembling, even inwardly, as he realized how close he had come to being caught. Suppressing an urge to slink, Schulz made his way towards the bar exit. He was just about to go through the swing door when he remembered the briefcase.

He froze. There was no question of leaving without it. He was not going to have time now to return and dig up the rest of the money. For an agonizing moment he considered brazenly retrieving it from Melfort. Then he suddenly realized that Melfort had not had the briefcase with him when he had been talking on the phone.

He made his way back to the table and, with a sigh of relief, saw the briefcase on the floor where he had left it. He quickly bent to pick it up.

'And where do you think you're going with that, sir?'

Schulz looked up in terror. A white haired old gentleman was now sitting where he had been sitting earlier.

'Pardon?' he said. There must be some mistake. What could the old man have to do with it? He looked like a veteran from World War I.

'Put that down! It doesn't belong to you!' the old man said indignantly. He was probably a colonel.

'Pardon?' Schulz said again, now completely bewildered.

'I know your sort! Petty sneak thief, that's what you are! Thrive in bars like this, don't you? It belongs to the fellow who was sitting *there*.' The old man pointed to the chair that Melfort had vacated. 'Put it down! Put it down, I say!' He was beginning to froth at the mouth and had grabbed the briefcase from Schulz.

'Let go!' said Schulz, forgetting about Melfort and losing his temper as he tried to wrench the briefcase out of the old soldier's grip.

'How dare you!' the old gentleman bawled self-righteously. 'Thief! In broad daylight too! While your countrymen are dying on the beaches of Dunkirk! Shame on you, sir, shame on you! Let go of it!'

Melfort, standing at the bar counter, heard the fracas and turned to see what the matter was. When he saw a tug o'war being fought over the briefcase he quickly made his way to the table.

'It's mine, you old fool!' Schulz was screaming now. 'Let go! Let go!' he shouted, knowing as he did so that the plainclothes men could very easily come across and open the briefcase.

A second later he wrenched the case free. Instantly he leaped towards the door.

'Stop that man! Stop him! Stop thief!' the old gentleman shouted, and felt a tap on his shoulder. He turned and saw the man who had given him the case to look after. 'After him!' he yelled, pointing towards the door. 'After him! sir! He's taken your case!'

'It's his case, not mine,' said Melfort calmly.

The old man's mouth fell open and he stared at Melfort in towering and speechless indignation. Melfort couldn't be bothered to explain and hurried out in search of the man in the plus-fours, who had forgotten his bowler hat.

Sam Maynard had propped his bicycle up against the hotel entrance and was describing the shape of a pair of plus-fours to the commissionaire who could hardly forget them. He nodded to the policeman and pointed inside the hotel, opening the door for Sam in his well-trained way. As he did so the man in plus-fours came flying out, colliding with Sam. They both fell down in a heap on the pavement.

'That's the one, Sam!' croaked the commissionaire, a proud veteran of the Boer War. 'That's the one I meant!'

Schulz recognized his cycling pursuer and at that moment spotted the conveyance he needed. He darted towards the bicycle as the commissionaire stepped bravely towards him.

'Here!' he croaked again, 'you can't do that! Leave that bike alone!'

Schulz swung his briefcase at the commissionaire's head, catching him a heavy blow on the mouth. The commissionaire staggered back into the arms of a tall thin man with a pencil-line moustache who was speeding out of the hotel lobby, while Schulz ran a few yards with the bicycle before swinging on to the saddle and pedalling off precariously.

'Stop him! Stop thief! Stop him!' shouted Maynard, rushing after him, now more concerned about his disappearing bicycle than the fate of the nation.

Schulz had managed to build up tremendous speed by pedalling furiously. In any case Maynard was now being impeded by the tall thin man who had run after him and was pulling him back.

162

'For God's sake leave the poor fellow alone!' cried Melfort. 'It's *his* case, officer, not mine!'

'I don't give a damn whose case it is, sir!' shouted Sam, wrenching himself free from Melfort's grip. 'I've every reason to believe that that man is a German spy! And what's much more important he's got my bloody bike!' It was only then that he realized that Schulz had also taken his helmet.

He lumbered after Schulz who had disappeared round a corner, leaving Melfort staring disconsolately at his retreating figure as he realized, for the first time whose briefcase he had been looking after.

The nine-days-wonder of the evacuation of British and French troops to the southern coast of England had only two days to go before Winston Churchill would stand up in the House of Commons when it was all over and declare, 'Wars are not won by evacuations'. All around the coast, ships, large and small, disgorged battered and bruised soldiers taken off the beaches at Dunkirk. Some, from the larger ships, disembarked on jetties, others jumped into the water from small boats and waded up the beach where they flopped exhausted on to the sand.

Meanwhile army lorries carried soldiers inland, winding their way through the rambling roads of Kent. One such fleet of lorries which had set out from Rye two hours earlier was meandering sluggishly along the A259 in the early afternoon hours of 2 June. As it approached the neat little village of Brooklands, deep in the heart of Walland Marsh and less than a mile from Brenzett, the driver of the front lorry suddenly spied a cyclist pedalling erratically towards him. The driver, who was himself in a state of near-exhaustion having ferried similar cargoes practically non-stop for four out of the last five days, rubbed his eyes in disbelief.

The cyclist was wearing steel-rimmed glasses, plus-fours and what looked like an old school tie and a policeman's helmet. He seemed quite oblivious of the effect his outlandish garb was creating and waved cheerfully at the driver. The expression on his face was one of blustering panic and amiable optimism by turns. He was soon past the convoy and away down the road towards the coast. The driver was well aware of the immense public sympathy that the evacuation had called forth. In the Channel, fishermen were braving the Stukas and mines in their trawlers, shrimpers and crabbers, to bring home the boys. But the driver could not imagine what earthly use this strange apparition of English eccentricity thought he could be to the evacuation. He shook his head in wonder: the spirit of Dunkirk was obviously highly intoxicating.

After the lorries passed him, Schulz decided to abandon the helmet which he had inadvertently grabbed in his struggle with the policeman, possibly confusing it with his wretched bowler. At least he had managed to ditch *that* monstrosity. He had not wanted to throw the helmet away until he was well clear of the hotel; it had occurred to him that it might lend him some kind of authority. This was, after all, a Sunday, and it was quite possible that a rural constable would dress in civvies but with a helmet as a gentle reminder of his official status. When he noticed how the lorry driver had stared at him as though he were a lunatic, however, he threw it in a passing hedge. He wondered idly why British troops should be driving *away* from the coast, but it was an unproductive line of thought and he had more urgent things to think about.

At every village he passed, he ran the risk of being stopped by a police check and, as he had noted earlier, there were practically no signposts. Unfortunately the compass supplied by Captain Ohm proved useless, not because it was not mechanically accurate to a thousandth of a degree, but because the road he was travelling meandered crazily from north to south and east to west. In the end he estimated that, on average, it was veering south: he would eventually, therefore, reach the coast. If it was nightfall by then, he decided, so much the better.

Above him the intermittent vapour trails from unseen

fighter planes no longer bothered him but he was continually on his guard for police – on foot or bicycle. He was now cycling along a road bordered on the left hand side by marshland and he guessed he must have entered Walland Marsh, part of an area of low-lying 'bog land' according to Captain Ohm's men and about which he had been solemnly warned in a geographical briefing.

According to their experts, the whole of the Thames Estuary was infested with agues, fever and noxious vapours, but no part of it was as poison-ridden as Walland and Romney Marshes which, he was assured, were still suffering from the Great Plague and in which malaria was rife. Though Schulz knew this was nonsense, having lived near Romney for two years without even catching a cold; the land had still been very marshy. Even now it had an air of mystery and he began to feel distinctly uneasy, as though he were being followed by an invisible evil presence. All that could be heard however was the occasional bleating of sheep and the muffled roar of bombers overhead. He prayed that the Marshes weren't flooded before he got out of them.

He had been cycling for well over an hour and was beginning to search anxiously for the coastline. Suddenly, out of nowhere, a car came streaking along the road towards him. Schulz just had time to catch a glimpse of blue uniforms and, terrified, turned his head, looking behind him. He did not turn his head back in time though and, as the car tore past him, two blue-helmeted faces locked eyes with his. Fifty yards further on, the police car skidded to a halt and two policemen stared out of the rear window.

By that time Schulz had turned off the road and disappeared down a small track into a wood.

'Was it him, do you think?'

'It could have been,' Sergeant Lewell said to Sergeant North. 'Plus-fours, bicycle, briefcase. Let's go back and have a look.'

'But he wasn't wearing the helmet,' said Sergeant North.

'That's true,' agreed Sergeant Lewell.

'Of course,' suggested Sergeant North, 'he might have got rid of the helmet.'

'Mmmmm,' said Sergeant Lewell.

Finally Sergeant North executed a U-turn and sped back in the other direction, swerving off the road and on to the narrow path, bumping crazily over the uneven ground. But there was no sign of Schulz.

'Hold it!' Sergeant Lewell suddenly shouted. He had seen something.

The car came to a violent halt.

'Back up!'

Sergeant North reversed the car back up the track and came to another halt. Both policemen leapt out and ran to the ditch at the side of the road. Sergeant North jumped down and lifted out of the ferns and nettles Schulz's abandoned bicycle. He peered into the woods that glowed in the late afternoon sunlight.

'He won't get far that way – not unless he swims for it,' he said wrily.

Sergeant Lewell nodded and got back into the car. Without bothering to close the car door he picked up the microphone.

'Hello?' he radioed. 'Car 27 here. We're just outside Haydon Farm. We've spotted him. He's on foot – heading for the coast.' As an afterthought he added. 'And he lost the helmet.'

Schulz stumbled on over rough fields, panting hard, his breath coming in great heaving gasps. Somewhere out there was the beach: he could smell it now, that faint, distinct, salty smell. He paused for breath, exhausted, and tried to fix his bearings. He took out the compass and waited for the needle to swing north. Then he picked up his briefcase and set off again, running south east.

The beach in Rye Bay was shallow and the smaller craft were gravitating towards it like bees to a honey pot. It was as though Henley Regatta had gone terribly wrong, with dozens of small boats bobbing up and down in the water or beached on the shore. Soldiers lay about everywhere: tired and filthy, smoking cigarettes and drinking tea. Some were talking listlessly to each other while waiting to be told where to go; others just sat gazing vacantly at the sea, trying to make sense of what had happened. A few larger boats were standing out to sea, one or two ferries and a destroyer pouring smoke over the whole scene to add to the gloom. At one end of the beach a group of ladies was manning a mobile tea urn and a queue of men stood shivering in their greatcoats.

A small boat with about a dozen soldiers was just landing. A sergeant major marched smartly towards it, pointing and shouting instructions at the men as the craft ran aground on the beach. The soldiers got out of the boat and made their way up the beach where they slumped down in groups. Two orderlies moved about with a huge flask of tea, dispensing it like nurses. Another boat was prepared to make the journey back across the Channel.

'Another bloody muck up, Joe,' sighed a soldier who had found himself a beachchair, watching the new arrivals crowding the beach as though it were bank holiday.

'Yeah,' nodded Joe.

'I don't know why we bother,' continued his more talkative friend.

'Nor me, Ernie,' said Joe, shaking his head.

Up at the far end of the beach was a small but sheer cliff. If any of the thousands of weary occupants of that beach could have been bothered to look they would have seen a small steel-rimmed pair of eyes looking down, in dismay, not at their plight, but at his own.

Schulz lay flat on his stomach on the cliff edge, appalled at the vision below him. His plan had been to steal a boat: his only worry had been of not finding one. Instead he had found hundreds of them, so many, in fact, that there was not a hope in hell of stealing one, let alone getting far in it. Especially in broad daylight. The whole mission had been a complete disaster. He let his head sink into his hands and brooded.

From the far, far, distance came the sound of dogs baying. He looked up, startled, his heart beginning to race.

Sergeants North and Lewell led the way, holding on the dogs' leashes. Behind them came PC Maynard, still livid about the theft of his bicycle and helmet, and Gerald Melfort, sprinted athletically but not, in fact, as quickly as the policemen, no doubt impeded by the bowler hat he was carrying. Further back, Barnes and his assistant, still raincoated, panting audibly, brought up the rear. The dogs were now yelping with excitement having picked up the scent, triggered by Schulz's bowler hat.

'Let 'm go, let'm go!' yelled Barnes. 'They can smell him!'

The sergeants leaned down and unchained the dogs who tore off in deranged pursuit.

Schulz had got to his feet and could now hear the dogs quite clearly. Clutching his briefcase, he turned and scrambled down the cliff, sliding and slipping as he half-climbed, half-fell, down the chalky face, wishing with all his heart at that moment that he could be back home with Frau Nusbaum.

A converted ship's lifeboat with a small canvas dodger round its bows lay at anchor just beyond the water's edge where there was some surf running. Its engine was still ticking over, its owner having just gone ashore, limping so badly that he had to be helped up the beach.

Schulz was also limping – and covered in chalk – as he approached the boat, having fallen the last six feet of his journey down the cliff-face. He threw his briefcase on board and heaved himself up after it. The anchor had dragged and the keel had just taken the ground so that the propeller was showing, but the boat was still lifting occasionally in the surf. A greasy overall was lying on the engine box and Schulz ducked down and put it on. Then he went forward to the anchor and was just about to haul it up when he heard a shout.

'Hey! You! Wait a minute! Wait!'

He looked up. Two soldiers were rising from their deck-chairs and pointing at him. They started running towards him, clutching their rifles. Schulz panicked. There was no way out. On one side of him was the sea, behind him more soldiers who were now looking his way, in front, the two soldiers who were fast approaching. He could do nothing. He did nothing.

'Just a minute!' shouted the soldier who had reached the boat. 'We'll give you a hand!'

'What?' mumbled Schulz in confusion.

Ernie and Joe put their shoulders to the boat's stern and gave it a shove.

'Right, push!' shouted Ernie. Schulz stared at him without moving. 'Come on,' Ernie repeated to Joe, 'push!'

The penny dropped. There was some kind of a relief mission going on and these two soldiers imagined he was on his way back to France to bring off more men.

The soldiers pushed once more but the boat didn't move. Then Schulz froze again: a sergeant major who seemed to be directing operations had spotted the two soldiers and was walking towards them.

'You there!' he bellowed. The men were still pushing. Schulz tried to hide himself inside the boat. 'You there!' came the sergeant major's voice again. 'Give those men a hand with that boat! Can't you see they need it! Move!'

Schulz peered out in astonishment: soldiers were running towards the boat from all directions. It seemed to him that a whole company was being deployed to ensure his safe escape from England. He hauled once more at the anchor rope and the boat started to slide into deeper water. The soldiers who had been pushing returned to the beach, all except Ernie and Joe, who stood there watching him. Schulz waved to them.

'Thanks!' he called.

'That's all right, mate!' called back Ernie. 'Good luck! Bring'm all back.'

'Yeah,' shouted Joe.

Schulz waved once more to them, pulled the cord of the outboard motor, which fired instantly, and took the rudder, steering the boat out to see. As the boat receded, Ernie, still waving goodbye, shook his head lost in admiration.

'"Men that go down to the sea in ships", eh Joe? Salt of the earth,' he said as they walked back to their beach-chairs.

'Brave as they come, Ernie,' Joe nodded.

'Couldn't wait to get back to them beaches – knowing he might never come back,' sighed Ernie.

'Yeah.' said Joe, considering it all.

'I'll tell you something, Joe,' Ernie added after a pause. 'If we had men like him at the top, we'd have won this war by now. Unselfish, that's what they are.'

Joe nodded. They had reached the chairs which were now occupied by two other soldiers. Ernie and Joe stared at them coldly.

'Do you mind?' said Ernie brusquely. 'Find your own chairs.'

'Yeah,' said Joe.

On the edge of the cliff the frustrated dogs were running first one way and then another, while Melfort, Barnes and the policemen looked at each other and at the tableau below them, baffled. Barnes's assistant was nowhere to be seen.

'Fancy a swim, Sergeant North?' said Melfort brightly.

The Channel was alive with boats, some broken down,

others jam-packed with troops, some drifting aimlessly. In some men were singing or in a dazed stupor. In one was Schulz, feeling like an alien bacterium that had found its way into the sluggish bloodstream of a shocked accident victim. He had no idea how much fuel he had, or even where the fuel tank was placed, and was beginning to wonder whether he would end his days alone in this boat, presumed dead and therefore low on the rescue priority lists. There was no contact between boats, and in his overalls Schulz was hardly likely to be conspicuous.

A naval launch, with a long string of lifeboats in tow, suddenly appeared to starboard and, as Schulz approached, a rope was flung to him without a word, so that he was able to attach himself to it. He now felt like the tail end of a long crocodile. After a time he began to see great palls of smoke over the French coast and could hear the noise of continual bombardment. Occasionally a ship could be seen being attacked from the air by tracer bullets and at times it seemed as though all the boats around him were under fire.

Suddenly there was an ear-shattering blast from the bows of the launch and flames shot up in the air, followed by billows of smoke. The launch had evidently been hit by a torpedo. Ahead of him was pandemonium; men from the launch were jumping into the lifeboats, regardless of whether they were full or not – which most of them were. Schulz wasted no time : he quickly detached his rope from the lifeboat in front, as though severing a new-born baby from the umbilical cord of its dying mother. His boat began to lurch helplessly : Schulz had stopped the engine earlier and had no idea how to start it again.

'What's up, monsieur?' called a Frenchman from a nearby boat, which seemed to be some kind of a trawler.

'Fuel !' screamed Schulz instinctively.

The Frenchman threw him a rope.

Slowly Schulz was trawled ever nearer to the hell that was Dunkirk.

'How many can you take?'

171

Schulz had just run aground on a small beach on the periphery of Dunkirk. Everywhere was noise, bombing, confusion.

'I said how many can you take?' screamed the army captain above the noise of gunfire.

'What!' screamed back Schulz, aghast.

'How many?' yelled back the captain, losing patience. Schulz thought quickly.

'Fuel!' he shouted. The captain looked blank. Schulz decided that it was not worth wasting time trying to explain.

'Fifteen!' he shouted. The captain nodded and turned to a group of soldiers waiting nearby.

'The first fifteen!' he yelled. 'Hurry up! We haven't got all day!'

The first fifteen soldiers came running towards the boat. Schulz stared at them in bewilderment. He had no intention of returning to England. In any case the boat probably *was* running out of fuel. As the first man clambered into the boat, Schulz clambered out.

'Where are you going,' cried the captain in alarm.

'I'm ... I've got a message for the beach commander!'

'I'll give it to him!' shouted the captain, starting to help Schulz back into the boat.

'No, no, it's personal! It's from his mother!' shouted Schulz, releasing himself from the captain's muscular grip. 'Where is he?'

'Over there!' yelled the captain, pointing to the far end of the beach. 'Hurry up! I'll get the men on board!' Schulz, clutching his briefcase underneath his overalls, turned and ran off in the direction the captain had indicated, while the latter directed the men on to the boat, shouting at them to hurry. Suddenly he stopped and turned, looking back at Schulz's retreating figure, now almost lost to view amid the crowds and turmoil along the beach.

'From his *mother*?' he said in deepest wonder.

Wherever Schulz looked, his eyes met long queues of soldiers, some asleep on their feet, many without boots and with horribly swollen feet, as if they had been marching for days. There seemed to be few Frenchmen in sight, however, and this gave Schulz an idea. If anyone stopped him he would reply in French.

He did not look behind him but hurried through the bombed-out shells of houses, some still smouldering, that made up the once-residential part of the town. Everywhere were stretcher bearers carrying out wounded victims of the bombings, infantrymen still lurking with tommy-guns, and Red Cross workers busily helping out where they could. Stray dogs were prowling the streets, having developed a taste for the bloody dressings of the wounded. There was still the distant noise of shelling. Occasionally Schulz tripped on a piece of rubble from a blasted building and, as he made his way to the edge of the town, he glimpsed a British patrol turning into the other end of the street.

He dodged into an open gateway, hugging the wall at his back as he waited for the patrol to pass by. Beside him was a window and he turned and glanced inside. A sad-looking coffin lay on a table, covered with flowers.

A hearse had come to a stop outside the courtyard, and an undertaker and his assistant got out, just as the patrol marched up from the other direction. The patrol halted in front of the undertaker and the corporal in charge questioned them. The undertaker showed some papers to the corporal, gesturing towards the courtyard. Having examined them to his satisfaction, the corporal handed back the papers. The patrol moved on.

Schulz had watched the whole ritual and, alarmed at the undertaker's evident intention, flattened himself desperately against the wall. Sure enough, they entered the courtyard and walked gravely towards the house, but without catching sight of him. The undertaker, a solemn little man with long white sideboards and immaculately dressed in spite of the destruction raging around him, rang the bell. As he waited he straightened his tie, brushing a speck of dust off the rim of his hat. The door opened, he bowed circumspectly, and entered the house followed by his assistant. Schulz darted from his hiding place and out of the gateway. On impulse, he paused by the hearse and looked inside. The keys were still dangling from the ignition.

Slowly and solemnly the undertaker and his assistant emerged from the house, carrying the coffin on their shoulders, followed by the weeping family mourners. They walked with dignity across the courtyard to the gateway. Machine-gun fire chattered in the distance, slowly dying away, and then returned again, this time much nearer. It sounded now more like the chug of a car engine starting. Puzzlement profaned the undertaker's impassive features as the chattering turned into a roar. He started to trot. The coffin swung precariously behind him and behind the coffin followed his astonished assistant.

'Stop! Come back! Stop thief!' screamed the enraged undertaker as the hearse moved rapidly down the street and disappeared round a corner. 'Stop! Come back!' His words were drowned by another burst of shelling.

The roads through the Dunkirk perimeter and along what remained of the Maginot line were littered with refugees on wagons, bicycles and on foot. Old crocks, driven for years and crammed with the freight of whole families, choked the thoroughfares. There were peasants with carts, carrying calves or pigs, women with prams and the occasional well-dressed farmer. The night sky was illuminated by the haze of distant fires, and Messerschmitts and Stukas were still doing untold damage to neighbouring towns.

Through the midst of this confusion Schulz drove the hearse, cringing from the sound of low-flying planes and artillery fire. At times it was impossible to move. He would hoot the car horn wildly, but nobody took any notice. In the end he gave up, allowing the hearse to crawl through the crush. By now he was so tired he was falling asleep at the wheel, which hardly seemed to make any difference most of the time. His route was taking him gradually south-east towards the German front, through Arras and St Quentin.

The further east Schulz drove the nearer to the battle

zones he found himself, and the more reluctant he was to return to the mad-house. At the back of his mind was an unformed plan to hide out the war in some deserted paradise. He was now deep in the heart of the champagne district and the lush countryside was whetting his appetite. He now made it a policy to drive along side roads, both to avoid the crush of traffic and because he was convinced that somewhere in the hinterland of France there was a wonderful woman waiting for him, ready to refresh his spirits and his manhood, and with whom he could bask out the rest of the war on his private fortune. One thing was certain: the operation had been bungled. Once he returned to Germany the notes would be useless. He would be demoted to private, excluded on grounds of rank and Bertha's congenital inhibition from ever partaking of her favours.

That was if he were lucky. If he were unlucky, Neuheim would have him shot. Schulz determined therefore to have one final fling before going back, or getting out. Unfortunately it did not appear that at that moment in French history there were many good times to be had. If there were any women left they were probably hiding deep in cellars. If his recent experience of England had been frenetic, France was in the throes of invasion and Schulz could almost smell her fear: she was like a hunted animal trapped in her lair.

In this uneasy frame of mind, Schulz found himself driving into the grounds of a deserted chateau which he had spotted from the road, some fifteen kilometres north of Vitry-le-François. He had been attracted by its imposing iron gateway, through which he saw a building of palatial dimensions. He parked the hearse at the side of the chateau and climbed stiffly out, his tweeds and plus-fours by now rather soiled and still faintly chalky. Around the chateau it was so peaceful that it was almost possible to believe that a wicked fairy had cast a spell of deep enchantment upon it. The grounds were beautifully landscaped and enclosed by old stone walls with sculptured animal heads. Tailored lawns stretched out behind. Schulz walked around to the main entrance. In the distance gunfire still thundered. Suddenly he heard a shrill cry coming from the gardens. A moment later, a peacock appeared: it had obviously been disturbed by the gunfire. A Rolls was parked outside the front door: it was empty.

The door was unlocked and Schulz found himself inside the most impressive looking house, outside a museum, that he had ever been in, not excluding the houses he had visited in Amsterdam and Zagreb with the Dutch banker. None of the curtains were drawn and he gazed at the great portraits in their gilt frames; the vast chandelier hanging from the main-hall ceiling; priceless antique furniture; precious silverware; a long, highly polished table with exquisitely carved legs.

'Anyone at home?' His voice echoed through the rooms, but there was no answering call and no one appeared. The chateau had obviously belonged to some wealthy aristocratic family who had fled from the approaching German army. Stealthily he mounted the stairs and turned into the landing. The first open door revealed a room of magnificent proportions, again lavishly furnished with splendid tapestries hanging from the walls. He stared in wonder at such impressive luxury, reclined on a chaise longue by the window, wandered on to the next room – a study lined with books bound in leather and gold. He sat at the elaborate inlaid desk and examined a letter which trailed off in the middle of a sentence. Next to it was a bottle of ink. Whoever had abandoned it had done so in a hurry. The lid had not been replaced.

Now completely satisfied that he would not be disturbed Schulz strode from room to room, examining delicate porcelain vases and intricate miniatures. Finally he lay down on the velvet quilt of an extravagant four-poster bed in what must have been the master bedroom and closed his eyes. All he needed now, he thought dreamily, was a rich, beautiful comtesse with whom to share all this opulence. The next moment he opened his eyes and his prayer was answered.

A magnificent looking lady with long auburn hair that fell almost to her waist was staring down at Schulz as if he were something that had fallen from the roof.

17

'And who, may I ask, are you?'

She spoke in French, with a deep, velvety voice that combined aloofness with condescension. In her hand was a hairbrush which she brandished like a riding whip and Schulz could well believe that he was one of the privileged few to have caught her with her hair down. She was looking at him with considerable distaste down a nose that had clearly evolved through the centuries for that purpose.

'I – beg your pardon, madame,' stammered Schulz, easing himself off the bed as unobtrusively as possible, 'but – I saw the open gate and I just wandered in.'

She tossed her head in anger and her bright green eyes flashed like emeralds.

'Then you'd just better wander out again,' she said, brushing her hair viciously, as if it were some therapy to calm her rage.

She picked up a chemise and walked through to a small dressing room which Schulz had not previously noticed. He followed and stood watching as she closed a suitcase. She was wearing a black tailored suit and elegant black high heeled shoes. She was in her forties and, with her fine cheek bones and exquisite nose, she resembled a splendidly bred Persian cat. Schulz suddenly felt very hungry.

'Madame – I haven't eaten for some hours,' he said. 'I was hoping to buy something to eat here.'

'This is not a cafeteria!' she boomed haughtily.

Schulz did not move. She eyed him for a moment and suddenly seemed to find a use for him. There was a loud explosion in the distance.

'If I can be of assistance, Madame?'

'Shut that case and bring it down to the car.'

She gathered up a mink coat and swept out of the room. Schulz, without questioning, leapt forward and shut the case, picking it up and following her down the stairs.

'Wait there.'

'Very good, madame.'

She went into another room and reappeared with another mink over her arm. Schulz stood aside to let her go first and followed her out of the front door.

'Are you any good with cars?' she said over her shoulder.

'Well ...' Schulz hesitated.

She stepped elegantly into her Rolls and turned the ignition keys but although the motor turned, the car refused to start. Schulz dumped her case in the rear of the car.

'It won't start!' she shouted at him furiously as though he had sabotaged it. 'Do something – or those German pigs will be here before you can say "knife".'

Something about the way she said this reminded Schulz of someone else, but he could not think who.

'Open the bonnet!' he now said.

'What?'

'If you'd be so kind, madame, there's a lever under the dashboard. Please pull it.'

The comtesse, for she could be nothing less, fumbled for the lever while he went to the front of the car. She finally found the lever and pulled. Schulz lifted the bonnet and examined the glass dome over the petrol dump.

'There's no petrol in it,' he announced.

'Rubbish!' she scoffed. 'I had it filled this morning!'

'Then somebody else has *emptied* it this morning!'

'Stolen it?' The comtesse's eyes flashed dangerously.

'If you prefer,' said Schulz. 'Someone has siphoned it off. One of your servants, perhaps?'

'Those thieving menials!' screamed the comtesse. 'Swine! There's your French worker for you! Thieves and swindlers, all of them!'

She began to swear fluently, storming out of the car and back inside the chateau, clutching her furs. For a moment Schulz stood there, not knowing quite what to do. Then he shrugged and followed her inside, still holding the briefcase. The artillery fire was getting louder all the time and aircraft were dive-bombing ahead of it.

178

In the hallway Schulz could hear her speaking on the telephone.

'Is that Monsieur Gaston? ... This is the Comtesse Monime. The car in your garage, does it have petrol? ... I'd like to buy it. How much is it? ... *Mon dieu*, I want the car, not the house as well ... I see ... Well, I'll take it. I can't give you cash, of course, but I have some jewellery ... Why not? ... But I don't have cash! ... Monsieur Gaston? Monsieur Gaston? ...' She rattled the receiver rest and then slammed the phone down angrily. 'Petit bourgeois pig!'

Schulz had gone out to the hearse and was about to start the engine.

'You! Is that your car?'

Schulz looked up. The comtesse was peering down at him from the hall window.

'In a manner of speaking, madame,' he replied.

'What sort of answer is that?'

'Yes, it is actually, madame.'

'Will it start? Has it got petrol in it?'

'Yes, madame, it has!'

'Come up here! And stop calling me "madame"! Comtesse Monime, if you don't mind!'

She withdrew her head. Schulz hesitated for a moment and then got out of the car again, still glued to his briefcase.

Downstairs the comtesse was nowhere to be found. Then he heard her pacing about upstairs. He found her in the bedroom.

'I'd like to buy your car,' she said impatiently. 'Naturally I haven't any cash – the banks weren't open this morning, but I suppose you'll take these.'

She was holding her necklace out to him. Schulz stared at it in wonder. It was studded with emeralds and diamonds and it was an exquisite piece of work. All the same, he shook his head.

'I couldn't possibly sell you the car,' he said. 'I need it myself.' The comtesse bridled.

'Typical!' she said, snatching it back from him and fastening it around her neck again. 'All the French worker

179

thinks of today is himself! No wonder France is on her knees!'

'A car is a very scarce commodity at the moment, madame,' said Schulz.

'Comtesse!'

'I beg your pardon. Perhaps, though, we could come to an arrangement? I've been travelling for some time. I really am starving.' The comtesse hesitated, eyeing his plus-fours.

'Come with me,' she snapped. She led him to a kitchen which was so large and well equipped it could have belonged to a grand hotel. On a long stone dresser was a stale roll. 'You'll have to hurry,' she said coldly as Schulz busily chewed. 'Why are you here?' she added with complete indifference.

'Antiques, comtesse,' he said, swallowing the last mouthful. 'It's a good time for bargains, as I am sure you will appreciate. I would not mind that necklace, as a matter of fact. I'll pay you handsomely.'

'What with?' said the comtesse sceptically. 'You don't suppose I'll take a cheque, do you?'

'Would five thousand pounds be acceptable?'

'Five thou –?' The comtesse was almost taken aback and touched her hair hesitantly. 'Did you say – "pounds"?'

'Yes,' said Schulz. 'English five-pound notes.'

She stared at him. Schulz was opening his case and beginning to count out the money. She took out her lorgnette and came and stood behind him, peering down at the rows and rows of white fivers. His head reeled with the smell of her perfume. *Her* head reeled with the smell of the money.

'English currency?' she purred in a rich honey voice, removing her lorgnette. 'Where did you get it?'

'It's a long story,' said Schulz, who was certainly not planning to tell it. He handed her a wad of notes and started to close the lid of the case, but she stopped him with a well-manicured hand.

'Is there . . . anything else in the chateau you fancy?' she said in a strange voice. She was smiling dazzlingly at him and was standing very close.

'Well,' Schulz cleared his throat, 'there's nothing I could

180

carry away and ... besides, it would hardly be fair to deprive you of things of great sentimental value.'

'Even things of great sentimental value can be bought,' she said in a low husky voice. 'They just ... cost a lot more, that's all.'

She smiled at Schulz again. Suddenly he understood: this elegant, beautiful, haughty aristocrat was prepared to throw herself at him on account of his money. From being a weapon of devilish ingenuity, the money had been transformed into a useful tool to get him back home and, as a bonus, a means of enjoying himself *en route*. The idea that it was anything more hadn't struck him until now. That was what money would do! he thought. His horizons had expanded with the touch of a hand.

Without saying another word, the comtesse swept out of the kitchen, beckoning him to follow. They went from room to room, the comtesse pointing out the value and history of every item, in that husky voice that made it impossible to keep one's mind on the treasures she was presenting. Finally they reached the master bedroom. A suit of riding clothes was hanging on the door of the wardrobe. Schulz lifted them down.

'Whose are these?' he asked.

'My husband's,' she said perfunctorily. 'Surely you don't want to buy those?' The sound of guns was growing louder and this fool was inspecting her husband's clothes. She looked anxiously towards the window which had begun to rattle.

'Comtesse,' said Schulz, 'let me be frank. There are things in the chateau I might buy, but – it's you who fascinates me.' There was a pregnant pause.

'Oh, I see,' she said at last in a flat voice.

Schulz began to wonder whether he had been reading the signals correctly. 'Well,' he said apologetically, 'you did say even things of great sentimental value could be bought.'

'Of course, of course,' she said grimly. 'I said, too, they cost a lot more.'

'Oh, naturally, but money, at the moment, is no object, and ...' He trailed off.

181

The comtesse, however, was equal to the occasion. 'Well?' she said with some dignity, 'you surely don't expect me to stand here and name a price, do you?'

'Of course not!' Schulz said hastily. 'Certainly not, nothing so vulgar! Suppose I were to reconsider and say that the necklace, after all, is worth twenty thousand English pounds and a lift in the car? What would you say to that?'

'Twenty thousand ... ?' If the comtesse had been impressed before she was now overcome. '*Mon Dieu,* monsieur I'd say you certainly know what you like! Shall we begin?'

She began to take off the square-cut jacket of her tailored suit, revealing a pair of feminine shoulders and a very well-bred figure.

'A moment, comtesse,' said Schulz, as she started to unbutton her blouse.

She paused.

'What's the hurry?'

'The guns, monsieur?' she said, leaving her blouse half-undone but folding her arms over her breasts.

'Oh,' he laughed, 'we mustn't worry about a little gunfire. I tell you frankly, comtesse, our little situation rather intrigues me.'

'I can't tell you what it does to me, monsieur,' she said heavily.

'I'd like to savour it a little – not rush it.'

'If you have in mind some unspeakable practices peculiar to yourself –' she said coldly, starting to fasten her blouse again.

'No, no – nothing like that!' said Schulz hastily. 'What do you take me for? But we ought to be more civilized. I thought – a little light lunch before we begin, a good wine, bottled, perhaps, on the estate? A stroll through the grounds and then, if we felt like it – which we probably shall – a little rest in the afternoon – up here?'

Schulz was extremely hungry – the roll had only stimulated his appetite – and he had no intention of letting what might be the only reward for his disastrous ordeal slip so quickly through his hands. But the comtesse was staring at him as though he were a madman.

182

'Do you think we've got all day?' she gasped. 'Those German pigs will be here any minute!'

'Oh, they're miles away,' said Schulz with a wave of his hand. He smiled. 'Will you see to the lunch then, my dear. Nothing elaborate, a little pâté, an omelette *fines herbes,* some cheese?' He held up the riding habit and looked at it. 'I think I'll change for lunch.'

They had used the main hall as a dining room. At one end of its magnificent table sat Schulz, now dressed in full riding habit, finishing his omelette. At the other, the comtesse, glaring at him impatiently, drummed her fingers on the table. Outside, the rumble of gunfire was now much louder and quite frightening, to the comtesse at least.

Schulz dabbed his mouth with a napkin and took another sip of the vintage wine which he had personally selected from the cellar.

'Excellent, my dear,' he said, licking his lips. 'You should have had some.'

'I wasn't hungry,' said the comtesse tersely. 'Are you ready to go upstairs now?' She bared her teeth at him in a smile.

'Just a little cheese. The chevre is excellent.' He smiled and stretched. 'I suppose this all seems a little curious to you?'

'A little,' said the comtesse.

'Do you think it is strange to try to forget the war for a moment?'

'I think it is very clever of you, considering the world is falling apart all around us.'

Schulz sighed. He gazed into the flickering lights on the silver candlesticks.

'This moment represents for me a little oasis in my life that I shall probably never stumble upon again. Can you blame me for making the most of it?' To illustrate his point he lit a cigar and gazed lasciviously at the comtesse. 'To eat a meal in these exquisite surroundings, prepared by a woman of breeding and beauty whom I might, who knows, but for an accident of birth, have called my wife?'

'That's what you think!' the comtesse snarled.

He laughed.

'Oh, don't spoil my little fantasy. I can't tell you the happiness these few moments have brought me, happiness that costs you so little –'

'Are you going to complain about the price, now?' she hissed.

'Good heavens, no! I was going to say, "Costs you so little and yet means so much to me".' He smiled even more broadly. 'Neither do I forget the happiness that is yet to come. I feel, comtesse, like a man about to enter Paradise...'

He was interrupted by the sudden reverberation of guns from somewhere very close by. The chateau seemed to rock to its foundations and a painting fell off the wall with a crash. The comtesse leaped to her feet.

'They're certainly closer than I thought,' remarked Schulz, rising uncertainly and moving towards the window.

The comtesse meanwhile had strode towards the door, where she stood with hands on hips.

'We must do it *now* or not at all!' she proclaimed.

'Of course,' Schulz demurred. 'Still, let's be tasteful – preserve the decencies.' He picked up his wine and looked expansively round the hall. 'Your class has taught us all so much, comtesse – the value of leisure, the refinement it can bring to the coarser human feeling –'

Another enormous crash shook the walls.

'Will you come upstairs *now* or do you want it on the floor!' the comtesse spat at him.

'I beg your pardon?' Schulz was not expecting such vulgarity. The comtesse grabbed him by the collar of his riding coat and shook him.

'*WHERE* DO YOU WANT IT?' she screamed.

Just then there was a high-pitched whine and a roar of aircraft engines outside. Then a huge crash came from the roof. The comtesse screamed and threw herself into Schulz's arms. For a moment he felt her warmth and softness, then they were both enveloped in falling rafters, plaster and brick dust as the roof caved in. Schulz collapsed immediately under a beam. The comtesse managed to free herself and crawled away towards the stairs, leaving him senseless amid the rubble.

She staggered into her bedroom almost in a state of collapse, crossed to the bed and picked up Schulz's clothes, wrinkling her nose in distaste for a second before rummaging through the pockets. She soon found the car keys. Hastily throwing the clothes in a corner, she picked up her minks and her necklace and was about to leave the room when she noticed the briefcase, stacked with fivers, which Schulz had left on a table. She picked this up too and hurried out. As she descended the staircase, Schulz, who had just come to, was crawling on all fours towards the foot of the stairs, still dazed. He held out a hand to the comtesse for help.

'My dear –' he gasped. The comtesse let loose a flying kick, the point of her elegant high heel catching him full in the face and sending him reeling backwards.

'Out of my way, you communist pig!' she shrieked, and hurried out of the front door. Schulz got painfully to his feet and slowly stumbled after her. As he crossed the threshold he heard the roar of his hearse as it tore off into the distance. He staggered out, holding his eye which was bleeding. The whole house seemed to be moving as though a small earthquake was about to swallow it, and from the lawns behind the chateau he could hear the incessant screeching of the comtesse's peacocks.

Then he understood.

Hordes of German motor cyclists and lorries laden with infantry were plunging through the main gate and skidding to a halt twenty yards from him. Schulz raised his arms above his head, staring in utter dismay as troops carrying rifles and revolvers jumped off the lorries and motorbikes, and bore down on him as though he were a citadel that was about to be stormed. The fact that at least two-thirds of them were taking possession of the crumbling chateau and its fabulous contents was purely academic.

18

Exactly a week later, on 10 June 1940, the Germans crossed the Seine and Mussolini declared war on France, hoping to get a share of the spoils. On 22 June at Rethondes in the Forest of Compiegne the German terms for an armistice were accepted.

In Paris Germans were everywhere, marching through the streets, and drinking aperitifs in boulevard cafés, while in Berlin tumultuous crowds cheered Adolf Hitler and his returning victorious soldiers. For the first time since 1871, German troops staged a victory parade through the Brandenburg Gate. Children scattered rose petals as the Fuhrer's Mercedes drove down Unter der Linden. With fewer casualties even than Germany had sustained in the Franco-Prussian War, Hitler had reversed the verdict of 1918. The German army was invincible and Germany was the Master of Europe.

In the offices of Dept VIB of the Sicherheitsdienst in the Delbruckstrasse, a celebration party was in progress. A dozen officers, and at least as many girls, were drinking champagne and singing 'We March Against England'. Some were watching from the windows as the victory parade passed by. Martial music could still be heard faintly in the street as a burst of cheering and laughter greeted the end of the song and glasses were raised.

'Ladies and gentlemen, a toast!' came the magnanimous voice of Major General Alfred Neuheim, and a hush fell over the assembly. 'To the Fuhrer, to the German people and to a great German victory!'

Cheers and hammering of feet on the floor and the clinking of glasses followed. Then Neuheim held up his hand and silence fell again over the company.

'One more toast!' said Neuheim. 'To the men of SS Counter-Espionage. And may I say that I, especially, do not forget those brave and unsung heroes who parachuted into enemy territory and never came back. Unknown to all except a few of us, they are the eternal glory of the Fatherland!'

Solemnly everyone drank. Then, movingly, a few people began to sing the '*Horst Wessel*' song. It was just getting into its swing when the door opened and a man entered. He was wearing a filthy riding habit, his face was severely bruised and he had a black eye. Behind him came two Gestapo officers.

Neuheim stared incredulously. One of the officers, a beaming, chunky, round-faced, bespectacled little man looked round the room and coughed.

'So sorry to interrupt the party,' he said. 'Major General Neuheim?'

'I'm Major General Neuheim.' Neuheim's voice had an oddly stilted quality, as though he had just been found in a highly compromising position.

'How do you do?' beamed the round-faced man. 'I'm Kruger – Gestapo. This is yours, I believe?' He pointed pleasantly at the riding habit and its contents. 'We found him about a fortnight ago in a bombed-out French chateau. Well, our troops did. They handed him over to us thinking he was an enemy agent. We were so busy we threw him in the Bastille and it was over a week before we got round to him. Wasn't it?' he beamed benevolently at the riding habit. 'Of course,' he said to Neuheim, 'we've questioned him. We thought he was an English spy. He kept telling us he was working for the SD but,' he laughed jovially at the riding habit, 'we didn't believe you, did we?'

'No,' said Schulz sullenly.

'Then,' continued Kruger, 'we thought he must be an escaped lunatic – an asylum had been hit by a bomb in that area and several were roaming the countryside. Well, look at him!' he laughed, obviously enjoying himself hugely. 'But it turned out he isn't a lunatic at all but a member of your staff, Herr Major General!'

'Have you quite finished?' said Neuheim in a grim, strangled voice.

'Oh, finished, finished,' replied Kruger. 'I must go!' He turned to Schulz. 'So sorry for the –' he touched his own face, '– misunderstanding.' He grinned at Neuheim and gave them all a chubby wave of his hand. 'Enjoy yourselves! If you've got any more like him in the SS I should keep them at home.' He went out, chuckling.

There was an appalled silence. Then Neuheim forced a smile.

'Well, come on, drink up!' he boomed heartily. 'More champagne, everyone!' Quietly he added to Schulz: 'Come with me!'

The party burst once more into life while Neuheim grimly led the way out to Schulz's office. As he opened the door he caught a glimpse of an SS officer with his hand buried deep inside the skirt of a tall redheaded girl who was lying across his lap. The couple leaped to their feet as Neuheim entered, guiltily adjusting their clothes and hurrying out. Neuheim slammed the door and turned to Schulz.

'I ought to have you shot!' he thundered. 'How dare you come back here alive?'

'I had no choice ...' said Schulz miserably. It was a question he had asked himself a thousand times during his week in the Bastille and the ordeal that had followed.

'SHUT UP! You imbecile!' roared Neuheim. 'To get caught by the Gestapo! YOU SHOULD BE PUT AWAY!'

He paced up and down furiously for a moment and then stopped and glared at Schulz.

'What happened? What happened over there?' He was eyeing the riding habit.

'It was a fiasco!' sighed Schulz.

'I didn't ask for a description, I asked what happened!' Neuheim rasped. 'I *know* it was a fiasco! Everything you touch is a fiasco!'

'It wasn't my fault,' replied Schulz somewhat self-pityingly. 'Our contact in England turned out to be working for the British Secret Service.'

'Melfort?'

'Melfort. They were waiting for me – literally. He was either always working for the British or the British turned

188

him. I could've been hanged.'

'Oh, stop moaning! If there's one thing I can't stand it's a moaner! What happened to the canister with the money?'

'It's buried somewhere in Kent,' said Schulz regretfully.

'So you accomplished nothing?' Neuheim screamed. 'Your sole contribution to the German war effort has been to take a canister of English money secretly out of Germany and bury it secretly in Kent?'

'I think that's a very jaundiced way of putting it, sir,' said Schulz stiffly.

'Do you know of a better way of putting it?' Neuheim replied coldly. Schulz could not actually think of one and Neuheim nodded, grimly satisfied. 'I want a full written report on the whole operation by tomorrow morning. Meanwhile, get out of those clothes and get back into uniform.' He started to walk out but paused. 'Where did you get them from, anyway?'

'A French countess, Herr Brigadier –'

'May I remind you, Schulz, that I am a Major General – and you,' he added darkly, 'can still consider yourself a private. Now, about this French –'

'I'll put it all into the report, Herr Major General,' Schulz said hurriedly. 'It's not something that can be explained in a few words.'

'I'm sure it can't,' grumbled Neuheim.

'May I ask, Herr Major General, what the Major General intends to do about the scheme now operating in Barracks 19?'

'I'm going to break it up, what do you think?' Neuheim stormed. 'There'll be no more notes coming from Barracks 19 because the war is over and we'll shortly have all the English money we need.'

With that he stalked out of the room and returned to the party, leaving Schulz's last flickering hope snuffed out.

Neuheim's optimism had been, once again, premature. On 10 July, the Battle of Britain began. In the first ten days of August the Luftwaffe lost several times more planes than the

RAF and early in September casualties sustained during bombing attacks on airfields and aircraft factories were beginning to make the Luftwaffe lose sight of their true objective – the destruction of the RAF. Many people both in and outside the SD were blaming this singular failure on the pompous Hermann Göring.

On 7 September came the first mass attack on London. 'This,' declared Göring, 'is the historic hour when our air force for the first time delivered its stroke right into the enemy's heart.' But in spite of the twenty-three day bombardment the Blitz was taking more out of the Luftwaffe than it was out of the heart of its enemy. By the end of October the Battle of Britain was over, but it became clear that the war would be going on and on.

Schulz was amazed at the way in which the SD and Neuheim in particular seemed to adjust so quickly to this dramatic reversal in fortunes. It was almost as if Neuheim welcomed the opportunity to prolong his association with the SS as a means both towards personal advancement and for his continued assault on his prime guinea-pig. Schulz meanwhile was settling down again to the masochistic routine of keeping office for Neuheim, his policy as always being to keep out of the Major General's way as much as possible. He still had his regular tour of listening duty at the Salon Kitty which drove him nearly insane every night, particularly as he now did not dare go near Bertha Freyer, whom both Neuheim and his master Heydrich had put out of bounds. Schulz often wondered if he might not have been wired up to detonate on sight of her, such was his paranoia.

He derived a little comfort, however, from one fact which Schumacher revealed. It seemed that three other agents had been dropped over England at the same time as Schulz. All three had had the full course of training, including wireless operation and parachute jumping. All three were caught within an hour and later shot. None wore plus-fours.

Another thought also sustained him. The thought of the brief but wonderful time he had spent in the chateau and the possibility of that delicious but unfulfilled final moment with the comtesse. All this had come about for one reason only – his wealth. He had seen a haughty, untouchable aristocrat melt at the sight of it and nearly abandon herself to him. It was a lesson he could never forget, and he brooded over it. The forged five-pound notes haunted his daylight hours and his dreams. Like intangible snow they seemed to flutter around his mind, lying thick and white and always melting when he thought too hard about them.

Sooner or later he knew he would have to do something about it and, inevitably, one day in early January 1941, he found himself once more at Fraulein Freyer's door.

'Countess! Chateau!' she taunted him, laughing helplessly. 'You don't seriously expect me to believe that, do you?'

Bertha was attempting to fix her make up, but Schulz was making it difficult.

'It's true,' said Schulz indignantly, watching her in the mirror.

'*Threw* herself at you?'

'There's no other way of describing it. When she saw all that money I could have had anything I liked.'

'Anything?' Bertha carefully applied fresh lipstick.

'Anything.' Schulz looked longingly at her mouth. 'I'm telling you, Bertha, if I could have brought home what I could have paid for –'

'You'd have returned with an expensive dose of clap – the French aristocracy's riddled with it.'

'Well – some of us like our game high.' He grinned.

She laughed and slipped off her robe, crossing the room to get her stockings which she started to put on while he stared at her wistfully.

'If I could only get Neuheim to start that scheme up again,' he said with longing.

'It wouldn't do you any good. Nothing does *you* any good in the end.'

'Why do you say that?' said Schulz, in a wounded tone.

'Because it's the truth.'

'You don't think much of me, do you?' he said, getting to his feet. 'But have you any idea what I accomplished?'

191

'It seems to me you've accomplished very little,' she said evenly.

Schulz was deeply stung by this remark and began pacing the room in excitement.

'I accomplished everything, everything!' he said. 'I built the greatest counterfeiting organization the world has ever seen.'

'That's just what I mean – nobody knew about it.'

'What difference does that make? I solved problems people said were insoluble! I created an organization that produced an English five-pound note acceptable anywhere – even in Threadneedle Street – and that fool, Neuheim, has thrown it all away.' While he had been talking his irritation had slowly evaporated as his sense of loss overwhelmed him. Now he sat down again, burying his head in his hands.

'I could have been rich,' he sighed. 'The money could be rolling off the presses at this very moment and this time some of it would have come my way, I'd have seen to that.'

'Not you,' she replied, and shook her head. 'There's something about you, Gerhardt – I don't know what it is, but ...'

'What do you mean?' Schulz raised his voice again in his irritation. 'Something about me? Be precise.'

Bertha paused from rolling up a stocking to study him.

'You're a loser,' she said. 'You're brilliant in some ways, and you're certainly wasted as Neuheim's clerk, but –' she searched for the right words, '– you're flawed.'

'Flawed?' said Schulz uneasily.

'You're – accident-prone. It's as if you were born with a stumble.'

'A stumble?'

Bertha nodded, now firmly convinced.

'An inbuilt stumble that always trips you just as you're about to cross the finishing line,' she continued. 'You're a born last-minute stumbler, Gerhardt, and I don't know what you do about that. It's as if ... you don't know how to hold on to things.'

He stared at her with some hostility and then laughed.

'And what are you, a winner?' he said sarcastically. 'What

have you ever won? What are you likely to win lying on that bed all day?'

'When the war's over I'll be comfortably off,' she replied, slipping into a black satin dress.

'Comfortably off! You'll have enough to buy yourself a sweetshop – if you're lucky! Oh, I don't know why I talk to you! Your mind is really too small to take in what I'm saying.'

'What *are* you saying, then?' Bertha was busy examining the general effect in the mirror.

'I'm saying that I saw the future, Bertha,' said Schulz agitatedly, '*my* future – and I won't settle for less! I saw how life *could* be –'

'In a French chateau?'

'Sneer all you like! I had fifty thousand English pounds in my hands – I could've bought anything I wanted. I could even have bought you, Bertha Freyer! From the tips of your painted toenails to the top of your peroxided head, I could have owned you body and soul. And all for a suitcase of fake fivers!'

'Not everything has a price,' she said, examining her profile.

'You're wrong,' said Schulz passionately. 'Money buys everything – people, goods, information, loyalty, service! It buys . . .'

He stopped abruptly, struck by a sudden thought. He seemed almost to quiver with it. Bertha turned to look at him. When she saw the expression on his face, she shook her head disapprovingly.

'Now what have you thought of?'

'Let me get this straight. You're suggesting that those foreigners who are secretly spying for us in their own countries should be paid in forged English five-pound notes?'

'Yes, sir.'

'You're suggesting,' said Neuheim, 'that we reward those brave friends of Germany who daily risk their lives to provide us with vital information – that we reward them in counterfeit money?' He was screwing his face up, almost like a camera's shutter.

'It's – very good counterfeit,' replied Schulz nervously.

'That's the most immoral proposal I've ever heard,' said Neuheim. The shutter had opened to reveal just how appalled he was.

'Yes, sir!' said Schulz stiffly.

'It is utterly dishonourable!'

'Yes, sir.'

Neuheim paused as though this totally immoral idea was slowly developing in the silver nitrate of his brain.

'And yet –' He turned away thoughtfully, pulling at his lip. A negative was gradually beginning to take shape. '– there's a devilish irony in it.'

'Irony, sir?'

'In England paying for the services of Germany's agents abroad,' mused Neuheim. Schulz laughed. 'And, when you think of it,' went on Neuheim, 'in paying those foreign swine who demand English currency in forged English fivers!'

'It serves them right for having so little faith in the German mark, sir,' said Schulz patriotically.

'Exactly!' agreed Neuheim, pounding his office desk. 'It's rough justice!'

'Very rough, sir. But that's not all. We could buy up all sorts of valuables in the occupied countries – jewellery, objets d'art –' Schulz was remembering the chateau.

'And England would be paying for them!' The print had emerged.

'Exactly!' Schulz laughed. 'It would be costing Germany nothing, sir.'

Neuheim began to laugh as he saw the humour of it.

'This could revolutionize the whole concept of war finance!' he said, now attempting an enlargement. 'It could become possible to fight a war entirely at the expense of the enemy!'

They both exploded into merriment until Neuheim, seized with another thought, stopped abruptly.

'Something wrong, sir?'

194

'You don't think the British are already doing it, do you?'

They stared frozenly at one another as the sobering thought struck them. Then, as one man, they dived into their pockets and pulled out German marks, holding them up to the light and examining them for signs of forgery – but on reflection Schulz shook his head.

'I don't think so,' he said. 'I'm sure they wouldn't think of it, sir.'

'No,' muttered Neuheim. Reassured, he looked at Schulz. 'I like it. We'll have to go into mass production, of course. We'll need to produce millions and millions of notes without loss of quality.'

'Millions, sir,' agreed Schulz, licking lips which had suddenly gone dry.

'We'll buy up Europe. We'll set up a distribution centre somewhere to co-ordinate all the activities, and find a brilliant financial brain to run it.'

'Not only brilliant, Herr Major General, but completely honest. The opportunities for corruption will be enormous. The man who runs this operation could make himself into a millionaire overnight.'

Neuheim was looking at Schulz rather oddly now. 'I hadn't thought of that,' he said pensively.

'Could I make a suggestion, sir?'

'You're right, of course,' Neuheim continued. 'The temptations will be enormous – and under the circumstances no one should be exposed to them but myself.'

Schulz nodded drearily. He'd stumbled already. Maybe Bertha was right. Neuheim continued to pace up and down as the bromide sharpened in his mind. 'I'll put it straight to the Fuhrer but I'm sure he'll agree, provided the whole thing is kept secret from the Ministry of Economics. As for you, you can begin straight away. You can open up Barracks 19 again and reassemble that team of crooks and swindlers that you got together before.' He paused, looking at Schulz with immense satisfaction. 'It's a wonderful idea, an idea that could save Germany millions! I wonder I never thought of it before.'

19

Operation Bernhard was officially approved by Neuheim's immediate superior, Schellenberg (who had more or less replaced Jost as boss of RSHA Dept VI), Heydrich, Himmler and ultimately the Fuhrer himself. What was then required was a super salesman who would be able to buy anything negotiable with the forged bank notes, including bonds and foreign currency, to pay Germany's network of foreign agents.

There was only one man who could conceivably fit the bill.

Frederico Schwend, alias Wenceslas Turi, alias Wendig Alisax, was an Austrian who had lived in America until the Fuhrer came to power, when he had returned to Germany and offered his services to Göring as an international contact man. He was introduced to Hitler who, suspecting 'this much-travelled cosmopolite' might be an enemy agent, ordered his house to be searched. Schwend, furious, returned to America but was now suspect there as well, because of his German associations, and at the outbreak of war he had returned to Europe and settled in Italy. There he was introduced to Schellenberg who, realizing his contacts could be useful, offered him a commission in the SS.

Major Schwend was given the job of liaising the distribution of the forged British currency, under Neuheim naturally. Once Heydrich was satisfied that the notes could pass as genuine, full-scale production had been sanctioned. But the notes had had to be tested once more. It was one thing for one first-edition five-pound note, so to speak, to be declared genuine by Threadneedle Street, as had happened during Schulz's brief trip to Switzerland, but quite another to get mass-produced copies past Germany's network of highly shrewd and naturally suspicious agents.

After a trial run in Switzerland and elsewhere, organized by Schwend, the newly printed forgeries were examined minutely on glass-topped desks illuminated by ultra high-powered magnifying glasses.

There were three groups of examiners, each with three inspectors, and all were under the command of Ephraim Solokoff. The first group assessed the colour and printing; the second, the watermark – Britannia; and the third, the texture and overall effect. Then the notes were classified. Class I notes were used solely for German agents sent to enemy or neutral countries, Class II for collaborators and blackmarket operations, and Class III for small-time operations which included buying from partisans the arms which the British were beginning to drop in Yugoslavia.

The day that the first foreign agent was paid with forged currency Neuheim called it the proudest of his life. Before long there were demands for notes of larger denominations. Solly was not too happy about this, a fifty-pound note, for instance, being so rare that bank officials were bound to examine them more closely. As it was, most of the fivers that were printed, in the beginning at least, were passed by hand down long files of prisoners so that they would have natural fingermarks and the grubbiness of everyday use. Bank-tellers' pencil marks were even placed on certain notes as if they had naturally passed scrutiny in English banks before being put into circulation.

Within six months of Operation Bernhard being given the official go-ahead, Barracks 19 in Sachsenhausen was transformed. New machinery was installed and more criminals recruited, again mainly from jails, to aid Solokoff. Again Neuheim launched the operation with a kindly word:

'Scum,' he shouted at them, 'crooks and enemies of the Fuhrer! Your profession is filth and you are a disgrace to the German people. You're all a pack of thieves and swindlers and you ought to be shot! However, the Fuhrer has ordered a reprieve and you will now be faking for the Fatherland!'

The forgers, as before, breathed a sigh of relief and set to work with a will. The photo engraving room, printing room and dispatch room had been streamlined, and output doubled, then quadrupled. Before long the finished notes were being moved regularly in bulk to the Schloss Laber, a small castle near the Austrian border that Schwend had taken over for his operations and which served as the distribution centre. The journey took just under two days and necessitated a stay at a hotel on the way for the messenger and the accompanying SS guard.

A system of accounting was set up in Sachsenhausen to ensure that none of the output was side-tracked, for, as Schulz had pointed out to Neuheim – to his eternal regret – the temptations were enormous. Additional security was involved since the Gestapo knew that something was up. Despite the fact that Hitler had given Operation Bernhard his blessing it was, technically, illegal and once the Gestapo got wind of it they spent much of the war trying to disrupt and discourage this enterprise and discredit the SS. They were jealous of its success and were to maintain that it should have come under their jurisdiction.

When the notes arrived at the Schloss, they were again accounted for and handed over to Schwend's couriers. The couriers then went on their various journeys through Europe buying up everything of any value at all. They paid enormous prices and had little difficulty since English bank notes were more acceptable to most people at that time than any other currency.

The scheme was in full operation and Schulz had been promoted to corporal by a for-once-grateful Neuheim, who himself had been awarded another Iron Cross personally by the Fuhrer and once again promoted, this time to lieutenant general. But Schulz's problem, as always, was how to get his hands on the notes, a problem which kept him awake at nights. By the summer of 1942, Schwend and his salesmen were demanding £5,000,000 worth of notes a week, but whereas earlier on Neuheim had shown surprising leniency when Schulz had been caught trying to bribe Fraulein Freyer, Sachsenhausen was more businesslike than Berlin and Operation Bernhard three times as big as Andreas. Schulz had even seen two guards shot out of hand after a few notes were found on them after a search.

In the course of his duties he often hung about in the machine shops talking to Solly. The sight of all that money coming off the presses nearly drove him insane. He watched it being printed, the numbers carefully noted down, tied into bundles, packed away and handed over to messengers for the journey to Schloss Laber until he had to go outside and steady himself. The only comparable experience in his memory was sitting on the end of a hot microphone listening to Bertha and one of her clients making love. The effect on him was the same. He felt like a chained tiger with the scent of blood in its nose.

Solly was very fond of Schulz, in fact Schulz always seemed to Solly like a fellow inmate rather than one of the guards. But Solly's career had nearly come to a halt when he had helped Schulz sidetrack the fivers before and this time he refused to be a party to any of Schulz's personal schemes. Schulz had decided by now that the only way to get at the money was to become a messenger and make a break for it out of the country. He knew that if a messenger fell sick while waiting at the camp for the money he stood a good chance of becoming a substitute. But he couldn't stand around waiting for it to happen. He had even applied for a transfer, hoping that his languages would stand him in good stead – but nothing happened.

One day he was talking to a big, beefy courier called Erhardt. In spite of his huge size, Erhardt was a harmless chap with not a single thing in his head except chewing gum of which he got through dozens of packets every week. Schulz had once asked him why he so often swallowed the chewing gum instead of chewing it.

'Because I don't like the taste,' said Erhardt.

'Then why do you eat it at all?' Schulz asked.

'Well, I've got this bad stomach and I always swallow a tablet to ease the pain,' explained Erhardt. 'I've always done it, ever since I started getting a bad stomach.'

'When was that?'

Erhardt thought for a minute. 'It must have been around the time I found out how good chewing gum was for it.'

Nevertheless this moron had unaccountably been employed as a salesman and was proudly telling Schulz about one deal from which he had returned with a carload of bars of gold, a crate of dollars, two crates of genuine fivers and a dustbin full of Swiss francs.

If a man with as little imagination and ability as Erhardt could net such profits, how far could he go, given the opportunity, Schulz thought. He saw very little of Bertha now that he was almost permanently attached to Barracks 19, and the occasional visit from Schumacher in which he would drop some chance mention of her only seemed to elevate her in Schulz's imagination as an unattainable object like the fortune that was passing daily through his hands.

One day in early July 1942 Schulz was in the printing room with Solly and a courier. It was over eighteen months since Schultz had first brought up the idea of Operation Bernhard to Neuheim. During that time Germany had seen a major setback in the East. On 22 June 1941 the German army had marched over the 2000-mile long Russian border. Military experts had predicted that Russia would be defeated in six weeks and Hitler, expecting victory before the leaves fell, made no provision for winter clothing or equipment. At first the German advance did indeed seem like a repetition of the 1940 blitz. Russian armies had been annihilated, hundreds of thousands of prisoners taken, and if Hitler had left his generals to their own devices they would have taken Moscow and no doubt have established a line to mitigate the worst rigours of the Russian winter. But as supreme commander the Fuhrer had scattered his objectives: he wanted Leningrad, Moscow and the Ukraine all at once. Even Schulz, who had never taken the slightest interest in the war, knew that it was better to do one thing at a time and began to wonder if the Fuhrer were not taking his bumble-bee philosophy too far.

Schulz was proved right. Hitler's Russian intelligence reports were faulty, his supplies and reinforcements inadequate for anything but a *blitzkrieg*. The brilliance of the initial advance had been deceptive. As the first German troops thrust into the Ukraine they were hailed as liberators, but behind the Wehrmacht came the SS Einsatz squads, the executioners and liquidators. Schulz had always known that the Fuhrer was mad but had sneakingly admired a certain simplicity about his logic with which he could identify. But now that seemed to have given way to manic brutality at all costs.

The Fuhrer, relying on his intuition, had begun to spread himself too thin over Europe, North Africa and Russia. Schulz was amazed when Hitler added to his folly by declaring war on the United States. It was one thing to have fights with your next-door neighbours but quite another to involve the whole street.

By July 1942 Rommel had taken Tobruk, advanced to El Alamein and was ready to capture Egypt. For what it was worth, then, Rommel's Afrika Korps had presented the Fuhrer with a lot of sand. Schulz could not understand why anyone should want so much sand except, possibly, to process it for the silver salts that were a crucial element in the printing of forged money. He was telling this to Solly and Solly was agreeing though he was a little abstracted by the fact that he was examining a plate. Eventually Schulz wandered away, closely followed by Schmidt, the courier. Schmidt was an easy-going, friendly sort of man with whom Schulz had struck up a good friendship, and who sympathized with Schulz's peculiar obsession.

'I never tire of watching those notes come out of that press,' he told Schulz as they finished their coffee. 'It's the most fascinating sight I've ever seen.'

At that moment a huge, thick-set SS guard with a surly face appeared at the door of the printing room.

'Are you ready, Schmidt?' he said in an even surlier voice. He was obviously a dedicated Nazi who would no more think of abusing the trust given to him by the SS than Schulz would in not doing so.

'Coming,' called Schmidt. As the guard left, he put his coffee mug down. 'Gruber, on the other hand,' he added to Schulz in a low voice, 'is the least fascinating sight I've ever seen.'

'Is he your new guard?' asked Schulz. Schmidt nodded. 'Why didn't you bring him in for some coffee?'

'He's got friends here he talks to,' replied Schmidt flatly, picking up his hat and coat. 'Well, thanks for the coffee, Gerhardt, I'll see you next month.'

Schulz picked up the large suitcase that was now stacked with piles of banknotes and handed it to Schmidt, almost caressing it as he did so. Schmidt laughed as he took it.

'I've been coming here for the last nine months and every time you hand me that case you get the same look on your face,' he said

'What look is that?' Schulz said lightly.

'Like you're handing over your life's work,' replied Schmidt.

'Don't run off with it,' Schulz grinned.

'Are you joking? With Gruber sitting beside me?' He turned to go but Schulz put a hand on his arm restraining him for a moment. Schmidt seem
ordinary people he might have ordinary feelings.

'You know,' Schulz began nervously, 'this is just a hypothetical question, Willi, but – supposing he wasn't?'

'Wasn't?'

'Sitting beside you?'

'There'd be somebody else,' said Schmidt and smiled. 'It's not so easy when there are two of you, and they keep changing you about.'

Once more he turned to go but again Schulz restrained him, speaking even more quietly.

'But suppose that *somebody else* was me?' He paused to see the effect of this on Schmidt but the courier just waited. 'If Gruber fell sick while he was here they'd send me in his place. It nearly happened once before. Suppose *I* were sitting beside you in the car instead of Gruber – what then?

There was a slight pause.

'You mean – hypothetically?' said Schmidt carefully.

'Absolutely.'

Schmidt hesitated again, looking round to make sure the conversation was not being overheard. 'Let me ask *you* a hypothetical question,' he said.

'Go on.'

'Why should Gruber fall sick here when he's as strong as an ox?'

'Because,' said Schulz who had been rehearsing this conversation for several weeks, 'a teaspoonful of copper sulphate in a cup of coffee could *fell* an ox. Hypothetically,' he added.

Schmidt stared at him.

'Look, Willi,' Schulz went on, 'they're all making a fortune up at that castle, you know that. Everybody up at that distribution centre who has a hand in spending that money is getting rich. Even that blockhead Erhardt. But not you, and not me.'

Just then there came the loud, impatient blowing of a carhorn outside. Neither Schulz nor Schmidt moved.

'There's half a million English pounds in that case,' Schulz whispered, lifting the case slightly. 'They've been accepted all over Europe for what they are – genuine fivepound notes. A man could buy his way into any country in the world with the contents of this case.'

Schmidt was thinking hard. 'What about travel documents – passports, visas?' he asked.

'Solly will make you the best travel documents you've ever seen. All he needs is your photograph. We do it all the time here – we've got a special unit.'

Schmidt's mind was a riot of indecision. He scrutinized Schulz for a moment longer, then turned and walked out of the printing room to the waiting car, deep in thought, and Schulz slowly followed him. As they stood outside, looking at Gruber, still blowing his horn, Schmidt seemed to come out of a trance.

'Are you sure you'd be chosen to take his place?' he said finally.

'Certain,' replied Schulz. 'All you've got to do is get him inside the barracks for a cup of coffee the next time you come. You can leave the rest to me.'

'Won't he taste it? The copper sulphate, I mean?'

'I'll put plenty of suger with it, don't worry.'

'Where would you go?' said Schmidt, still eyeing Gruber.

Schulz shrugged. 'Switzerland?' he replied. 'From there, anywhere.'

Schmidt considered this. 'All right, he said at last. 'Start it rolling. I'll see you in a month.'

'In an unprecedented move that shows how crucial is the conquest of Stalingrad in the Fuhrer's victory plans, he has personally taken over command of Army Group A and has set up his HQ in Vinnitsa in the Ukraine. Complete German victory is now assured. In the desert German and Italian tanks are valiantly overcoming Montgomery's Eighth Army which has been cornered at Alam Haifa Ridge ...'

The radio in the printing room blared out the good tidings to a knot of prisoners and guards who were listening intently. Schulz was wondering how the Fuhrer could hope to take personal command of an army that was nearly a thousand miles away. It also seemed odd to him that Rommel should be changing his tactics, which had previously been successful because of his ability to sit tight and wait to be attacked. Perhaps the Fuhrer had also taken personal command of the Afrika Korps ... His mind wandered back to more important things.

It was now nearly September 1942 and nearly two months since Schulz had first mentioned his plan to Schmidt. The next time the courier had called at Barracks 19 he had brought a selection of photographs of himself which Schulz had surreptitiously handed to Solly. Now, as the voice of the news announcer droned on triumphantly, Solly signalled Schulz to join him. They found themselves an unobserved corner and Solly discreetly pulled out Schmidt's passport, visa for Switzerland, transit papers and other documents.

'Careful,' he whispered, 'the ink's not absolutely dry on the visa signature.'

'They're beautiful,' said Schulz in awe.

'Well, I hope you make it.'

'You should have come with us. We could have worked it. We could have smuggled you out.'

'No,' said Solly, shaking his head. 'If you're caught you'll go to jail, but if I'm caught ...' He drew his finger across his throat.

'Don't you think that's going to happen anyway?' Schulz replied quietly. 'They're all maniacs here, you know that. If we win they'll have no more use for you, and if we lose – they'll do it out of spite.'

'Probably,' Solly nodded.

'Why not, then?'

'Because I give less for your chances *going* than I do for mine staying. If I'm going to die, I'd like to feel that the least possible blame attaches to me.'

'Well,' replied Schulz, 'if I get to Geneva, I'll open an account for you.'

'That's all I want,' said Solly. 'If I ever do get out of this mess I'd like to know I've got somewhere to go in my old age. And if I don't, well, I shan't need much where I'm going.'

So Solly wasn't coming. But Schmidt certainly was. The next time the courier visited Barracks 19 Schulz handed him his forged documents and they arranged the final details. Schulz had managed to obtain some copper sulphate which was used in the printer's ink. The date was now set for early November.

'Aren't you coming in?' said Schmidt as he got out of the car.

'No,' said Gruber, still seated in the car. 'I'll wait here.'

Schmidt was taken aback. Operation Coffee hadn't begun yet and already there was a ridiculous obstacle.

'Oh, come on, Gruber,' he said, 'stretch your legs a bit.'

'I said I'll wait here,' Gruber repeated and folded his arms.

Resigned, Schmidt walked over to the gate and entered the building. In the dispatch room, a big iron safe was being emptied of its contents. Large piles of notes were being counted and stacked neatly on a table. A prisoner acting as clerk was calling out the beginning and end serial numbers of each packet of notes to Schulz who was entering them with dates into a huge leather-bound ledger.

As Schmidt walked in he jerked his head at Schulz.

'Take over here,' said Schulz to another prisoner and went over to Schmidt. 'Your consignment's nearly ready,' he said loudly to the courier as they shook hands. 'Did you have a good trip?' Then, more quietly: 'Where's Gruber?'

'He's outside,' said Schmidt.

'Well, bring him in,' said Schulz. 'The coffee's ready!'

'He won't *come* in,' Schmidt hissed.

Schulz instantly saw his whole scheme about to flounder because a man wouldn't get out of a car. He trembled inwardly.

'Perhaps we'd better forget it?' said Schmidt nervously.

Schulz glared at him. 'I've got all the travel documents ready – everything!' He thought desperately for a moment. 'Tell him both of you have to sign for the money. Tell him it's a new rule. Tell him *anything* but get him in here.'

Schmidt looked doubtfully at him, then pushed his hat determinedly on his head and turned to go.

'Willi,' Schulz added, 'bring him into the printing room. I've got the coffee there.' Schmidt nodded and went out.

Schulz turned to the prisoners. 'Pack Herr Schmidt's case ready for him to leave,' he called out. 'He'll be back in a minute.'

In the printing room Schulz carefully poured coffee into three mugs. It was, for once, the real thing, not ersatz, which Schulz sometimes reflected was the only thing he had got out of the war so far. He added sugar, stirred, and carried the mugs over to a bench, putting them down in a row. Then he dipped a teaspoon into a tin of dark liquid, poured the spoonful into the middle mug of coffee and stirred vigorously. He replaced the spoon quickly as Schmidt entered, followed by Gruber.

'Gruber!' he effused. 'How nice to see you! Did you have a good trip down?'

He handed Schmidt the end cup of coffee. Schmidt put his hat down on the stool and took it.

'All right,' said Gruber, impatiently. 'Where's the book I have to sign?'

'It's in the dispatch room,' replied Schulz. 'There's plenty of time. I've just made some coffee. Here, have a mug.' He grinned proudly. 'It's real coffee, not ersatz.'

He offered the middle mug to Gruber.

'I don't like real coffee.'

A stunned silence followed. Then Schulz laughed. 'What do you mean you don't like real coffee? Everybody likes *real* coffee,' he said heartily.

'Well, I don't. I like ersatz coffee. Now where's the book you want me to sign?'

Schulz looked from Gruber to Schmidt, who looked back at Schulz disgustedly.

'Oh, let's get the cash and get out of here,' said Schmidt putting down his mug in resignation.

He turned to go, followed by Gruber. Schulz stared disconsolately down at the row of mugs and followed them both. On their way out they passed Solly who was returning to the printing room carrying a half-printed note which he was studying intently, holding it up to the light.

Solly paused by the bench, noticing the mugs of coffee and picked up Schmidt's.

'Your coffee's over here, Solly,' called a prisoner.

'Thanks,' said Solly, putting Schmidt's mug down next to Schulz's, and wandering away to drink his own coffee which he took without sugar.

In the packing room the suitcase containing a million pound notes was being closed and locked, while Gruber signed the book.

'I'll see you outside,' he said curtly and left the room.

Schmidt gave Schulz a look like a pint of milk that had turned sour. Then he signed the book too, picked up the suitcase and went out, Schulz following him in deep depression.

'How was I to know he didn't like real coffee?' Schulz said to Schmidt as they re-entered the printing room. '*Who* doesn't like real coffee?'

Schmidt picked up his hat which he had left on a stool and put it on his head. 'Forget it, Gerhardt,' he said glumly. 'Luck doesn't run your way. I must have been mad even to think about it.'

He picked up the end mug but suddenly hesitated. 'Which is mine?'

'That one,' Schulz nodded, and Schmidt drank it down quickly. 'Let's try again?'

'Look, what are you trying to do to me?' said Schmidt. 'I've got a nice little number picking up cash and delivering it to the castle. For that I get well paid and nobody bothers me. I must have been insane, listening to you.' He gulped down the rest of the coffee and replaced the mug, pointing to the one in the middle and laughing.

'I should get rid of that one before you accidentally kill someone.'

Shaking his head, he picked up the suitcase and walked to the door, highly amused. He was just about to open the door when the copper sulphate hit him like a runaway bus. He let out a ghastly scream and froze, dropping the case and clutching his stomach.

Schulz, who had been emptying what he thought was Gruber's mug, also froze. He looked up to see Schmidt turn slowly towards him, his mouth open, his hand still holding his stomach. Schulz's own mouth fell open as he looked from Schmidt to the empty mug in his hand.

'But that's impossible –'

'Aaaaahh!' howled Schmidt as he slumped to the floor.

20

'Poor Schmidt, eh?' said Gruber, hands firmly gripping the driving wheel of a car that was speeding south towards Leipzig. Next to him in the front seat was Schulz, now in civilian clothes, as required of a courier. They had been driving for over an hour and this was the first time Gruber had spoken.

'Yes,' said Schulz glumly. They drove on in silence. Eventually Gruber spoke again.

'So sudden. I don't understand it – to be taken ill like that.' Again he lapsed into silence. They by-passed Leipzig and were on the road to Nuremberg when he spoke again. 'What do you think it was?' he asked, shaking his head.

'Burst appendix, probably,' said Schulz. They did not speak again for two or three hours. There had been no interference from the Gestapo and they were making good time. The plan was to spend the night at a hotel in Oberammergau and then reach Merano by the following midday.

'It just shows, you never know,' Gruber suddenly said, as they were heading for Munchen. 'It could've been me, it could've been you.'

'No,' said Schulz after a little pause, 'it couldn't have been me.'

Gruber looked at him suspiciously.

'I've had mine out,' Schulz said.

Gruber still looked at him suspiciously.

'Appendix,' Schulz added. They drove in silence again, but Schulz could not resist remarking quietly, 'But it could've been you.'

As the evening closed in, Gruber's silence, which Schulz had greeted with relief, became oppressive. No doubt he was annoyed at having to drive with a new courier and no doubt he did not trust Schulz an inch. Earlier on he had cursorily asked Schulz if he knew the routine.

'Yes,' Schulz had replied, not wanting to appear stupid. Now he decided it was worth at least one effort to test Gruber's fanaticism. Some of the most brutish looking and dedicated conmen at Barracks 19 could, if required, present a facade of patriotism.

'It must be a great temptation to the unscrupulous to take advantage of this situation,' he said.

Gruber eyed him dangerously for a moment. 'Just you

try,' he said grimly. 'If I turn up with an empty case, I'm for it, so – just you try.'

Schulz said no more.

By the time they arrived at the hotel it was dark. Schulz parked the car and kept the keys – that was the routine, Gruber had said. He saw Gruber talking to two burly, sinister-looking SS men but he avoided them and waited for Gruber to join him at the dinner table. A waiter brought over two dinners and they ate in silence. Halfway through the meal, two equally sinister men walked in and sat down at a table some distance away.

'The enemy,' whispered Gruber.

'Good God, British agents?' hissed Schulz dramatically.

'No, you fool, the Gestapo.' They finished their meal in silence.

Finally Gruber said good night to Schulz, reminding him they must leave at the crack of dawn.

'That's a bit early,' said Schulz.

'That's the routine,' replied Gruber impassively and went off to his room. Schulz undressed and got into bed, but he could not sleep. The moment he'd waited for for two years had come and the only thing that was inhibiting him from grasping it was a dim-witted *Oberscharfuhrer* and his SS pals. The chances of being caught in the mountains were minimal and it could well be easier to take the opportunity now, rather than wait until they reached the castle. On the other hand, the whole thing might be a trap.

Finally, at 3.00 a.m. he got up, dressed and crept to his door. The corridors were quiet. He stepped out noiselessly and went downstairs. There still wasn't a sound to be heard. He let himself out of the door and went round to the car. It was just as he had left it. If he pushed it back and then forward, he could roll it to the top of the drive, then roll it down to the slope and he would not have to start the engine. Releasing the hand brake, and sweating and straining, he pushed and pulled it to the top of the slope. Then he got in, rolled away and started the car. He was away.

It was all so easy. He was less than a hundred miles from Switzerland; he was fully armed with identity cards and visas, and a million pounds was sitting in the boot, waiting to be spent. He drove slowly, without lights. Five miles from the hotel, as the dawn broke, he emerged from the mountains on to a wooded road. Switzerland was now a mere hour's drive away.

At the next turning he drove straight into a road block. Three Gestapo officers stepped out of nowhere. They looked at him coldly and asked for his papers, which he showed. One of them demanded the car keys. Schulz started to protest, but then he noticed that another had a Luger trained on his nose. He pulled the keys out of the ignition and a third went round to the back of the car and opened the boot.

It's all over, thought Schulz in despair. He considered making a run for it but knew they would have him before he got more than two yards. The boot of the car went up and the third Gestapo man flashed his torch into it. There was nothing there.

He closed it down and returned the keys to Schulz. 'Where are you going?' he asked.

'To the Schloss Laber at Merano on behalf of General Neuheim,' Schulz replied, his head spinning.

'We'll get you Bernhard boys one day,' said the most evil-looking of the three. 'You think you're clever but we know what you're up to.' They stood aside and Schulz got back into the car in deep shock. His hands were shaking so much that he could hardly start it.

He drove on for a mile without daring to think, now totally confused. Where was the money? It dimly occurred to him that the best thing would be to return to the hotel and, at least, salvage his position vis-à-vis Gruber. He was just about to turn back when three more figures stepped out of the side road. Schulz couldn't believe his eyes.

It was Gruber, carrying the case, and accompanied by the two SS officers whom he had seen earlier.

'Where have you been?' said Gruber impatiently. 'You were supposed to meet us at dawn – you know the drill.'

They put the case in the boot and got in the car.

'Come on,' said one of the SS men, 'let's get to the Schloss. We've wasted enough time already.' He chuckled. 'The Gestapo fall for that trick every time.'

Schulz stared at him in bewilderment. Then it dawned on him: This was the 'routine' which Gruber had mentioned. Instead of running off with a fortune, all that had happened was that he had done his job.

'Yes, I've got all that,' General Alfred Neuheim was busily scribbling information on a pad as he spoke into the phone. 'And it's Djevo, you say?' He got up, still holding the phone, and looked for the spot on a wall map. 'Djevo? ... Yes, I've got it. It's right up in the Julian Alps near Trieste ... Well, the courier I'd send isn't actually here but I'll find someone. You'd better give me that list again – item by item. Right.' He sat down at his desk. 'How many rounds of amunition? ... Yes, I've got that. Grenades?'

The door opened and Neuheim's secretary walked in. She was a very well-built and mature looking young woman with the sexiest eyes that Neuheim had ever seen, which was why he had employed her.

'The messenger from Barracks 19, Herr General,' she said. Neuheim cupped his hands over the phone.

'Bring them in,' he said and returned to the phone. 'Yes, I'll send someone down to negotiate. How much? ... Yes, we've got that much here. You can expect them in a few days.' He hung up just as Schulz and Gruber were shown in by the secretary.

Schulz was staring at her, and thinking that she had the sexiest eyes he had ever seen. She had somehow managed to undress both Schulz and Gruber with them and even Gruber's normal poker face was beginning to redden. She seemed to generate heat around her as Schulz generated catastrophe. Now she was wrapping herself round a filing cabinet and Neuheim observed with quiet pleasure the disturbance that her presence created.

'They phoned me from the Barracks and told me Schmidt had collapsed,' he said. 'What's wrong with him?'

'It looks like a burst appendix, Herr General,' Gruber replied dutifully.

'I see.' Neuheim's look penetrated Schulz for a moment and then he took the case and documents from him. 'So they sent you in his place?'

'Yes, sir,' said Schulz, noticing that Neuheim had been awarded another Iron Cross and was sitting behind a desk that was large enough to store a small tank. Neuheim opened the case on his desk and then walked over to a safe which he also opened. It was stuffed full of notes.

'How much did you bring?'

'A million, sir.'

'Top quality?'

'First grade, Herr General.'

'Good, I'll need them.' He began to stack the notes in the safe. 'You've never been up here before, have you?'

'No, sir,' said Schulz. 'You seem to have everything very well organized, Herr General.'

Neuheim nodded with some satisfaction; the Fuhrer had promoted him to full general on the strength of it.

'It's the best day's work I ever did,' he agreed. 'It's amazing the things there are for sale in Europe at the moment. Do you know what that is?' He pointed to a small painting, newly framed, propped against a wall. 'A courier bought it for me in Milan.'

'A Canaletto, Herr General.'

Neuheim was slightly taken aback. Until the previous day, he himself had thought that Canaletto was tinned pasta.

'Yes,' he said. 'How did you know?'

'The style, sir,' said Schulz. 'It's unmistakable. Is it genuine?'

'Of course it's genuine! You don't think I'd buy a fake, do you? The courier's an expert on art.'

'It must have cost a fortune,' commented Schulz.

'Not really,' said Neuheim smugly. 'Ten thousand pounds. I'd say that was a bargain, wouldn't you?'

'Oh, yes, sir! Absolutely!' Schulz laughed. 'Especially as we make the money ourselves.'

Neuheim eyed him, a little disgruntled. He had genuinely forgotten for the moment that he had paid in fake money and considered it tasteless of Schulz to have brought the matter up. He continued putting away the money.

'How is everything at the Barracks?'

'Very good, sir,' replied Schulz. Gruber was apparently lost in contemplation of the secretary's shapely buttocks around which her tight-fitting dress seemed to have been sewn like a second skin. It was impossible to see how she managed to get in or out of it. 'We're producing about a million notes a week, cut and dried, that is,' Schulz went on, tearing his eyes off the secretary's behind. 'Half of those are top quality.'

'How would you like a trip out?'

'Out, sir?'

'To Yugoslavia? You speak Serbo-Croat, don't you?'

'Yes, sir.'

'I need someone to take a million pounds into Yugoslavia, buy up some arms and organize the shipment back here.'

Schulz swallowed hard. 'Did you say "a million pounds", Herr General?'

'That's right. There's a group of partisans here.' He tapped vaguely at the map, long enough for Schulz to note that it was not too far from the Adriatic coast. 'The British keep dropping them arms, though the partisans keep telling them they don't want any more and have all gone home.'

'It's the Anglo-Saxon mind, sir. If you try to cancel a magazine they keep sending it to you for weeks afterwards.'

Either Neuheim wasn't listening or chose to ignore this remark. It was as though he had deliberately cultivated such an ignorance about the British that he could no longer compute even the idea of them.

'Well,' he went on, 'this group has now accumulated so many arms they've offered them to us. Germany needs arms. The only courier I've got who speaks Serbo-Croat is away in Italy.'

Schulz stood stiffly to attention. 'I'd consider it an honour and a privilege, sir, to go on such an important mission.'

'Good,' said Neuheim and he smiled with benevolence. 'And you can take Gruber with you.'

Schulz's face fell.

'You'll leave in a couple of days,' continued Neuheim. 'I'll have all the travel documents ready by then. Well, go and get yourself a room and a meal. You'll find the food here is excellent. I should take advantage of it if I were you.'

Neuheim himself looked as though he had been taking advantage of that and a lot of other things for the last year. He was like a well-fed cat who no longer needed to chase mice to survive – which only made them more of a rich source of amusement. Schulz swore to himself at that moment that, one way or another, he would cease to be within clawing distance.

Schulz decided to turn in early after dinner and explore the Schloss Laber the following day.

Unfortunately by the time he woke next morning it was almost lunchtime, so he quickly headed for one of the several bars dotted about the castle. This one seemed to have been reserved for middle-ranking SS officers but though Schulz was only a corporal, no one was taking much notice of him. He ordered himself a Scotch and soda and then sat back listening to the mostly male company chatting around him. He caught snatches of conversation which were mostly about the attempts of Heinrich Muller and the Gestapo to foil Operation Bernhard. Indeed it seemed as though guards, officers and couriers alike feared the Gestapo's intervention far more than the possibility of any leaking to the British that German agents were being paid with counterfeit money.

Schulz ordered another Scotch. He was just thinking it was about time he had lunch when he felt a tap on his shoulder. Turning, he found himself face to face with Schumacher, fatter and sleeker and sporting a major's insignia.

'Hello, Schulz,' he grinned.

Schulz wondered what kind of doodlings could promote

one so rapidly up the ladder. Then he remembered that Schumacher was still working for Kube who, though previously Neuheim's deputy, had been on a par with him since the shutting down of Andreas.

'Well, Gerhardt,' Schumacher said, 'one of your chickens has come home to roost.'

'A fat lot of good it's done me, Albert,' Schulz replied. 'What are you doing here?'

'I commute occasionally from Berlin with Kube. It makes a change from the Salon Kitty, though.'

'You mean you're still in the boiler-room?' said Schulz looking at his stripes.

'Not exactly,' said Schumacher blandly. 'I'm more of a supervisor these days. I have to attend to the various needs of the girls as well. It's such a nuisance. It means I can't see enough of Johann.'

There was a silence while Schulz considered the irony of this. Another of his intuitions had apparently been proved correct. After the obligatory small talk he risked the question he was itching to ask.

'How's Fraulein Freyer?' he said casually. 'I don't suppose you see much of her nowadays?'

'No,' said Schumacher, looking perfectly disgusted.

He was about to say more on the subject when Kube suddenly appeared.

'Corporal Schulz? This bar is for senior officers only,' he said, escorting Schulz to the door without another word. At the door Schulz caught a glimpse of Schumacher still at the bar, talking to a good-looking young major. Johann, he thought.

The rest of the day Schulz wandered about the castle. The encounter had depressed him. How unfair that Schumacher had been elevated to a position where he might have been able to take advantage of such little luxuries as Bertha Freyer. He wondered what Schumacher had been going to tell him but he was nowhere to be found. Gruber too seemed to have disappeared and he himself would soon be on his way to Yugoslavia ... If only he could think of some way of getting rid of Gruber for good, the world could be his oyster. Gruber could hardly be drinking with the senior officers upstairs, but he certainly was not with the rank and file, the clerks, secretaries and telephone girls who floated around the bars and the ballroom. This was a small patch of floor where an orchestra pumped out the same sugary music that haunted the Salon Kitty, attempting to create the impression of a tinsel-sweet fairyland. It was no more than an illusion, and Schulz spent most of that evening getting quietly drunk, while he dreamed of what might have been and what could still be.

Then on his second day at the Schloss, something odd happened. He would catch glimpses of Neuheim's secretary at odd times in odd places, floating around the ends of corridors where the NCOs and other underlings were billeted. What made it odd was the frequency with which she appeared and disappeared. It was as though she were always hovering in his vicinity. When he went down to breakfast in the mess, she seemed to be gazing at him from the other side of the room. Later, when he went for a walk in the grounds, he caught yet another glimpse of her, wandering through the trees ahead of him. Was he imagining it?

He told Erhardt, the gum-chewing brute of a courier, about it, when he bumped into him in a bar.

'You're lucky,' said Erhardt. 'She never seems to notice me.'

Schulz found that difficult to believe because Erhardt was so big. But it was not, he decided, the physical but the mental that turned women on. Was it possible, that Neuheim had let slip to her that the whole idea of Bernhard had originated not with Kube but with Neuheim, no, not even with Neuheim but with Schulz. Who is this Schulz? the incredible secretary might have said. Oh, nobody in particular, Neuheim might have replied. You'd hardly notice him. Oh, but I'm intrigued, she might have protested, thinking to herself, with a mysterious smile on her lips, that a man who can conceive all this must be rather special ...

Schulz had never thought of himself as attractive physically, but he could imagine a beautiful woman like Neuheim's secretary growing tired of the constant attentions from handsome young SS officers without any brains or originality between them. After all, thought Schulz, the Fuhrer himself was not by any stretch of the imagination a handsome man, but women flocked to see him throughout the 1930s and there was no doubt that his presence, his mind, his genius, had a strong sexual magnetism which would attract women of all classes. All that he, Schulz, had hitherto lacked was success; it was the one ingredient that would be guaranteed to make women 'come across'. Bertha had said as much to him that night in the boiler-room at the Kitty, and the comtesse's reaction to his wealth had been instantaneous.

By the evening of the second day, however, Schulz had fallen into a mild depression again, as he sat alone in the bar. He had began to dream of Rembrandts and Canalettos and his own private chateau, when he suddenly felt the presence of a woman nearby. He turned round on his bar stool and Neuheim's secretary was standing a foot away from him, looking quizically at him through half-closed eyes.

'Hello?' she said in a voice that was low and husky. 'We meet again.' She took the empty seat next to him and gave him a ravishing smile. Schulz leaped off his stool and bowed stiffly and formally.

'Fraulein!' he said. Even seated she was taller than him, and his eyes were immediately accosted by an expanse of thigh, tantalizingly encased in black fishnet.

'What do you think of our little, old, fairy castle?' she murmured in a voice like syrup, with the trace of an American accent. She must be bored out of her mind by the brutish SS men she saw daily. Schulz's intuitions had been right all along.

'It's wonderful,' he said, feeling giddy at the smell of her perfume. 'May I offer you a drink. Fraulein?'

'Gertrude – Gertrude Steiner.'

'Gerhardt Schulz – at your service.' He gave another formal little bow and sat down again.

'How polite you are! I do like polite men. I'll have a Dubonnet.'

'A Dubonnet and a Schnapps,' Schulz said to the barman whose eyes were popping at the sight of Fraulein Steiner. She had somehow managed to change her tight-fitting dress of two days ago for one that was, if anything, even tighter. Schulz found it very hard to stop his hand shaking as he handed her her drink.

'I don't suppose you know anyone here?' She said, undressing him with her eyes as she had done previously.

Schulz decided that knowing Gruber and Schumacher was not particularly to his advantage.

'Not yet, Fraulein,' he said coyly.

She laughed.

'Lucky for me, then!' She sipped her Dubonnet without taking her eyes off his. 'Gertrude,' she added.

'Gertrude,' Schulz repeated, smiling. 'What a wonderful time you all have here,' he added.

'Oh, it's all right.' Again she half-closed her eyes. 'But I love meeting new people, don't you?'

'Some new people,' said Schulz, significantly.

'Oh, well – one should be discriminating, I agree. But then, when you've been here for a while you're just glad to meet anyone. It soon gets dull, you know.'

'Where would you like to be?'

'Oh, I don't know. Trieste? Do you know Trieste?'

'Before the war,' said Schulz, calculating busily. 'It was a gay spot.'

'It still is,' said Gertrude, again half-closing her eyelids and half raising pencil-fine, arched eyebrows that made her look even more like Marlene Dietrich at her most seductive. 'You can have a *wonderful* time in Trieste.' She shook her head. 'I certainly wish I were there now.' She opened her eyes wide and blazed them full on Schulz.

'As a matter of fact, Fraulein –'

'Gertrude.'

'Gertrude, then.' Schulz shifted uncomfortably. 'I'll be passing through it shortly.'

'Lucky you! I spent my last leave in Trieste. I had a *wonderful* time.' Out of the corner of his eye Schulz could see that she was slowly and rhythmically caressing her

219

thigh. She laughed huskily. 'You don't want a passenger, do you? No, I shouldn't ask that.' Her eyes smouldered. 'I just thought a few days in Trieste might be rather nice. It was only an impulse.' She smiled dreamily. 'I really am the most impulsive girl when you get to know me.' Her hand had miraculously moved to Schulz's thigh.

Schulz caught his breath and there was a slight pause. Schulz sipped his drink thoughtfully, trying not to be distracted by Gertrude's impulsive fingers.

'How would you explain your absence?' he said.

'Absence?' she said, withdrawing her hand and now letting it caress her other leg. 'Oh, that's no problem. I've got a few days' leave coming to me, I can take them when I like.' She laughed. 'But it's quite against the rules to give people lifts. I shouldn't *encourage* you. I'm liable to get you in the most *awful* trouble.'

'Oh, I've been in trouble before,' Schulz laughed. 'Trouble's no stranger to me.'

Gertrude was staring at him, suddenly serious. 'No, I'm sure it's not. You look like a man who's ... seen a lot.' She paused and lowered her eyes to her magnificent body. 'Well, I'm glad we've met, aren't you? Let me buy you a drink?'

'Absolutely not!' Schulz was playfully severe. 'The drinks are mine. Will you have the same?'

'Actually,' said Gertrude slowly, 'I've got a bottle of five-star Napoleon brandy in my room. Would you like to try it? You look like a man who knows his brandy.' Now she lowered her eyes to his body.

'In your room?' Schulz's heart was pounding.

'Why not?' said Gertrude. 'We're all free and easy here, you know.' She gazed at him for a moment. 'You know,' she added, 'you have the sexiest eyes of any man I've ever met.'

21

'What would you really like to do? If you had the chance?'

'Oh, go abroad, sit the war out in some gay place.' She put the bottle down and handed him a glass of brandy. 'Still – it's all dreams. To get away you'd need a lot of money and, if you're a girl, the right sort of man to go along with.' She laughed. 'That's a combination that's very hard to find. Take you, for instance. You'd be perfect – but you haven't got any more money than I have.'

She smiled brilliantly at him and slowly got up from the sofa, kicked off her shoes and, then, as if it were the most normal thing in the world, began to unhook her dress. Schulz sat watching her, stunned.

'I'm glad you came,' she went on. 'To be frank, people here are rather boring and terribly unsophisticated. The men especially.'

She had managed to peel herself out of the dress which now lay on the floor. Absently, Schulz picked it up, folding it neatly and laying it over a chair. Meanwhile Gertrude had flipped back the cover of her bed and slipped inside, pulling the sheet up to her chin. She started to wriggle out of the rest of her clothes, one by one.

'You can't have a serious conversation with any of them,' she remarked. 'They're only interested in one thing.'

Her naked arm emerged from under the sheet and dropped a fishnet stocking to the floor. Again Schulz stooped and picked it up, examining it professionally.

'One thing?' he repeated.

'Well, you know.' Another stocking floated out and Schulz stooped once more and picked it up. 'Of course, you're different, I can see that. One could talk to you about many things.'

Next came her suspender belt. Schulz took it from her and laid it neatly away with her other underwear.

'Books, for instance, music, theatre,' she went on. 'I'll bet you even like grand opera.'

'Yes, I do, as a matter of fact,' said Schulz, feeling rather pleased. 'Do you know *Travatore*?'

'Is it near Trieste?'

Schulz wondered if he had overestimated her intelligence.

A pair of French knickers appeared and floated down to the floor.

'Would you really like to go to Trieste?' Schulz said, staring at her.

'With *you*, oh yes! Anywhere! Of course, if we really had a lot of money – I mean, an awful lot, we could just take off for Switzerland.' She giggled. 'I'm terrible, aren't I? But to tell you the truth, you've rather bowled me over.'

Her brassière dropped from her well-manicured hand on to the floor and she lay back, pulling the sheet over her now-naked body and smiling brilliantly at him. He picked up the brassière thoughtfully, staring at it. He could still feel the warmth of her body in the thin material.

'As a matter of fact,' he said, 'I'll be carrying a lot of money.'

There was a slight pause.

'Really?' said Gertrude softly. 'It seems almost like Providence.'

'How would you get out? I mean, I couldn't be seen giving you a lift.'

'I'd just take the bus to the village but get off halfway and wait for you.' She stretched, languorously, exposing her naked white shoulders, and smiled at him. 'I told you I was impulsive.'

'The trouble is,' said Schulz, frowning, 'Gruber's coming with me. Do you know him? He's a last-ditch type – he'll never give you a lift.'

'Oh, I'll deal with Gruber,' said Gertrude. 'You can leave him to me. I'll let him think he's in for a night with me in Trieste on his way back. He'll agree like a shot.' She smiled and moved sensuously about under the sheet. 'Oh, this bed is so big and cold.'

222

Schulz moved towards her in a trance and pressed his lips against her naked shoulder, while she stroked his head. His mind was whirling. He could feel power coursing through his veins once again. What money couldn't buy!

'We'll have to dump him on the way,' he said breathlessly.

'Of course,' she breathed into his ear.

'Up in the mountains,' he moaned.

'Right – so it takes him a long time to walk home,' she sighed.

'You're wonderful,' he gasped.

'So are you,' she whispered. 'What do you think – shall we leave this mad world behind us, risk everything and escape from it all?'

'Yes, yes!' he said hoarsely. 'Let's do it, shall we?' He was shaking all over.

'All right – you've persuaded me,' she said dreamily. 'You're an amazing man. I'll get some sleep now. Put the light off as you go out of the door.'

For the next two days Schulz seethed with impatience. He met Gertrude several times and the promise of paradise was ever present in her smile and talk. Whenever he saw Gruber in the corridor, he couldn't help feeling a little sorry for him, and made up his mind to set aside a small sum for Gruber's enjoyment after the war – if he survived, that was. When Schulz went into Neuheim's office to check the details of the trip, Gertrude mouthed two words at him on the way out: 'It's fixed.'

Sure enough, later that afternoon, Gruber came to his room, looking a bit shamefaced.

'Look, I know it's against the rules and regulations,' said Gruber, 'but would you mind if we took my girlfriend and dropped her off at Trieste for a couple of days? We could pick her up on the way back?'

'Well, it's strictly against rules, Gruber,' said Schulz, 'but all right. I know how it is. She's probably pining for the bright lights.'

223

Gruber seemed mightily relieved. 'I thought you were one of those fanatical SS men,' he said.

They picked up Gertrude about five miles outside the Schloss. She was waiting by the bus stop in the village and at first she didn't see them. Schulz jumped out of the car and went over to her, taking her suitcase.

'We'll have to ditch Gruber,' he reminded her in a whisper.

'I'll tell you when,' she said.

Schulz opened the car door. 'Allow me,' he said.

'Thank you,' she returned, smiling. She quickly winked at him and climbed in the front seat next to Gruber. Schulz got in the back.

'Schulz here is a friend,' said Gruber.

They drove on into the Alps, saying little. Gruber had to concentrate on his driving as they wound round the narrow mountain roads, sometimes passing small convoys. Even so, he was more talkative than on the journey to Merano. Schulz, in the rear, fingered the revolver in his pocket. One million pounds of perfect English fivers rode in the boot. Every now and then, Gertrude would turn round and wink at Schulz, but he didn't dare wink back in case Gruber should see him in the mirror. He did, however, allow himself a quiet smile of satisfaction. Poor Gruber. He wouldn't know what hit him.

At one point, it seemed such a good spot to dump Gruber that he actually drew the revolver from his pocket and pointed it at Gruber's back, but Gertrude shook her head warningly and he put it away quietly. She rewarded him with a wide, warm, reassuring smile and another wink.

They were now deep into the Alps and miles from anywhere. Schulz was beginning to get anxious. Surreptitiously he again half drew the revolver out of his pocket.

'Cigarette?' Gertrude suddenly said.

Schulz looked up. She was holding out a packet of cigarettes to him. He let the gun fall back into his pocket and took a cigarette.

'Light?' she added.

Schulz leaned forward to take a light. It was the biggest lighter he had ever seen. In fact it was not a lighter at all: it was a Mauser and Gertrude's delicious fingers were wound round it and it was pointing straight at him.

The car's brakes squealed.

'What's going on?' said Schulz.

'You're not for one,' said Gruber. 'Out!'

He gave a grunt like a pig and brought the car to a skidding halt.

'Out? Out where?' squeaked Schulz.

'Out!'

Gruber had got down from the front of the car, drawing his own Luger and opening the door for Schulz who still sat there in utter disbelief. He looked at Gertrude and pointed at Gruber.

'But it's him who ... ?'

She shook her head slowly and a little sadly.

'In love,' she said, 'you have to wait for the right moment and the right man.'

'But ... Gruber ... !' Schulz's horror almost superseded his terror.

'Out!' repeated Gruber.

'It was always him,' said Gertrude. 'We've been planning this for weeks. Schmidt would never have fallen for it, darling.'

'Don't Darling him. Out!' said Gruber, pulling Schulz's gun out of his pocket and throwing it away down the mountainside. He held out his hand.

'The key to the suitcase!'

'Oh, come on, Gruber!' Schulz was trembling uncontrollably. Then something snapped inside him. 'THAT MONEY'S MINE! I MADE IT!' he screamed.

Gruber didn't answer. He just waited implacably. Finally Schulz dug in his pocket and resignedly took out the key. Gruber snatched it and waved his gun.

'Start walking.'

Schulz looked beseechingly at Gertrude who blew him a kiss. Gruber got back in the car.

Schulz watched the car disappearing into the mountains with Gertrude and all the money. Dusk was gathering. Disconsolately, he pushed his hands into his pockets and trudged down the road, a solitary figure on the mountainside.

'Go on,' snapped Neuheim. He was standing in his office with the Canaletto in his hand, looking for a place to hang it while at the same time listening to Schulz's story. Schulz hesitated.

It had taken him nearly eight hours to get out of the mountains. Finally he reached a cluster of buildings which turned out to be a military police barracks. Foolishly Schulz had asked them to get him back to Merano, but the commander wanted nothing to do with the SS and sent him under guard to the headquarters at Trento in Italy. The officer there didn't want to get involved in SS business either and rang the Gestapo in Munchen. Fortunately before the Gestapo could arrive – and the prospects of being caught by the Gestapo were now more sinister to Schulz than being caught by the British – he had been mysteriously whisked back to Merano by two SS guards who had said nothing on the journey back.

Neuheim paused from placing his Canaletto and swung round to fix Schulz with his eye. 'Go on,' he repeated.

'Then Gruber stopped the car and pulled a gun on me. He ordered me out and took the keys to the suitcase. Then he drove off again, Herr General.'

'And where do you think Gruber is now?'

'I don't know, Herr General. He's probably slipped across the border into Switzerland where he'll just drop out of sight.'

'You think so?'

'I do, sir – though I sincerely hope we catch him. He deserves to be shot.'

Neuheim smiled at Schulz. 'But we *have* caught him. And he has been shot.'

There was a stunned silence. Schulz paled visibly.

'Caught him, sir? Shot.'

'Not by us,' said Neuheim, returning to his Canaletto. 'He was stopped by the Italian police and – would you believe it? – elected to shoot it out.' He smiled again. 'He lost the election.'

And Gertrude? thought Schulz, waiting for the inevitable.

'One thing you omitted to mention in your story was that my secretary, Fräulein Steiner, was in the car with him. She works for me, of course. You don't think a beautiful, intelligent woman like Fräulein Steiner would stoop to anything so disgusting as theft, do you? Two birds with one stone, Schulz, two birds with one stone.'

Schulz gasped. Then Neuheim had been behind the whole thing. At least, he consoled himself, she had had more taste than to go off with a thick-headed SS thug like Gruber.

'In that case, sir, I suppose you know everything?' he said, faltering.

Neuheim put his nose an inch from Schulz's.

'Everything!' he bawled. 'YOU ARE A TOTALLY CORRUPT HUMAN BEING! SHIFTY, SLIMY AND SLY! All you've ever thought about is lining your own pockets and, by thunder, you'll pay for it! Guard! Guard!'

The door opened and a weasel-faced SS guard entered.

'This man is under arrest!' screamed Neuheim. 'Take him to the guardhouse!'

'Yes, Herr General!' The guard turned to Schulz. '*Achtung!* Quick march!'

Neuheim scratched his head. He still couldn't decide where to hang the Canaletto.

Neuheim had not allowed Schulz to fall into Gestapo hands: that would have been disastrous. There was no telling what Schulz might have blabbered about the formation and running of Operation Bernhard. On the other hand he was not inclined to have him shot. Schulz was far too useful to him.

Instead Schulz was courtmartialled for the first time in

his military career. The president of the courtmartial had probably been a headmaster in civilian life. He was morally upright, correct to the last detail, and unbelievably pompous.

'I find no extenuating circumstances,' he told Schulz who stood before him flanked by SS guards. 'You fell from the very high standards of personal conduct set everywhere by the SS and abused a position of trust ...'

Schulz blinked glumly.

'... While all around you worked selflessly for nation, party and Fuhrer, giving no thought to themselves, you thought only of personal gain. I have no hesitation in sentencing you to three years in a labour camp where I sincerely hope some effort will be made in the direction of your personal and political regeneration ...'

22

The tide of war had turned. The Afrika Korps had been defeated at El Alamein, the Sixth Army at Stalingrad; Cologne, Hamburg, the Ruhr, Berlin itself, had been heavily bombed; the Allied armies were pouring through Europe towards Germany – despite the rantings and ravings of the Party leaders the situation was becoming clear to everyone. The Fuhrer's thousand-year Reich would be lucky if it lasted even twelve.

Schulz was not much concerned with the outcome, since he could never see why Germany had gone to war in the first place. He was far more tormented with the thought of all the money that was still being manufactured at Barracks 19, all the Canalettos being brought to the Schloss Laber, and all the women upon whom the money was being lavished. While he, the man who had invented the whole idea, was behind barbed wire, grateful, it is true, for not having been shot but so utterly depressed that he sometimes cried out aloud in the night.

Ebensee, on the River Traun near Salzburg, was a transit camp. There were a few local quarries where the prisoners were set to work, but it was not too strenuous and because Schulz was still officially in the SS he was treated fairly well. By the personal orders of the Fuhrer, no one who was party to any secret was to be put at risk of being captured and interrogated, so in a strange way Schulz's knowledge of Operation Bernhard served as a kind of lifebelt.

He had been at Ebensee for twenty-seven months when a convoy of army lorries, followed by a huge staff car, drove through the gates and halted beside a row of empty huts. Schulz, among a squad of prisoners, digging a row of latrines as inefficiently as they could without drawing attention to themselves, seized the opportunity to down tools and watch. SS guards from the convoy took up positions round the vehicles, while from the last truck in line a number of prisoners jumped out. Schulz thought there was something familiar about one of them. Then his mouth fell open in astonishment.

'So this is where they sent you,' said Solly.

'They send me this one and they send me that one, a few hundred here, a few hundred there. "Don't worry, Globke will find room for them!"' The camp commandant was looking most unhappy as he watched Neuheim unpacking crates of personal belongings and files, aided by his driver who kept on bringing in more. 'Doesn't matter if I have to double up prisoners already doubled up or cut everybody's rations by ten per cent,' Globke grumbled on. 'Just send them, then they'll be Globke's problem.'

'My dear Globke,' said Neuheim who was looking for somewhere to hang his Canalettos, 'I understand your problems but I've got problems of my own.'

'Who are these prisoners, anyway?' said Globke sourly. 'They look different. What's in all the crates you brought?'

'Special equipment,' said Neuheim airily. 'The prisoners are special, too, they'll stay under my command. Here are the papers. We're a special unit of SS Counter-Espionage and as such you needn't regard us as part of the camp.'

'Except for food and facilities, I suppose? What exactly will you be doing here?'

'Making money,' replied Neuheim loftily. 'English money to be precise, and very good English money, too.'

Globke stared at him. 'You mean you're forging it?'

'Exactly. Those men out there are all skilled professionals.'

'What a dirty business war is.' Globke looked genuinely shocked. What would have shocked him much more, if it had occurred to him to ask, was why the operation had been moved to Ebensee.

The money that constantly rolled off the presses in Barracks 19 with such ease and in such quantities had started to become a threat to the stability of the European economy, as Dr Funk at the Ministry of Economy had predicted. Now it threatened the Nazis as much as anyone. The SS had found it almost impossible to resist temptation. Neuheim had been threatened with a transfer to the Russian front unless he put a stop to the corruption, but he had found that whoever he employed to check the output of notes, sooner or later was found to be involved in sidetracking them.

As things went from bad to worse in Germany, the corruption spread like a cancer. SS generals were still constantly requisitioning vast sums, on all sorts of trumped-up excuses which Neuheim could not prevent, and it was clear that they were salting away the money against the certainty of German defeat. Constant complaints now flowed back from the Schloss Laber that there were cash shortages in all moneys being delivered, and that the shortages must originate from the camp. Neuheim was ordered either to plug the holes or move the operation to a safer place. He chose the latter course.

Ebensee had finally been selected because it was spacious and, perhaps more important, its situation was ideal. The new quarters for Operation Bernhard within the camp complex included an approach leading to huge caves cut into the granite slopes of a mountain. It was here that the printing presses were to be installed. Neuheim had every intention of also using the caves to store his own personal fortune before Operation Bernhard disintegrated altogether. Kube had already disappeared on the journey south and Neuheim was now totally in control.

'Whose idea was all this?' said the camp commandant when he had recovered from the shock.

'As a matter of fact, it was mine but I was given a few tips by a brilliant little clerk who used to work for me,' said Neuheim offhandedly and remarkably generously.

'Where is he now?' asked Globke.

'In a labour camp somewhere,' replied Neuheim. 'He was caught trying to steal a million and sentenced to three years.' He suddenly grew nostalgic. 'What a character!' he said wistfully. 'A brilliant fellow, full of ideas, one of the great unsung geniuses of the war, a man so full of –'

He stopped abruptly. He had turned and found himself looking straight at Schulz who had been standing in the doorway listening to this unexpected eulogy.

'You . . . !' he gasped.

'You know this prisoner?' said Globke in surprise.

'Certainly!' said Neuheim. 'That's the crook I was telling you about. What the devil are you doing here?' he added to Schulz.

'They sent me here, sir. I've been here over two years.'

'Well, I'll leave you to it,' said Globke impatiently to Neuheim. 'If there's anything at all you need, please don't ask me, I haven't got it.'

He slammed the door behind him. Neuheim and Schulz stared at each other.

'Well, well!' said Neuheim cheerfully. 'Fancy you turning up here! You've lost weight.'

'Yes, sir,' said Schulz cautiously. 'Well, it's not exactly a holiday camp.'

'No, I can see that. Don't think I haven't thought a great deal about you, Schulz, because I haven't.' He returned to his unpacking. 'What do you want?'

'My sentence will be finished in a few months, sir. I'd like a chance to redeem myself. I'd like the privilege of

231

rejoining your staff.'

'Quite out of the question, Schulz. You are, let me remind you, a traitor to the Third Reich. We are surrounded by traitors these days.' He was carefully unpacking a Rembrandt.

Schulz tried again. 'What's needed, sir, is someone who has everything to gain in being honest, and nothing to lose.'

'Fool!' Neuheim swung round, eyeing him evilly. 'Nobody gains by being honest.'

'A prisoner would,' replied Schulz. 'I would.'

'I'm sure you would. What you really mean is you'd like to get near those notes again.'

'Oh, no, sir. I've learned my lesson,' said Schulz meekly.

'And so have I,' replied Neuheim grimly.

'I thought you might need a clerk, sir. They're very short-staffed here and you don't seem to have brought one with you.'

'My driver's my clerk, Schulz, I don't need you. But don't worry, you'll get your chance to redeem yourself when you leave here – at the Russian front.'

Schulz left the office more depressed than ever, while Neuheim looked round for a place to hang his Rembrandt.

Schulz knew that once Neuheim had registered his presence he would soon find a use for him. It was simply a question of speeding up the moment of realization.

One day, about a week later, Schulz happened to pass Neuheim's car parked in the camp grounds. The driver had jacked it up, having taken off the front wheel, and was underneath it, hammering away at something. Schulz walked past the car and then paused as a soldier emerged from a nearby door and got into an army truck parked in front of Neuheim's. The truck was a winching vehicle and the hooks were hanging down.

Schulz looked at the jack holding up Neuheim's car and the feet of the driver sticking out. He glanced round. No one was about. He took the hook, stooped quickly and slipped it round the jack. Then he walked on.

232

As he passed the army truck he heard its engine start and the gears engaging. Despite himself, he screwed up his face in a grimace of vicarious pain as he anticipated what was to come.

The truck started and almost at once there was a grinding, metallic sound followed by a piercing, heart-rending howl of agony.

'...Lastly, in view of the rapidly deteriorating situation and the proximity of allied armies necessitating the possibility of another move I shall wait for the situation to stabilize itself before starting up production again.'

Neuheim stopped pacing up and down. 'Get that typed up and give it to the dispatch rider when he comes,' he told his secretary. 'Mark it "secret".'

'Yes, sir,' replied Schulz.

'Did you enquire after my driver?'

'Yes, Herr General. I phoned the hospital, sir. He's as well as can be expected – considering his leg's broken and he's got a dislocated hip.'

Neuheim shook his head. 'I don't understand it,' he grunted. 'He was never that careless before.'

'It needs just a moment's lapse of concentration, sir,' said Schulz impassively.

'Yes-s-s-s.' Neuheim eyed Schulz for a moment with just a glimmer of suspicion. 'All the same, it was an extraordinary coincidence.'

'Sir?'

'Him having that accident, wouldn't you say?'

'Amazing, sir. And very fortunate, too, that I was here to take over. Will that be all, Herr General?'

Three weeks after Operation Bernhard moved to Ebensee, Adolf Hitler, with his world collapsing about him, decided to proclaim his 'Scorched Earth' policy, telling Speer, when he protested:

'If the war is lost, the German nation will also perish.

233

This fate is inevitable. There is no need to take into consideration the basic requirements of the people for continuing even a most primitive existence ... Those who will remain after the battle are those who are inferior; for the good will have fallen.'

Among those who had made up their mind to remain inferior and alive was Gerhardt Schulz. As the last titanic struggle took place Schulz was becoming ever more hopeful, but, at the same time, desperate. The prospect of getting his hands on the millions of fivers which had eluded him for five years was once more becoming feasible. He was sitting outside the huts in a pool of March sunshine while the other prisoners gathered round the radio listening to the gloomy newscast.

'... the German High Command announced that after fierce fighting German troops have withdrawn from Mannheim which is now occupied by the Americans. Fierce fighting continues along the front. In East Prussia, Russian troops are said to be regrouping for a major assault ...'

Solly wandered out to join Schulz. 'The Americans are beyond Frankfurt and the Russians are preparing a final assault,' he said quietly.

Schulz nodded. 'The war won't last long,' he said anxiously.

'What's going to happen here?' said Solly.

'I don't know,' Schulz replied and sank into a preoccupied silence. Suddenly he broke it. '*Where's* the money, Solly, what has he done with it? You brought all the equipment from the camp and Neuheim closed the castle down, so what has he done with all the money that was printed and never spent?'

Solly sighed. 'The whole world's collapsing and all you think about is the money –'

'Oh, to hell with the world!' Schulz broke in impatiently. 'The world's getting what it deserves. The point is the war's going to end soon and when it does the chance of getting any of that money will be gone for ever!'

'Is that all the end of the war means to you – the end of the money?' said Solly, exasperated. 'Have you thought

234

what might happen to *us* when the SS realize the war is lost?'

Schulz stared at him, stunned. The thought had gone completely from his mind and Solly could see that it had.

'I dread the end of the war,' he went on. 'I've been dreading it for weeks and so has everyone in Hut Seven.'

Schulz wasn't listening: he was again deep in thought.

'Solly,' he finally said, 'I'll make a bargain with you. If I can persuade Neuheim to carry on with the operation and you can increase your production by two notes in every hundred, we can split the proceeds fifty-fifty. What the accountants don't see they'll never miss. As for what will happen to us – what have you got to lose?'

For once Solly had no answer.

'Trust me, Solly,' Schulz pleaded.

'You're a fool, Gerhardt,' said Solly, but he agreed to go along with him.

'You're a fool Schulz,' barked Neuheim.

'The situation is getting desperate, Herr General,' said Schulz with passion. 'We have the men, the machinery and the experience. And as you know, sir, the orders are still flooding in.'

It was true, Neuheim had to admit. SS generals were still demanding cases of Bernhard money and Goebbels himself was still putting in his special order for anti-British propaganda stamps, giving Stalin and George VI Jewish noses. If they were going to print worthless stamps at this stage of the war they might as well do some real fiddling while Berlin burnt, and carry on printing money.

'All right, Schulz,' said Neuheim finally. 'But if I discover that a single five-pound note goes missing, you will be sent straight to the front line where you belong and this time I mean it. Plug the holes or a hole will be plugged in you.'

So Operation Bernhard slowly ground back into action in the first week of April 1945. In the end Solly was confined to producing the special propaganda stamps, as he had been doing for the past two years. Schulz did however manage to persuade another printer to produce the extra notes and within less than a month he had stacked away £50,000 under his mattress. Neuheim had even recommended him for promotion to Senior Private.

Things were thus going extremely well for Schulz, who was again dreaming of a life of post-war ease, but very badly for Germany. Schulz's only fear now was that the crumbling fronts would cave in altogether before he had had time to gather a nest egg worthy to carry back to Berlin and present to Bertha Freyer.

'Schnapps or Vodka?' said Neuheim, as unctuous as a bartender.

'Vodka,' snapped Kaltenbrunner. 'We may as well drink it while we've got it.' He looked tired and dispirited but he was no less direct and brutal than usual. Ash dropped from the cigarette that permanently hung from his thin lips.

'The news is bad? Very bad?' Neuheim was treating the head of the security services with the deference he would give to an unexploded bomb.

'I have to tell you that if you're expecting last-minute miracles there won't be any. It's all over – in two weeks at most. Where's Globke?'

'He went over to Landsberg to quarrel with the camp commandant,' said Neuheim lightly, hoping that Kaltenbrunner would find this amusing. 'He keeps sending Globke prisoners and claiming he's got no room for them.'

Kaltenbrunner frowned. 'Well, all that doesn't matter any more.' He raised his glass. 'Your health – what's left of it.'

Neuheim choked a little but managed a smile. 'And yours, Herr Oberst!' he grinned and bowed low. They drank.

'This forgery operation – I understand you packed up £500 million in bales and brought them with you?'

'That's correct,' said Neuheim a little smugly. 'They're locked up under guard at the railway station. No one, apart from me, knows what's in them.'

Kaltenbrunner nodded and lit another cigarette. He was

smoking two at the same time.

'I'll tell you what's been decided. Colonel Skorzeny is making a last-ditch stand up in the Austrian Alps. The money is to be taken up to him to help finance his resistance. Now, your forgery operation must be disbanded at once and all traces of it, destroyed,' he went on. 'It's vital that the Allies learn nothing about it. The decision is that you will take the machinery and equipment with you and dump the lot in the lakes up there.'

'Of course, Herr Oberst, an excellent idea,' agreed Neuheim smoothly.

Neither of them heard Schulz entering the outer office.

'What do I do with my team?' added Neuheim as blandly as before.

'The prisoners? They must be liquidated,' replied Kaltenbrunner without expression. 'We can't risk them falling alive into enemy hands.' He helped himself to more vodka.

'Then I'll need your signed orders to that effect to pass on to Globke when he returns.'

'Very well,' snapped Kaltenbrunner. He turned to the open door of the office and spotted Schulz standing as if in a frozen trance. 'Is that your clerk?'

'Yes, Herr Oberst,' said Neuheim apologetically.

'Take this down,' Kaltenbrunner called to Schulz.

Schulz put a sheet of paper in his machine, his heart beating madly. The SS chief dictated from the open door.

' "To Camp Commandant Standartenfuhrer Globke, Muhldorf Camp, 17 April 1945. In view of the worsening military situation and the need to maintain strict secrecy concerning the activities of those prisoners under the command of General Neuheim, all steps will be taken to ensure that under no circumstances will they be allowed to fall alive into enemy hands." Signed : Kaltenbrunner, Oberstgruppenfuhrer, Head of Reich Security Service.'

He waited. Schulz finally ripped the sheet out of the typewriter and handed it smartly to him. Kaltenbrunner signed it, giving it to Neuheim who folded it and put it in his pocket.

'Well, I'll be on my way back to Berlin,' said Kalten-

237

brunner, 'What's left of it.'

A look of deep concern crossed Neuheim's face. 'How *is* the Fuhrer?' he asked with feeling. 'How does he feel?'

'Terrible,' replied Kaltenbrunner, shaking his head. 'How would you feel? He's determined not to survive the war – and I've decided to share his fate in the Bunker.'

Neuheim was genuinely moved. 'This is a great moment in history, Herr Oberst.'

'*I* certainly shan't forget it, I can tell you that,' snarled Kaltenbrunner savagely. 'By the way –' he closed the door to Schulz's office and lowered his voice '– I'm – a little short of cash ...'

'Of course, Herr Oberst, allow me,' said Neuheim obsequiously, reaching for his wallet.

'No, no – I think British currency might be more useful from now on.'

23

'I not only saw them, I typed them!' Schulz hissed. 'And Kaltenbrunner signed them! And Globke will carry them out!'

He and Solly were sitting in a corner of Hut Seven and Schulz's urgency was beginning to get through to Solly who was now nodding slowly.

'You've got to get out of here, all of you!' added Schulz.

'What do we do, blast our way out?' Solly laughed and shook his head. 'No – we'll wait.'

'For what – a bullet in the head?'

'Your way's no better,' said Solly quietly and calmly. 'I told you once before, if I'm going to die I'd like someone else to be responsible.' He noticed Schulz's sceptical face and shook his head again. 'Look, there's no way out of here alive. I've known that for some time, so have the rest of us. Either we throw ourselves at the gates or just wait – it's

238

all going to come to the same thing. And in the end, it's better just to wait.'

He glanced over at two SS guards sitting at the other end of the hut, casually reading the paper, then turned back to Schulz.

'Save yourself,' he added. 'In a short while, that uniform won't be too popular with a lot of people.'

'I suppose you're wondering, Neuheim, what possible use I could have for British currency in the Bunker in Berlin?' said Kaltenbrunner, as they emerged from the railway shed. A cigarette drooped as ever from his lips. Neuheim relocked the door, once more noting wistfully that the pyramid of waterproofed bales had been reduced considerably in height.

'It – had crossed my mind, Herr Oberstgruppenfuhrer,' he said respectfully, as they walked back to the car.

'The answer's quite simple. It's none of your damned business what I want it for.' He climbed into the car throwing two heavy suitcases in beside him and snapped at the driver 'Drive on.'

Neuheim watched the car disappear north towards Berlin, admiringly. Then he went to the boot of his own car, opened it, and pulled out two suitcases of his own. He marched determinedly back into the shed, closing the door behind him.

An hour later Neuheim burst into the office in a great hurry, carrying the suitcases and looking like a carpetbagger about to make a fast exit.

'Come in here!' he snapped.

Schulz rose and followed him into his office. Neuheim had put one suitcase on the floor and the other, which he was now opening, on the desk. The contents were carefully covered over with a white cloth, but Schulz had no doubts about what they were. Neuheim seemed to have been drinking. He was unusually talkative and he was going through cupboards and drawers, taking out personal items and throwing them into what space was left in the open suitcase.

'Schulz, the war's over. For the moment, Germany's finished. The German people have proved utterly unworthy of the Fuhrer.' Neuheim was almost singing.

'He was always too good for them, sir, they never deserved him,' said Schulz.

'Ungrateful swine! However, Colonel Skorzeny is making a last ditch stand up in the Alps and I've got a task for you. In a shed in the railway yards are a number of waterproof bales. They contain top-secret Intelligence files vital if Germany is to rise again. I want you to take them in a truck up to Skorzeny.'

'Yes, sir,' said Schulz, trying to conceal his rising excitement.

Neuheim had a Canaletto in one hand and was studying a signed and framed picture of the Fuhrer in the other, unable to make up his mind which to keep. Finally, he dumped the Fuhrer into the waste bin and the Canaletto into his case.

'Skorzeny is about here –' he tapped the wall map, 'forty miles south-west of here on the River Enns. You will also take all the counterfeiting equipment and dump it in one of the lakes. It's vital that we destroy all traces of this operation.'

'Yes, sir.'

'I need hardly tell you that the British won't take kindly to those who tampered with their currency.' Neuheim had, by now, thrown so much stuff into the suitcase that he was having difficulty closing it. 'Of course,' he went on, 'that doesn't affect me because I've decided to join the Fuhrer in his bunker. He's determined not to survive the war and neither shall I.'

He had managed to get the locks closed and lifted the case off the desk. The locks flew open again and the lid fell down, spilling the contents, including all the money. There was a stony silence. Neuheim looked momentarily embarrassed, then feverishly began scooping everything

240

back into the case while Schulz stooped down to help him. Their eyes met for a second.

'I need another bag,' barked Neuheim.

He got up and crossed the office to fetch a haversack that was hanging on a peg. Quick as a flash, Schulz scooped up a pile of notes and dumped them in the waste-paper bin. Moments later, Neuheim returned and between them they stuffed as much as they could into the case and what was left over into the haversack. This time the case locked.

They stood up and again their eyes met.

'I suppose you're wondering, Schulz, what possible use British currency will be to me in the Bunker?'

'It's none of my damned business, sir!' said Schulz, standing smartly to attention.

'You're damned right it's none of your business,' replied Neuheim grimly. 'And just remember that. Oh,' he added, pulling a folded sheet of paper from his pocket, 'here are the orders relating to the prisoners. See that *Standartenführer* Globke gets them on his return.'

'Yes, sir,' said Schulz, pocketing it. Neuheim, about to leave, paused and looked round the room and then affectedly at Schulz – conscious, suddenly, of the greatness of the hour.

'The Third Reich was a glorious adventure, Schulz.'

'Yes, sir.'

'Germany may be on the point of collapse, but it will rise again while there are men like us to make heroic sacrifices.'

'Yes, sir.'

Neuheim paused: he couldn't think of anything more to say.

'It was good while it lasted,' he finished lamely.

'It was a whole lot of fun, sir,' said Schulz reassuringly. 'It really was. People will miss it.'

Neuheim nodded sadly and then, perhaps thinking of the money in his cases, he seemed to brighten, giving Schulz a quick, brave smile before going out.

Schulz immediately leapt to the waste bin and pulled out the wads of notes, feverishly stuffing them into his pockets

241

while he calculated their probable value. Then there was the money underneath the mattress. This could quite conceivably double his wealth. And of course there were the waterproof bales in the railway sheds: even with his suitcases stuffed to overflowing, Neuheim quite obviously would not have been able to take away all the money. There could be a fortune waiting for him ... Suddenly his attention was drawn to the orders that Neuheim had given him, and which were still in his pocket. He frowned.

'I'm to give them to Globke when he gets back,' said Schulz quietly to Solly who was looking at Kaltenbrunner's signed orders. 'I thought I might give him these instead.' He handed Solly another apparently identical sheet of paper which Solly began to read.

'But these aren't signed,' said Solly, looking from the typed sheet to Schulz.

'I know. I've just written them. You sign them.'

'Me?'

'You've forged a signature before, haven't you? Forge his.'

Solly gazed at him for a moment, then looked across at the card-playing guards. There was a desultory air in the hut: everyone was waiting for something to happen.

Solly made up his mind. 'Get me a pen and ink,' he said, smiling for once.

'Oberstgruppenfuhrer Kaltenbrunner was *here*?'

'Yes, sir,' said Schulz impassively.

Globke was in a very bad temper. He held a torn-open envelope and a sheet of paper. 'Couldn't he have waited?' he said fussily. 'Everybody's in such a hurry! Where is General Neuheim?'

'Gone, Herr Standartenfuhrer.'

'Scuttled, I suppose!' Globke said scornfully. 'Run off! By thunder, the Fuhrer knows who his friends are now.'

'General Neuheim, sir, has gone to Berlin to join the

Fuhrer in his Bunker,' said Schulz stiffly.

Globke was taken aback. 'Really?' he said. 'Well, well, perhaps I spoke hastily.' He examined the sheet of paper in his hand once more. 'Well, here are your orders. You will carry them out to the letter!'

'Sir!' replied Schulz, springing to attention.

'You will take all the prisoners in Hut Seven,' Globke read out, 'remove all the machinery from the cave and the secret files at present stored in a shed at the railway yards, and proceed to the general area of Radstadt where you will report to Colonel Skorzeny in the redoubt. Map references are given. There you will set up the presses and begin printing money for use by the forces of the resistance.'

They were on the move within an hour. They drove in convoy, and the moment they left the camp it was obvious that the roads were in a terrible state. Bombing had started in the area, and bunches of soldiers who had lost their units, and escaped prisoners from neighbouring camps, were wandering about aimlessly. The convoy averaged no more than fifteen miles an hour.

In the cabin of the front truck sat Schulz next to the driver who, in spite of his tough appearance, seemed to be in a nervous panic and frequently wiped his sweaty brow with a dirty handkerchief. Between Schulz's knees lay his haversack, containing a few personal belongings carefully concealing the fifty thousand pounds from his mattress and the wads of notes he had retrieved from the waste-paper bin. Neuheim's dispatch case containing the sealed orders was chained to his wrist. Behind them trundled lorries, trailers and a van, containing prisoners, machinery, and the still unopened waterproof bales.

After driving for nearly three hours they were approaching a sharp bend in the steep mountain road, when Schulz turned to the driver.

'I think we should stop here for five minutes,' he said.

The trucks slowly came to a halt. Schulz and the other drivers and co-drivers jumped down. While the drivers went to the side of the road to relieve themselves, Schulz approached the two guards in the back of the prisoners' truck.

'You go,' he said. 'I'll watch these.'

The guards jumped down, clutching their submachine guns, and joined the others at the side of the road. Schulz looked up and caught Solly's eye. They nodded to each other.

'Don't shoot, don't shoot, they'll kill me!' Schulz's voice rang out suddenly. 'Don't shoot!'

The guards spun round and stopped dead, some with their flies still open.

Solly had Schulz's head in a vicious-looking arm lock, and was pointing Schulz's gun, straight at his head.

'If you move we'll kill him!' shouted Solly, sounding unusually desperate.

'Do as he says,' screamed Schulz, rolling his eyes. 'They'll kill me!'

No one moved. Then one of the prisoners jumped down and ran round to the driving cabin. He climbed in and the engine burst into life; the truck pulled out of line and shot forward. Solly let Schulz go.

Schulz dived to the ground as those guards with guns handy fired a fusillade of bullets. But the truck had disappeared around the bend. Schulz had kept his side of the bargain.

The drivers and guards rushed back to their trucks.

'Wait a minute, wait a minute!' shouted Schulz in alarm. 'Where are you going?'

'After them!' screamed a guard.

'What's the point?' shouted Schulz. The guards paused. 'You won't get them back without a struggle and they're no use to us dead.'

'No, but we can get the bastards!' screamed another guard.

'And maybe they'll get one of us,' persisted Schulz. 'Look, who are we kidding, fellows? The war's over, nothing we can do will change it. Do you know how lucky we are to have survived this long? What's the point of getting killed now?'

'You swine!' spat the guard. 'You did it deliberately! You let them go!' He swung round at Schulz but his companion pushed the gun down and a burst of bullets buried itself in the earth.

'He's right,' said the second guard. 'The war's over! Let's go home! He threw the gun over the cliff and his own after it. Then he pointed at the trucks. 'What do we do with these?'

'I've got strict instructions,' Schulz declared firmly. 'Nothing must fall into enemy hands. We must find somewhere to dump the equipment.'

It would just be a question of waiting for the right moment he reflected. While the guards were dealing with the machinery, he could simply melt away with some of the bales.

'All right,' the more voluble of the guards conceded. 'Let's get started.'

Lake Toplitz was shrouded in mist. Over the neck of the narrow end of the lake was a high bridge. A gravel road ran down to it leading to a long wooden pier jutting out into the lake.

They drove the lorries along the pier. The first few trucks were driven straight in, the drivers jumping out before they reached the end. After eight lorries had been disposed of the pier started to collapse. After that the heavy crates were manhandled into boats which dropped them into deep water.

Schulz watched the lorries disappear one by one with a mixture of relief that he was no longer to be hampered by the cumbersome disposal operation, and regret that each disappearing bale of 'files' might be the last of a fortune in forged notes. By dawn it was all over. Schulz had been able to hide two boxes, which he hoped might contain at least something of value, in a hole in a bank by the lakeside. He was covering up the traces as machine-gun fire began to rattle loudly from the hills. Planes were now flying over regularly. Schulz grabbed his knapsack, dropped his SS uniform with a stone wrapped in it into the lake, and made himself scarce.

An hour or so later when things had quietened down a little a strangely scarecrow-like figure returned to the lakeside. Crouching down by his cache, Schulz opened the crates. Inside he found piles of reports, files on espionage operations, lists of payments made to agents – all the painstaking bureaucracy of the SS. Despite his disappointment Schulz found them fascinating and he read them for over five minutes before flinging them all away in disgust. The last he saw of the papers they were being chewed up by a cow.

He didn't stop walking all night. He wanted to get as far away from the lake and the SS files as possible. He still hadn't been able to count the money and as soon as it was light enough, he sat down in a field and began to laugh. He had managed it. He had come through the war and was through with Neuheim too and he had rescued a share of the money. The Alps were bursting into life in the late April sunrise. Buds were opening beneath his feet. He felt like a tourist: he even had a knapsack.

He took out the money and laid it on the grass. The notes were all Grade 1, and he counted them as he had seen Solly count them so many times, professionally licking his thumb and turning each bundle over when he had counted them. There were over fifty thousand pounds in all, which, added to the fifty thousand from the mattress, left him with over a hundred thousand.

Schulz was overjoyed. As he got to his feet he heard the call of a cuckoo. This time, he mused, as he walked on, the cuckoo had struck. He laughed again. Immediately a fusillade of shot broke out, rapid automatic fire that tore the leaves off the trees all around him. He flung himself to the ground. The firing stopped. All was still. Then a voice spoke.

'Stay still! Don't move!' Schulz stayed still. He didn't move. There was the sound of running feet and then the voice again, now quite near. 'Okay, bud! On your feet! Up!'

Schulz got shakily to his feet, holding his hands above his head, including the haversack. Six fresh-faced, plump, healthy looking GIs with carbines, led by a corporal, closed in a small circle menacingly around him.

24

'Where did you get these – off a scarecrow?'

A young, lean American lieutenant was walking around Schulz a touch theatrically, his eyes fixed on him. He was pushing and pulling at Schulz's clothes.

'No sir – they're mine,' said Schulz nervously, looking around at the rather ordinary room in the rather ordinary house which advance guards of the 91st US Infantry Division had taken over as a field centre. A local man had been helping the lieutenant round up strays. The local man had shaken his head when he saw Schulz, who thought that it meant that he didn't recognize him as a war criminal. What it actually meant was that Schulz wasn't local.

'Like hell they are!' said the lieutenant whose name was Carson. 'I'll bet my boots I know where yours are – buried in a field somewhere, eh? SS uniform?'

'No, sir!' said Schulz earnestly.

'Can't get'm off quick enough, can you!'

Schulz didn't answer. The fact that he spoke English made it all the more easy for Carson to concentrate on him. The lieutenant went over to the table where the money was now stacked up in neat little piles.

'Where did you get it?'

'I found it,' said Schulz innocently. It was true in a sense.

'Found it? Where?'

'On the hillside, sir. In that haversack. It was just lying there. Someone must have dropped it.'

'Fifty thousand pounds?'

'They must have been in a hurry,' replied Schulz and then hesitated. 'A hundred thousand,' he pointed out.

'Pardon me,' said Carson.

'I thought there was a hundred thousand there,' said Schulz politely.

Carson pushed his face up into Schulz's. 'Are you implying something, Kraut?' he said equally politely.

'No, sir,' he swallowed. 'I must have miscounted.'

Schulz could not believe his ill-luck. He had somehow walked into the arms of the American equivalent of Neuheim and this time their interests were in no way mutually advantageous.

'You bet your sweet ass you miscounted,' said Carson very quietly. 'Corporal!' he screamed. Then he added to Schulz in a voice like bad eggs: 'Something smells about you and I don't know yet what it is. But my guess is, mister, you may not get home for a long time after the war.'

'Quite a little travelling bank, isn't he?' said Browne, in a frigid English drawl. He was examining a five-pound note through a magnifying glass. Carson was chewing some gum rather noisily in Browne's ear.

'Well, are they yours?' said Carson. 'Are they Bank of England notes?'

Browne finally lowered the glass. 'They're Bank of England notes.'

'You mean they're genuine? Those notes were made by you.'

'I didn't say that,' said Browne who found Carson's crudity a little distasteful. 'A Bank of England note is something that looks to the Bank of England like a Bank of England note. This looks to me – and believe me, sir, I'm an expert – like a Bank of England note. If it's a fake, I can't tell the difference.'

Carson whistled softly. 'I haven't heard about any forgery operation, have you?'

'No,' replied Browne. 'And I'd stake my life that if these were some of them, the Bank of England would have no grounds for refusing payment on them. The question is – if they have been printing them – how many have they printed?'

'I'll get the guy who maybe can tell you,' replied Carson.

He went to the door and signalled to his corporal, who followed Schulz into the room.

'I'll leave you to it,' said Carson, still chewing.

He and the corporal went out and Browne indicated a chair for Schulz. Then he pointed to the wads of notes on the table.

'Quite a little travelling bank aren't you?' he repeated his well-rehearsed joke but Schulz was too glum to respond. He had seen the Englishman draw up in a staff car, a tall, fair-haired man in his late forties, thin and with a fair moustache streaked with grey: another schoolmaster, Schulz had thought dismally.

'Where did you get these?'

'I found them lying in the wood, sir,' replied Schulz, wondering if Browne was a currency expert.

'Now you don't expect me to believe that, do you?'

'No sir.'

'Then tell me the truth.'

'I found them lying in the wood,' Schulz repeated doggedly.

Browne decided to try another tactic.

'Do you know what a monstrous crime it is to forge somebody's currency?'

'Yes, sir,' replied Schulz. Browne sounded just like Funk's deputy.

'Have you ever thought of the harm it does to the savings of widows and orphans, or how it destroys the value of hard-earned pensions? Don't you think that's a horrible thing to do?'

'Yes, sir.'

'I don't suppose you can understand this but inflation – which is one of the main results of this sort of thing – can ruin a society overnight. But you probably wouldn't know about that would you?'

'Yes, sir.'

'Do you know that the deliberate forging of an enemy's currency,' went on Browne obliviously, 'might be considered a war crime?'

'Like the forging of clothing coupons and ration books, sir?'

'No – not at all like the forging of clothing coupons and ration books. The two things are entirely different. Forging German clothing coupons was just a joke, really, a bit of fun. Good God,' Browne said, getting rather heated, 'don't you Germans have any sense of humour.'

'Not a lot, sir.'

'But forging an enemy's currency is a criminal act of wanton recklessness that has no regard for the rules of war or the elementary decencies.' Browne was growing red in the face. 'You can't fight wars like that.'

'Why not, sir?'

'Well, for one thing,' he shouted, astounded at Schulz's obtuseness, 'nobody would know who was paying for them! That would destroy the whole purpose of war! The loser might be better off in the end than the winner – you couldn't have that!'

'No, I can see that, sir.'

Browne began to feel he was getting somewhere at last. 'Well, then, look here,' he went on in a calmer voice, 'I can see that you intend to be reasonable. Now, it's vital for us to know the names of those involved in the operation and how much of this stuff is still lying about.' He had no idea if there was an operation but it was worth trying. 'Suppose I were to say – here's ten thousand pounds, eh? A reward for information leading to etc., etc.'

He had picked up an armful of money and brought it over to Schulz, who stared at him and then at the money. His mouth watered. His hands went out and touched it. Then he looked again at Browne and thought of Solly.

'It hurts like hell, sir,' he said with difficulty, 'but the trouble is, I found this stuff lying in the woods.'

Browne exploded. 'You bloody swine! You horrible man!' he shrieked. 'I'll have you tried and shot as a war criminal! You're not fit for human society! I'll see that you stay in jail long after everyone else has gone home!' He strode to the door and opened it. 'All right, Lieutenant, I've finished with him!' he called.

Carson returned with the corporal.

'Lock him up for further interrogation,' said Carson. The corporal bundled Schulz out of the room. Carson looked at Browne. 'No go, eh?'

'Damned fellow wouldn't talk,' said the Englishman.

'Perhaps he's telling the truth?'

'Perhaps. I don't like the look of him, though. He looks damned untrustworthy to me.'

'I suppose you'll be taking charge of this cash?'

'Yes,' said Browne. 'I'd better take over.'

'I'll get a receipt,' said Carson.

Browne was again examining the notes with his magnifying glass.

'You know,' he said, 'it's possible that there are millions of these notes out there, all of them fakes, and each one, in its own way, like a rat gnawing at the foundations of the Bank of England.'

'I never thought of it like that,' said Carson politely, but clearly unimpressed.

'How much is there here?' said Browne, still looking at the notes.

'I don't know,' replied Carson, looking him straight in the eye. 'We haven't counted it yet.'

'I see,' said Browne thoughtfully. They stared at each other. 'Well, perhaps I'd better count it.'

He started to count the bundles of notes. About ten bundles had, however, somehow got pushed to one side of the table. Pointedly, Browne ignored them, counting only the main pile. 'Thirty thousand?' he said.

'Yeah,' replied Carson, 'That's what I figured – thirty thousand.' Browne split the separate little pile neatly in half.

'What about that?' said Carson. 'You making it the same as me?'

The 'further interrogation' with which Schulz had been threatened proved futile. He stuck to his story and there was no way that they could make him change it. Moreover it was impossible to prove that the notes were forged and, in spite of the fact that Schulz had lost his little nest egg, he was, a week later, relishing the prospect of being set free when an odd thing happened.

At a village further down the Traun, a local angler had been startled to make out what looked like a shoal of fish floating downstream towards him on the surface of the water. When he looked more closely he realized that they were not fish but bits of paper and not just any bits of paper but bank notes. Soon the villagers and the American troops in the district were scrambling madly for the notes. The Americans, who turned out to be slightly more patriotic than Lt Carson, handed over the money to SHAEF whose Intelligence officer, quickly established that these were not just any bank notes but part of the consignment of forged British notes known to have been concealed in crates on lorries that had been sunk in one of the deepest lakes in Austria.

On 15 May 1945, just as Schulz was about to be freed by Lt Carson, he was arrested by SHAEF. It was obvious that they knew far more about Operation Bernhard than Carson or Browne had done and that honesty would be the best policy. Schulz asked to speak to the chief American Intelligence officer, hoping that if he volunteered information about Bernhard, he would be given preferential treatment. He also knew that if they found out he was in the SS he would not get off lightly.

He was grilled by SHAEF and British Intelligence, and in return for his co-operation he was taken back to Ebensee Concentration Camp to be confronted by SS guards and Bernhard workers being held for interrogation. Solly, he was happy to see, was not among them.

The guards verified that Schulz had been a prisoner there and later released when he had been seconded to work for General Neuheim. The workers confirmed that he had treated them leniently. Schulz was sent to an internment camp in Linz where he was kept for seven months. Then, one bleak morning in January 1946, he was pushed out into the world, the cold, grey world of post-war Germany.

25

On the night that Operation Bernhard had sunk like a stone into the depths of Lake Toplitz, the Fuhrer had committed suicide with his long-time mistress and wife of a few hours, Eva Braun. Like that short-lived matrimonial bond, the money in Schulz's haversack had been wedded to Schulz for only a few hours after many years of unsatisfactory court-ship before Schulz was parted from it for ever.

During that first winter of peace, twelve million Germans were expelled from their homes in Poland, Czechoslovakia and Hungary. Hordes of homeless people crossed the ruined landscapes and cities, riding in trains little better than cattle cars, sleeping in fouled air-raid shelters. The mark was as worthless as it had been in the inflation of 1923. Cigarettes became the only true form of currency.

That winter when Schulz was again ejected like yet an-other unwanted pfennig from yet another slot machine on to the streets of Linz, he thought seriously and calmly at times of ending it all by jumping into the river. The thought did not proceed from some inner sense of melancholia or from some need to make a bitter if once-and-for-all gesture. It was simply that, carefully considered, if one could but triumph for a brief moment over those idiotic inner voices that screamed hysterically against it, to end it all had more point than going on with it.

He was cold, hungry and depressed. There was not the slightest prospect of regaining any of the fortune that he had helped to create. He was, as Bertha Freyer had once said, a stumbler, or as Neuheim had often said, a fool.

And yet, the prosaic fact was that it was too cold to leap into the river. He knew by instinct that the shock of icy water would revive his ebbing spirits, that the moment he struck it some tiger inside him would be unleashed that would struggle wildly, simply to get out of the cold. In that mood the tiger was not to be reasoned with. If he were to end it all, he knew, in his heart, he must wait till summer.

By April 1946, as the waters of the River Traun were becoming less icy, though still cold, and his thoughts of ending it all were subsiding, Schulz had found a job waitering and washing up in a small café in Linz. It was hardly how he would have chosen to live it up in peacetime but he had very little choice. Until he could earn enough to make the journey to Berlin, where he still dreamed of finding Bertha, he had to be content with what he could get. What he also got was a landlady even plumper and more elderly than Frau Nusbaum had been, but Frau Vogel would no more have dreamed of allowing Schulz into her playroom than Schulz would have had the slightest wish to do so.

Linz was, like other German cities, a place of misery and despair, a shattered town full of shattered people, many of its buildings half-demolished and its streets still littered with the rubble caused by American shells.

It was through the debris of one such street that Schulz was trudging one night towards a tram stop when a cruising car skidded to a stop beside him; the door was flung open and a man got out, pointing the snub nose of a Luger in his face.

'Get in,' rasped the man.

'What?' said Schulz, bewildered by this sudden intrusion and thinking for a moment that this was the Gestapo. Then he sighed with relief: the war was over.

'Get in!' repeated the man and pushed him violently into the car. The driver turned and levelled another pistol at him while the first man slipped in beside Schulz, slamming the car door and pushing the gun up into his terrified face.

Then the car drove off at high speed.

The house was a tall, imposing, three-storey building and, except for some damage to the top floor, surprisingly intact, standing as it did in a street of partially demolished ones. The car came to a screeching halt outside the gate, its doors opened and Schulz was shoved out on to the pavement. The two men got out and pushed him through the gate and towards the house.

Schulz could now see that the man who had grabbed him off the street was wearing a very expensive looking Italian overcoat. He looked vaguely familiar. When Schulz glanced at the other man, he noticed that he had a very bad limp and then he recognized him. It was Neuheim's driver, whose feet beneath a jacked-up car, was the last view he had had of him. Schulz's heart began to pound. They were inside a very grand, well furnished house whose walls were covered with Italian paintings.

A door opened and a tall, thin man with a black patch over his left eye and wearing a tuxedo appeared. Schulz still had nightmares regularly about him.

'Well, well,' said Neuheim cordially, 'we thought they'd never let you out.' He grinned maliciously. 'Thoroughly denazified, are you? Thoroughly deloused?'

Schulz glared at Neuheim, immediately back under his spell and trying hard to fight it. 'I don't understand,' he said nervously. 'What am I doing here?'

'My dear Gerhardt – you don't mind if I call you Gerhardt?' Neuheim said smoothly. 'The war's over now, we can be completely informal. You can call me Herr Neuheim.' He poured himself a brandy and sat down in a deep armchair by a blazing fire.

'I'm not going to call you anything!' shouted Schulz, completely outraged. 'How dare you kidnap me off the street and –'

He stopped short as the man in the overcoat lifted his Luger.

'No, no, Walter, put it away,' said Neuheim, affably waving his hand. 'We shan't need that, we're old friends.'

'How did you know where I was?' said Schulz, seething.

'We've already established an old-boy network, Gerhardt,' replied Neuheim, still calm and unflappable, 'a sort of SS brotherhood, just to help one another, you know. It took a little time but we found you. Catering seems to suit you, Gerhardt. Walter, here, has nothing but praise for your splendid performance as a waiter, haven't you, Walter?'

The man in the overcoat, whom Schulz now recognized as a recent diner at the café, grunted.

Schulz was speechless.

'Why don't you sit down, Gerhardt.'

Schulz shook his head but one of the thugs pushed a chair over and Schulz into it.

Neuheim got up and leaned over Schulz menacingly.

'What did you do with them?' he snarled.

'Do with them? Do with what?' Schulz was trembling.

'Still the cuckoo, eh, Schulz?' Neuheim bared his teeth. Then his expression changed. 'The trucks that you took to Skorzeny?' he growled ferociously. 'They never got there.'

'Of course they didn't get there, we dumped them. We found a deep lake and dumped them!'

Now Neuheim was speechless. He stared at Schulz as though he were something that should have been dumped in the lake too.

'You what?' he finally said, very quietly.

'We dumped them, there was nothing else to do, the area was crawling with Americans.' He stared back at Neuheim nonplussed. 'Well, you didn't want all those files falling into enemy hands, did you?'

'Files?' repeated Neuheim aghast. *'Files?* My God, didn't you realize what was in them? Don't you know what those files were?'

'Yes,' said Schulz nervously. 'I read some of them, they detailed payments to agents and so on ... ?' He trailed off.

'There were only *two* crates of files. Everything else ...' Neuheim did not have the strength to go on.

There was a stunned silence. Schulz stared white-faced at Neuheim as the truth slowly penetrated his tortured brain.

'Oh, no! Oh, no ... !'

'There were five hundred million top-grade English pounds in those crates!' hissed Neuheim. 'All cashable.

256

All the money that had been printed and never spent was bundled up in them! And you dumped them all in the lake!'

'No, you can't mean that, you . . .' Schulz began hoarsely.

And then, suddenly, all the years of frustration, all the madness and incompetence he had had to deal with, all the hypocrisy and opportunism that had festered around him for so long, burst inside him and he flung himself blindly at Neuheim, screaming at him, while Walter and the driver, struggled to hold him back.

'WHY DIDN'T YOU TELL ME IT WAS MONEY, YOU FOOL!' he screeched. 'WHY DIDN'T YOU TRUST ME! You brainless idiot! You bungling, clumsy half-wit! You never did anything right in your whole life! Never! Never! Never!'

Neuheim stood perfectly still, shaken by the outburst, but unflinching. Schulz had fallen back in his seat. He started to laugh and then cry and then both together as he collapsed in hysterics.

'What do you have to do to win – just once?' he moaned. 'You have ideas, you work hard, you bring off the impossible – and still you come out the loser. I'm cursed, cursed, cursed!'

There was a long, depressing silence. Schulz was still picturing the crates that he had hidden in the bank by the lake, certain at that moment that fate had carefully manipulated them to be the only two that genuinely contained secret files. If he had taken any other crate . . .

'What happened to the money you took with you?' he suddenly asked Neuheim in a weak, toneless voice.

'Look around you, my dear Gerhardt. You don't expect me to live in a seedy little attic like you, do you? Besides,' he added, looking pained, 'I ran into some Italian partisans who took half of what was rightfully mine. They even took my Canaletto, the thieving swine. Typical! I got away by the skin of my teeth. Fortunately, I had the presence of mind to throw some of the money into a rubbish bin while they were not looking. I retrieved it afterwards, of course.'

He smiled smugly for a moment and then looked again at Schulz. 'Well, you're no use to us. You're a bloody waste of time, you always were.'

Neuheim's henchmen had put away their guns. It was now clear to Schulz that he was as free to go as a rather bothersome little fly. He sighed and got up to leave, but at the door he hesitated. It had suddenly occurred to him that he might be walking out on the only man alive who had knowledge of Operation Bernhard, even though Neuheim was hardly human. But if he could use Schulz, then Schulz could use *him*.

'If we could get some diving gear ... ?' he hesitated again.

'Diving gear?' said Neuheim, looking up.

'Naval gear. We dumped the crates in Lake Toplitz. There was a naval experimenal station there. They'd built a pier out into the lake. We ran the trucks off the pier, then they destroyed it, but I remember where it was.'

Neuheim was rising from his seat, smiling.

'He remembers where it was,' he said genially to his little army. He put an arm round Schulz's shoulders. 'My dear Gerhardt, you remember where it was? *Exactly* where it was?'

'Yes, sir,' replied Schulz, falling back unconsciously into his subservient role. 'But you'll need a professional diver.'

'Nonsense,' grinned Neuheim. 'You can do it. I know you can.'

Schulz bridled. 'I think you forget, *Herr* Neuheim,' he said politely, emphasizing his civilian title, 'that the war is over.'

'Is it, Schulz, that's the question?'

Willi and Walter stood smartly and threateningly to attention, Lugers raised.

'But the lake's very deep!' spluttered Schulz.

'Well, we won't send you down without a suit!' said Neuheim generously. 'We'll do it properly – oxygen and everything. Have you ever done it before?'

'Never!' gasped Schulz, remembering the parachute.

'You'll enjoy it!' Neuheim beamed. 'I'm reliably informed it's very invigorating. Something to do with the silence.' Schulz opened his mouth to speak, but Neuheim slapped him on the back. 'Now don't worry,' he boomed, 'I'll raise the money somehow. I know a chap, a sailor, he's bought a whole load of naval surplus. We'll buy the gear and we'll go back up to the lake.'

Schulz had no doubt that Neuheim was now living the life of a fully fledged gangster working the black market. He was utterly convinced, for once, that Neuheim would honour a promise.

There were, by this time, quite a number of people who knew or thought they knew that there was an awful lot of money in the lake at Toplitz. But the lake was huge and deep and no one knew exactly where to dive for it.

This, however, was a minor matter which did not bother Neuheim in the least. He had Schulz and Schulz knew where the lorries had gone in. Schulz had needed neither inducements nor blandishments: the mere sight of the Lugers had instantly reminded him of his patriotism and he had agreed like a shot.

'It'll be like old times,' beamed Neuheim to his former clerk a few nights later as they sat once more in Neuheim's living room, planning the operation.

'We'll take you up to that lake and you'll put that gear on and you'll go down to the bottom of that lake a poor man, a man without a pfennig to his name!' said Neuheim, pouring himself another brandy and not offering a glass to Schulz. 'But, by thunder, when you come up again, Gerhardt, I'll – you'll be rich, rich! As so shall we! There's enough in one of those black crates to set us all up for the rest of our lives!'

It took another fortnight to acquire all the necessary equipment, all, as Schulz had correctly guessed, via the black market.

'You'll have me in the boat working the equipment and that should give you every confidence,' said Neuheim to Schulz as they drove late at night through the Alps, trailing the boat behind the car. 'Unfortunately, we shall have to work at night because the Austrians have forbidden diving in the lake.'

Schulz, sitting in the back seat, was already shivering, even though it was early May. They were nearing the lake, which, in comparison with the broad expanse of Grundlsee, was a gloomy, eerie region, once more shrouded in mist as it had been a year earlier.

They set up camp that night in the hills. Apart from Willi, who had had a little experience of diving before his regrettable accident underneath Neuheim's car, they were all complete amateurs. The diving equipment was ancient. It took two days to get it working. In the first hour of darkness they would trundle everything down to the lakeside on a kind of sledge. There were two diving suits with helmets, air pipes and a rusty old winch and pump which was operated from the boat. The noise of the pumping engine was loud enough on its own to raise the dead let alone the Austrian police.

As dawn was breaking on the third day they were sitting huddled around a small fire eating their meagre rations. Schulz, who had just shed his diving suit, was shivering and sweating at the same time, with a mug of hot ersatz coffee in his hands and a blanket round his shoulders.

'You should have held on to it, you fool!' Neuheim was grumbling at him. 'You had it in your hands! You panicked, that's what you did, and let it go!'

'You try working down there in sixty feet of water,' shivered Schulz through chattering teeth.'

'Well, at least he saw one of the crates and touched it,' rasped Willi, who had a little sympathy for Schulz's plight. 'We'll have another go at it tonight.'

'It's not easy,' complained Schulz. 'There's a whole false bottom of sunken tree trunks down there. It keeps shifting about. And now and then one of them breaks loose and comes up and clouts you on the way up.'

Walter nodded.

'There are one or two logs floating about, too,' he agreed. 'You'll have to watch out for them in the dark.'

'You don't realize how easy it is to get trapped down

260

there,' said Schulz.

'Oh, stop moaning!' barked Neuheim. 'You can't achieve anything without a little effort. I'll send Willi down with you next time to give you a hand.'

Willi looked uncomfortable but he shrugged it off.

'Yes, don't worry!' he said. 'This time, I'll be with you. All you need is a little nerve.'

'Exactly!' cried Neuheim. 'That's the real SS talking!'

'Could I have another blanket?' said Schulz who had begun to sneeze.

'Oh, give him another blanket before he dies of a cold!' sneered Neuheim disgustedly.

They tried again the following night.

'That's Willi's line jerking!' Walter whispered excitedly, peering over the side of the boat. 'Pull him up, pull him up!'

'I can't,' Neuheim whispered back, 'it's stuck!'

'What do you mean, stuck? Here give it to me!'

Walter grabbed the handle of the winch and started turning it, but it jammed.

'What's the matter with it?' he yelled hysterically, forgetting that they were supposed to be whispering.

'He must be caught on something down there!' hissed Neuheim.

'Oh, my God, he must be trapped in those sunken logs! Help me free him!' screamed Walter.

Neuheim was pulling at a piece of piping in the water. It had obviously gone in deep but it was coming out very quickly and easily, as though there were nothing on the end of it.

'It's Willi's air-line!' said Neuheim wonderingly. 'It's come adrift!'

'How could it?' cried Walter in horror. 'How much did you pay for those suits?'

'All the money I had, what more do you want?' snarled back Neuheim menacingly.

'That's Willi down there and you sent him into sixty feet

of water in a cheap diving suit!' Walter yelled at him.

Neither was sparing a thought for Schulz.

'Cheap?' yelled back Neuheim. 'I paid three thousand cigarettes for those suits!'

'Three thou ... ? You cheapskate!' Walter flung at him. 'You can't buy a pair of pyjamas for two thousand cigarettes let alone a diving suit! Oh, my God, Willi, Willi! Let's get him up!'

They both began dragging frantically on the line.

Suddenly they felt a tug and the line began to move, though heavily.

'He's free! He's come free!' said Neuheim triumphantly, anxious to vindicate his equipment.

Slowly, and with great effort, they pulled at the line. The diving suit containing Willi finally appeared on the surface, floating like a dead fish. Together, Walter and Neuheim dragged it on to the deck and began unscrewing the helmet.

'Oh God, Oh God,' moaned Walter, 'he's going to be dead, I know he is, I know it! We went all through the war together and I just know he's going to be dead!'

'You *don't* know it!' thundered Neuheim who was trying to get Willi's helmet off. 'You know nothing of the sort. Do you want to put the mockers on him? He'll be all right, I tell you, I can see his lips moving! People have been drowned and brought back to life before! Don't you have any faith? Willi's as tough as old boots and if he's dead I'll eat my –'

He had got the helmet off and had slipped his hand inside the suit feeling Willi's heart.

'How is he?' gasped Walter.

'Dead,' Neuheim nodded.

A small sob escaped Walter and even Neuheim was shaken.

'That bastard!' roared the ex-SS General. 'He sold me a dud suit! The rubber hose must have perished.' A sudden thought struck him. 'My God, I could have gone down in it myself!'

For the past three minutes Schulz's line had been jerking more and more violently. Neuheim now got up and went over to the wheel, turning it furiously.

'Not so fast, do you want to kill him, too?' whimpered Walter.

Neuheim slowed down a little. A floating log bumped heavily against the keel and Walter pushed it away with an oar. A few moments later Schulz broke the surface of the water holding a waterproofed bundle.

'He's got it, he's got it!' shouted Walter excitedly, forgetting his grief.

While Schulz was climbing the ladder into the boat, helped by Walter, Neuheim pulled the package on board. Walter unscrewed Schulz's helmet.

'Is Willi . . . ?' Walter nodded sadly. 'I saw the pipe come away,' gasped Schulz, still out of breath, 'but there was nothing I could do. Help me out of this. I never want to go down there again as long as I live.'

Neuheim was hacking away feverishly at one corner of the bundle. He finally made a hole large enough to put his hand in.

'Shine the light over here!' he said in a strange voice.

Walter turned the lamp on to Neuheim and all three stared down at the bundle of perfect English five-pound notes in his hands.

'We've done it!' he said in a voice that oozed with satisfaction. 'There must be five million pounds in here.'

Schulz forgot about the recent agony of his subaquatic ordeal. The impossible had happened. Neuheim was the first to rise. 'Let's go back to the car,' he ordered.

'Wait a minute,' said Walter. 'What about Willi?'

Neuheim looked thoughtfully at the body, and then across the lake.

'He hated the water,' protested Walter.

Neuheim glared at him. 'It's an honourable way to go, Walter,' he said. 'Some of the best people are buried at sea. Besides, we can't risk taking him ashore.'

Schulz shook his head. 'We might just as well have left him down there.'

The other two frowned at this piece of crass insensitivity.

'It's not the same thing at all,' said Walter. 'Come on.'

They lifted the body, still swathed in the diving suit, and carried it towards the side.

'We should've had a flag, a German flag,' Walter said, disapprovingly.

'You can't *get* German flags at the moment,' said Neuheim. 'They're not popular. Look, Willi will understand, he wasn't one to stand on ceremony. He never cared where he slept so why should he care where he's buried? And anyway, he'll be down there among the fivers. Isn't that where we'd all like to be when we go?'

There was no answer to this. Walter nodded however, profoundly moved. 'Say a few words, then,' he said in a hushed voice.

Neuheim thought for a few seconds. 'You come into this world with nothing and it is certain you can take nothing out. Amen.'

The body was pitched into the water.

'Let's get going!' shouted Neuheim, clambering over to the engine and started it. Walter took over the steering. As they neared the shore, the engine was cut and they drifted towards land. Neuheim told Schulz to be ready to jump ashore. This had been Willi's job previously.

'Just hold the bow to stop us touching,' Walter explained.

Schulz could hardly see what he was doing; the engine was still smoking and in any case there was a thick pre-dawn mist. He jumped too soon and found himself up to his waist in water but this time without a diving suit on. He slipped and went under, but recovered his balance, and had started to pull the boat towards the shore, lifting the bow, when he suddenly froze.

Car headlights flashed on to them and there were cries coming from the shore.

'Halt! Stay where you are! This is the police!'

'Turn the boat round!' Neuheim was screaming. 'Turn it round!'

As Schulz swung the boat out towards the middle of the lake the engine roared into life once more. The boat leapt forward with Schulz clinging to it.

'Wait! Wait for me!' he yelled but the thrust of the boat

was far too powerful. It shot away; leaving him floundering up to his neck now in the water. He stood there, helplessly gazing after the rapidly receding boat as several Austrian policemen rushed up and grabbed him.

Schulz made no effort to resist.

By the time the police had sent a motor launch out to search for Schulz's accomplices, they found an upturned boat adrift in the middle of the lake, and no signs of the diving gear, its two passengers or the opened bale. A semi-submerged log floated nearby. Since Schulz insisted that he had been on a pleasure trip, and had stuck to his story, the police could not prove otherwise. He was offered the choice of paying a fine or going to prison for a month, which in his case was no choice whatsoever. What meagre savings he had accumulated from his café job had been 'lent' to Neuheim towards the diving equipment. He spent the rest of May and the early part of June in the same prison camp in which he had been interned the previous year, and swore to himself that not only would he abandon any thoughts of going back for the money which he had come to associate with disaster and ruin in his life, but he would never again allow himself to be manipulated by Alfred Neuheim.

Neither event was likely in any case. The security precautions around Lake Toplitz now made it practically impossible for any further pleasure trips to be taken on its waters. As for Neuheim: a few days after Schulz's release a body was washed ashore on the banks of Lake Toplitz. It had been eaten away by various forms of marine life and was unrecognizable. Schulz was not called in by the Austrian police to identify the body.

26

When Schulz came out of prison yet again in June 1946 he knew it was time to make a serious assessment of his life and prospects. His first priority was to salvage what was left of his confidence and self-respect. He had had enough of Germany for one lifetime, so when he met a man who offered him a job as a barman in a hotel in the coastal resort of Bandol, near Marseilles, he jumped at it. He soon quietly submerged himself in Provençal life, even acquiring a taste for dominoes and baccarat. He had, it is true, been tempted to the roulette wheels at Monte Carlo in his second summer, where he lost all his money minutes after nearly winning all of the bank's. After that he never went near a gambling table. His employers treated him well and he was regarded by the Bandol regulars as a quiet, meek little Swiss with a flair for languages, who had spent the war years quietly working in the post office in Zurich.

Nevertheless he occasionally found himself trembling when a wealthy customer, usually English or American, but occasionally Swiss or even French, would hand him an English five-pound note, telling him to keep the change. In spite of the voluntary block he had put on that particular avenue in his brain, Schulz had acquired, and still retained, a second sense as far as Bernhard notes were concerned. It was something to do with the texture that was a fraction too crisp, like a shirt that had been marginally overstarched, that would tell him that the note was forged. Fortunately for his peace of mind it never did. It seemed as if the last of the notes slumbered among the bones of Alfred Neuheim, deep below the surface of Lake Toplitz.

Then, one evening at the end of May 1950, he was handed a shirt that was too starched and the top began to spin. He had not been paying much attention to the customer, who was bronzed and bearded and richly dressed, like so many other foreigners at this time of the season, but when the five-pound note crackled Schulz slowly looked up: the man was about his height and his age, though much plumper, with a vaguely moon-shaped face, luxuriously covered by a reddish beard.

'Excuse me, sir,' said Schulz peering at his vaguely familiar eyes. 'Haven't we met somewhere before?' The man stared at him.

'I don't think so,' he said offhandedly. 'I'm from Zurich and unless –'

'What a coincidence, sir,' said Schulz, mentally stripping the man of his beard, 'so am I.' The man looked slightly relieved.

'Well, in that case, perhaps we have,' he said, glancing with less interest than before at Schulz. Then he paused. Schulz, like most of the barmen in the area, had grown a neat little moustache and had taken to wearing contact lenses, a small luxury which was just becoming fashionable and which made him look younger and less owlish. Now the man was mentally stripping him of his moustache and imposing a pair of steel-rimmed spectacles.

'*Mein Gott!*' he whispered. 'Schulz!'

'Schumacher!' said Schulz at the same moment.

'Bless you,' said a nearby customer, looking up at the sound of the sneeze.

Schulz and Schumacher stared with astonishment at each other.

'I never thought I'd see you again,' said Schumacher. 'I assumed you'd perished in Austria or had got hold of some more Bernhard money. I'd have thought it would come easy to you,' he added in a whisper.

Schulz wasn't sure whether he was talking about perishing or stealing forged notes. For painful reasons he had found both equally impossible. He quickly filled in his former colleague on his experiences since they'd last met. Schumacher listened with rapt atteetion, nodded sympathetically now and again, and laughed grimly when Schulz

267

described Neuheim's watery end.

'So now you're Swiss, like me,' Schumacher laughed finally.

'Yes,' agreed Schulz philosophically. 'Swiss and poor.'

'No,' replied Schumacher. 'Swiss and rich.' Schulz eyed Schumacher's affluence with new interest, noticing for the first time a diamond ring on his finger.

'What did you do, Albert?' Schulz joked. 'Meet an heiress?' He had not forgotten that the ex-major was a blatant homosexual.

'No, Gerhardt,' said Schumacher brightly. 'I worked on Operation Bernhard.' Schulz suddenly remembered the five-pound note he'd just been handed. He stared at Schumacher incredulously.

'WHAT?' he said. A few people in the bar turned to look at him. 'But – *how*, Schumacher, *how*?' he whispered. He felt weak at the knees.

'Quite easily, really,' replied Schumacher, also whispering. 'When Kube and Neuheim were ordered by Kaltenbrunner to move the Operation down to Ebensee, I was ordered to close down the Kitty – after helping to clear out the Schloss, that is. Kube was in such a hurry to get out with the money that he left some of it lying around. I asked him where he was going with it and he said –'

'It was none of your damned business . . .' replied Schulz weakly.

'That's right, how did you know?' Schumacher was looking distinctly smug.

'How much?' whispered Schulz. He thought he was going to be sick.

'Oh, about a million. By the time I got to Berlin –'

'A million pounds!' Schulz whispered, not because he was trying to keep his voice down but because he'd lost the use of it.

'No, notes,' replied Schumacher. 'By the time I got to Berlin –'

'*Five* million pounds?' yelled Schulz, his voice returning with a vengeance. Now *everyone* turned to stare at him.

'Ssshh – not so loud, Schulz, you never were discreet,

even Johann said so,' whispered Schumacher in irritation.

'Who's he?' said Schulz miserably. Schumacher opened his mouth to reply when Schulz interrupted.

'Don't tell me, I don't want to know.' He was in no mood to hear how Schumacher squandered his millions on some pretty little former SS officer.

'Five million,' Schulz repeated wistfully.

'No,' said Schumacher sadly. 'That was what I was about to tell you, but you keep interrupting. I've noticed that about you, Gerhardt, you're an interrupter. By the time I got to Berlin and had bribed all the Americans and Russians in the Salon Kitty to leave and let me and Johann go, we were left with barely a tenth of the money. And then we had to get out of Berlin . . .'

'Still,' said Schulz with a touch of sarcasm that was lost on Schumacher. 'I expect you and Johann have been able to struggle along on half a million.'

'Just about,' said Schumacher breezily. 'But Johann always did have expensive tastes.' At that moment a beautiful looking man dressed in the latest fashion walked in to the bar and approached Schumacher. 'Ah, there you are, Johann!' beamed Schumacher.

The man was certainly good looking in the old blond Aryan way that Schulz never wanted to see again. A woman had followed him in and, from what Schulz could see of her, she was devastating. She was however standing in Johann's shadow. Schulz now understood what Schumacher meant by expensive tastes. He actually felt pity for Schumacher, unfortunate enough to have hitched his wagon to a bisexual. Johann and his expensive taste were probably living with Schumacher as a ménage à trois, milking the poor man dry.

'Johann, you remember Gerhardt Schulz, don't you?'

Schulz stared at the man. He didn't look at all familiar. So that was where Schumacher used to disappear to at Dusseldorf and Berlin. Schumacher laughed.

'I knew it!' he said, slapping the palm of his hand on the bar counter. 'I often used to say to Johann that you preferred men to women, Schulz, but she wouldn't have it.' The man was blushing with embarrassment. Schulz had turned crimson with confusion.

'She?' he repeated, staring at Schumacher in astonishment.

'I knew you'd remember her,' replied Schumacher chuckling. 'Gerhardt, allow me to introduce you to my wife, Bertha-Johanne Schumacher – I call her Johann, it's our little joke – but, of course, you probably remember her by her maiden name – oh,' he added, winking at Schulz as if to say he understood his sexual preference 'this is Paul, her brother.' Paul extended a smooth white hand and smiled coyly.

'Hello,' he said in a gentle, almost feminine voice. The dazzling vision of German womanhood stepped sinuously out of the shadow of her younger brother and looked Schulz deep in the eye. The glass he had been wiping dropped from his trembling hands and fell to the floor with a smash.

'Hello, Gerhardt,' said Bertha Freyer.

The rest of the evening was a nightmare, intensified by her gentle laugh, and the occasional searching gaze that seemed to question and tease and ask forgiveness at the same time. Schumacher, meanwhile, kept slapping his back, joking about his bad luck and generally needling him, while Paul dropped shy, furtive glances through long eyelashes. Schulz tried to busy himself with other customers but it was impossible to avoid the Schumachers, who ordered cognac after cognac, and then switched to Scotch. By the end of the evening Albert and Paul were thoroughly drunk, but Bertha-Johanne was as cool and sober as she had been at the beginning. When she disappeared to the Ladies, Schumacher took the opportunity for a confidential chat.

'Well, Gerhardt,' he winked, 'what do you think? Isn't she wonderful? I don't understand you, I must admit. I could never see why you didn't want to just grab her and rip her clothes off – she's so ... delicious, edible almost. Mind you, it wasn't easy to get hold of her. She had a psychological block, you know. Couldn't do it with anyone below major.

Whenever I saw her I had to go and take a cold shower. Fortunately that problem was solved later on. And the money was a great help, I can tell you.' He swallowed down his whisky and ordered another one for both of them. 'Mind you,' he went on, slurring his words and grinning lecherously, 'you probably had other fish to fry. What do you think of Paul here? More your type, eh?' He giggled inanely.

'Oh, shut up!' Schulz screamed at him. At a nearby table Paul stared at him in surprise and Schumacher himself looked quite offended. Schulz tore off his white barman's jacket and stormed out of the bar. As he flung open the exit door, he caught a glimpse of Bertha-Johanne, reappearing from the Ladies. It might have been his imagination, but she looked as though she had been crying.

It was still there. That is to say, it hadn't been built over. It was, of course, mostly ruined. Where the roof had been, there was now a gaping hole, and most of the front façade and the main hall had been blasted. Where ten years earlier there had been a stretch of lawn, immaculately cut and symmetrically divided by a stone stairway that led down to the River Marne below, there was now a sprawling mass of undergrowth, with no sign of the peacocks, or indeed of any animal or human life. Schulz stood before the entrance door in a daze.

He still didn't know why he was at Vitry-le-François, except that the chateau had been drawing him like a magnet for years. Ten years ago, on 5 June 1940, he had stood in the same spot, but then he had had a very different goal: to stay alive. Now he had come back to find out what he had stayed alive for. Perhaps he had imagined for an absurd moment that the comtesse would be in her bedroom, brushing her hair and waiting for him with aristocratic impatience. But she must be in her fifties by now and probably cruising around the world with his money. That's if she'd got hold of the briefcase. He'd never quite been sure. Maybe he even thought that the Gestapo would somehow have missed spotting it: he really didn't know.

He had packed up his job at Bandol the morning after he had been catapulted out of his stretch of normality. The maître d', a fat, kindly man, who had treated Schulz almost as a son, wept, pressing into his hand an envelope which Schulz assumed contained a monetary token of his gratitude. When he had returned to his room for the last time, and opened it, he discovered inside a sheet of the hotel toilet paper on which was scrawled in lipstick: 'I told you, we're both out of the same Berlin gutter. Love, Bertha.' Underneath, as a cruel afterthought, she had printed a kiss. He didn't know whether to laugh or cry. Instead, he had torn up the toilet paper and flushed it down the toilet, before going out and getting paralytically drunk.

Now he clambered over piles of broken stone and rubble that half blocked the entrance. Although it was still light outside, inside it was dark and gloomy. Fortunately Schulz had brought a torch. He shone the beam inside the entrance hall, appalled, even though he could hardly have expected anything else. The former treasure house of elegance and grandeur, a miniature version of Versailles, Fontainebleau and Compiègne, was now a shattered, ransacked warehouse. Even the marble slabs from the fireplace had been removed. He felt like a pathologist performing a post mortem on a long-putrified body. The wallpaper had been stripped, light fittings torn out of their sockets, wiring plundered. Because he had come this far, and because he wasn't doing anything that night, he decided to explore the rest of the chateau.

Upstairs the picture was much the same. The rooms were unrecognizable but he remembered that the master bedroom was on the right of the corridor. Out of curiosity, he clambered through torn rafters and chunks of plaster into the room: cobwebs hung from broken beams; the windows were now jagged holes, and shards of glass littered the floor. Even the birds' nests on the window sills had been abandoned.

In the midst of this rubbish dump Schulz sat down and cried for his lost youth and dreams and his lost inheritances, and for a woman who had only done what he would probably have done himself in a similar situation: after all they were kindred souls. He half expected to hear the roar of bombers ripping through the stillness but the only sounds were the sighing of the wind and the low sobbing from his abdomen: he was extremely hungry.

Gently he got to his feet as if not to disturb the dead and groped his way out. As he pushed open the door that had swung back on its rusty hinges, he shone the torch idly on the opposite corner and noticed something. Bending down, he pulled from a heap of plaster and rotten wood a stiff colourless piece of material that – in spite of the years of rain and snow which had mildewed and rotted it into a bizarre and unrecognizable shape – was still decidedly tweedy. After ten years, Schulz was reunited with his plus-fours.

By the light of the torch he identified the tie, a faded strip of linen, the tweed jacket and, finally, a filthy mis-shapen brogue shoe. After another search he found its partner. He wrapped the shoes and tie in the plus-fours and jacket and stumbled out. On the staircase he slipped on a missing rung and toppled down to the floor below where, the next morning, he was found by some children playing among the debris.

27

They thought he was dead at first, and ran screaming back to the village. Their parents called the police and two gendarmes arrived at the chateau half an hour later, dis-covered that his heart was still beating, and radioed at once for an ambulance. An hour later Schulz was admitted to hospital and by late afternoon he came to in an accident ward.

'You are very lucky, monsieur,' a neat, cultivated young doctor with a pointed little beard was saying. 'You have had slight concussion and sprained your ankle and wrist. There

are also some bruises to your back, but no broken bones!'
He looked disgruntled, as though he had been cheated out
of a nice fat wage packet.

'*Schuhen . . .*' groaned Schulz.

'Monsieur?' said the doctor, leaning closer. He looked
at the nurse. She shrugged her shoulders.

'*Schuhen . . .*' repeated Schulz who couldn't remember the
French for them.

'*Chouan?*' repeated the doctor. Was the patient a guerilla,
a member of the Resistance, left over perhaps from the
war?

'*Souliers, chaussons . . .* shoes!' Schulz gasped.

'*Ah, oui, monsieur, des souliers . . .*' repeated the doctor
in triumph. He looked again at the nurse. They both
shrugged. He stared at Schulz. 'What about them?'

'I must have them . . . very important!' gasped Schulz
again, trying to climb out of the bed, and crying out in pain.

'*Mais non, monsieur,* you must rest! said the nurse, a
pretty redhead. She forced Schulz back between the sheets
with the grip of a weightlifter.

'But . . . my shoes . . .' he moaned impotently. The doctor
and nurse looked at each other meaningfully. *Concussion
more serious than first assumed*, wrote the doctor, with
some satisfaction.

'Go to sleep now, monsieur, and when you wake up we
will have a long discussion all about your shoes,' said the
nurse. The doctor moved on to examine the next patient.

'Doctor, *please!*' Schulz began.

'Monsieur Schulz –' said the nurse firmly.

'How do you know my name?' said Schulz in surprise.

'Your passport and identity card were in your jacket,
monsieur. Naturally –'

'Then you've got my shoes as well?'

'Yes, monsieur?' the nurse replied with a sigh.

'I must see them at once, nurse. I promise not to get out
of bed,' said Schulz, taking command of the situation. The
nurse hesitated. Perhaps he had a gun concealed in them.
However he did not look as though he would know how to
use one. He *was* German though.

274

'Very well, monsieur,' she nodded. A few minutes later she returned with a pair of shoes covered in hygienic wrapping paper.

'You must not open them in the ward, monsieur. Germs.'

'They're not the ones!' said Schulz in exasperation.

'I'm sorry, monsieur, but they are. We do not make such mistakes in this hospital. You were wearing them when you were admitted!' She was beginning to raise her voice.

'But I'm talking about the others. The ones I wrapped in my plus-fours!'

'You mean the rags you had with you when they found you in the bomb site, monsieur!' She was too young to remember the chateau. 'They've gone to the incinerator. Germs, monsieur.'

'*Incinerator?*' repeated Schulz.

'Yes, monsieur, they were infested with germs. Now you must get some rest –' But Schulz had no intention of resting. He had climbed out of bed again, and this time the strength of ten weightlifter-nurses would not have been able to hold him down. He limped with amazing speed out of the ward into the landing, and down the stairs. In the main reception area he rushed up to the first nurse he could see; a plump elderly woman.

'Excuse me, mademoiselle, where is the incinerator?' he asked. 'I have to inspect it.'

She stared at his pyjamas.

I am carrying out an inspection for the Health Department!' said Schulz. 'We believe your incinerator is dangerous.'

By reflex she pointed to the far exit.

'But monsieur –' she started to say.

But Schulz had already retreated down the corridor towards the exit.

The orderly had been working at the hospital for under a month. He was anxious to perform his job well, and equally anxious to get the rubbish loaded into the garbage truck as quickly as possible. He had ten minutes to shift the last bin, tidy up and cycle home. He had a date with Monique and she didn't like to be kept waiting.

He wheeled the last bin out to the waiting truck, heaved the contents over the side, signalled all-clear to the driver, and turned back to the hospital yard with his attention firmly set on the evening ahead.

One might therefore say that Monique had a lot to answer for.

A hunched figure in a shabby brown overcoat plastered with old medals, and a beret, was proceeding slowly down the avenue, his hand cupped over his eyes to protect them from the glare of the setting sun. He paused at lamp-posts and trees to catch his breath, since he was suffering from asthma and twinges of gout. His feet were hurting him particularly: they were covered in old sores and blisters but he couldn't afford new shoes. In any case he was proud of his old army boots. They were a souvenir of the war he had fought for the Kaiser a few years earlier.

As he approached the exit gate to the hospital yard he stumbled. Painfully he stooped down and picked up a brown paper bag, sealed with tape. It must have fallen out of a dustbin. Out of curiosity he began to tear it open.

The orderly was locking the gates as a pyjama-clad figure erupted from the service door, made for the line of bins and proceeded to tip them over in turn like a row of dominoes, screaming with mounting incoherence as each bin emitted a drum-roll of emptiness. The obviously deranged patient then turned and hobbled straight for the now-terrified orderly, the gates and, presumably, freedom. All thoughts of Monique wiped from his mind; the orderly watched aghast as the wretched lunatic desperately clawed at the wire mesh and rattled the bars of the gates, while the disappearing garbage truck lurched and bumped over the potholes of the avenue, trailing a long plume of dust.

The elderly tramp squatting on the pavement muttering

to himself paid no attention to the disturbance. He was concentrating on a pair of badly misshapen brogues into which he was fitting a pair of equally misshapen feet.

Suddenly the orderly remembered his position of trust and responsibility. Grabbing the would-be escaper and twisting his arms behind his back, he frog-marched him across the yard.

'I think, monsieur, you are making a big mistake,' moaned a subdued Schulz.

'I think, monsieur, you are out of your mind!' replied the orderly, much relieved to see two nurses and a porter coming to his assistance.

They carried Schulz back into the hospital. He was immediately sedated heavily and returned to the accident ward. He was still groaning about his shoes when he awoke the following afternoon. He was now very weak, not having eaten for two days and was fed and sedated again. The next morning he woke up in high spirits. The old man must be a local: it would not be difficult to trace him; he was bound to keep his find, like any old rubbish.

A week later, on a bright sunny morning in mid-June, Schulz walked out of the hospital and was immediately arrested by the French police.

Kurt Erhardt threw himself into the shadow of a shop doorway and swallowed a stick of chewing gum. In the distance he could hear the mournful wail of a ship's siren from the Hamburg docks; from somewhere nearer, a police car siren screeched along the Reeperbahn. He waited for it to fade before slinking back into the street. Suddenly he heard a police whistle behind him.

'There he is, get him!' cried a voice. He tore down the block, turning into an even shadier street, ran halfway along it and scrambled up a fire exit. From below he could hear shouts and footsteps, police whistles and dogs barking. *The game's up*, he thought, *I should never have got into it in the first place*. Times had been hard, though, since the war had ended and he'd been pressganged into the robbery.

All he'd got out of it was a bleeding shoulder when he'd followed the others out of the jeweller's window. Before he could make it to the getaway car it had sped off with the diamonds. He paused for breath at a landing, one floor below the top of the fire exit. More police whistles came from above him.

'You can't get away, scum!' came a voice. 'You're surrounded! Give yourself up!'

Kurt looked round desperately. There was a door at the far end of the landing. He hurled himself towards it: it was locked. He banged on it in a frenzy, not because he expected anyone to be there at this time, but because there was nothing else to do. Suddenly the door opened. A tall thin man, wearing a ridiculous blond wig and dark glasses, appeared in the shadows.

'What on earth do you think you're doing?' he barked. 'Do you know what time it is?'

'You've got to help me, mein Herr!' whispered Kurt frantically. He saw the scar on the man's cheek and made a wild guess. 'In the name of the Fuhrer!' he added. There was something familiar about the man in the wig.

There was something familiar about this huge lump of beef, thought the man in the shadows. Could he have been one of the couriers, or maybe a guard? Then he recognized him. He pointed to the lavatory door.

'You can thank the Fuhrer I've got a kind heart!' he snarled. Kurt could have wept.

'Thank you, mein Herr,' he whispered. 'I'll never forget.' He scampered into the lavatory and closed the door. Seconds later the police rushed in. Seconds later they rushed out of the front door, through which, the man had told them, the thief had made his escape. When Kurt had finally slunk out of the lavatory, the man was sitting in an armchair. He had removed his wig.

'Aren't you – ?'

'Hold your tongue!' snapped the man, now folding a newspaper which he had been reading with deep interest. He took a sip of brandy and chuckled to himself.

'How would you like to work for me again?' he ordered.

278

It might take years, but it would be worth the wait.

'I still can't get over it, Herr Schulz! I never thought I'd see you again.'

Schulz nodded glumly at Frau Nusbaum. He was thinking the same thing, though with less ecstasy than his former landlady. Since Hamburg was still entered in his passport as his town of residence he had inevitably found himself back in her front room, staring dutifully at the untwinkling eyes of Herr Nusbaum that still regarded him sternly from the mantelpiece. He had to admit though that his old room was cheap and, when Frau Nusbaum had put on the kettle and informed him that she was changing the sheets in his honour, he had felt relieved. Hers was at least a familiar face and it was quite probable that her playroom was now firmly locked up for good.

'Funnily enough, Herr Schulz, I was clearing out the playroom only this morning and it seemed quite sad and empty,' she said. 'It's been eleven years since we played in it, you know.' She smiled happily. That was when Schulz remembered that today was Saturday.

He smiled politely back and drank some ersatz coffee, hoping that Frau Nusbaum had not been reading the local paper too closely. His deportation had not made the headlines, certainly, but it had been reported on one of the back pages under the heading: HAMBURGER CAUSES FRACAS IN FRENCH HOSPITAL OVER SHOES. Underneath was a short explanation:

Gerhardt Schulz, 42, was deported last night from France, following an incident in a Vitry hospital. Schulz, a patient, caused a disturbance because, he later claimed, they had tried to set fire to his shoes. A hospital spokesman denied this: 'His own shoes were locked away with his clothes when he was admitted. Those he claimed were burnt were English shoes, infested by microbes, which we confiscated and destroyed in accordance with hospital regulations.' Schulz later commented: 'Fortunately the

279

hospital was so incompetent it couldn't even burn them. An old man stole them before I got the chance to get them back.' Schulz, claims the French police, was a leading Nazi and his presence in France is undesirable. German authorities are taking no action on this, although he will not be permitted re-entry to France for four years and must report monthly to the Hamburg police.

After finishing his coffee and giving Frau Nusbaum a doctored account of his distinguished war career, he asked casually if he could borrow the paper to do the crossword.

'Certainly,' replied Frau Nusbaum merrily. 'You make yourself comfortable while I go and have a bath. What a terrible business that war was. Still, it cleared the air. Though I doubt whether things will ever be the same,' she added sadly. At the door she paused. 'I think I'll be popping out to buy some refreshments, Herr Schulz: our little treat.' She beamed at him and sighed. 'It will be quite like old times.'

Schulz also sighed, with relief that she had not yet had time to read the paper and in apprehension at the forthcoming visit to her no-doubt-roomier-than-ever playroom.

For the next four years Schulz resigned himself to the life of a solid German citizen. After all, what else could he do? He had little money – there was no point in going to England because he had more or less completely forgotten where the canister was buried and in any case he was expected to report to the police once a month. After the first few months though it was obvious that the police took the matter as lightly as he did and by tacit agreement they both forgot about it. But by that time Schulz had found himself a lucrative job of sorts.

In spite of Frau Nusbaum's ignorance of his police record, both before and after the war, it was impossible to conceal it from prospective employers. This had persuaded him to throw himself on the mercy of Herr Krauss. Though the office proved to have been demolished along with Herr

Krauss, it did not take him long to track down Krauss's nephew who had set up business in another part of Hamburg.

Hans Krauss had been little more than a child during the war years and, now in his early twenties, he was full of evangelistic zeal for the new Germany and the economic miracle which he was convinced was about to take place. Schulz was himself looking for an economic miracle and was therefore happy to fall in with his plans. Hans had inherited a small shipping firm from his father and was only too delighted to hire Schulz and his five languages. Ships docked at Hamburg travelled all over the world. Schulz however was principally interested in those that called at Southampton, Hull and Liverpool, and particularly London. Although he was not able to return to France for four years, there was nothing to stop him making a trip to England for a reconnoitre – except time and money.

Meanwhile he was bolstered by the secure knowledge that two million pounds still lay buried in a canister somewhere in a field in Kent. Like the canister the knowledge lay somewhere just under the surface. It did not obsess him night and day: it warmed him with a pleasant glow – his time would come. Occasionally he still had nightmares of Neuheim and Kube and Heydrich and all the other SS crooks, and would wake up sweating with fear. Sometimes, too, he thought of Solly. Even if he had managed to survive he might have been handed over to the Soviet troops as a Russian national and was probably living out the rest of his life in abject poverty behind the Iron Curtain. He consoled himself with the thought that Solly was a professional prisoner who would have felt instantly at home in the communist state provided he was allowed to forge for Stalin or his successors. He rarely thought of Bertha-Johanne.

He prepared for his return to France in June 1954 for months. From his earnings he had bought a secondhand Volkswagen. His plan was to find the old man, offer him a substantial sum for the shoes and head for England. Frau Nusbaum was heartbroken about his intended departure, as was Herr Krauss. Schulz had been an invaluable asset to

281

the company: profits had doubled since his arrival at Krauss Shipping. This was not unconnected with Schulz's regular and ingenious doctoring of accounts, which was unlikely to be discovered until he was out of the country, if indeed it were ever discovered at all. Meanwhile he had earned for himself and for Herr Krauss a large bonus. Every Deutschmark would be necessary for the successful execution of his final attempt to benefit from the proceeds of Operation Bernhard. Naturally he felt guilty that it was necessary to bite the hand that fed him. It was not done in a spirit of vengeance for the meanness of Hans's uncle. He was genuinely grateful for Hans's generosity and he fully intended to return to Germany and give him a substantial share of what he now thought of as his Anglo-German inheritance.

Nevertheless he felt distinctly uneasy when Krauss handed him a cheque for a thousand marks, shaking him warmly by the hand.

'You are leaving at an auspicious time in Germany's history,' said Hans with great passion. Schulz had been hearing these words all his life. 'We are on the edge of an economic miracle and you should have been here to share it with us,' added Krauss with tears in his eyes.

'Don't worry, Herr Krauss,' replied Schulz, just as passionately, 'I *shall* be sharing it with you.'

He shaved off his moustache before leaving Hamburg. He would be living in the vicinity of the hospital at Vitry and he did not fancy another four years' deportation.

'You look quite your old self, Herr Schulz,' said Frau Nusbaum, also with tears in her eyes.

'So do you, Frau Nusbaum,' said Schulz jovially. Actually it was true: Frau Nusbaum had settled into middle age fourteen years ago and had decided to stay there.

'I know you'll be back so I'm keeping your room just as it is. Why are you leaving anyway?'

'To pick up some valuable footwear, Frau Nusbaum,' said Schulz mysteriously.

'Oh, you're teasing me again, Herr Schulz,' she giggled. 'Two can play at that game.' Schulz felt her foot tickling his underneath the table. He didn't want to hurt her but had decided to leave before she could make any further suggestions. He stood up.

'My dear lady,' he said gently, 'just wait till you feel the quality of the footwear I shall be bringing back with me. It will be worth the wait.

'I really think you mean it,' she said looking at him wistfully.

28

Schulz took up residence in a small *pension* near the Place d'Armes in Vitry. It was central enough to allow him an uninterrupted view of three busy thoroughfares in the heart of the town, but he soon tired of sitting in his room and chose instead a café in the main street, just off the square.

As July gave way to August, Schulz began to lose sight of his reason for being there. He thought he had memorized the old man's face, dress and general physique, but soon discovered that the *Place* was full of old men in overcoats with medals, berets, and even brogues, though never *the* brogues. He was vegetating himself. Although he had made attempts to chat to the old folk and question them, he rarely drew them out with more than a *oui* or *non* or *c'est ça*. He tended however to keep to himself, not wishing to attract too much attention. So far he had been successful in avoiding the friendly solicitations of the old spinster on the floor below to join him for tea. Occasionally she bumped into him on the landing and, having discovered that he was born in Berlin, never tired of telling Schulz of her brother who had returned to Berlin a few years ago to see it one last time before he passed away. Schulz himself had only bad memories of Berlin and could not understand why anyone should want to return there.

As September came and the first leaves of autumn fell, Schulz grew desperate. He had searched through all the secondhand shops and cobblers, he had tried the local *dépot de mendicité*, where all the tramps and beggars were housed. He had even placed adverts in *tabac* windows, but apparently none of Vitry's senior citizens could read. It was of course, possible that the old man had died, in which case the brogues might remain stuffed in a wardrobe or drawer or under a bed in some little hovel in or around the town. He could hardly call from house to house without a valid excuse. The only people who did that were charity workers and *chiffonniers* – rag and bone men: both alternatives were out of the question ...

He purchased a false beard and grey wig, an old shabby suit, collarless shirt and red-spotted scarf. To complete the image he acquired a cart and horse from another *chiffonnier* who, having argued that Schulz was taking away his livelihood, had finally agreed to a figure that was half of Schulz's savings. The Volkswagen was parked in a garage on the outskirts of Vitry, not far from the ruined chateau. The horse and cart were stabled in an old shed nearby. Every morning he dressed in his best suit and tie and left for work at 9.00 a.m. He would then walk across Vitry to the shed, change into his *chiffonnier* garb, beard and wig, and make his house calls. After three months he had tried nearly every house in Vitry, asking particularly for old unwanted shoes, especially brogues. Vitry's population was about ten thousand and there were three thousand houses to visit: he averaged fifty calls a day. Often no one was at home or the door was slammed in his face. Even so he now had a huge collection of old shoes, all unwanted, especially by Schulz. And a garage-full of other useless junk.

The only unvisited houses were those in his immediate neighbourhood. As Christmas approached he had had enough of being a rag-and-bone man. It was beginning to snow and although his desire was as tenacious as ever, he decided on a more direct approach. He resold the cart and horse for a fraction of the price he had paid for it to another *chiffonnier*, its original owner having probably hopped it to the Riviera. Now he visited the houses on the neighbouring blocks, explaining that his uncle had died and he had come to collect his property, describing the old man and the shoes in detail. He was so convincing that he soon had another collection of useless junk and was now in a quandary. He decided to cut his losses – or gains – and abandon the search. Perhaps if he stopped looking, they would find him: he still remembered Ebensee. Instead he would remain in Vitry and find work. His savings had dwindled to practically nothing. At least Mlle Eclaire was too old to enjoy playrooms, let alone attics.

He began as a secondhand dealer, renting a shop in Vitry to which he transported the junk from the garage in the Volkswagen. For the next few years he toured St Dizier, Chalons-sur-Marne, Reims and other neighbouring towns for worthless nick-nacks which he tried to sell at inflated prices. He even went to Paris, visiting the bookshops down by the Seine, but soon ran out of money and returned to Vitry determined to make a profit out of his wasted time. Unfortunately there was not much profit in old shoes and nick-nacks in Vitry at this time and finally he sold his entire stock to another *chiffonnier* for a pittance.

He returned to the *pension* and within three weeks made plans to return to Germany. He was about to pack on Christmas Eve, when there was a knock on his door.

'Come in,' he said despondently, already guessing who it was. Sure enough Mlle Eclaire appeared in the room with a bottle of wine in her hand and a smile on her lips.

'*Bon Noël,* monsieur,' she said merrily, hesitating when she saw signs of packing. 'I thought, as it was Christmas, you might like to join me for a festive glass.'

Schulz also hesitated: he had no desire to hear more stories about her brother. Then he smiled.

'Of course, mademoiselle. I would be delighted.'

Her flat was exactly as he had imagined. The front room,

in which he was seated by the fire, had an old-fashioned, musty air. Framed photographs of long-dead relatives lined the mantelpiece, old postcards of Paris, Berlin and Nice at the turn of the century, and artificial flowers in ornate vases, and the faint aroma of camphor, rose petals and moth balls made him shudder.

'I haven't seen much of you, Monsieur Schulz, in the last few months,' said Mlle Eclaire, a birdlike little lady, as she poured him another glass of wine and handed him a plate of biscuits.

'Well, you know, I've been rather tied up,' replied Schulz, glancing at a photograph of a young German soldier, obviously taken during or after the First World War.

'Ah,' she smiled with deep satisfaction. 'I see you have found Wilhelm.'

'Mademoiselle?' said Schulz.

'My brother Wilhelm. Yes, it's a German name, Monsieur Schulz. Our mother was German and poor papa was French. He died in the trenches. My brother fought on the opposite side.' The memory still made her cry. 'Wilhelm was named after the Kaiser, you know. He was born in the same year that Kaiser Wilhelm II came to power, 1888. My mother was heartbroken after the news of poor papa's death and we moved back to Vitry, where my father's family used to live, but Wilhelm – my brother, that is – always considered himself German. Have some more wine, Monsieur Schulz.' She poured him some more, while Schulz looked discreetly at his watch.

'Of course he was young then and handsome,' she prattled on. 'You would have liked him. But the war broke his spirit, monsieur. And he suffered badly from *la goutte*, especially his toe. Also he had trench fever, you know – and his feet had the gangrene. But he still wore his old army boots, he was very attached to them. As a matter of fact, monsieur, he wrote to me recently asking me to send them, but the post is so expensive nowadays and alas, I have not been well.'

'Your brother's still alive then?' asked Schulz without much interest.

'Why, yes, of course he is, though he has been very ill in recent years, both in body and in mind. That's why I begged him not to return to Berlin. But he's a stubborn man, monsieur, and he'd made up his mind. I have a more recent photo of him somewhere.' She got up and went over to an old oak sideboard and started to rummage through a drawer. Schulz cleared his throat, looking again at his watch.

'It really doesn't matter if you can't find it, mademoiselle,' he began to say. 'I mean, I would prefer to remember him from this photo in the German army.'

'So would he, Monsieur Schulz,' she sighed. 'Ah!' she suddenly shrieked, 'Here it is.'

She handed him a small, dog-eared photo. Schulz examined it politely. It showed an old man in a beret and a shabby overcoat with stout shoes. He wrily thought of all the similar old men he had seen in his first three months at Vitry. He didn't even notice them nowadays, they were as familiar as the birds on the trees ...

'*Mon Dieu!*' said Mlle Eclaire from somewhere near his ear. Schulz jumped.

'What's the matter, mademoiselle?' he said in alarm. But he then saw that she was looking distastefully at the photo. 'Well,' he added tactfully, 'we all grow old.'

'*Non*, monsieur, it's those shoes, they were so *dégoutant*. Rat-infested, if you ask my opinion. But Wilhelm grew quite fond of them. He always wore them and he used to say they were good for his feet.'

'Really?' said Schulz politely. It was time he made some excuse to leave.

'Yes,' went on Mlle Eclaire. 'He brought them home one day a few years ago, in a paper bag. He said they were special hospital shoes – but that's because he found them in the street by the hospital.'

'*Really?*' said Schulz who had suddenly gone very pale.

'*Oui*, monsieur, I said that he should burn them but he said they were worth a million.'

'Two,' whispered Schulz, starting to tremble.

'Monsieur?'

287

'Mademoiselle Eclaire,' said Schulz ingratiatingly, 'I would be most honoured to make the acquaintance of your brother in Berlin and –'

'Why, monsieur!' cried Mlle Eclaire in delight. 'You have taken the words out of my mouth. I didn't know how to ask you. You see I did say I would post them and I saw that you were packing and wondered –'

'Post what?' said Schulz excitedly.

'Why, the shoes, monsieur.'

'*You mean – you've got his shoes!*' screamed Schulz.

She looked at him rather curiously. 'But I've already told you, monsieur. I have them here.'

Schulz tried to contain himself, but he shook with excitement as Mlle Eclaire pulled an old pair of boots out of the dresser drawer.

'But – these aren't them!' he said, crestfallen.

'Yes they are,' said Mlle Eclaire. 'They're the boots Wilhelm asked me to post.' Suddenly Schulz understood.

'I shall be delighted to give them to your brother personally,' he said. 'I expect you will be glad to feel that he has got rid of those other shoes – the disgusting pair in that photo – and I will be happy to dispose of them for you.'

Mlle Eclaire smiled. 'You are too kind, Monsieur Schulz. Now, let us have some more wine.'

'I'm afraid I really must be going now, Mademoiselle Eclaire,' he said hurriedly. 'But of course you must give me your brother's address ... in Berlin.'

She looked a little disappointed and sighed. 'I understand, monsieur, there is perhaps something – or someone – dear to your heart in Germany and you cannot wait to be back with them?'

'You are a very perceptive woman, mademoiselle,' replied Schulz, beaming.

My dear Frau Nusbaum,

It does seem such a long time since I have written and for that I can only apologize from the bottom of my heart. However I hope to be back in Hamburg in a few months time and look forward immensely to renewing our acquaintance. I am at present staying in Paris. It is such a magnificent city and one to which I sincerely hope that I will be able to return and set up business after I receive a little windfall which I am expecting imminently. In connection with this I shall be travelling to Berlin, and can be contacted during the next fortnight care of Herr Eclaire, at the following address:

> Das Raftenbauen 417,
> Frankfurter Strasse 60
> Berlin

I would be obliged if you would do me a slight favour, dear lady, which I hope will not inconvenience you. Could you deliver the enclosed letter immediately (that is most important) to Herr Krauss, my former employer.

I hesitate to write to him direct in case, though I know it is unlikely, he has moved his office and I cannot afford a delay in this confidential matter. I do hope that your corns are not plaguing you. I trust also, of course, that your little playroom is not too lonely.

> Your former tenant and permanent friend,
> *Gerhardt Schulz*

Dear Herr Krauss,

I have never forgotten your kindness and generosity to me while I was in your employ and, during the last few years I have thought often of you and of how I have hoped to repay you. Unfortunately until this time that has not been possible but in the near future I am expecting to inherit a great deal of money. As a token of my gratitude I am looking forward to offering you a share of this, which, I can assure you, will be very substantial indeed. It is difficult to elaborate in this letter on the nature of this inheritance, but suffice it to say that I have recently discovered a very valuable item of footwear which is at present in the possession of a gentleman whom I shall be visiting shortly. Meanwhile I would like to ask one rather large and last favour of you. I am at the present

P.S. – K

time a little short of funds. I hesitate to take advantage of our relationship, but I would be eternally in your debt if you would be prepared to loan me a small sum – say, a thousand marks, which sum, let me assure you, will be repaid many times over. If you are able to accommodate this request would you please send me a cheque to that amount as soon as possible, care of Herr Eclaire, at the following address:

> Das Raftenbauen 417,
> Frankfurter Strasse 60
> Berlin.

I am, as always, your humble servant,
Gerhardt Schulz

In the years since his last visit, Berlin had been given a complete facelift, after being bombed out of recognition. Modern apartment blocks had sprung up like symmetrical mushrooms all over the western sector, though the old building in the Delbruckstrasse was still standing, and he half-expected to see Neuheim swaggering out of the door. But it was only a momentary lapse. Beside him in the Volks-wagen were Eclaire's army boots in a canvas bag and in his pocket was a letter of introduction from the old man's sister. Soon the brogues would be his.

The Raftenbauen proved to be a symmetrical mushroom. As Schulz pressed the lift button to the fourth floor he could hardly believe that the old man would prefer to live here than in Vitry, or at least some less faceless part of West Berlin, or Germany.

'I don't want any more charity,' said Eclaire as he opened the door. He looked much as he did in the photo, except a little older, more hunched, and even more depressed. Schulz couldn't blame him.

'I'm a friend of your sister's, Monsieur Eclaire,' said Schulz hurriedly, before the door could be slammed in his face. 'She gave me this to give you.' He pulled out the letter and photograph.

'*Herr* Eclaire,' replied the old man with a frown. 'Well,

you'd better come in,' he added grudgingly, taking the letter from Schulz and wandering back inside. Schulz followed, nervously clutching the canvas bag.

'Adele is always fussing,' Eclaire wheezed, folding up the letter. 'One reason why I came here was to get away from her. To get a bit of peace.'

Schulz looked around at the bare little room. 'Well, it's certainly peaceful here,' he said.

'Too peaceful,' grumbled the old man. 'The Kaiser should never have abdicated. The peace terms were a mockery!'

'I've brought your boots,' Schulz said after a pause, pulling them out of the bag.

'Well, you'd better put them down,' Eclaire wheezed.

Schulz had not been invited to sit down but he did so nevertheless. Eclaire did not seem to stand on ceremony.

'Your sister mentioned –'

'She's always mentioning,' grumbled Eclaire, wheezing again. While Schulz waited for him to finish he looked round the room. There was a pleasant view of the trees of the Grunewald in the distance. Otherwise it was as austere as Eclaire himself. The only decoration was a collection of World War I memorabilia, including some evil-looking guns and medals and a helmet. Eclaire was placing his boots next to the collection with a great deal of care and pleasure.

'She told me that you had some ... shoes which I gather were of no further use to you,' said Schulz.

'I told you I didn't want charity,' repeated Eclaire, scowling ferociously.

'Oh come, Herr Eclaire, it's hardly a question of charity, it's simply that now you've got your boots back, I wouldn't have thought you'd need –'

'Of course I need them,' grunted the old man.

'The boots?'

'Yes!'

'But not the shoes?'

'Well, obviously I need the shoes. What am I supposed to wear?' the old man snarled.

Schulz was confused. 'The boots?' he suggested.

'Are you mad?' Eclaire glared at him. 'I can't *wear*

them. I need them for my collection.'

Schulz stared at the memorabilia with dismay. 'But you shouldn't be wearing those shoes,' he said. 'They're bad for your feet.'

'How *dare* you!' screamed Eclaire. 'Who are you? Are you one of *them*? What business is it of yours how my feet are? In any case those shoes are brand new. Look!' Schulz looked: M Eclaire was wearing a shiny brown pair of shoes.

'But what about the shoes you found in the bag?' he said, 'by the hospital ...'

'You are one of those damned charity people, aren't you?' yelled Eclaire hoarsely, reaching for an enormous blunderbuss.

'For God's sake, don't shoot me, Herr Eclaire!' Schulz cried out in fright, raising his hands above his head. 'I swear to you I'm not from any charity! I'm a friend of your sister's.' The old man regarded him ferociously for a minute and then lowered his gun.

'Well,' he grunted, 'you don't look like one of them. Called themselves charity workers or social workers. Said I had no business to be wearing them. Looked more like thugs to me, especially the one in the blond wig, and dark glasses.'

Schulz felt the icy waters of Toplitz lapping round him, the roar of the boat's engine as it sped off into the dawn mist and out of the headlights of the police cars, in a futile attempt to escape. It wasn't possible, he thought. One of those confounded logs *had* struck the boat; Neuheim and Walter *had* been flung overboard; the money *had* gone down with them. Anyway, what about the body that had been washed ashore? Even if it wasn't Neuheim – or even Walter – it was inconceivable that either of them could have slipped through the police net that had surrounded the lake. But he shivered with the creeping apprehension that for the past fifteen years Neuheim *might* not only have been alive but have quietly been keeping tabs on him, waiting for him to pick up a pair of brogues. Who else shared his obsessive interest in them? – apart of course from Eclaire. But then, the old man didn't know about the heel.

'You didn't ever have those shoes mended did you?' he stuttered, as the new thought struck him.

'How did you know that? I didn't tell those thugs?' said Eclaire.

'You mean you *knew* about the heel?' asked Schulz going even paler.

'Of course I knew about the heel!' wheezed Eclaire. 'Wore them for ten years. The most comfortable shoes I've ever had. But the heel was worn down so I sent them to the cobbler's. I'm going to collect them this afternoon.'

Schulz took a deep breath. 'Herr Eclaire – this ... social worker, the one with the wig – did he have a scar?'

Eclaire began to raise his blunderbuss again. 'You *know* him?' he cried. 'You're one of them!'

'Herr Eclaire – in the name of all the brave and loyal Germans who died in the trenches for the Kaiser – I am not one of them!'

The old man eyed Schulz fiercely, wheezing atrociously, and finally seemed to make up his mind. He nodded, and lowered his gun.

'I told them I'd got rid of the shoes but they wouldn't believe me,' he snorted. 'They even tried to threaten me. One of them had a gun. But I showed those little pipsqueaks. I was a lieutenant in the Kaiser's Army!'

'You didn't shoot them, did you?' asked Schulz hopefully.

'I didn't get a chance. They shot out of the door like mice, the cowards!' he jeered, waving the gun. He suddenly paused in mid-gesture. 'Can't understand it: a lot of damn fuss over a pair of old brogues.'

Schulz thought quickly.

'Herr Eclaire, I must tell you that those shoes were no ordinary brogues. There was something important hidden in the heel.'

'Really?' said Eclaire. He looked suspicious again. 'How do you know?'

'It's a long story, Herr Eclaire, but one day I will tell you about it. I was a secret agent in the war – for the Fatherland, of course. Those men who visited you are traitors. The future of the Empire is at stake. The theft of those shoes could cost millions!'

Eclaire looked very impressed.

'What are we to do?' he said.

'Give me the receipt – the one the cobbler must have given you. I must get them back for you and for Germany – before they get into the hands of traitors!'

'Of course, of course!' said Eclaire, stumbling to a little chest of drawers. Presently he handed Schulz the slip of paper with trembling fingers.

'The Kaiser would be proud of you, Lieutenant Eclaire!' said Schulz, saluting him, and turning to go.

'Wait a minute –' began Eclaire.

'I can't stop, Herr Lieutenant, Germany needs me in this dark hour!' Schulz called out from halfway down the corridor. As he pressed the lift button he could see the old man running painfully towards him waving his gun and screaming at him. It was only when he reached the ground floor that he realized what Eclaire had been holding in his other hand.

When Eclaire opened his door again he was cursing and waving his gun around dementedly.

'I'm sorry, Herr Eclaire – I believe you've got a letter for me,' said Schulz sheepishly.

'Why do you think I was chasing after you?' wheezed the old man. 'To shoot you?' He broke into a renewed fit of wheezing. 'I've lost my glasses, I want you to read this letter that came for me. I can't read without them. Do you think it's from *them*?' He held out a letter which had a Hamburg postmark and was addressed to Schulz in Frau Nusbaum's familiar flowery handwriting.

'Actually, Herr Eclaire, this letter's for me,' said Schulz apologetically.

Eclaire screwed his eyes up and lifted his gun again. 'Don't you play games with me, young man. This is *my* letter. It arrived a few days after Christmas.'

It was an argument that could go on for the rest of the day and might end in bloodshed. Schulz opened the envelope and skimmed the contents. Frau Nusbaum was ecstatic to hear from him and hoped his health was good. Her corns were playing her up ... She rambled on about her health for a few more sentences.

'It's from the Kaiser's intelligence section,' Schulz said aloud.

'Aha!' Eclaire's eyes gleamed.

Now I must tell you about poor Herr Krauss, whose letter you asked me to forward. My dear Herr Schulz, this will come as a shock to you but ...

'We charge you in the name of the Kaiser to render every assistance to our emissary, Gerhardt Schulz, in a secret and highly important mission to regain valuable German intelligence before it falls into the hands of traitors to the German empire,'

'Upstarts!'

... soon after you left us, Herr Krauss was accused unjustly of embezzlement and was imprisoned for six years in Hamburg. What a terrible calamity to fall upon such a fine young man. Whoever responsible should come clean. What treachery ...

'Well? Any more about these traitors?'

'They're wanted for embezzlement,' said Schulz, feeling weak at the knees.

'I'm not surprised. Germany's gone to pot since Versailles. They say the Kaiser's dead, but *I* know he's alive. He'll put it right again.'

However as I'm sure Herr Krauss would love to hear from you – I still visit him and he always says how you were a loyal and devoted employee – I took a bus down to the prison the moment I got your letter and handed it in to the authorities and I'm sure you'll be hearing from him in due course ...

'Well, go on!'

Schulz was finding it difficult to digest the contents of the letter. He was naturally upset about Krauss but he was far more worried about Neuheim's reincarnation and all he wanted to do was retrieve the brogues from the cobbler before Neuheim got to them first.

'In the name of Kaiser Wilhelm I we salute you as a loyal patriot,' he continued, but stopped. Eclaire had picked his blunderbuss up again.

'You're making the whole thing up!' he roared, snatching the letter from Schulz before he could read more. 'Everyone knows the Kaiser's dead. He died in 1888. What year do you think we're living in?' Schulz was lost for words. 'I'll tell you then,' went on Eclaire, wheezing atrociously. '1920! I think you're one of those pipsqueaks. Give me back the receipt.' He aimed his gun.

This time Schulz didn't stop until he was out of the building and down the road where the Volkswagen was parked.

29

It was after six o'clock when he turned into the shop doorway, and the cobbler was shutting up the shop. Schulz pleaded silently through the glass door and finally the cobbler relented.

'I have a life to live you know,' he grumbled, locking the door again. He looked slightly familiar: perhaps all cobblers were alike with their polished foreheads and laced-up mouths, tongues neatly in place. Then Schulz remembered: this was the man from whom the brogues had been purchased by Ohm's technical division.

'Couldn't it have waited until tomorrow?' said the cobbler brusquely. He was now an old man, but he wore the same half-moon spectacles and his hands were still strong enough to rip off a sole with ease.

'I'm sorry,' said Schulz. 'I'm in a bit of a hurry.' The cobbler glanced at him, then peered at his face as though it were a damaged boot.

'Haven't I seen you somewhere before?'

'Yes,' said Schulz, smiling with relief. The cobbler might be better disposed if he remembered him. 'I used to work not far from here,' he explained, handing over the ticket. 'A long time ago.' The old man examined it and then stared at him curiously. 'Is anything wrong?' Schulz added.

'So they're *yours*,' said the cobbler, waving the ticket.

'Mine?'

'The brogues.'

'Yes,' Schulz replied firmly. 'Of course they're mine.'

The cobbler scratched his head. 'Well, that's rather odd. They were collected only an hour ago by an old man. The one they belonged to.' *Oh, Christ,* thought Schulz miserably. Eclaire had beaten him to it. He must have sprinted there. But he could hardly walk! 'They *were* the ones sent to me for repair by Herr Eclaire?' added the cobbler.

'Yes,' said Schulz gloomily. He did not look forward to tackling the old man again, with or without his blunderbuss. In any case the SS were probably lying in wait for him on the way. 'He's my father,' he added in a mutter, 'he must have collected them himself.' He turned to leave.

'Just a minute, Herr Schulz.'

His heart missed a beat. Perhaps the cobbler had a gun too. 'How did you know my name?' he whispered, turning back to face the new enemy.

The cobbler was looking very pleased with himself.

'I never forget a face,' he grinned.' 'Especially after he mentioned your name. That triggered off my memory, I can tell you.'

Schulz was puzzled. He surely hadn't given Eclaire his name. Then he remembered the letter.

'Now then – those brogues,' the cobbler was saying, still looking rather smug. 'They were soled and heeled – *and* I had to fumigate them.' He grinned at Schulz once more, but there was now a question in his smile.

Schulz hesitated.

'They were a very curious pair of brogues, Herr Schulz,' the cobbler went on. 'Do you want to know why?' Schulz already knew why. He slowly nodded, waiting for the inevitable.

The cobbler was enjoying himself immensely. 'Then I'll tell you why,' he went on. 'One of those brogues had a trick heel. When I started to remove it, it twisted round. The inside was hollow. Then, when I let it go, the heel snapped back again, as if by a spring. That's why I call them curious.'

In the cobbler's half-moon spectacles Schulz imagined he could see the secrets of the universe, twinkling like stars that could be observed but only half understood.

'Were they *really* yours?' insisted the cobbler. 'I mean after they were bought from my shop in 1940?' Schulz stared at him in awe. 'Oh yes, Herr Schulz,' went on the cobbler, 'I forgot to tell you – I never forget a pair of brogues either. Well, were they?' Again Schulz nodded. 'There was something inside,' said the old man, at last getting to the point. 'A map printed on silk. It was remarkable, Herr Schulz. After twenty years it was in perfect condition – without a single crease. Highly ingenious.'

'You don't ... you haven't ... kept it, have you, the piece of silk, Herr ... ?' Schulz said hoarsely.

'Krum. The name's Krum. Naturally I couldn't help looking at it. It was a map of Southern England.' He paused.

'Herr Krum –' Schulz began.

'What were you – a spy or something?' said Krum, removing his glasses so that he could see Schulz better. 'I never met a spy before. 'Do they get paid well – spies, I mean?'

Schulz looked at him wistfully. 'I was once one of the richest men in Germany,' he said in a faraway voice.

Krum wagged his head. 'Amazing! Tell me, are your lips sealed? Or have they released you from your oath of secrecy? The old man told me a little but I must admit I find it fascinating.'

'I don't think you'd believe me if I told you,' said Schulz. 'I doubt if anyone would ... You say the old man told you?' he added, sceptically. 'But Eclaire didn't know anything about it, not the real story at least. Anyway he was living in France.'

'Oh, that wasn't his name,' replied Krum knowingly. 'Eclaire was the one who brought them in here in the first place. But the old man knew about it all right. As a matter of fact he said he'd known you quite well for many years. He said he was going to keep it for you though he didn't expect to see you again.'

Schulz was dumbstruck. Then he remembered what he had come for.

'Herr Krum, did you keep the map, or –' he swallowed '– did you give it to him?' It must have been one of Neuheim's ploys.

'Of course I gave it to him. He paid me enough for it. He said he wanted it as a souvenir. Funny thing was – he paid me in British currency.' He pulled open the till and brought out a crisp five-pound note.

Schulz stared at it with beating heart. 'I don't suppose you remember his name, do you?' he asked miserably.

'I told you, Herr Schulz. I never forget a name. It was Solokoff. Ephraim Solokoff.'

'It must bring back the memories, eh, Gerhardt?' said Solly, looking from the map to Schulz, still amazed to see him again. Schulz nodded affectionately, both at Solly and the map. If he had expected Solly to be living in style on Bernhard money that particular illusion had been banished the moment he set foot in the cosy little West Berlin flat.

'An incredible story, Gerhardt. Amazing. And so, there are millions of my notes at the bottom of Toplitz.' He sighed. He, like Schulz, had been convinced when they left Ebensee that 'his' notes, as he liked to think of them, had been snatched up by Neuheim and Kaltenbrunner. 'And so the note I gave Krum really was the last one,' he sighed again. 'I kept it as a souvenir, you know,' he added guiltily, for the third time.

'I understand, Solly,' said Schulz. He hadn't mentioned that another enormous share had gone to Kube, and that what Kube had missed Albert and Johanne Schumacher and the last-ever clients of the Salon Kitty hadn't. But he did tell Solly about the ten-year search for the shoes which were now sitting safely by the hearth.

'You know what I was going to do with that map?' said

Solly. 'I was going to frame it. I was going to hang it on my wall, over the fireplace, say, pride of place. And then, please God, when my sons' children ask me for a bedtime story, I'd tell them how you dropped over England in the Great War.' He laughed, 'I never did forget those *mashugenah* shoes!'

Schulz chuckled along with Solly. It was hard to believe that the old man had only recognized the brogues in Herr Krum's window by chance, nor did he seem to appreciate the true value of the map.

'Yes,' he said. 'It will be a good story to tell your family, I suppose. But the truth is, Solly, I wasn't really thinking of framing it.'

'You weren't?' said Solly, pouring out the last of the Schnapps.

'No. I'll tell you what I was thinking of. I've searched for ten years for that map because twenty years ago I buried a canister in a field in Kent. As you well know, that canister contained two million pounds which are still waiting there to be discovered. And now I've got the key.'

Solly stared at Schulz as though he had just proposed starting another World War.

'You're not serious, Gerhardt?' he said. 'I always said you were mad!'

'And I'm not the only one who appreciates the value of this map,' went on Schulz, ignoring him. And he described the extraordinary reappearance of Neuheim – or someone very like him. 'Who else could know about it? It *must* be him!'

'But how did he find out about this old Frenchman?' said Solly, who was beginning to change his mind about framing the map. If Neuheim could threaten one old man he could also threaten another, and Solly didn't have a blunderbuss.

'That's what I've been trying to work out all day,' replied Schulz, sipping at his Schnapps. 'The only person I gave his address to was my old landlady in Hamburg, in case there was anything to be forwarded to me before I left for England – I didn't want to waste time. But she's not likely to be in league with Neuheim –' he hesitated.

'What's the matter?' said Solly.

'Oh, it's probably nothing,' Schulz had turned pale. 'It's just that . . . I also wrote to Krauss.'

'Who's Krauss?'

'He was my employer in Hamburg, a very decent man. In shipping.' Schulz had lapsed into thought. 'At least he was – he's . . . in prison now.'

Solly could hardly believe his ears. 'You mean you wrote a letter to a man in prison telling him of your intentions?'

'I didn't say much,' replied Schulz defensively.

'Gerhardt – you *are* crazy! Haven't you heard of postal censorship?'

Schulz stared at Solly dumbly. How could he have forgotten?

'In the war postal censorship was a vital function of the OKW. It employed thousands of workers and controlled more than two dozen postal and telegraph stations in Germany and the occupied territories,' chanted Solly, sounding like one of the SS manuals that had littered the Delbruckstrasse and Sachsenhausen. 'Of course, in peacetime, both before and after the war, postal censorship tends to be confined, Gerhardt, to prisons and, in case you've forgotten that too, the prison in Hamburg where you and I served time was, and still probably is, very hot on postal censorship. Furthermore, friends of mine who have been released from Hamburg in recent years tell me that the prison staff is now made up of ex-SS men. In short, Gerhardt, Neuheim has been waiting to hear from you for years.'

Schulz was silent.

'Did you hear me, Gerhardt?' said Solly irritably. Schulz seemed to have lapsed into a brooding silence. 'Look, Gerhardt,' Solly said more gently, 'don't worry. Just forget the whole thing. Neuheim doesn't know I've got the brogues and there's no reason why he should.'

Schulz slowly raised his eyes to Solly's; a sly smile had crept into his face.

'Oh, yes there is, Solly,' he said.

* * *

'You are kidding me, Gerhardt, yes?' said Solly. 'You are exposing me to incredible risks.' His keen eyes flashed like twin lighthouses warning of imminent disaster.

'It's foolproof, Solly!' cried Schulz with evangelistic fervour. 'Didn't I get you out of Nazi Germany alive when six million of your compatriots were murdered?'

'And now you want to get me murdered by one of the most fanatical Nazis of the lot. Haven't you heard of ODESSA?'

'Trust me, Solly! One last time! I promise you that not only will Neuheim not be able to touch you, but you'll have that map back, framed for all your thousands of descendants to see. And not in this poky little flat but in the richest mansions of Germany, or France, or ... wherever you want to go!'

Solly shook his head sadly.

'You still don't understand, Gerhardt, I'm too old to move.'

'Then do it for me. Unless of course you don't think you're up to it,' Schulz added. 'I must admit that it will need a delicate hand to do it properly and perhaps ...' He lowered his eyes doubtfully at Solly's fingers.

'There's nothing wrong with my hands, Schulz,' said Solly indignantly. 'And to prove it –' He stopped abruptly as he saw the trap Schulz had led him into.

'It will be your last forgery, Solly, and your greatest!' said Schulz with eyes that shone as they had not done for a dozen years.

Schulz finally convinced Solly that there would be no danger to him or his apartment, and they sat up till midnight planning the final details of Operation Gerhardt. Solly agreed to lend him part of his savings to tide him over the next few days in case there were any complications. 'Who knows,' Schulz had said, 'Melfort may still be looking out for me.' And they both laughed.

Schulz slept fitfully, dreaming of tracker dogs and English policemen carrying truncheons and blunderbusses, and millions of fivers, while Solly sat up working at his desk and did not go to bed until dawn.

The following morning Schulz caught a plane to Heathrow – by courtesy of Solly's savings – and Solly set out for Hamburg. He had friends to visit in the prison, the only part of the city which he knew and where he felt completely at home. First, though, he had to deliver a letter on which he had carefully fabricated the postmark dated 5 January. The envelope was marked 'Urgent' to ensure that it was just as urgently opened by the censors. Solly had another letter with him, also written by Schulz and addressed to Frau Nusbaum, introducing her to one of his dearest friends and asking her if she would be good enough to help him find accommodation for the next fortnight.

'Hello?'

'Hello? Who's that?'

'They call me Whitey but that's only a nickname.'

'Alfred – is that you?'

'Of course it's me – who else still knows the code?'

'Schulz?'

'Yes . . . well, that's why I'm ringing. Now, listen, Melfort, I think I've tracked it down.'

'Tracked what down?'

'The map, of course. Is your memory as rotten as the rest of you?'

'There's no need to be rude, Alfred. I've helped you a lot in the past, with very little recompense I might add.'

'Nonsense, I could have had you shot as a traitor to the Fuhrer, which you undoubtedly were.'

'You'll never understand fieldwork, Neuheim. I had to make my cover convincing.'

'It was so convincing that you bungled a simple plan that would have led to the total destruction of the British economy. If it hadn't been for a few useless bits of information you passed on later in the war –'

'Which helped you get out of Germany at the right time.'

'At the right time for the Russians, you mean. They took

303

half of the Bernhard money – which I had hoped to get through to the Fuhrer, of course. The rest is still in Toplitz.'

'A lost cause, Alfred.'

'So are you. But we are still sitting on a fortune. My colleagues in postal censorship have, as always, been most diligent and Schulz is still the obsessive and greedy little crook he always was. He should have been sent out to the front line before he wormed his way into the SD. However, his self-serving interest has, as I predicted, led him into yet another indiscretion.'

'Really, Alfred, you and your idiotic little corporal!'

'He may be an idiot, Melfort, but I selected him for intelligence work and he's not a fool. He's quite a clever little chap, actually. Totally dishonest, of course. But even Schulz appreciates that it would be impossible to dig up the canister without the map.'

'Is there any reason for this call, Neuheim, or did you just want a social chat?'

'I'm ringing about the map, you fool, and the brogues ...'

'Oh, not those ridiculous brogues again.'

'... Schulz has revealed their whereabouts. They are – or were – in the possession of a crazy Frenchman who thinks the Kaiser is still alive. He lives in Berlin. How he got them is a mystery. As you know, the last I heard of them was when Schulz was deported from Vitry and my men ransacked the town back in 1951 soon after he returned to Hamburg.'

'Perhaps you didn't look hard enough.'

'I hope that was meant to be a joke. I paid undercover agents to sit around in the square in brogues. Most of them got so lazy they stopped looking altogether. They're probably still there today. I even got a man to make house calls, pretending he was a rag-and-bone man. Collected all kinds of useless junk. Complete scoundrel: disappeared to the South of France. The trouble was Schulz was the only one who knew where the shoes were. So we just had to wait.'

'Until he led you to this Frenchman?'

'Exactly! Anyway, the man's dangerously unbalanced.

He tried to threaten me with a blunderbuss.'

'Who – Schulz?'

'No, the Frenchman, you idiot! But now that little babbler has revealed his plans to us again.'

'Who – the Frenchman?'

'No, Schulz. Is your brain as muddled as your filthy English roads? He's written another letter to his former employer who's in prison for embezzlement. If you ask me, Schulz is behind that as well. Anyway he's done our work for us.'

'Who – Schulz's employer?'

'No, Schulz! Are you doing this on purpose? The shoes are now in the hands of a criminal called Solokoff. An arch forger – he worked for me printing some of my money at Sachsenhausen. Schulz is spending a few days with this Solokoff. He's even supplied us with the address. I'm going over there tonight with two of my most trusted colleagues.'

'And you think the three of you will be able to get hold of the map?'

'No, the two of us – and my Luger.'

'Supposing Schulz suddenly decides to slip away to England before you arrive?'

'Impossible. The letter was only posted yesterday. Herr Ditzer was very speedy in handing it over to me, especially when I offered him some silk underwear. So if Schulz has left Germany he will only just have arrived in England. That's where you come in.'

'Me?'

'I want you to look out for him just in case. Report to me the moment you sight him. Shoot if necessary!'

30

The flat was unnaturally quiet considering it was only nine o'clock in the evening.

'Ring the bell again, Kurt,' Neuheim snapped. Kurt swallowed some gum and rang the bell again. They waited for another minute.

'Do you think they've gone to bed?' said Kurt sullenly.

'At this hour? Well, if they have, we'll just have to wake them up. Try the lock!' Kurt tried the lock, using a skeleton key which snapped after a few seconds. Kurt stared at it and Neuheim in wonder.

'Force it,' barked Neuheim. Kurt tried to force it with a penknife and then with a boot. The door didn't budge.

'Use the Luger, you fool!' snapped Neuheim. Kurt used the Luger. The explosion echoed up and down the staircase. The door did not move. 'Try firing into the keyhole, you brainless scum!'

Kurt tried firing into the keyhole. There was a light on in the front room and signs of a meal having been recently eaten. While Kurt checked the other rooms to see if they might be hiding in a closet, Neuheim systematically went through the drawers, scattering the tools of Solly's trade haphazardly on the floor. He checked behind the bookcase, snatching books and atlases one by one and shaking them open in case the map were concealed there. He was prepared to make Kurt go through the apartment with a fine toothcomb if necessary – and of course they were bound to come home sooner or later. He was quite looking forward to meeting Schulz again. It would be like old times to detect the invisible twitch that would register panic and fear beneath his meek little countenance.

'There's no one there,' said Kurt watching Neuheim on his knees peering under the carpet.

'Well, don't just stand there!' roared Neuheim. 'Help me look!' Kurt got down on his knees and peered under the carpet while Neuheim went out to the kitchen to find something to drink. He returned a moment later. 'There's nothing to drink!' he said furiously. 'Why didn't you bring something with you?'

'Do you want me to go and buy some?' said Kurt, brightening.

'Of course not. Keep searching,' growled Neuheim, sitting

down in an armchair. He took out his cigarette holder and lit a cigarette.

By eleven, Kurt had been through every room in the apartment. He had peeped behind all the framed prints on the walls and even inside the lavatory cistern, since Neuheim remembered that the silk was waterproof. Between them they had ripped apart the clothes in the wardrobe and checked in the larder, spilling food all over the floor. The apartment looked as if it had been blitzed. After that, they sat down to wait.

'It looks like they've hopped it,' said Kurt at twelve o'clock.

'Don't be an idiot! Schulz stated categorically in that letter that he would be staying here all week. They're probably out drinking somewhere. We'll just have to be patient!' Neuheim barked impatiently.

'He might have changed his mind.'

'Shut up!' bawled Neuheim.

They were both beginning to doze when they heard a sound at the outside door.

'Get them!' snapped Neuheim. While Kurt left the room with Luger raised, Neuheim prepared himself to meet Schulz. The door opened. 'So we meet again!' he purred with a cordial smile.

Kurt entered, clutching his Luger sheepishly, followed by a hungry cat that purred back at Neuheim.

He stared malevolently – first at the cat, then at Kurt – and then swore at the top of his voice.

At two o'clock Kurt got up to go to the lavatory. Presently he returned carrying a brown paper bag.

'I found this!' he said. Inside was a pair of brogues. Neuheim glared at him.

'That's the last place they'd hide it,' he said, dismissing them.

'That's probably why it might be hidden in them,' said Kurt.

'Then why didn't you find them before?' Neuheim

snapped, grabbing the shoes and tugging at the heel of one of them. It remained firmly heeled.

'I wasn't looking for them. We were looking for the map,' replied Kurt.

'Where do you think the map was originally hidden, numbskull!' barked Neuheim, trying the other heel, again with no success. He paused. 'Why, in that case did you bring them in now?' He grunted from the strain of his renewed efforts on the first shoe.

'Because I hoped you'd let me wear them,' replied Kurt flatly. 'My feet feel very comfortable in them.'

'Your head won't feel so comfortable in them,' rasped Neuheim, flinging one at him. 'You try!' Kurt tried. Again the heel didn't budge.

'Try the other one.' Kurt tried the other heel.

'They're very well-made shoes,' he said.

'Of course they are, fool. We made them!' thundered Neuheim. 'Use your penknife!' Kurt tried to slide the blade into the heel. It glanced off the shoe and plunged into his hand.

'Idiot!' yelled Neuheim as Kurt licked his wound. 'Here, give it to me!'

Kurt gave Neuheim his hand.

'The shoe!' Kurt passed the shoe. A minute later Neuheim's finger was also bleeding. The shoe was unscratched. 'Get me a bandage before my finger drops off!' he screamed. After another five minutes Kurt re-emerged from the bedroom with a swatch of silk.

'I found this in a drawer,' he said.

'What bloody use is that?' screamed Neuheim whose hand was now dripping blood. 'I'm bleeding to death!'

'But you said –'

'I said get me a bandage! Now get me one!'

'But it's a –'

'Don't argue, lout!'

Kurt was still pointing indifferently to the silk.

'– map!' he said.

'Where?' said Neuheim, wiping off the excess blood on

the silk and looking behind him to see what Kurt was pointing at.

'In your hand,' said Kurt glumly. Neuheim stared with horror at the silk. Beneath the bloodstains he could make out the printed curving lines and place names of an intricate map.

'Quick! Get me something to clean it!' he screamed. 'I've found what we're looking for!' He spread the bloodstained silk on the table, screwing his eyes up as he tried to read it. Kurt returned a moment later with a bottle of liquid, which Neuheim snatched and poured over the silk. 'Now get me some soap!' he snapped. 'Water's not going to get this blood off.'

'But that's bleach,' said Kurt evenly.

'What!' exploded Neuheim: he gazed impotently at the wet material. The print was now barely visible. 'You fool!' he screamed. 'You blundering idiot! You've just destroyed the chance of regaining two million pounds for the German nation! Do you realize what this was? It was a map of southern England!'

Kurt retreated into a corner. 'No, it wasn't,' he said dully. 'It was a map of East Berlin.' Neuheim stared at him for a moment and then grabbed the still-soaking silk which had turned pink as the bleach neutralized the bloodstains. One corner was still dry. He took out his magnifying glass. The print was still legible: ... *Touristik und Wandern der DDR, Unter den Linden, 36/38, Berlin*, it read. He stood rooted to the spot, speechless. Then he looked at Kurt.

'Well – don't just stand there! Get me a bandage!'

By the time Kurt had returned with a piece of cotton wool and a handkerchief, Neuheim was struggling with one of the brogues again.

'I wish I could remember which one it was,' he muttered. He was standing on the shoe, trying to force the heel apart with his other foot, but he kept slipping off.

'Maybe they've taken out the map and glued the heel back on,' said Kurt. This hadn't occurred to Neuheim. 'Or maybe they can't open it either,' Kurt added. This hadn't occurred to Neuheim either. He scratched his head. 'Heat melts glue –' Kurt went on.

'Get a match!' snapped Neuheim. Five minutes later the dead contents of a box of matches lay littered all over the floor. Kurt was rubbing grease on Neuheim's burnt fingers. 'Use the Luger!' Neuheim snapped. Kurt pointed the Luger at his master's fingers. 'On the heel, you cretin!'

'But you might rip through the map,' Kurt protested.

'Well, you think of something,' Neuheim sighed. 'Don't leave it all up to me.'

Kurt thought for a minute. 'I suppose we could try the catch – it might still work,' he said.

'Catch – what catch?'

'This one,' said Kurt, pressing the catch. Neuheim grabbed the shoe from him and tugged the heel with all his strength. It still didn't move.

'Of course it doesn't work,' he said. 'Don't you think I'd have tried it long ago if I'd thought it possibly would.' He threw the shoe on the floor and sat down again, totally frustrated. Kurt picked up the shoe, examining it thoughtfully and pressing gently on the side of the heel. It swivelled open with ease. 'Stop wasting your time on that shoe,' said Neuheim irritably. 'We'll just have to wait for them to come back.'

'I think there's something inside it,' said Kurt.

Neuheim eyed him incredulously. 'Are you mad?' he stormed. 'Of course there's something inside it. Why do you think I've been trying to get it open?' He glanced at the shoe which now sported a hollowed-out heel and then stared at it. 'How –?'

He grabbed it from Kurt and stuffed his fingers eagerly inside the heel and triumphantly pulled out a carefully folded toffee wrapper.

By four in the morning, Neuheim was ready to go home. He got up from the armchair, stretching and glancing vacantly at the framed print above the fireplace.

'Let's get out of here,' he said.

Kurt picked up his overcoat and glanced carelessly at the framed print above the fireplace.

'Isn't that a map?' he said, pointing at it.

'Don't be ridiculous!' barked Neuheim. 'You've already looked behind there – twice!'

'But – isn't it a map?'

'Of course it's a map. What do you think it is – the Mona Lisa?' he sneered, pulling it off the wall. His mouth dropped open.

It was a map of a small area of south-east England, of Kent in fact, with a cross in the middle, next to which the symbol '£' had been carefully marked. Various local sites such as churches and footpaths had been indicated in the same ink as the cross; longitude and latitude numbers were given. It was stamped with the SS insignia and coded 'RSHA VIF5' – Captain Ohm's department, the technical division.

Neuheim hastily broke open the frame and removed the glass and cardboard backing. The map was printed on super-fine waterproof silk. He began to fold it. By the time he had finished, it had compressed almost to nothing, obviously the work of a dedicated expert. He slowly looked up at Kurt and folded his arms. Then he unfolded his arms, and unfolded the map again. There was not a single crease in it.

'If I'd left it to you, we'd never have found it in a million years,' he said with a sardonic smile. Then he pointed to the cross. 'On that spot, Kurt, the very spot where they were buried twenty years ago, lie two million pounds, which we – you and I – are going to collect. The man who buried them has lost his nerve – not that he ever had much.'

Kurt stared at the cross on the map, and then nodded glumly at Neuheim's nose.

'Yes, Herr Neuheim,' he said.

When Gerhardt Schulz was afraid he trembled. He was afraid now. He was afraid of what he might do next. The

311

truth was that he had lost his nerve – *not that I ever had much*, he thought glumly.

He stared again at the cross on the map to make absolutely sure. There could be no doubt. Even though it was nearly five o'clock and the dusk was gathering there could be no doubt that this was the spot, nor even that the brick walls of the public convenience were a tasteful yellow. In fact it was tastefully situated altogether, at the border of a park area. On the other side of the convenience was a large new factory and the country had all been tastefully re-arranged around it, with a road laid down to accommodate it. There was a fair amount of early evening traffic either coming from both directions between London and the south coast. A little necklace of trees had been planted by the road. Considering everything it was all very tasteful and attractive, and there was only one thing he could do.

He walked inside and relieved himself.

Schulz stood looking at the tiles underneath his feet, and wondered whether the canister could have come to light when they had dug up the ground. It was entirely possible that it had. But even if it hadn't, how on earth was he to get at it?

He thought of all the people to whom he had made promises: Solly, whose last savings he had 'borrowed'; Frau Nusbaum, who had really been very kind to him over the years; Herr Krauss who, entirely innocent of the crime for which he was now in prison, still no doubt thought of Schulz as a good and faithful servant. And even though it was now unlikely that Krauss had received either of the letters he had written to him, he *had* promised him a share of the money and he *had* intended to keep his promise.

He thought of the promise he had made to himself, again and again, that one day he would come back to England and collect his wages. It had been, not an obsession, but a warm, pleasant glow under the surface. as when the central heating was turned down low, and it had kept him alive.

Finally he thought of Bertha Freyer – Frau Schumacher – for whom he had promised it all in the first place. If it hadn't been for her, his life might have taken a different course. He might have quietly waited for the war to end, like Schumacher, doodling away his days in the Delbruckstrasse and waiting for some other idiot to come up with a brilliant scheme so that he, Schulz, could net the profits. On the other hand, he reflected, he might just as easily have been sent out to the front line and, by now, be underneath the ground himself.

He sighed. The lavatory was unattended and he had been standing there for some considerable time. He had, by this time, stopped trembling and begun to think logically. He started to walk around, trying to remember the shape of the culvert near which he had dug the hole twenty years before. In his mind's eye he drew a line from the distant church spire that gave him the exact bearing. It seemed to him that the natural shape of the culvert had been retained, although the stream which had been there had been diverted. The only problem was that to search he would have to go through layers of concrete where the road was banked up. He would, in other words, have to blast through either the road or the lavatory, and he couldn't possibly do that on his own.

He sighed again. It seemed as though all the trouble he and Solly had taken over Neuheim had been wasted. It would have been far more fitting if he had just let Neuheim find the real map and let Neuheim dig his way through the lavatory. Knowing Neuheim, though, he would have commandeered every criminal he could find to dig the road up for him.

'Excuse me, constable, I wonder if you could tell me the way to the nearest prison?'

The policeman automatically looked at his watch.

'Seven-thirty,' he said and then stared blankly at Schulz.

'Did you say ... prison, sir?'

'Yes,' said Schulz just as blankly.

'Well, now, let me see. There are quite a few prisons. Do you want a small prison or a big prison?' the policeman replied. Schulz considered this for a moment.

'Oh, a big prison. The bigger the better,' he said firmly.

'Well ...' replied the policeman, removing his helmet and scratching his head, 'That would probably be Maidstone Prison, sir, but it's about twenty-five miles away.' Schulz considered this. 'It's a very big one,' added the policeman encouragingly.

'Then it will do nicely,' replied Schulz, satisfied.

'Going to give yourself up, sir?' said the policeman humorously.

'No,' chuckled Schulz. 'On the contrary, I'm – just recruiting for a robbery.' The policeman laughed uproariously and after a moment Schulz joined in.

'That's very good, sir, I must remember that one,' said the constable.

'I'd rather you didn't,' said Schulz.

The policeman stared at him again and then laughed even louder. 'How many millions are you going to steal, sir?' he chuckled.

'Oh – only two,' replied Schulz, and quickly disappeared into the night.

'Is your room all right, Mr Schulz?'

'Very nice, Daisy, thank you.'

It was the next morning. The barmaid at the Prisoner's Arms had unaccountably taken a liking to Schulz. He did not flatter himself: he was now fifty and though still amazingly youthful looking – he could still pass for late thirties – his singular lack of success with women told its own story. He had come to the conclusion, however, that Daisy had a taste for Germans with dark pasts. Since Schulz's past was practically opaque and Daisy was a buxom, attractive brunette, they were getting along like a house on fire.

'It doesn't bother you being able to see the prison?' she said as she wiped some glasses.

Schulz was sitting on a stool at the bar. 'Not a bit,' he said cheerfully. 'Anyway, you can only see the end of it.'

'You *are* German, aren't you?'

'Yes, Daisy.'

'I thought so.' She was looking rather dreamily at him. 'You're the first German we've ever had staying here, since I've been here anyway.'

'And how long has that been?'

'Oh, about a year.'

'Well,' replied Schulz, 'I don't expect many have come since the war. 'You know, the English have long memories. Perhaps Germans have not been made to feel welcome.'

'They certainly couldn't have been made to feel welcome during the war, could they?' said Daisy. She had learnt that at school.

'No,' said Schulz. He'd learnt that from experience.

'Anyway, it's all over now, isn't it?' said Daisy, putting away the glasses. 'Are you here on business?'

'Sort of business, Daisy, yes.'

'What made you come and stay here?'

'Oh, I don't know,' said Schulz, fingering his glass. 'It looked a very nice pub.'

'It wasn't because it was right near the prison was it?' She leaned forward conspiratorially. 'You don't have to worry about me, you know,' she whispered. 'You can trust me.'

'That's nice of you, Daisy,' replied Schulz, relieved.

'My brother did a spell in there,' she whispered again, jerking her head, in the direction of the prison. 'Of course, he's straight now.'

Schulz nodded politely. There was a slight pause.

'Visiting someone, are you?' she asked.

'Well, not exactly. I'll have another, Daisy, please.' He pulled out a pound and placed it on the counter. 'There – and keep the change.' It was a lot of money to him at the moment but he reckoned it might be a good investment.

'Oh, that is nice of you,' replied Daisy. 'Thank you very much, Mr Schulz. Same again?'

'Just the same,' said Schulz, watching her pour another Scotch. 'I suppose they release someone more or less every day from the jail.'

'Oh yes, usually around midday. And I'll let you into a secret, too.' It had been an investment. 'First thing they'll do is come straight in here.' It hadn't been an investment. Schulz laughed.

'I'll bet they do. That's sort of –' he leaned towards her and said more quietly '– well, why I picked this place.'

'I thought it was,' said Daisy darkly. 'I'm not usually wrong. Well, have a very nice stay, Mr Schulz. And anything you want, just let me know.' She gave him a wink, patted her bouffant hairdo and took her tray of glasses down to the other end of the bar. Schulz looked thoughtfully at the pub clock. Twenty minutes to go.

Schulz had a very logical mind. Once he had decided that the best way to recruit criminals was to find them in the nearest prison – the only place where they did not avoid advertising their trade – it was simply a matter of waiting for them to drop into the Prisoner's Arms. But he had been waiting for forty minutes and there was no sign of a criminal type, apart from Daisy, who had a little way to go yet.

At 12.20 he got up and strolled out into the street and hung around the prison gate. He had smoked six cigarettes and the hands of the town clock had turned to 1.00 p.m. when Schulz, checking with his watch and debating whether to forget the whole thing, noticed that a small door in the great prison gates had been opened by a uniformed warden, to let out a big, burly man in a fawn mackintosh carrying a brown-paper carrier bag. An interchange of banter was going on between the two. Finally the big man grinned, put two fingers up in the warden's face, and walked off while the latter slammed the door shut, muttering grimly to himself. Schulz hurried after the man determinedly. As expected, he turned into the Prisoner's Arms. Schulz followed him in and watched as the big man ordered himself a Scotch and took it over to the corner table to read his papers. Schulz strolled over and sat down casually nearby.

'Nothing much in the papers,' Schulz said at last.

'No,' said the man, picking up his Scotch and swallowing half of it before putting it down again. He turned a page of the paper and folded it back in such a way as to make it obvious that he had no wish to talk to Schulz. It was just as obvious to Schulz, though, that the man could hardly read. An archetypal criminal.

'Good to be out, eh?' Schulz tried again. The man looked up and stared at him, as though Schulz were a psychopath. The man had eyes like broken glass and a chalky-white complexion – prison pallor, Schulz mused wrily.

'What?' he said.

'It's all right,' said Schulz, winking at him. 'I've been inside myself.'

'Oh?' said the man.

Schulz noticed his massive shoulders, perfect for digging.

'I saw you being let out,' he went on. 'I followed you in here.' He laughed. 'I used to do the same – made straight for the nearest pub. Tastes good, doesn't it?' The man seemed to understand this.

'Yeah, tastes very good,' he croaked. 'What were you in for?'

'Oh, this and that,' Schulz laughed. He hesitated and stared once more at the broken-glass eyes. 'I'd like to talk to you,' he said confidentially.

'What about?'

'A job?' said Schulz. There was a pause. The man looked inscrutably at Schulz. 'Can I get you another drink,' Schulz added.

The man nodded. 'Thanks,' he croaked, draining his glass. Schulz took it over to the bar. He could see the man looking at him. Good, he thought, the thug was interested: he blocked out half the window and could probably shift the whole lavatory in a few hours.

'Hello, again,' said Daisy, a little flirtatiously.

'Two Scotches, please, Daisy,' said Schulz. While she poured out the drinks Schulz studied the man again. Their eyes met and Schulz gave him another wink. He was perfect. Daisy brought the glasses over and leaned forward again in her conspiratorial manner.

'Did they let out anyone today?' she whispered.

'Just as you said, Daisy,' Schulz whispered back. 'About 1.00 and he came straight in here.'

'I told you – they all do.' She looked around the bar, puzzled. There were quite a few customers now. 'Which one is it?'

'Him,' whispered Schulz, nodding across the room.

Daisy's jaw dropped. 'Oh, my God!' she said. 'You must be crazy.'

'I don't think so, Daisy. He's just right for the job I have in mind.'

'But he's one of the screws!' she whispered.

'What?'

'He's a screw going off duty!' she said. 'Can't you tell the difference?'

Schulz swayed, steadying himself with a hand on the bar. He looked at the Scotch he had picked up from the counter, looked at the man he had bought it for and then drank it himself in one gulp. He put the empty glass back on the counter.

'Give him the Scotch, Daisy. I'm going up to my room. If he asks about a job, tell him – tell him I decided he was unsuitable. Not the right type at all.'

The next day, Schulz tried again. As the town clock struck one, the door in the prison gates opened again and another man wearing a belted coat stepped outside. The door slammed behind him and he set off across the street. Once more Schulz hurried in pursuit to the Prisoner's Arms.

'A pint, love, and don't put any head on it,' said the man to Daisy. 'I don't want a load of froth,' he added

'I know how to pull a pint,' replied Daisy, offended

'Hurry up, then, love, 'cos I'm thirsty.'

Daisy pulled the pint as Schulz entered the pub, his eye instantly on the man who had his back towards him. He was of medium height but he had a short, thick neck and, again, Schulz noticed with satisfaction, a pair of powerful shoulders. Schulz caught Daisy's eye, pointing at the man's back and giving her an enquiring look: she nodded. He went up to the counter and stood next to the man just as Daisy put his pint down in front of him and took the money.

'A pint please, Daisy,' said Schulz. While she pulled his pint, he stood at the counter, watching the man drain half the glass in one go.

'I'll bet that tastes good,' said Schulz encouragingly, grinning and raising his eyebrows in an effort to disarm him.

Without looking round, the man made himself clear.

'Piss off – or I'll knock your head off,' he growled, picking up his beer and going off to a table with it. Schulz stared after him, somewhat nonplussed.

'He won't have much money in his pocket,' whispered Daisy. 'Wait till he's finished, then offer him another.'

Schulz watched him drain the rest of his pint, picked up his own drink and wandered over, sitting near enough to speak but not obviously at the same table. Again, without turning his head, the man glanced at him sullenly.

'Are you following me?'

'Of course not,' said Schulz. 'I just wondered ... if you'd like another drink?'

'Why?'

'I've been inside myself,' said Schulz understandingly. 'I know what it's like.'

The man stared at him in astonishment. 'How do you know I've been inside?' he growled suspiciously.

'I saw you being let out,' said Schulz with a wink.

The man frowned. 'You got a proposition?' he growled.

'Maybe. Same again?'

'All right,' the man nodded, his thick neck bulging below muscular jaws. 'Same again. With a chaser.'

Schulz went over to the counter.

'What's he like?' Daisy said, smiling.

'He looks a bit thick to me.'

Daisy laughed. 'Well, you won't be getting university graduates coming out of Maidstone Prison, will you? Does it matter?' she added, eyeing him curiously.

'Not much,' said Schulz. 'Bring it over, would you?' She nodded.

Schulz returned to the table and sat down again.

'My name's Schulz – Gerhardt Schulz.'

'Gerhardt?' growled the man suspiciously. 'That's not English.'

'No, it's German. What about you?'

'Stanley Kemp,' said the man flatly.

'It's nice to meet you, Stanley,' said Schulz amiably.

'German, are you?' said Kemp, studying him for the first time. 'I don't like Germans as a rule.'

'Well, there's not too much I can do about that, Stanley,' said Schulz patiently. Kemp stared at him, not sure if he was being made fun of.

Daisy came over with the beer and Scotch. They drank and Kemp put his beer down, wiping his mouth.

'What were you in for?' said Schulz.

'Robbery with violence,' replied the bear.

Schulz had been expecting something a little less unpleasant. 'I see,' he said nervously. 'Someone got hurt, then?'

'Naturally,' growled Kemp. 'A sub-postmaster.' He glared at Schulz. 'But it wasn't my fault,' he added morosely. 'It was his – he kept getting up: I had to keep putting the boot in, you see?'

This wasn't really what Schulz wanted at all. 'Was it worth it? I mean – did you get away with much?'

'Oh, yes,' said Kemp proudly. 'Nearly six hundred pounds.' He had another gulp of beer. 'You're in the market, are you?' Schulz nodded. 'How big is it?'

Schulz hesitated again.

'It's very big,' he said at last.

'Well, I've done things before. What do you call big?'

Schulz looked at him cautiously to see how he would take it.

'Two million pounds?' said Schulz.

Kemp stared at him in amazement.

'Well,' he said, 'I . . . haven't done anything quite as big as that before.' He paused. 'What is it – a bank?' Schulz

320

shook his head. 'A bullion job?' Again Schulz shook his head. 'What are you?' Kemp growled. 'Some kind of nut? Where are you going to find two million?'

'I've found it, Stanley. I just need help to get at it,' said Schulz.

Kemp stared at the strange little man with mounting scepticism. 'Oh, piss off!' he growled. 'You must think I'm barmy! Two million nikker!' Suddenly he leaned across to Schulz, grabbed him by the shirt front, and pulled him over the table. 'You crummy Kraut, who do you think you're kidding? I've a good mind to push your face in.'

Schulz took a long deep breath.

'Listen, my friend,' he said coolly but forceably, 'your kind come ten a penny in any jail in any country in the world. You can push my face in but you haven't the brains to keep yourself alive. You rode on a star out of that jail, today, straight to me and if you live to be a hundred you'll never know why. There were things happening in the war beyond your wildest dreams and I was part of them. Do you want in or out? If it's out – stop wasting my time, I'll find somebody else.'

There was another long pause while they both drew breath. Schulz's complete self-assurance had shaken Kemp to the core and had shaken Schulz himself just as much. It was probably the most he had ever said to any stranger about himself and the intensity released in him was formidable.

Slowly Kemp let him go. 'Who *are* you?' he said in an awed tone.

'Never mind who I am,' said Schulz tersely. 'You'll know it all in good time. I just need some help, that's all,' he went on in a gentler tone. 'You – and three others.'

Kemp thought for a moment. 'Cracksman, geli-man – what sort of help do you want?'

'Nothing skilled, nothing professional,' replied Schulz calmly. 'Just straight labour, that's all. You'll get all the details when you get me the labour. It'll be the easiest money you ever earned in your life. And you'll never ever again have to put the boot in, Stanley, I promise you.'

Kemp's face fell a little. 'Well, of course I don't enjoy doing that, you know,' he said hastily. 'But if you kick a bloke in the head and he keeps getting up, what can you do except keep kicking him?' He looked appealingly to Schulz, who laughed.

'You really do have the divine gift of expression, Stanley. I've never heard that point of view put so elegantly. And what fun you must have had in the war!' If he had been German, Kemp might have risen to the rank of general in the SS, Schulz thought ruefully.

He finished his beer and stood up. 'I'm going to make you rich beyond your wildest dreams,' he announced. 'You'll be able to buy anything you want. As for me, I'll settle for a sun-drenched beach in Hawaii and a girl with a flower in her hair.' He was thinking of something quite different but he dismissed the thought automatically and returned to the present. 'I'll give you two days to get in touch,' he added, shaking Kemp's hand. 'After that, I'll look for someone else.' He turned and walked off.

Kemp stared after Schulz, not quite sure whether he had not imagined the whole conversation. The nick sometimes seemed quite a sane kind of place, he thought.

31

Solly was feeling homesick. He had spent the last three evenings drinking endless cups of coffee with Frau Nusbaum.

Frau Nusbaum had been most distressed about the fate of Schulz's former employer and had expressed her horror to Solly on many occasions that a fine man like Herr Krauss should have been forceably incarcerated inside such a monstrous prison. The more she talked, the more Solly had missed the homely comforts of prison life: the lack of responsibility, the absolute security, the friendly chitchat with old pals and the gossip. But he had to admit there was something completely different about the atmosphere of the old prison. It was not just that a new maximum security wing had been built. Nor that the inmates and officers that he had seen in the visitors' room in the last few days were also different. It was that the smell had changed. It smelt unkosher.

Nevertheless, he still had some old friends in there, lifers who had somehow got through the war without knowing of the horror. They had dismissed his whispered stories of Operation Bernhard as fantasies, though one or two seemed to know more than they let on – and this struck Solly as equally strange. As on the previous days Solly had returned to the prison, spending the time until visiting hours wandering among the geraniums in the prison garden. They at least were just the same.

He was gazing up at the windowless, drab prison wall which, in his eyes, stretched maternally and protectively around its children when a face poked itself out of one of the only open windows.

'Hey, you!' said the face. 'Off the geraniums!'

Solly jumped.

'I'm sorry, Herr Beck,' he said instinctively, stepping back to the concrete courtyard. The face stared at him with fascination.

'Why, if it isn't our little forger!' said Beck. 'Had all your presses confiscated by the Russians, eh? Wait there!'

A minute later Beck appeared at the entrance, beckoning Solly to follow him.

'It looks a bit marshy out there,' said Kurt Erhardt, as he and Neuheim diverged off the small side road on to a footpath. In the distance was a church tower and Neuheim had calculated that the canister was buried halfway between these two points. There were, of course, more detailed location points on the map, and, once they had approached the general area Neuheim would be able to take more precise bearings. He looked at his watch: it was 10.15 a.m.

Today was 9 January. Neuheim had cabled Melfort to

323

meet him at the largest hotel in the nearby village the previous night. Since, however, there might have been some confusion about which hotel that was, and since in any case Melfort was constitutionally incapable of keeping appointments – as the mess-up in 1940 had proved – it was hardly curious that he had not turned up.

It would have been useful, though, to have had Melfort with them. Kurt didn't speak a word of English, while Neuheim himself had got a little rusty. Also Melfort was marginally more intelligent than the blockhead walking beside him. On the other hand, Melfort's absence had its advantages. It would mean that Neuheim was not obliged to force Kurt to use the Luger. It might also be difficult to bury Melfort alongside Kurt in the hole where the canister was going to be dug up.

'This is a great day for the German nation!' he said, ignoring Kurt's comment, and striding along ahead, carrying a large briefcase. Kurt, lagging behind with the spade, stared at Neuheim's receding figure with utter indifference. Neuheim had promised him, however, that after this trip Kurt's debt to Germany would be paid, and he would be free to go. And Neuheim, he consoled himself, never forgot his promises.

About noon on the same day, Stanley Kemp sat talking quietly and seriously to three of his fraternity, two of them figuratively, by virtue of their trade, and one literally by virtue of blood.

'Now, as I see it,' Stanley lectured them, 'there's two alternatives: either he's a nut or he's not. If he's not, then we're in business.' They considered this for a moment and then Harry Moore, who was short, fat and amiable, stubbed out his cigarette and yawned.

'And if he is?' he said.

'Then we bounce him on his head all the way down to the coast and chuck him in the sea,' growled Kemp.

'Are you sure he said two *million*?' asked Fred Gorman, a wiry-thin cockney-Irishman, sceptically.

'That's what he said.'

'And we don't have to knock over a bank or cosh anyone?' said Gorman in disgust.

'He never mentioned it,' replied Kemp, commiseratingly.

'You must've got it wrong, Stan,' said Moore.

'I'm telling you,' growled Kemp, 'that's what he said and he'll tell you himself when he gets here!'

'*If* he gets here,' said Gorman. 'I reckon he's one of them jokers. While we're waiting here for the next two hours, he'll be sitting on a train somewhere, laughing his head off.'

This possibility had never occurred to Kemp and suddenly it seemed awfully real. The silence was suddenly shattered by the ring of the door bell.

'Practical joke, eh?' Kemp growled triumphantly. 'Why don't you leave things to me? And by the way,' he added, 'he's a Kraut, but just remember he can understand every word you say.' He walked out to answer the door.

The men got up and stood around awkwardly, until Kemp came back with Schulz. They stared at him and Schulz stared back at them, sizing them up, while Kemp introduced them.

'Now I want to make one thing clear right from the start,' said Kemp, once they had all shaken hands. 'Mr Schulz, here, is a Kraut, but we don't hold that against him.'

'We've got nothing against Krauts, Stan,' said Moore generously. 'My old man did a stretch in Hamburg and said he'd go back there any time.' Schulz remembered Beck and thought Moore's father, like Solly, must be crazy.

'You see?' Kemp turned to Schulz. 'These boys are without prejudice. You couldn't have a better group. Now, I've told them what it's about and the fact is, they don't believe me.'

'That's a long story,' Schulz said and paused. 'I'm trusting you with my life.'

'It couldn't be in better hands,' replied Kemp promptly, 'could it, Harry?'

'Definitely not,' agreed Moore with a grin.

'Well ...' began Schulz, 'being German, I was naturally

on the other side during the war.'

'There's no hard feelings about that,' Kemp broke in quickly, turning to the others. 'He had no choice, did he?'

'Of course not!' said Moore. 'A lot of people didn't. Poor Melvyn, here, was a prisoner of war for six years.' He indicated Kemp's brother, a vacant-looking man who said very little and thought less.

'In Germany?' asked Schulz with mild interest.

'No, in Aldershot,' replied Melvyn.

'Go on,' said Kemp to Schulz, who had decided he would have to tread carefully.

'Well, I wasn't an ordinary soldier, you understand? I was a ... secret agent. And I was dropped over Southern England in 1940 with a canister containing nearly two million pounds and instructions to finance and organize networks of sabotage.'

'Two million quid?' Moore whistled.

'I told you!' said Kemp beaming. 'Go on,' he added to Schulz.

There was a stunned silence when Schulz finished. Even in the highly simplified version that he offered it was one of the most extraordinary stories they'd ever heard and they were not sure whether to treat it as anything more than just that. Gorman was, however, and if Gorman did the others would go along with it.

'Christ!' he said hollowly. 'You never know what you're pissing on these days.'

Kemp shook his head and whistled softly. 'I never heard of anyone robbing a lavatory before.'

'It's very easy,' replied Schulz patiently. 'You just pick up pneumatic drill and some shovels and picks, knock of some boards which say "Urban and District Council" "Road Works" and things like that and start digging.'

Gorman was aghast. 'You can't do that!' he said scornfully. 'You can't just go digging up a public lavatory when you feel like it!'

'Who's going to stop you? Do you ever know if a man digging up the road has authority to dig it up? The only people likely to know are the Town Clerk or the Borough

Surveyor's Office. It could be days before they hear of it. But for us it's only a matter of hours.'

Kemp stared at him with admiration. 'You German spies are certainly cool customers. Whereabouts is this public lavatory?'

'Ah – that I can't tell you, not now,' said Schulz who had been waiting for this. 'But if you're in – I'll take you to it. And we'll split fifty-fifty.'

The men looked at each other and slowly began to nod, taking their cue from Kemp.

'It's a deal,' said the latter. '*We'll* knock off all the equipment and *you* take us to the spot.' Schulz took his hand. 'Our word's our bond. Just give us a couple of weeks and we'll be in touch.'

This was something that had been worrying Schulz a lot recently. 'I'm afraid two weeks will be too long,' he said. 'You'll have to have the stuff by tomorrow.' The men stared at each other.

'Tomorrow?' said Gorman. 'Forget it! Where do you think we're going to put our hands on all that road gear in one day?'

'Where do you think you're going to put yours hands on a million pounds in one day?' countered Schulz.

The men stared at each other once more. It looked like stalemate.

'I know where,' said Melvyn suddenly. The stares turned on him.

'Well, go on then – where?' said Kemp.

'In the bank on the corner of the high street,' Melvyn replied smugly.

The men rolled their eyes.

'Go back to sleep,' growled Kemp looking with disgust at Melvyn.

'Wait a minute, Stan,' said Moore. 'Isn't that where they've got the road up?' Again the men stared at each other.

'All right, Mr Schulz,' said Kemp, 'we're in business.'

* * *

'Quite like old times, Solokoff,' rasped Beck, offering him a lukewarm cup of coffee. Solly nodded wistfully, still eyeing Beck with a certain amount of distrust. The old prison warden was being surprisingly pally with him.

'I'm sorry to hear about Herr Untermeyer,' he said. 'A sad loss.' In fact he hadn't been at all surprised. As Schulz had predicted back in 1940, the strain of holding a regular prison together when it was being encroached on daily by the sinister bureaucratic demands of the SS had proved too much for Untermeyer. He had been one of the last of a dying breed. Beck was another, but he had, at least, survived. Although more cynical than the idealistic Untermeyer whom Beck had always considered quite unsuitable for the job, in his old age Beck had mellowed.

'You know, Solly,' said Beck, addressing him for the first time ever by his first name, 'Untermeyer may have had his head in the clouds but deep down ... shrewd old bird.' He paused and his eyes wandered off towards the window, beyond which clouds drifted without apparent direction. 'Got out at the right time. World's gone mad.'

Solly nodded again. He knew that only too well.

'Bit of a shock to see you out there, you know,' went on Beck. Solly glimpsed once more those stumps of teeth, like lumps of brown sugar, as Schulz had once unkindly said. He realized the old boy was grinning with something like affection. 'Not many of the old-timers left,' Beck went on. 'Quite a different class of prisoner nowadays. Quite a different class of officer too. Can't say I can stomach either of them.' Solly nodded again : he didn't really know how to answer this; it was the first time a prison officer had ever confided in him. 'Thoroughly bad hats. Complete frauds – all of them,' Beck muttered. 'Like that little conman – what was his name? – Schulz!'

'He wasn't all bad, you know, Herr Beck,' said Solly defensively, marvelling at his memory.

'All bad,' said Beck, shaking his head. 'I remember – I said to him : "You'll be back" – and d'you know? he was. Dressed up as an officer. SS. Disgraceful.' He shook his head again mournfully. Obviously he had forgotten what Schulz

328

had come back for. 'They're all like that Schulz character now,' went on the warder. 'Thought I'd seen the last of them when that crazy war was over but they're all coming back.'

Solly wanted to ask Who were all back Where? But he nodded instead.

'Even the Governor's one, you know. SS. Nazi. Hitlerite. Thorough bad hat.'

Solly stared at Beck, stunned to hear the words, especially coming out of a prison officer's mouth.

'Back in the old days it was different,' went on Beck nostalgically. 'A lag was a lag and a screw was a screw. Nowadays you can't tell them apart. Take yourself, Solly,' he said, winking confidentially. 'You're a forger – a bit of a con, maybe you faked a few marks here, a few francs there.'

Solly nodded. 'That sort of thing, Herr Beck,' he said, 'though I think of myself as more of an artist than a criminal – you understand?'

Beck eyed him for a moment and frowned. 'Well, that's as may be. But I'm talking about something different altogether. There are men in this prison who –' He hesitated.

'Yes, Herr Beck?'

'Mustn't go further than these four walls, Solly,' Beck, looked anxiously round at the intercom to make sure it was switched off.

'Trust me,' said Solly, wondering where he had heard these words before, quite recently, in fact.

'You won't believe this,' Beck whispered, 'there was a scheme . . . in the war, you know . . . they printed money. SS printed it. British pound notes. Thousands of them. Not just hundreds of thousands but thousands of thousands. Millions. Maybe thousands of millions. What do you think of that? Takes the biscuit doesn't it?'

'Ingenious!' said Solly.

'Monstrous more like. Despicable! Tell you something else: they were going to build a tunnel under Britain. Plant all these fake fivers there.' Solly suspected that Beck had taken the word 'undermined' literally. 'Even paid their agents with it,' Beck went on. 'German agents paid with forged English money! What's that got to do with war? Worse than war. Perverted. Like everything nowadays. Topsy-turvy. Don't know where you are with it all. Tell you something else.' He drew even closer and Solly got a nostalgic whiff of skilly and carbolic. 'Want to know how I know?' Beck whispered.

Solly nodded.

'They're all in here. *All* of them. That's what I mean about different class of prisoner. Got away with it for years, they did, but they've all been caught. Trying to pass off forged British money. Want to know a funny thing?' Solly nodded again. 'They were perfect. That's what made it so criminal. That's why I say it's out of your league, Solly. No way of detecting them, you see. But not any more. Want to know why?' Solly nodded again, by now listening intently. 'British found out about it, see. Couldn't keep it a secret any more. Came out in a magazine last year. Raised ten million of them from some lake. They'd been buried there. All these years. Took them away in a wheelbarrow. So, guess what the British did?'

Solly had already had a pretty good guess.

'Withdrew them from circulation. That's how they all got caught. All those rotten apples!'

'Well?' said Kemp, after Schulz had left. 'Does he sound like a nut?'

'Definitely not,' said Moore. 'He's got his head screwed on.'

Gorman wasn't so sure.

'A German spy!' he shivered. 'God, it gives you the creeps!'

'Exactly!' said Kemp. 'That's just what's been going through my mind. Now, here's how I see it. I reckon, as Englishmen, we've got more right to that money than a bloody German and I'll tell you why. First of all,' he said, holding up a finger as he had seen politicians doing on television, 'it's English money, he said so himself. Secondly,' he held up two fingers, 'it's buried in English soil.' The others

330

gazed at the two fingers.

'What do you suggest then, Stan?' said Fred.

'Simple,' replied Kemp with a smirk. 'When we've got the canister we just dump him.'

'Suppose the money's not there?' said Moore.

'Then, like I said, we'll bounce him on his head all the way to the coast and chuck him in the sea. My time's too valuable to be wasted by clots like him.'

'Queer bunch they are,' Beck was saying. 'Not like the old timers.' *At least*, thought Solly, *he's not disgusted with me.* Solly himself felt more apprehensive than disgusted. Poor Gerhardt.

'One's an American,' went on Beck, screwing up his face in contempt. 'Claimed he found them in a wood. In a wood!' He chuckled. Then he screwed up his face again, ferociously. 'Want to know what I think? Pinched them, that's what. One of those Yanks who occupied south Germany after the war. Carson's his name. But he made a big mistake. Guess what?'

'What?' said Solly, quivering anxiously. Beck's ferocity brought back memories.

'He went over to Germany to spend the money! Serves him right!'

'Who else have you got?' said Solly, curious.

'Who else have we got? Who else *haven't* we got!' replied Beck distastefully. 'There's even an Englishman. Calls himself a currency expert. Forgery expert, more likely. Browne he calls himself. Carson calls him Tommy, though. Carson grassed on him. Said it was all Tommy's fault. Tried to get immunity. They should both be immunized!' He roared with laughter and Solly joined in weakly. 'Then they both blamed it on someone called Jerry,' Beck continued. 'Said Jerry was to blame. Kept changing their story. Said Jerry found them in the wood. Pack of lies, the whole thing.' He spat on the floor. 'Tell you what: money supposed to be forged by Jews, all sorts – even Russian.' He eyed Solly curiously. 'You're Russian aren't you?'

'So they're all foreigners are they, these forgers?' said Solly nervously, thanking God that he'd never benefited financially from Operation Bernhard.

'All sorts: American, Russian English ... They even say there's a Frenchy in the women's block. Calls herself a countess. I call her a counterfeiteress!' Beck broke into guffaws of laughter and spat again. 'Been living in Switzerland. Spent most of it. Came into Germany to buy a Mercedes. Caught redhanded. How does that strike you? A French countess living in Switzerland stealing English money forged by Russian Jews employed by Nazi Germans paying foreign agents! Ever heard anything like it?'

Solly nodded. Schulz had told him all about the countess.

'Most indignant she was. Said they'd been planted on her by a communist who blew up her chateau and stole her Rolls. More likely she stole his! Reckons she's got rich English friends who'll get her out, that one. True aristocrats she calls them. Apparently they own half of Yorkshire. That's in north England, you know.'

Solly was puzzled. All the prisoners seemed to be foreigners. 'Aren't there any Germans in prison who were involved in this ... forgery, Herr Beck?' he asked.

Beck paused. He grew even more confidential and got even closer to Solly.

'Funny thing! Very few. Mostly idiots.' He paused to think, knitting his brow in concentration. 'Course there's some Swiss. Swiss-Germans. One's a businessman from Zurich. Very rich, very prosperous, came into Germany and got caught. The Swiss swizzler got swizzled!' He guffawed again. 'Doodles all the time. Probably doodling pound notes. Won't do him much good though. Tell you the wicked thing: he says the Governor used to be his boss. In the war. What's his name? ... Like a cobbler ... Schumacher!'

'Schumacher!' whistled Solly in astonishment.

Beck had been looking at him oddly. 'Know him then, do you?'

'No ...' stamered Solly, 'I just thought ... well, it's funny for a prison governer to be a shoe-maker.'

332

'Got it wrong,' said Beck, shaking his head. 'Schumacher's the swizzler, not the Governor. Governor's name's Kube. Rum fellow. Sinister if you ask me. Know what *I* think?' Solly shook his head. 'SS,' said Beck darkly. 'Written all over him. Gets others to do his dirty work. Never lifts a finger. They're all like that.'

'Who?' said Solly, still puzzled. He'd never met Kube though everyone at Barracks 19 had heard of him. Operation Bernhard had been named after him. He was really the chief of the whole outfit.

'Screws. Not like the old bunch. Rum lot. Queer crew. All SS. All very rich. Not like me. Only kept me on 'cause they thought I'd ask no questions but I keep my eyes and ears open. Kube's the richest of the lot.'

Solly nodded. It made sense of course.

'Tell me, Herr Beck,' he said, 'when all these forgers and fences were caught ... what happened to the money?'

'That's another funny thing. Supposed to be destroyed. But I reckon it wasn't. Want to know why?' Solly nodded again. 'Still valid in some countries. Swizzler told me that. Very miserable, he was. Said he should have known and got out. Won't get out, not now though. In for life.'

'Life!' said Solly.

'Life,' repeated Beck, nodding his head sagely. 'Wicked offence, worse than war.'

Solly had to get away: somehow he had to ring Schulz to warn him. Schulz had told him to contact him, if there were an emergency, at the Swan Inn in Appledore. Solly could leave a message there for him, Schulz had said.

'This is all incredible, Herr Beck,' he said, getting up from the table, 'but I really must be going.'

'Haven't finished your coffee,' said Beck looking hurt. 'Haven't told you the rest –'

'I'm sorry, Herr Beck, I'd love to hear more about it, but ... You understand.' Beck understood. He'd been in prison all his life. He didn't have anyone to meet or anywhere to go.

'Goodbye, Herr Beck,' said Solly. 'I'll see you ... again.' He had no intention of returning of course. Most likely one of the officers would recognize him from Barracks 19 and he'd spend the rest of his life behind bars. On second thoughts ... 'I'll see you tomorrow,' he said decisively, and left.

Beck was looking forward to seeing old Solly again. He could tell him all about the rum types who were now employed as postal censors, like that Herr Ditzer who was always going on about reforming prison underwear – he seemed to have made it into a crusade. Ditzer maintained that silk was most fitting for the rehabilitation of a prisoner. He said that it would redeem the most lost of souls in the spiritual values of life. Beck also wanted to tell Solly about the strange characters who came and went, to and from the prison, never speaking to him but only to Kube. They all came in with their empty briefcases and left with them bulging. The swizzler said they were off to Peru but Beck didn't really believe him. One of them had tried to get pally with Beck though. He was the rummest of the lot. He wore dark glasses and a blond wig and he seemed to switch from outrageous flattery to gross hostility every other minute. Kube kept him at arm's length, and told Beck not to speak to him. Said he'd committed some crime against the prison authorities and would never be forgiven. Beck shook his head: they were all as bad as each other, he concluded, and finished Solly's coffee, which was now stone cold.

32

'Are you sure this is the place?'

'Of course I'm sure. It's marked on the map, isn't it?

Ex-SS-General Alfred Neuheim was struggling with rage and confusion. He was standing on a patch of relatively firm ground. But most of the land around him seemed to be one enormous bog. It seemed inconceivable but the map indicated that Gerhardt Schulz had buried a canister containing two million pounds in the heart of the one genuine marsh in the whole of Romney Marsh.

'You don't think he could have got it wrong, do you?' said Kurt.

'Shut up and keep digging!' barked Neuheim.

That wasn't so easy since Kurt was now up to his waist in muddy water.

Of all the regions in Romney Marsh, the only land that was, and is, so low that natural drainage is impossible is an area called the Dowels. The Dowels are on the north-western tip of the Marsh, which is an area of a hundred square miles, shaped rather like a birthday cake that has been more than half-eaten. The bit that has been eaten makes up the coastline and the uncut part forms an arc extending from Dungeness to Hythe. Even though the Dowels have been drained artificially, the area is still full of dykes, ditches, cuts, guts, sluices, streams and pits. Kurt therefore had the misfortune to be standing in *the* marsh in *the* marsh in The Marsh.

But the signs were that even if Schulz had got it wrong, he had not deliberately bungled it. Why else would he have spent the last ten years searching for the map? And, as Neuheim had pointed out to Melfort, Schulz might be an idiot but he was no fool. Perhaps he should have put that the other way round. Neuheim didn't know any more.

'Are you sure he didn't get it wrong?' Kurt repeated miserably.

'Of course he didn't get it wrong!' snarled Neuheim. 'If I had him here instead of you I'd have got it by now.'

'Then why didn't you wait for him to come back and get him to go with you?' asked Kurt.

Another loaded question. Ever since Neuheim had met Schulz he had found himself gravitating towards him. He needed Schulz because Schulz had always had the pertinent answer, the missing piece of the jigsaw. But to take the other side of the coin, Schulz always seemed to land him in deep water. Like now, he thought, staring malevolently at the marsh. Like in Lake Toplitz, beneath which he would not have found himself had it not been for Schulz. Fortunately Neuheim was essentially a man of action, especially when it came to fleeing from the Austrian police, and while it had been Walter's idea to cut the engine, pour himself into the diving suit and slip away in the mist, that was probably the only good idea Walter had ever had in a life which had ended that night. By the time his body had been washed ashore, Neuheim was in South America, with as many of the notes as he had been able to rescue from the bale when he went down. The money had stood him in good stead with ODESSA and, of course, with their paymaster, Freidrich Schwend. Neuheim was a survivor as was Schulz. But Schulz carried the seed of disaster and ruin around him like a disease. That was one reason why he hadn't got Schulz to come and dig up the canister. There was another.

When, in early 1950, Neuheim had been kicked out of ODESSA's headquarters in Peru for insulting Martin Bormann, the Fuhrer's Deputy, and now the chief of ODESSA, he had returned to Hamburg with a new name and identity. After a while he had reverted to his old name. But he was still anxious to regain his personal prestige with ODESSA. It had been such a small thing. He had simply reminded Bormann of the story of the bumble bee. He was, however, out in the wilderness, and the day he had read in a Hamburg newspaper that Schulz had been deported from the very town where he had been picked up by the Gestapo in 1940, minus his brogues, Neuheim had known that once again he had the power to bludgeon fate into his arms. For the past ten years the thought of the canister had been a flickering flame in his darkest hours. Now his time had come round again. And this time he was anxious to prove that he didn't need Schulz. Kurt, of course, was hardly in the same league, a complete blockhead, and Neuheim only needed him to do the spadework.

'I could spend the rest of my life digging up this marsh,' complained Kurt.

'I see no reason why that can't be arranged,' said Neuheim. It would be getting dark soon and this was no weather to be out in the middle of a bog. Perhaps they should leave it till tomorrow. He'd give it another half an hour and then arrange to meet Melfort at the hotel. It looked as though he was going to need him after all.

In all the excitement, Schulz had quite forgotten about Neuheim. Operation Gerhardt had seemed so perfect, so foolproof. Neuheim would burgle Solly's flat in order to steal the map. It was likely that Neuheim would hope to steal Schulz too – much more fitting to get the man who buried the canister to dig it up. Of course he would be disappointed to discover Schulz was out but would not hesitate to turn the flat upside down. To guard against this they had aranged for the map to be instantly discoverable yet not in such a way that it would give cause for suspicion.

Solly had suggested concealing the map in the heel of the shoe, saying that this, being the last place anyone would look, would be the first place that Neuheim would go to. Schulz had objected that, on the contrary, because it would be the last place anyone would look, it would be the first place any intelligent person would look and therefore the last place that Neuheim would look. They finally agreed that Neuheim would hardly avoid seeing it if it were framed above the fireplace. They had returned the shoes to their original brown paper bag and placed them in the most prominent position they could find, directly facing the entrance door, so that Neuheim could hardly fail to spot them.

Solly had then wondered whether even if a five-year-old could open the hollow heel, Neuheim might not find it impossible. Schulz agreed that this was possible. They set the catch so that it only needed a gentle press on the side of the heel to open it. Anyhow, Schulz said, even if it took Neuheim a week to find the map it would not matter, because they would be at Frau Nusbaum's. They could find out from a neighbour whether the flat had been entered, and whether the map were missing. If it was, it would only prove that Neuheim was up to his knees in a bog digging. Even if he got someone else to do the dirty work, he would certainly sit around nearby, supervising the digging day after day, getting soaking wet until either the spade or his spirit broke. Schulz didn't really mind which came first.

But ever since he had discovered the public lavatory, Schulz had been so obsessed with his plan that he had quite forgotten that today was 9 January. And 9 January, as he and Solly had agreed, was the first possible date Neuheim could arrive in the area. Solly had naturally emphasized the risk.

'Are you an idiot as well as a fool?' he had said. Schulz wondered if they should be the other way round but he said nothing. 'You spend six years of your life trying to get out of his clutches –'

'Seven,' Schulz had reminded him. 'He turned up again in Linz in 1946.'

'All right, then, seven. And now, after another ten years, you get your hands on them and what do you want to do? Invite Neuheim over to share in the proceeds? You're out of your mind.'

'Solly, how many times do I have to tell you,' Schulz had replied. 'I'll be long gone by the time he arrives in England – *if* he arrives. I'm just giving him a taste of his own medicine, that's all.'

Now however things had changed. There was a real danger that Neuheim might pop out in his inimitable manner just as the money was recovered. Speed had become a vital factor. Just in case there had been any unforeseen developments at Solly's end Schulz decided that the best use he could make of his last free evening in England would be to return to the White Swan to see if Solly had left a message.

'Hello –'

'Hello? Who's that?'

'They call me Whitey but –'

'Oh, for God's sake, Melfort, can't you forget all that mumbo-jumbo – the war's over, you know.'

'Alfred, is that you?'

'Well, of course it's me, who else did you think it would be?

338

'Schulz?'

'Schulz? Don't be ridiculous! He's still in Berlin looking for the map with his greasy little forger.'

'Isn't that where you're ringing from?'

'Of course it's not where I'm ringing from. I told you, I've found the map – you were supposed to meet me in the White Swan last night. Where were you?'

'I was at the White Swan looking for you, old chap. All I could see was a load of fairies. There was one about your height, Neuheim, wearing a blond wig of all things. He looked ridiculous! Hello ... ? Are you still there?'

'That was me in the blond wig. Haven't you heard of undercover work?'

'Good God, my dear fellow, I'm so sorry, I really had no idea you were going to be under ... so much cover.'

'Anyway, Melfort, we're wasting time. There's been a last-minute hitch. Schulz went and buried the canister at the bottom of some bog. Erhardt's been helping me dig all day, but it's going to be a long job.'

'Gerhardt? But you said he was in Berlin?'

'Not Schulz, you fool! Kurt Erhardt – my assistant. I've just sent him upstairs to have a bath. He's covered in slime.'

'You're surely not recruiting me instead, are you?'

'No, I've got a more immediate problem. My language.'

'Well, you could always try washing your mouth out with –'

'English – you fool. I haven't spoked the language for a few years.'

'You should have used Schulz. His English was impeccable.'

'Melfort, if you don't want me to report you to ODESSA as a subversive, you'd better listen. I will need you to help me to get out of the country. As soon as my man's out of the bath, I'll be in it. Then I'll eat some of your filthy food. If it doesn't poison me I expect to see you here at nine o'clock punctually. Don't be late!'

As soon as Neuheim slammed down the phone in his room

it rang again. It was probably Melfort again, but Neuheim was not prepared to go through the code mumbo-jumbo again, so he simply lifted the receiver and barked: 'Neuheim!'

There was a startled gasp at the other end and the phone went dead.

Damned little Englishman, thought Neuheim, one small puff of wind and you could blow him into the sea. He'd probably only rung to add some stupid facetious comment. It was time to drag Kurt out of the bath.

Far away in Hamburg at the other end of the phone, Solly trembled as he thought of the danger that Schulz was in. Could Neuheim have already forced him into his services, with the aid of the Luger that he used to be so fond of carrying? Solly sighed. He had warned Schulz all along of the danger, but that stubborn German had not paid any attention. It would serve him right if he ended up in the same hole he'd come to dig up.

He stared at the phone. The least he could do was to warn Gerhardt that the fivers were no longer legal tender. Knowing Schulz's luck, he would be arrested as soon as he changed the first fiver to have a cup of tea. How could Schulz have been so reckless, so stupid? Why hadn't he found out about the currency change beforehand? There was still a slim chance that Schulz had found the canister and had left England. But why, in that case, had he not sent the cable with the single-word message 'Found' which they had agreed he should do?

Solly was in a dither. He should have been more careful. He had simply asked to speak to the German staying at the hotel and the switchboard had put him straight through. Perhaps he should ring again and ask to speak to Schulz. No, it would be better just to ask for him by his first name. After another five minutes' hesitation, he picked up the phone again and asked the operator to put him through to England.

Kurt was fed up to his back teeth. He was just wondering whether he couldn't somehow creep away and head back for Hamburg when the phone rang.

'Answer the phone!' yelled Neuheim. 'It's probably Melfort to ask the way to the hotel.' Kurt answered the phone.

'Is there a German gentleman there called Gerhardt?' came the voice of the hall porter.

'Erhardt? That's me,' said Kurt.

'Go ahead, caller,' said the porter in his best operator voice. There was a click and then a crackling sound, as though the phone had been linked to a shortwave radio on a sinking ship.

'Is that you, Erhardt?'

'Yes,' said Kurt. It was a foreigner, talking in German: it must be Melfort.

'Listen, you've got to get out of there.'

'What? Why?' said Kurt petrified.

'Neuheim. He's in the hotel.'

'I know he is,' said Kurt.

'What?' exploded the voice at the other end of the line.

'But he's not here at the moment. He's soaking wet.'

'Thank God for that!' came the foreign voice sounding very relieved. 'What about you. Have you got the canister?'

'Oh, that. It's a waste of time. I doubt whether I'll ever dig it up. I doubt whether it's even there.'

'Are you all right, Gerhardt? It doesn't sound like you.' Kurt wondered how Melfort would know what he sounded like. They'd never met or spoken to each other.

'Well, how would you be if you'd been digging around in the marsh?'

'Did you get wet in The Marsh too?' asked the caller. 'I said you would.'

'Soaked. It was absolutely filthy in there. But I'm quite dry now.'

'I told you. You should have taken my advice. Now listen. You must get out of the country. He'll kill you.'

'What? Who?' said Kurt in alarm.

'Neuheim, of course. And for God's sake, don't go anywhere near Hamburg! It's crawling with SS and you don't

341

stand a chance. They're all in it. Police, prison officers. Even the prison governor. It's Kube!'

Kurt swallowed. He remembered Kube very well.

'And, please God, whatever you do, don't spend a single one of those fivers in England or Germany, Gerhardt. They've withdrawn them from circulation. They're illegal. Probably in France and Switzerland too. You'll be arrested at once.'

'Oh, I don't care about those stupid fivers,' Kurt whispered. 'I only did it because Neuheim made me.'

'Gerhardt, are you sure you're all right? You never talked like this before. Pull yourself together. Think of all your good points. You are one of the cleverest people I've ever known. You are brimming with ideas. Crazy ideas, true, but ideas. You should be so down now when you've come this far. Think of all the time you spent searching for the shoes.'

'Oh, you mean those shoes with the hollow heel. Yes, it took ages to find them – and I wasn't even looking for them. But I was the one who found them, I suppose. I wanted to wear them, you know. They were very comfortable.'

'Gerhardt? ... Well, what about the map, remember how long it took to get hold of that map?'

'Yes, you're right, I did get hold of it before Neuheim. But so what? What did I want with an old map?'

'It's a shock to hear you in this mood, Gerhardt. I don't know whether to be happy or sad. But I'm glad you've seen sense at last.'

'What do you think I should do?'

'Well, you've always been the one with the ideas, but ... well, I can understand it. You were nearly there and now this ... Well, come to my place then, Gerhardt. He won't think of looking for you there. Only to start with though. I think it's best that you should leave the country. Find yourself a nice woman. Settle down.'

'Is that still Melfort on the phone?' boomed Neuheim who had been dozing in the bath. Kurt froze: how could he have forgotten what Melfort had just told him about Neuheim. He cupped his hand over the phone.

342

'Yes,' he said nervously.

'Whats he doing, discussing the state of the economy?' boomed Neuheim with a chuckle. The bath had restored a certain amount of good humour to his jaded nerves. 'Tell him to get a move on. He's supposed to be here at nine.'

'All right,' said Kurt. He spoke into the phone again. 'He's expecting you here soon,' he whispered.

'What? Who is?' said the foreigner.

'Neuheim. He'll soon be out of the bath. What shall I do?'

'I don't know,' Melfort seemed to be trembling. 'Leave as soon as possible. Come direct to my place. Don't go to Hamburg. Did you say he expects *me* to go over there and join you? You must be out of your mind! He'll probably put me in a gas chamber. You come *here*. And remember, Gerhardt, I may be the only friend you've got.' The phone clicked dead.

Schulz walked briskly through to the reception desk at the White Swan. The porter was talking to a huge brute of a man who might have passed for an SS guard except that he looked as though he had been pulled out of bed in the middle of the night by the Gestapo. He was trying to make himself understood in a hopeless pidgin-English, while groping at his clothes as if to make sure he had them all on. Most of them were there but they didn't look very happy about the fact. They had been fastened together so peculiarly that it was clear that the man was either permanently out of his mind or had just had a very bad shock.

'Can I be of any assistance?' said Schulz.

'Not unless you work at the local asylum,' replied the porter calmly. 'This man's a nutter.'

'No, he's not,' said Schulz, 'he's German.'

The huge brute turned and stared at Schulz.

'Amounts to the same thing,' said the porter as calmly as before. Neither Schulz nor his compatriot were prepared to defend this point of view: both had more urgent considerations.

'My name's Schulz,' he said to the porter. 'Are there any

messages for me?' The porter went off to consult his message pad. The brute still stared at Schulz with a look of desperation. He might very well be a nutter, thought Schulz.

'You're Schulz,' he said. 'You've got to help me.'

Schulz gaped at him in astonishment.

'Remember Barracks 19?' said the man.

Schulz began to tremble. Even if he wasn't a nutter, the man's presence here could only mean one thing. 'How did you know I was here?' he said hoarsely.

'Neuheim –'

Schulz didn't wait to hear more. He shot out of the reception area and through the hotel entrance into the street. Outside, a policeman was just propping up his bicycle against the wall. Schulz swung out into the street, tumbling over the policeman and his bicycle.

'What the –' began Sam Maynard, staring at the demented figure who was getting to his feet and running off down the street. His eyes opened even wider when a much bigger and even more demented figure rushed down the steps of the hotel entrance after him. When Kurt saw that Schulz was getting away he did the only sensible thing.

As the old constable watched the huge brute grab his bicycle, throw himself on the saddle and speed off down the street, he stared after him muttering: 'It's just like the war all over again.'

Schulz was almost out of breath. Somewhere very close behind him, Neuheim's henchman was still keeping pace without any apparent need to exert himself at all. Schulz forced himself to keep running, not daring to turn round. Whoever the hulk was and however bizarre he appeared, he was in peak condition and very dangerous, almost certainly an ex-SS guard. Probably Neuheim had two or three of them digging up the marsh and they'd decided to recruit more workers. Probably Neuheim had said: *If only I could get my hands on Schulz, I'd make the little criminal work for me*. It would be ironical if Kemp and his men turned up with their equipment at the public lavatory while Schulz was up to his knees in a swamp digging for Neuheim. But of course, he had only himself to blame. Solly had been right after all.

He had left the village and was running south along the country road. Now practically exhausted, he threw himself under a hedge. Instantly his pursuer swept past him.

'You've got to help me, Schulz,' he heard him scream. Neuheim's going to eat me alive! I don't know what to do!'

Schulz sighed with relief. There was no accounting for tastes.

33

It was eight o'clock in the morning of Monday 10 January. On the road outside the yellow-brick public convenience stood a compressed air generator, its motor already chugging. Gorman was trying to keep himself warm by jumping up and down, and breathing in his cupped hands: there was a bitter wind and the remains of last night's frost. As far as he was concerned, the whole thing was a waste of time. The German was a con-artist of the first order. He would watch him like a hawk.

Out of the distance came the sound of a lorry, and Gorman pretended to busy himself, fiddling with the generator. A builder's truck was drawing up by the lavatory, its engine coughing and spluttering, and finally giving out altogether as it pulled into the side of the road. Kemp jumped out from the driver's seat, looking very disgruntled. From the passenger seat, Schulz climbed out. Moore and Melvyn climbed out of the back.

'Couldn't you have knocked off a better truck than that?' Kemp yelled at his brother.

'It was all I could find,' replied Melvyn.

'It would be all the same if we was doing a smash and grab job,' said Kemp disgustedly. 'Now let me get this straight, Mr Schulz,' he added. 'You're still saying it's

345

fifty-fifty: we get a million and you get a million.'

'I've already told you,' said Schulz.

'Right then, let's get on with it,' growled Kemp. 'Fred, give this engine a going over!' While Kemp and Schulz walked round to the lavatory, Moore and Melvyn started emptying the rear of the truck, which was full of tools, drainpipes and boards announcing road works, bearing an assortment of different Councils' names.

'Is that the spot?' Kemp was watching Schulz who had been looking round the interior and was now staring down at the middle of the floor.

'I think so,' said Schulz. 'It must be about there.'

'What makes you so sure?' Schulz didn't answer. He was looking at the sketch map. Then he walked outside, followed by Kemp.

'The bank was about four to five feet high,' he explained. 'They built that road along the top of it. The lavatory's been set at the level of the road so they must have built it up.'

'Why would they do that?' said Kemp.

'Drainage,' replied Schulz. 'Water flows better when it's going down than when it's going up.'

'I see,' Kemp nodded. 'Yeah, it would.' He paused. 'But how do you know that lavatory's right on the spot?'

'Because there's a milestone back there which they left – out of historic interest, I suppose – and this spot is just two hundred yards from it. It's got to be here,' he went on confidently. 'Tell them to bring the tools in.' He walked back into the lavatory.

'All right, Harry,' called Kemp, 'bring the stuff in!'

The signs had been hung on the railings and propped on the ground. The 'new' drainpipes were lying on the road. Gorman had given up trying to sort out the lorry's starter and was helping the others to unload. Melvyn, who was carrying a pick in one hand and an 'Out of Order' sign in the other, clumsily dropped the pick, narrowly missing Gorman's foot. Gorman looked at him disgustedly, grabbing the sign and pointing at it.

'They ought to make you wear that permanently on your head,' he said. 'Just to warn people!'

346

'I'm not looking forward to this,' said Moore to Kemp. 'Digging's hard work if you're not used to it.'

'Three or four feet of hole with two million nikker at the bottom of it and you call that hard work?' said Kemp.

'*If* it's there,' said Gorman under his breath.

Kemp heard him. 'It had better be,' he said.

Inside the lavatory Schulz had squatted down and was touching the floor with his hand, as if he could almost feel vibrations coming from the canister. In a few hours the money would be his. Then it would simply be a matter of a few finishing touches. He was tingling with expectation.

'Right, let's get to work,' said Kemp who had just walked in. 'Bring in the drill here.' Moore put the blade of the pneumatic drill to the floor. A moment later there was an ear-splitting noise as it began biting into the concrete. Schulz's heart leaped. It was noisy enough to wake the dead. He stared, fascinated, as the concrete was slowly torn apart.

Outside on the roadway, Gorman was directing traffic with a STOP-GO sign. A country bus pulled out past the generator and the truck, while two cars waited to pass on the other side. The bus driver acknowledged Gorman's help with a wave of his hand. Meanwhile Gorman turned the STOP sign round to GO and the two waiting cars moved on.

'No sign of it,' came the voice of Harry Moore. He was taking a brief rest from digging a wide hole that was now over four feet deep. Moore was at the bottom of it.

'Keep digging,' said Schulz.

'Come on, Melvyn,' came Moore's voice, 'start shovelling.' Melvyn jumped back into the hole and picked up the shovel.

Outside, Gorman was watching with some anxiety as a policeman approached on his bicycle.

'What's going on?' said the policeman, getting off his bike.

'Drains are playing up again,' replied Gorman nervously. 'Can't you smell'm?'

347

PC Maynard sniffed. 'No, I can't.'

'You must have a cold,' replied Gorman. Maynard gave him a look: he might very well be catching cold. He had a rotten headache and had been up half the night looking for his bicycle. It had been handed in early that morning by a boy who had found it dumped by a hedge a quarter of a mile down the road from the White Swan. Propping up his bike, he walked round to the lavatory.

Moore and Melvyn were busy down the hole, while Schulz and Kemp, sitting back on their heels, looked on. Moore stopped digging and stared at something beyond and above them. They turned and saw the policeman, peering down into the hole.

'Drains, is it?' he said, sniffing.

'Yes,' Kemp nodded. 'Drains.'

'You're going down a bit for drains, aren't you?' There was a silence for a few seconds. Kemp's hand closed around a pick handle as he looked blankly at Schulz, who was thinking that the policeman looked familiar.

'Are you an expert on drains, officer?' Schulz said sternly.

'Not an expert, no,' said PC Maynard, wondering where he had seen this man before. 'Who are you?'

'I'm from the Borough Surveyor's office. I *laid* these pipes.'

'Oh well,' Maynard laughed, still eyeing him a little doubtfully. 'I bow to superior knowledge.' He looked back into the hole. 'Have you dug that this morning?'

'Of course we have,' said Kemp, tightening his grip on the pick handle.

'You certainly don't waste time,' said Maynard, looking at his watch. 'Well, the wife'll have lunch on the stove. Steak and kidney pudding. I'd better get moving. Knowing you council workmen you'll be here for a month.' He eyed them all once more and then walked back to his bike. The men sighed with relief. Kemp looked at Schulz.

'Pretty smart, aren't you?' he said.

'I've had to be,' replied Schulz.

'Then where's this bloody canister?' snarled Kemp.

348

'They're down there nearly five feet and there's no sign of it.'

'It's there,' said Schulz firmly. 'Just keep digging.'

'It had better be there,' replied Kemp menacingly.

Outside, Gorman was tinkering with the truck's engine again when Schulz came out on to the road and stood staring about him. Schulz was getting very worried. It was now almost 1.00 p.m. and they were getting nowhere. Was the canister still there? Were they in fact digging in the wrong spot? He studied the layout of the land again. There had been an ugly note in Kemp's voice and even Moore had begun to mutter. He *knew* he was in the right place and yet ... ? He looked down at the road and then from one side of it to the other.

'Found it yet?' said Gorman sceptically from the truck.

'I think I've found out where it isn't,' said Schulz, hurrying back to where Moore and Melvyn were still digging, and Kemp was still looking ugly. 'We're digging in the wrong spot,' Schulz announced.

Moore and Melvyn stopped digging. There was a deathly silence. Kemp looked like the boot was going to go in.

'What did you say?' said Kemp threateningly.

'It's the wrong spot,' replied Schulz with as much calm as he could muster. 'I made a mistake.'

Moore was outraged. He had stopped being amiable hours ago.

'A mistake?' he shouted. 'Look at my hands!'

'It was a natural mistake,' added Schulz hurriedly. 'I assumed the road was as wide as the bank but it's not, it's wider. They've built the road a couple of feet beyond the bank and shored it up with earth.' He walked over to the side wall of the lavatory and pointed at it. 'Don't you see?' he went on excitedly, 'I thought this wall began where the bank ended but it doesn't. They've built the bank out to support the road. The canister is under the road.'

'Under the road?' Moore laughed. 'Forget it! I've had

349

enough! He threw down the pick. 'Melvyn – out! One out, all out!' He started to climb out but Kemp put a hand in his face and pushed him back into the hole.

'I'll tell you when you're coming out!' He turned furiously to Schulz. 'You expect us to start digging up the road now?'

'No,' said Schulz, irritated at Kemp's obtuseness. 'We can reach it from here.' He went over to the side wall. 'We go down the same distance and then start digging inwards. We'll be under the road.' There was another pause while they stared at him with blank hostility. 'For God's sake, it's worth it, isn't it?' Schulz added passionately. 'Do you want to give up just because it wasn't right under your feet?' He waited, tense with anxiety. He was under no illusions about what they would do to him if they failed.

'Get the drill,' said Kemp at last, nodding grimly. 'We'll start again.'

Moore and Melvyn climbed out of the hole. Even Melvyn was now muttering as he went outside to call Gorman to start the generator. Moore picked up the drill while Kemp turned to Schulz.

'Just remember,' he said darkly. 'It's these boys who are doing the digging. They don't like digging. If they don't find anything, they're going to put that drill on your head and set it going – OK? All right, Harry, start it up.'

Once again Moore inserted his blade into the concrete floor, this time by the wall. Again, the noise was ear-splitting as the blade started to chew up the floor.

Schulz was sitting on a lavatory seat. He was suffering from acute nervous strain. His face was lined and tense with anxiety and he felt drained of energy. It was becoming obvious to him at least that something was very wrong and that the wisest thing for him to do was to vanish while he could. The men were getting more and more bad-tempered by the minute. Quietly he crept out of the lavatory.

Inside, the drill had been packed up hours earlier and now all that could be heard was the 'pick-pick' of Moore and Melvyn as they dug on. The hole was even deeper, though less wide, than the previous one and they had started to dig out the side under the road. Kemp stood watching them. He too was beginning to get the feeling that the canister wasn't there. He turned and walked out of the lavatory to look for Schulz.

The cabin doors of the truck were hanging open. Schulz stared at the truck. Even after ten years of searching and the constant obsession of regaining the money, his overriding impulse in life, and especially at that moment, was to save his skin. He was being seized with an irresistible temptation. He moved a little so as to see the dashboard and the keys which were still hanging from the ignition. He stared at them. They were the keys to safety. He turned and looked down the road: Gorman was preoccupied with the northbound Greyhound Express, which had been stationary for the last ten minutes because of a queue of traffic that was crawling south on the other side of the road, and which Gorman was directing like a matador. As the Greyhound crawled past, Gorman stared at a passenger wearing dark glasses, a blond wig, and a furious expression on his scarred face. Schulz noticed the Greyhound too and caught a brief glimpse of Neuheim – for the first time in fourteen years – and beside him a forlorn figure despondently chewing gum. The vision made him smile briefly. Neuheim had mesmerized another rabbit. At least, he thought, Neuheim was going according to plan. Neuheim had been the only thing that had been predictable in the last few days.

The bus flashed past and Schulz's smile faded. He was now in desperate trouble. If he didn't find the canister and Kemp's boys didn't get him, then Neuheim would. He turned back to the truck. After a moment's hesitation he moved towards the cabin door, but froze as Kemp suddenly stepped in front of him. For a moment they stared at each other. Then Kemp leaned inside the cabin and pulled out the keys.

'Very careless, leaving keys in trucks. After all, that's how we got it, didn't we?' He scowled at Schulz.

* * *

The light was fading with the first hint of dusk. Moore was burrowing inside the trench he had dug under the road, using a spotlight to see better.

'There's something there,' he shouted.

'A drain probably,' said Kemp, now convinced that Schulz was a nutcase and wondering how he was going to get out alive himself when the lads found out.

'It don't look like a drain,' said Moore excitedly. 'It looks – silvery.'

Schulz jumped with excitement.

'Let me have a look,' he shouted, jumping down into the hole and snatching the flashlight from Moore. He peered into the cavity. Kemp and the others, watched him, holding their breath.

'Well?' said Kemp impatiently. Schulz re-emerged hind-first from the trench.

'That's it,' he said, looking up in triumph. Kemp was astonished.

'You sure?' he said after a pause.

'Positive,' said Schulz. There was a moment's stunned silence: then they all broke into a spontaneous cheer.

'Found something,' said PC Maynard, standing at the entrance door. He walked over and looked down into the hole. Then he turned and glared at them.

'It's the broken drain,' said Kemp hurriedly, breaking the silence. PC Maynard scrutinized them penetratingly. His eyes narrowed.

'You're the best bunch of bloody workmen I've ever seen!' He looked again into the hole and shook his head. 'Well, the wife's got supper on the stove. Sausage and mash tonight. I'll be getting along.'

'Christ,' said Moore, when Maynard had gone, 'what an exciting life that copper leads.'

'Come on, come on!' snapped Kemp, 'dig it out!'

Outside PC Maynard was picking up his bicycle. He nodded at Gorman.

'They've found the drain,' he said.

'Oh yeah?' Gorman replied politely.

'The broken one.'

'Oh, that one!' said Gorman, trying to conceal his amazement.

'That's a fine bunch of mates you've got in there, son,' said PC Maynard. 'They're a credit to the country. I haven't seen anything like it since Dunkirk.'

'I'll tell'm,' replied Gorman, turning and walking quickly into the lavatory.

Dunkirk, thought Maynard affectionately. He hadn't thought about it for years. Of course he had fought his own war then, against one of the most dangerous agents Jerry could throw at the British. He would never forget the man in the plus-fours who had stolen his bicycle.

'There it is, it's coming!' Moore shouted with excitement as Gorman came in. Moore and Schulz were frenziedly hacking away at the earth surrounding the canister. It was, just as Schulz remembered, as big as a medium-sized suitcase. They were digging out the earth around the ends in order to get a grip on it.

'Go easy, easy, don't wrench it!' yelled Schulz with surprising concern, considering his impatience to get at it. Moore stared at him.

'What do you mean "go easy"? It's not going to explode, is it?'

'It might,' said Schulz.

'What?' gasped Moore, drawing back in fright.

'Give it here, give it here!' growled Kemp impatiently.

By now Schulz had got the canister free and was holding it in his outstretched arms. Kemp grabbed it from him with ease, pushing him aside. As Schulz scrambled out of the hole after him, Kemp grabbed a chisel and a hammer and was about to prise open the lid.

'Don't do that!' ordered Schulz sharply.

'What?' said Kemp, looking uglier than ever.

'There's an explosive device inside,' said Schulz nervously. 'You'll blow us all to bits!' There was a stunned silence. Then Kemp laughed.

'Who are you kidding?' he jeered.

'I'm telling you, it's true,' said Schulz earnestly. 'Let me do it, what difference does it make?'

'I'll do it myself!' snarled Kemp evilly. 'No Kraut tells me what to do. You chump! You'd believe anything!' He put the chisel to the edge of the canister and raised the hammer again. Schulz got up hastily.

'I'll wait outside,' he said and hurried out of the lavatory, Kemp hesitated. He looked at Moore, Gorman and his brother whose faith in his leadership was fast wavering. Then he snorted and lined up the chisel again.

'Explosive device!' he muttered scornfully. He raised the hammer and Moore, Gorman and Melvyn all bolted at once for the exit, leaving him with the unexploded canister, utterly alone, the hammer frozen in mid-air.

At a little distance from the lavatory, the others waited tensely. Then, instead of the shattering explosion they had been expecting, Kemp appeared, and went over to Schulz.

'All right, clever – you open it,' he muttered. 'And no tricks.'

Schulz led the way back inside.

Schulz put his hand on the small knob at the end of the canister. He thought of Captain Ohm who had designed it; of Neuheim who was waiting for it; of Hans Krauss, still hoping for his economic miracle, of Herr Krum, the cobbler, who would have been amazed to witness this moment; but as he steadied himself, pushing a small button and then turning the knob first one way and then the other, he thought of Bertha as she had looked when he had walked out of the Bandol hotel ten years ago. There was the sound of a click.

He relaxed. Then he looked at the others and smiled. His face was pouring with sweat and he was still trembling with excitement. Slowly he rolled back the steel lid that ran the length of the canister. They all stared down into it.

Inside lay row upon row of perfect white five-pound notes, stacked in perfect order. He was in a trance, but so were the others. None of them, apart from Schulz, had ever seen so much money before in their lives. For Schulz it was the end of a long road that stretched back twenty years through France and Germany and back again twice. He could hear the twang of Hawaiian guitars, the gentle sounds of accordions in Parisien cafés, where a woman no longer looked through him but deep into his eyes ...

There was a long silence.

'There's nearly two million pounds there,' said Schulz finally.

'Jesus Christ!' murmured Gorman in awe. There was another, but this time heavier, pause. Schulz closed the lid of the canister, picked it up and stood up. The others stood up with him. He looked at them all, one by one, hugging the canister to his chest. There was something about the way that they were standing there that ...

'Fifty-fifty – we agreed,' Schulz reminded them nervously.

'That's English money you've got there,' growled Kemp darkly. 'We can't let no Kraut steal English money – it wouldn't be right.'

The others nodded primly.

'There was nothing in writing,' said Kemp.

'An Englishman's word is his bond,' said Schulz. He'd read that when he was at school in Kent.

'I never heard of that before, have you, Harry?'

'Never,' said Moore aimiably.

These men had obviously never been to school.

Kemp took a grip on the canister. Schulz trembled.

'All right,' said Schulz desperately. 'Equal shares for all five.'

'Equal shares for all *four*!' said Kemp.

He put a hand on Schulz's chest and shoved him violently backwards. Schulz let go of the canister and fell back into the hole. Kemp towered above him.

'This'll pay for some of the damage you did,' he said, indignantly tapping the canister.

'But *I* didn't do any damage!' gasped Schulz who had hurt his back.

'Oh, no?' said Kemp. 'What about Coventry?'

'Exactly!' said Moore to Schulz. 'What about Coventry?

355

I had an aunt in Coventry,' he added to Melvyn.

'This is reparations,' said Kemp.

'Right!' agreed Moore. 'Reparations.'

'Of course,' said Kemp self-righteously, 'if you Krauts had paid us some reparations the first time round we wouldn't have had to do this.'

'Yeah,' agreed Moore. 'We weren't tough enough with you after the First bleeding World War, were we, Stan?'

'Right,' nodded Kemp, 'that's why you got too big for your boots again.'

'Come on,' said Kemp, 'I'll buy you all a drink.'

'Why don't we buy the pub,' said Melvyn, as they walked back to the truck, 'and then we won't have to pay for the drink.'

34

Schulz stared after them, almost as stunned by their complete ignorance of history as by the fact that, after all this time, he had yet again been frustrated so near to his goal.

Melvyn and Gorman were climbing into the back of the truck and Moore was climbing into the driving seat while Kemp, clutching the canister, was walking round to the other front seat. A country bus had stopped further down the road, Schulz came charging out of the public convenience gripping a shovel. He had never committed a wilful attack on another person in his life, apart from the kidnapping of the British officers and the incident with Neuheim's driver. Schmidt's death by poison didn't count. But that was all war. This was much more serious. A bunch of criminals were making off with his future.

He rushed after Kemp, fetching him a blow across the back of his head with the shovel. Kemp staggered, still clutching the canister. Schulz dropped the shovel, snatched the canister and, ran for the bus – which, to his relief, was marked Hythe.

The bus was just pulling away from the stop. Schulz sprinted after it desperately, and got his hand on the rail, swinging himself and the canister on to the platform.

'You could've got yourself killed doing that,' said the conductor disapprovingly.

'After him, after him!' screamed Kemp who was recovering from the blow to his head. Gorman, though, was again fiddling inside the bonnet.

'It won't start!' he screamed back. As he said it, the engine suddenly burst into life and the truck shot off. Moore, who was at the steering wheel, immediately braked, and waited for Gorman and Kemp to catch up and climb in the front cabin.

'I'll kill him! I'll kill him!' Kemp screamed as the lorry started up again. 'I'll pull his bloody arms out! Can't you drive this thing any faster?' The bus was now disappearing into the distance.

'It won't go any faster, there's something wrong with it!' replied Moore.

'I know that!' screamed Kemp.

'We're catching them up, anyway,' said Melvyn. It was true: imperceptibly the distance between the bus and the lorry was diminishing.

Schulz, with the canister squeezed between his knees, stared anxiously back at the truck which slowly seemed to be moving towards them. Although it was not exactly breaking speed limits it was going faster than the bus which crawled along with agonizing sluggishness. He looked desperately at the conductor.

'Can't we go any faster?'

'Faster? Faster?' said the conductor indignantly. 'We're ahead of schedule! We shouldn't even be here, yet. And don't think you'd have got there any sooner if you'd waited longer at the bus stop and we'd arrived on time, because you wouldn't. I keep explaining that to people but they never understand. It's a matter of schedules and regulations.'

'Got him! Got him!' yelled Kemp triumphantly as he saw the bus coming to a halt. At the same moment the truck's engine began to splutter and a moment later died altogether. 'What's the matter with it?' he screamed.

'It's that bloody carburettor!' screamed back Moore. He was pressing the starter repeatedly with no results. 'It's full of rubbish!'

'Oh, for Christ's sake!' said Kemp. The truck ground to a complete standstill. The starter motor whirred and whirred as Moore tried unsuccessfully to start it again. Kemp, now desperate, could see the bus, not a hundred yards away and still waiting at the stop.

Inside the bus, Schulz was still staring anxiously back at the truck. Suddenly he saw Kemp climb down from the cabin and run towards the bus, sprinting like a hundred-metre champion.

The conductor was standing on the platform, watching Kemp running for the bus like a Harrier. He put his hand on the bell but waited before pressing it to signal the driver to start. Kemp was no more than twenty yards away and was obviously going to make it. But he had reckoned without the peculiar psychology of the British Bus Conductor: with no more than a few yards separating Kemp from his goal, the conductor looked at his watch and pressed the bell. It was 4.40 p.m. and important to stick to the schedule. The bus was due at Hythe by 5.00 p.m.

'Wait! Wait!' gasped Kemp as the bus pulled away. The conductor stared at him expressionlessly for a moment and then turned to Schulz.

'He's a very good runner, that bloke,' he said knowledgeably. 'Got a very nice action. I used to do a bit of running myself. I was the Green Bus Cross-Country Champion for two years.'

Kemp, his face set and grim, sped on, like a marathon

runner, his eyes fixed unwaveringly on the back of the retreating bus.

Moore was still pressing the starter motor wildly. It was
beginning to sound distinctly tired.

'Oh, come on,' said Gorman, who was in the back with
Melvyn. 'Let's have a look at that bloody engine or we'll
be here all day!' They both jumped down on to the road.
At the same moment the engine burst into life again and
the truck leaped forward. Gorman and Melvyn rushed after
it. 'Wait! Wait!' screamed Gorman. 'Wait, you stupid sod!
Wait!'

But the truck rolled on. Melvyn, in frustration, picked
up a rock and threw it after them but it fell far short. The
truck came to a halt beside the panting Kemp who opened
the door and climbed in, slamming it shut. Immediately the
engine died again. Scarcely able to draw breath, Kemp
stared in outraged amazement at Moore. He opened his
mouth to say something but he was too winded to talk. Instead he opened the cabin door again, got out and started
running, even as Moore was hammering away at the starter
button.

The bus was entering the outskirts of Hythe. Schulz glanced
through the rear window and noted to his relief that there
was now no sign of the truck. The bus pulled up at a stop
and passengers started to get on and off.

'Next stop – Terminus!' called the conductor. He rang
the bell and the bus started off again.

Schulz turned and looked once more through the rear
window. To his utter dismay he could now see the truck
charging down the street towards him. Instinctively he
clutched the canister more tightly to him. It was obvious he
would stand more chance fleeing in the crowds than staying
on the bus.

The bus slowed down and stopped at the lights. Schulz

got up. He could make out the lorry wedged inside a stationary line of traffic. He slipped off the bus and ran.

Inside the truck Kemp suddenly spotted him. 'There he is!' he shouted. 'You follow in the truck!' He opened the door and jumped down. On the platform of the bus, the conductor stared open-mouthed at Kemp, who suddenly appeared from nowhere, sprinting along the pavement and passing the bus as if he had followed it on foot all the way.

'That man's a marvel,' he murmured to himself. 'A bloody marvel! He's better than Zatopek!'

Shoppers parted like the Red Sea before Schulz as he raced through the streets of Hythe. Some way behind came Kemp. After running and dodging for some time, it looked to Schulz as if he had finally given his pursuer the slip.

He made his way down to the sea-front in the gathering dusk. Perhaps he could find some refuge, some shelter where he could spend the night. It would be cold and uncomfortable but at least he would be safe. Then first thing in the morning he could get on a train and catch the ferry back to Hamburg.

Schulz walked down the steps on to the beach, pausing to gulp great breaths of air and relax for the first time in many hours.

Kemp was in a black mood: he had lost the Kraut in the High Street over an hour ago and since then he had been searching the town for him. It was like looking for a needle in a haystack. He had, though, found Moore and the lorry, and Moore was now as hard to shake off as Schulz was to find. For the last half hour they had been combing the beach in the darkness. Although it was midwinter and not exactly Blackpool, Schulz might have taken it into his head to find some little cave or hidey-hole further along. Moore was grumbling that it was a waste of time, and Kemp was also privately admitting that once again the Germans had got away with it, when he suddenly spotted a figure carrying what looked suspiciously like the canister.

'There he is!' he shouted to Moore, and began to run towards the figure which was some hundred yards away. The moon had risen and the canister was quite visible, gleaming silvery in the moonlight.

Schulz heard the shout and ran, faster than he had ever run in his life. After five minutes he paused momentarily to catch his breath and to look round: but Kemp was still running and even starting to gain on him. Further back, Moore was hastily waddling along, though not with the same furious urgency. Schulz started to run again and suddenly noticed in the far distance a boat lying upturned on the shingle: it was now his only hope. If he could get himself and the canister into the boat and row out to sea he would be free of Kemp – unless he was also an Olympic swimmer. Then he could either row back to some other part of the coast or keep on rowing until he reached France or Belgium or Holland – or even Germany.

He sprinted towards the boat in a final burst of energy. When he reached it, he put the canister down on the shingly beach, grabbed the side of the boat with both hands and heaved and strained until it turned right side up. Then he started dragging it to the water, lifting first one end and pulling it round, then the other. It was heavy, heavier than anything he'd ever moved before. It shifted inch by inch and all the time he could hear Kemp's and Moore's footsteps on the shingle coming closer and closer, their shouts more distinct and louder.

Slowly he was able to get one end of the boat into the water and it began to move a little more easily. Sweating and straining he made one last, almighty effort and pushed it clear. The boat was floating.

A flood of exaltation swept over him as he realized that he was at last going to get away. He pushed the boat out a little further to give himself enough water to use the oars and then turned round and rushed back to fetch the canister. He picked it up with shaking hands and paused, looking back.

Kemp was now running hard towards him. Schulz had about fifteen seconds left, ample time. He raced back to the boat which was bobbing up and down in the water and threw the canister into it.

There was a blinding flash and a roar like thunder.

Kemp was still some distance away. He stopped dead as a great gust of wind tore at his hair and clothes like some passing cyclone. After long, long minutes it subsided and was replaced by a terrible silence.

There was no sign of the boat, only pieces of wreckage floating about. The canister itself had entirely disappeared but an inert body lay in a crumpled mass on the beach, the water lapping at its feet.

His clothes were torn and full of holes where the blast hit him and there were burns on his hands and face. A charred five-pound note, solitary survivor of millions, had miraculously landed upon the outstretched palm of his hand.

The feel of it seemed to have some mysterious life-giving property, for his fingers closed over it like a blind man's sensing it out by touch, feeling its texture, which still possessed that odd, crisp quality. It was the only thing in the world that could be calculated to bring him back to life.

Schulz sat up, looking like a tailor's dummy rescued from a fire, and stared down at the note.

'You fool! You fool! You bloody fool!' Kemp growled at the wreckage of the mad German. 'What d'you do that for? I ought to kick your head in!'

For a moment Schulz didn't move. Then, slowly, and with a terrible, almost majestic dignity, he turned his ravaged face around.

Kemp stared, disconcerted, uneasy, almost awe-stricken. Further off still, stood fat Harry Moore, unable to see, let alone comprehend, what had just taken place. But Kemp understood.

The look on Schulz's face spoke of more human misery than Kemp had ever dreamed existed. It did something to him. Without another word he turned and walked away.

The sea lapped and rolled, deaf to explosions and the wrecking of human hopes alike. But Schulz continued to sit there and stare on the edge of the sea, on the edge of time and the universe, like a Yogi who had been there for days and was about to become one with the infinite. The moon went behind a cloud and the light faded, but Schulz never moved, only sat and stared. The moon emerged from the cloud and filled the sea with silver and only then did something begin to move.

Two large tears welled up in his eyes and rolled silently down his cheeks.

35

'The clouds of war are gathering,' muttered Ephraim Solokoff to himself behind his morning paper, 'and this time there's going to be a holocaust. No more Geneva Conventions. The United Nations is a joke. Khruschev, Kennedy – East and West – it's all the same. The world is heading for nuclear war and there's nothing anyone can do about it. The point is what can we do to get out of it?'

What Solly really meant was: 'What can I do to get out of it?' Prison was no longer a security against nuclear attack.

'I think there's going to be a war this time, Herr Solokoff,' his landlady said to him as she put down his morning cup of ersatz coffee, 'and personally I would welcome it. It will clear the air.'

'It will certainly do that,' said Solly, turning to the

financial page. The mark was steadily going up and the pound steadily going down. It was time that he began to think seriously about work again. It would not be too difficult to get hold of some plates to produce the marks. But it would be supremely difficult without someone to organize the operation. 'It may clear a lot of other things too,' he added.

'Thank goodness they've sealed off all those Reds,' said Frau Nusbaum. 'It's like that operation I had done last year. It wasn't nearly as bad once they stitched it all up.'

Solly tried not to think about the sealing off of the Berlin Wall which was still making headlines that August of 1961. As for the thought of Frau Nusbaum's bowel operation, he began to feel a little queasy.

' "Now don't worry, Frau Nusbaum," that young doctor said. "I'm removing the attic not the playroom".' She smiled coyly at Solly whose eyes flicked dutifully up over his paper. 'Herr Nusbaum would have approved of that. Herr Nusbaum had such a sense of humour. He was quite noted for it. What a pity you never met him.'

Solly smiled weakly. Herr Nusbaum's image stood on the mantelpiece. If the eyes had ever twinkled they didn't now. Next to them the eyes of Gerhardt Schulz looked positively manic with humour.

'I wonder where he is ...' he sighed.

'I don't think there can be any doubt about that question, Herr Solokoff,' replied Frau Nusbaum sternly, 'Herr Nusbaum was a man of the highest principles, who attended church every Sunday.'

'I don't doubt it, Frau Nusbaum, but I was thinking of Gerhardt.'

'Ah, Herr Schulz,' sighed Frau Nusbaum a little tearfully. 'It is disturbing that we haven't heard from him for so long. Do you think he's all right? Maybe he's had an accident. Is it possible, do you suppose, that he might be dead?'

Solly considered this for a moment.

'No, I think he's still alive, but whether he's all right is another matter.'

'That's what I think,' replied Frau Nusbaum firmly. 'Of course I didn't tell that hussy anything of the sort.'

'Which hussy, Frau Nusbaum?' said Solly curiously.

'The one who rang the other day, I forgot to tell you. She said the last time she saw him was in a hotel in the South of France ten years ago and that they used to be quite close. Apparently they met in Berlin during the war. If you want my opinion, I think she was the one who walked out on him.'

'Fraulein Freyer ...' murmured Solly.

'You *knew* her?' Frau Nusbaum looked shocked.

'I never met her, but Gerhardt used to talk all the time about her.'

'That must have been the one. Anyway, I soon put her in her place. I told her that Herr Schulz was now living in England and that he was very wealthy and didn't need her sort, thank you very much. Easy come, easy go, that's all these young people know.'

'Did you really, Frau Nusbaum?' said Solly, looking a little alarmed.

'I most certainly did. "In that case," said she, "I will just have to find him".'

'Did she really?' said Solly in astonishment.

'Yes, she did, if you please. Well, I told her she was going to find that rather difficult. In fact, I said, it would be impossible – like looking for a needle in a haystack.'

Solly was inclined to agree.

'But do you know what she had the nerve to say then, Herr Solokoff?'

'No?' said Solly.

'She said – and I still don't understand it – she said, "Have you ever heard the story of the bumble bee?" And then she rang off, without another word. Whatever do you think she could have meant?'

Solly wasn't sure, but it seemed to ring bells in his mind. So did Frau Nusbaum's high tinkling laugh in hers as she suddenly remembered what day it was.

'I think I'll be popping out to buy some refreshments, Herr Solokoff. I quite forgot – today's Saturday.'

Solly smiled weakly again.

'Do you know, Herr Solokoff, my little playroom hasn't felt nearly so empty since you've come to stay.' Her plump little hand stretched out reaching for his.

Solly let her take it. He couldn't afford to offend Frau Nusbaum. Times had been difficult since he had returned to Berlin to find his flat completely ransacked, and Frau Nusbaum's kind offer had come at the right time. His room was very cheap and comfortable and there were little things on the side which he appreciated. One of the little things on the side that he did not appreciate was Frau Nusbaum's playroom which he felt obliged to enter every Saturday night. It was excessively roomy ...

36

It was a wet day in February 1962 and chill gusts of wind were throwing spray over the second-class passenger deck of the Hull-Cuxhaven ferry churning south towards Germany, through the North Sea. Children played on the deck, a few passengers sat in chairs or strolled unsteadily about. One man was standing alone by the rail staring out to sea.

Gerhardt Schulz gazed into the depths of the water, remembering the time in Linz when he had nearly plunged into the River Traun, but had thought better of it. Although the years had tempered his manic depression, he was as low as he had been since those far-off days. In contrast to his mood, however, was the dark suit which he was wearing, which was the epitome of expensive good taste. He looked to all intents and purposes a wealthy businessman, but his entire wealth had gone into the suit. He had bought it the day after he had left the hospital, two weeks after the canister had exploded into the English Channel and, between them, fire and water had swallowed up his hopes for happiness.

He had paid in cash. It had cost him sixty pounds and

it was only after he had left the tailor with the suit that he remembered that it was the only cash he had left apart from an odd note. He had immediately gone to a bar to have a drink to steady himself and later that evening had been arrested for passing a forged five-pound note. Since Schulz had no identification on him and preserved a stony silence through the arrest and trial he was assumed to be a common thief and was sentenced to two years at Maidstone. On his release he had been handed his only possessions, the suit and his shoes. Inside a pocket he had discovered a crumpled piece of paper which had somehow been overlooked. It was a ferry ticket.

He had walked into the nearest travel bureau and explained that, due to a serious illness, he had been unable to make use of the ticket two years earlier. The company rules did not allow for the ticket to be transferred, said the girl behind the desk, but then she had seen the look in his eyes. She had pursed her lips and handed him a new ticket without another word.

Now he shivered. In spite of the suit, clean shirt and tie, he had no top coat and the biting north-east wind blew down his shirt. He pulled up the jacket collar round his neck and walked sadly inside to the saloon on Deck B. He took a seat in the warmth and comparative comfort of the saloon hardly noticing the other passengers around him. Beside him on the floor and on the seat was a pile of somebody's beautiful pigskin luggage. His eyes travelled from this to a huge cigar which had been abandoned, virtually unsmoked, in the ashtray. He glanced around. No one seemed to be interested in him or the cigar. He picked it up, took a match from his pocket and lit the cigar. He gazed at it, admiring the look and the taste.

A woman in an expensive mink coat that swished and twirled and moved about in the way that only expensive mink coats do, was walking towards the saloon exit. Schulz gazed at her more in reverence than anything else. She represented everything he had schemed for, suffered for and that was now forever gone. Suddenly the woman stopped dead and stared at him.

He automatically pulled the cigar out of his mouth. She had probably recognized it as one belonging to her husband.

'You!' she said. Her voice sent a thrill of memory through him.

'You!' he gasped, staring at her, the cigar now poised in mid-air.

'I ... didn't expect to see you here!' she said, gazing at his expensive suit. 'I thought –'

'But you look ... wonderful!' he said in a trembling voice. 'In fact, you look ... incredible.'

She seemed to flush, as if ice cream had suddenly turned to hot lemon meringue. Over the years his memories had been replaced by romatic images and he had sometimes admitted to himself that if he were ever to meet her again, she could not possibly live up to his idealized notion. But she was even more beautiful than he could have dared to imagine. Obviously she had aged: she must now be in her early forties. Her face was a trifle harder than it had been, but there was a glow in her eyes as she looked at him that left him breathless. It was as though the centuries of elegance and breeding that he remembered in the comtesse had been transfused into her without spoiling her natural warmth and sexuality. He shivered again. She had been staring at him too, no doubt shocked by the change in him from the youthful optimist who had promised her the world.

'You're looking magnificent!' she said finally.

Schulz looked down at himself. She was obviously trying to be kind: couldn't she see?

'Oh, well,' he stammered. 'Me!' He shook his head. 'I don't know what to say.' He was too embarrassed to say anything. 'You've done well, that's obvious,' he mumbled.

'Yes,' she replied quickly, as though not wishing to rub it in. She smiled. 'How are things with you?'

Schulz waved his cigar, trying to appear breezy and carefree. 'Couldn't be better. I've just closed a very big business deal in England. Very big.'

She stared at him for a moment and then nodded. 'Yes, I ... heard about it.'

'You heard about it?' said Schulz in astonishment.

'Through the grapevine, you know.'

Schulz was amazed.

'I'm glad,' she went on hurriedly. 'I'm really glad. It's lovely that we've both done so well ... After all this time.' She paused. 'I haven't forgotten the last time we met,' she added quietly. She laughed again. 'I can't get over seeing you here ... Are you married?'

'Good heavens, no!' replied Schulz. 'I ... never found the right person. Anyway,' he added quickly, 'I'm having too good a time. And you? – I mean,' he corrected himself, 'how's Albert?'

'Oh, he's ... doing very well, 'she replied blushing. 'He's an industrialist now, you know. He's in Brazil at the moment. I'm travelling with one of our oldest friends, she's a countess. We've just been staying with some English people. They own an estate in Yorkshire. They own half of the East Riding practically. We're ... old friends of the family.' She sighed and gazed at him again. 'It is good to see you again, you know.'

Schulz didn't know: he was bewildered. She and money went together. Just as much as Schulz and money didn't. There were some who knew how to make it and some who knew how to keep it. He shook his head and smiled.

'Wonderful, wonderful,' he said.

She looked round a trifle nervously. 'Well, I must be going,' she said. 'We'll soon be in Cuxhaven. It's lovely to see you.' She gazed at him again.

'And you,' Schulz nodded, swallowing. 'Wonderful. You ... look amazing.' He would have liked to turn her into liquid and bottle her, just as she was, so that he could sip her slowly for the rest of his life.

Her eyes, her hair, her perfume – her perfume?

'Thanks,' she said. 'Well ... goodbye.' She didn't seem to want to go. She looked round nervously again.

'Goodbye Fraulein – Frau Schumacher ...'

'Oh, please call me Bertha,' she said quickly.

'All right, then, Bertha.'

They touched hands and she hurried off. He watched her go, sniffing again the invisible mist of perfume that trailed behind her. After a few moments he followed.

She hurried along the deck. She stopped, glanced round, then took off the mink coat and carried it on her arm further down the deck. She had meant to tell him but her pride hadn't let her. Just like the last time. There were tears in her eyes.

She paused by the aristocratic, haughty-looking woman in her sixties who was seated in a chair, holding a pekinese dog. Bertha started to drape the mink around the shoulders of the Comtesse Monime, who snatched it from her.

'It took you long enough,' snapped the comtesse. She had aged considerably in the twenty years since Schulz had last seen her. The brief stay in Hamburg had not rejuvenated her much either. Schulz, who was watching the little drama from his vantage point a little way along the deck, knew nothing of that, though. He stared in astonishment at the two women who had represented the sublime gifts of life to him for so long. One was a dried-up stick, the other a deceiver. At least – she'd deceived him. But then, thought Schulz, he'd just lied to her. They were, after all, kindred souls ...

'I'm sorry, Comtesse, I ran into an old friend,' said Bertha in a contrite voice.

'I don't pay you to stand gossiping with old friends,' barked the comtesse. 'And I forgot to tell you to bring my pills from the cabin. You'd better go back and get them.'

Bertha sighed and turned to go, but stopped. Schulz was still standing there. He had seen and heard all.

Hurt and humiliated, she tossed her head defiantly and set off for the pills. She tried to walk past him but he put a hand on her arm.

'Bertha!' he said urgently.

'Let me go!' she whispered, pulling his hand away.

'Bertha!'

'All right!' she said, glaring at him furiously. 'I didn't want you to know but now you do anyway. It's not my coat, it's hers! She's not an old friend of the family, she's my employer and she pays me very well!'

'Bertha!'

'I left him years ago. I left him after I saw you in Bandol. I couldn't bear it. All the lies and deception. I came here to find *you* but I couldn't and now it's too late. You know what I am now. I'm a parasite: a lady's companion! Well, I like it. I've got a room to myself and –'

'Would you buy me a drink?' said Schulz quietly.

' – every Sunday off and –' she went on and then stopped abruptly. 'Buy *you* a drink?' she gasped.

Schulz gave a quick shrug and smiled wrily.

'I'm broke – and I could do with a drink.'

'What made you follow me?' she asked, staring into his eyes.

'Two things,' said Schulz.

'You always did have a logical sort of mind,' she smiled.

'One: the perfume,' went on Schulz.

'What's wrong with my perfume?' said Bertha, looking hurt. 'It's very good perfume. It's French.'

'That's how I recognized it,' said Schulz. 'It was the same French perfume you always used to wear in Berlin, and it didn't go with the coat.'

'Why not?' she said. 'What's wrong with the coat? It's a very expensive mink. Very rare.'

Schulz smiled at her. 'Exactly,' he replied. 'That's how I recognized it. I last saw that mink coat at a chateau in Vitry in June 1940, minutes before it was bombed by the Luftwaffe.'

'The comtesse –' she gasped.

'I told you at the time but you wouldn't believe me,' he said sadly.

'So, she's the one you used to go on about,' said Bertha archly.

'No,' he replied. 'You were the one I used to go on about. It wasn't her, Bertha. All she had was breeding and ... something else ...'

'What else?'

Schulz looked down at his hands. 'She ... looked as though she knew how to hold on to money.'

'And you never could?'

'I never could.'

'Well, that's what I used to tell you, Gerhardt. I always thought you were a last-minute stumbler. But you certainly looked as though you'd changed. You looked so prosperous. And then Frau Nusbaum said –'

'Frau Nusbaum?'

'Yes, I told you, Gerhardt,' she said, in her turn looking down, for the first time. 'I've been looking for you for the past ... well, I think I've been looking for you since the last time I saw you.'

They stared at each other.

'And I've been looking for a way to get you ever since I met you!' he said passionately.

'Really, Gerhardt!'

'It's true! That's why I suggested ... Anyway, what did she say?'

'Frau Nusbaum? She said you were very rich and living in England and –'

'She said that?' How on earth had Frau Nusbaum formed that conclusion?

'Well, you look rich.'

'I told you, it was just the cigar. But you look like a million.'

'It was just the mink coat.'

Schulz shook his head. 'A mink coat – a cigar ...' he said wonderingly. 'It's amazing the confidence they inspire in people.' He smiled at her. 'We *were* born out of the same gutter, Fraulein Freyer, you were right. We'd make a great team.'

She looked at him dubiously. 'For what?'

'Oh, I'd think of something,' he replied breezily. 'My head's teeming with ideas. You and I could tickle all sorts of trout. We just have to find the right tickle and the right trout. What do you think?'

Bertha stared seriously at Schulz for a moment and then put down her drink. 'I'll tell you what I think, Gerhardt. Why don't you stop playing games, I'm not the person you thought I was and you're certainly not the person I thought you were. Let's forget it.'

Schulz heard the words like a death sentence.

'The people we were,' went on Bertha. 'The games. The money. The plans. Whatever you've got in your mind. You always were a dreamer, Gerhardt, and it's time for you to wake up.'

He gazed at her with a heavy heart.

'Now why don't you listen to one of my fantasies for a change,' she went on. Schulz remembered a time when he did nothing else but that, in a hot boiler-room and through a pair of cumbersome headphones. 'I've saved enough money to open a little boutique or maybe a restaurant in Paris. Now, a man helping about the place would be welcome and if that's what you have in mind I'd be very agreeable.'

He could hardly believe his ears. 'But ... that's exactly what *I* had in mind, Bertha. I've been dreaming ever since the war of a little place in Paris with you.' He paused and looked at her again to check that he had got it right. 'Was ... was that a proposal?'

'Yes,' said Bertha, smiling.

'I accept – unconditionally,' he stammered.

Now she was taken aback in her turn. 'You mean – you'd marry me? After the Salon Kitty and ... Neuheim and Albert and ...'

He regarded her seriously, and then smiled. 'That was war,' he said. 'This is different.'

She burst into tears. 'I left him because of you. I wanted to explain to you at Bandol but I couldn't ... Then, you *were* looking for me?'

'I told you I was but I didn't have anything to offer you.'

'Oh Gerhardt, you *fool*,' sighed Bertha. 'I wasn't able to tell you then, but I've developed this psychological block. Ever since the war. I can't do it with anyone who's rich. That's why I wanted to marry you in a way. You see, I didn't believe Frau Nusbaum.'

'Why not?'

She hesitated. 'I'm not sure – she sounded too ... confident. I've never trusted people who are too confident. In any case, a woman has to hedge her bets.'

They gazed at each other for a moment and then burst out laughing. Suddenly she stopped. 'Haven't we got this the wrong way round? I mean, shouldn't *you* have asked me to marry you.'

'But I did, Bertha, about twenty years ago. You just weren't listening. Now, why don't you go and tell the comtesse the good news?'

She wiped her eyes again. 'I'd better get her pills first. She's going to need them when she knows.' She paused. 'Are you really broke?'

Schulz shrugged apologetically.

'I hate to see a man without money,' she said. 'It's just that I can't love a man *with* money.' She opened her bag and fumbled inside. 'Here – *she* gave it to me. The comtesse. You can have it.' She pressed a note into Schulz's hand and walked off. He opened his hand and unfolded the note, and then stared down at it. It was an English five-pound note. One of the new blue ones. A genuine one. He felt it between his fingers. There was a crispness to it that was somehow over-crisp, as though a shirt had been over-starched, very fractionally....

Postscript

In the notes that Peter Eton wrote about his interview with John Otto Rasch, the model for the character of Schulz, he wrote the following:

'Rasch wanted no money for the information he had given me in Bandol apart from a small loan which he promised to repay, and though I didn't believe him, I let him talk because he told such a colourful story with such a wealth of detail that I hoped some of it might indeed be true. On my return to England, as Operation Bernhard was still classified, I was unable to check it for some time. Later, in 1953, when I was living near Romney Marsh in Kent, I met little John again. He had been in the district for a few days, he said, and was shortly leaving for Geneva. I asked him jokingly if he had returned to look for the canister, which, according to his description, was hidden only a few miles away. He ignored my sarcasm and repaid me the small loan I had made to him in France. Perhaps the two fivers he'd given me were Bernhards, I suggested. He was not amused.

'A week later I spent my £10 at a local restaurant. The notes were counterfeit.

'Eventually the threatened prosecution was withdrawn, I compensated the restaurant and persuaded the authorities to return the Bernhard fivers – as souvenirs.'

Peter Eton never saw Rasch again, though it is faintly possible that he is still alive. Eton, however, had his own conjecture about this.

'The day after Rasch repaid his debt,' Eton wrote, 'five gentlemen who attempted to hold up the van carrying the weekly pay packets to men building the Dungeness power station were arrested by the police at Swamp Crossing, beside a gravel pit. Three months later the level-crossing gate-keeper at Swamp Crossing was arrested after trying

375

to pass eight counterfeit five-pound notes which he claimed he found floating in the gravel pit. And in 1965 the remains of a human skeleton were found in the gravel pit.'

This is all documented and, without doubt, true. Based on this evidence Eton then conjectured that Rasch had collected the canister, and set off in his hired car to wait at the rendezvous in Rye for the launch.

'Driving down the side road,' Eton conjectured, 'he came up unexpectedly behind a group of fierce looking gentlemen with tommy guns. He was not to know that they were even more surprised than he was. He thought the bandits were waiting for him and determined, one last time, not to be robbed of his fortune. He jumped out of his car and flung the canister out of harm's way into a nearby gravel pit, a miniature Toplitzsee, caught his hand in the ropes binding it and was, himself, catapulted into the lake, bound to the money for which he had searched for so long. At midnight there was an ominous rumble from the bottom of the gravel pit. The waters seethed and then grew calm. Nearly thirteen years later the destructive device had worked. Neither man nor money remained.'

Though Eton's account is entirely possible I tend to doubt it for a simple reason. The pathologist who investigated the remains of the skeleton was Francis Camps, who was not exactly an amateur. He established that they belonged to a man aged 21 to 25. If John Otto Rasch had in fact fallen into the gravel pit in 1953 it would therefore imply that he had been inducted into the SS in 1939 at the age of eleven as an intelligence worker. Alfred Naujocks could not possibly have executed such a monumental error of judgement.

It is on the other hand remotely possible that the canister remains in its original burial spot, somewhere in Romney Marsh, John Rasch having intended to use it as a savings bank to which, some day, he might and still may return . . .

M.R.N.

Author's Note

Operation Bernhard is described in *The Guinness Book of Records* as the greatest counterfeiting operation of all time and Alfred Helmuth Naujocks, its initiator, as the greatest forger in history. Set up in Nazi Germany in 1939 to print hundreds of millions of pounds worth of counterfeit British banknotes to be dropped over England in order to ruin the country's economy and win the war for Germany, it failed owing to a series of incredible bungles by the SS. And at the bottom of Toplitzsee, the deepest and most sinister lake in Austria, lies to this day the Operation's unused output of half a billion pounds in perfectly forged £5 notes – now alas no longer legal tender.

In the early 1950s Peter Eton, the late radio, television and film producer, was tipped off by a journalist friend, Alex Werth, to research the true story of another major German debacle, Operation Cicero. He was given the address of a Herr John Otto Rasch who, Eton had been told, had been closely involved with the enterprise. Rasch, who spoke perfect English, told him about Cicero, the German undertaking in which Elyesa Bazna, the British Ambassador's valet in Ankara, Turkey, was bribed by the Nazis to steal the Allied plans of the Second Front from the Embassy safe. They paid Cicero, the agent, £300,000 in British fivers, then failed to act on the information, which they suspected was false.

'We now know that the plans were genuine,' said Rasch. 'It was the notes that were counterfeit. I worked for the SS outfit, Operation Bernhard, that produced them – that's a far more interesting story.'

Rasch went on to tell what he claimed was the true story of Bernhard. 'Although,' Eton said, 'I was fascinated by his ability to tell a tale, I disbelieved most of it until, on checking the facts later, I found many of them to be true.'

What was particularly extraordinary about Rasch's story was his claim that it was he, Rasch, who had initiated the Operation and provided most of the ideas at every single stage of its planning. But time after time, he claimed, Naujocks, and later Bernhard Kruger who replaced Naujocks when the latter fell out with Heydrich, took the credit for masterminding the forgery, while Rasch became the resident fall-guy whenever the SS wished to test the efficiency of the plan.

'In his reminiscences,' said Eton, 'John Otto Rasch revealed himself as a brash individual. His squabbles with the SS hierarchy, his ability to snatch defeat from the jaws of victory, his chronic incompetence and amazingly consistent record of failure, all combined to make him an unsympathetic character. During his talks with me, Rasch showed himself to be so narrow-minded and egotistical that, without realizing it, he reduced the war into a series of mini-combats between his own greed and incompetence and the ineptitude, rapacity and short-sightedness of his superiors. It was quite startling how he managed to turn stunningly dramatic situations into almost nothing.'

Nevertheless, the facts of Rasch's story combined two vital ingredients towards creating genuine farce: fundamental absurdity and remorseless logic. The fact that the farce was true and that it concerned the activities of one of the most loathsome and inhuman organizations ever created – Heinrich Himmler's SS – made it difficult for many years after the war for Eton to persuade others that there was a potential for human comedy to be extracted from the authentic elements of Nazi Germany. The only kind of comedy that seemed permissible involved crude caricaturing of arguably demonic figures – Hitler, Himmler, Goebbels – in order to defuse the fear that had been inherent in the threat of a Nazi apocalypse. The problem was compounded by the fact that Peter Eton was primarily a producer and was particularly keen to produce a film or television series based on the life of Rasch.

In the early seventies, however, he did manage to interest Jack Pulman in the idea. Pulman became as intrigued as Eton in the character of Rasch, and eventually wrote a television screenplay which is the basis for this novel. Although Gerhardt Schulz, the fictional Rasch, remains the self-professed instigator of the plan that led to Operation Bernhard, and the ready-made fall guy of the SS, he thereafter becomes the irrepressible, thwarted and much-put upon hero, determined to get what he regards as his just deserts and, in surges of well-planned enthusiastic activity, always nearly succeeding.

In the process of fictionalizing the story many of the facts have inevitably been altered. Of course, Alfred Neuheim is based on Alfred Naujocks, the man who triggered off the Second World War in Poland; kidnapped the two British agents at Venlo on the Dutch border (which Rasch again claimed he himself was actually responsible for at the vital moment – Rasch's own account in a transcript of his interview with Eton is quite extraordinarily bizarre); supervised the monitoring of the Salon Kitty brothel under Heydrich; and took charge of Operation Andreas, the pilot scheme which later became Bernhard. And although Bernhard was actually named after Bernhard Kruger (who becomes the shadowy, sinister Kube) who replaced Naujocks, Neuheim – like Schulz – is too irrepressible to be got rid of so easily.

Before his death in July 1979 Jack Pulman had planned to write the novel himself. It was not an easy thing for him to do: while he had emphasized the purer comedy elements in the screenplay, he was desperately concerned that the novel should bring out the hidden rumblings and peculiar echoes of the story, the background in twentieth-century German history that could create such an absurdity, however frightening and destructive as it was at the time, as the Nazi Party, as well as the inherent logic, however flawed, in the character of Schulz himself, that would somehow reflect all this madness. He did complete the drafts of the first few chapters, and of course he left a screenplay brimming with brilliant, biting and very funny dialogue. I have felt it necessary at times to elaborate the story, as both Pulman and Eton were anxious should be done, since the the frenetic odyssey of Gerhardt Schulz could not be contained by the inevitable limitatons of screen drama.

In late December 1979, a few weeks before I had planned to show Peter Eton the manuscript of the novel, he died tragically after a fall at his home in Ashford. It is extremely sad that neither man has been able to see either the novel or its publication and I hope that *Private Schulz* will be received as a tribute to them both – Pulman as a brilliant writer, playwright and television adaptor, as well as a promising novelist, and Eton as a fertile and creative man of ideas. And I hope that a little of each of these qualities has been immortalized in their story. I would also like to acknowledge the help of Jack Pulman's wife, Barbara Young, in what has been a very distressing period of her life.

In a draft introduction Jack Pulman put the following words into the mouth of a fictional journalist who had agreed to tell Schulz's story. I believe they also reflect Pulman's own view of his creation.

'I have decided to tell Schulz's story. I don't like breaking a promise and I have thought long and hard about it. There seem to be two sound reasons why I should do so. First, the story really is extraordinary as those who know it only in outline will readily testify. As he told it to me it was, in my opinion, both exciting and outrageously macabre. The man was, in some ways, a natural philosopher, sensitive to the madness of his times in a way that I know of in no other person. And this brings me to the second strong reason for telling his story. It seems to me the only story I had heard that in a way explained the madness into which Europe plunged between 1920 and 1945. It is certainly true that more people took leave of their senses in Germany than elsewhere but it cannot be denied that the madness was general. Somehow Schulz's story captured that for me better than any story I had heard.

He was a Schweik figure, and just as all the idiocies of the old Austrian régime were suddenly revealed as if through a prism by that insanely sane old man, so Schulz's view of the world he lived in put it all in a sudden perspective that was quite new to me, though I had been immersed in the period myself. I believe it will be new to many others. I think they will look at this period in a different way as a result of Schulz's story. In his own way he was a poet capable of painting a familiar story in a totally different line, capable of making the scales fall from our eyes. That is why I believe his story should be told. And, as I've said, because it is extraordinary.'

Martin Noble, London, 1980

GESTAPO
by Edward Crankshaw

The mastery of the Gestapo extended from the Atlantic to the Volga, the North Cape to the Mediterranean, and it held Europe in an iron grip.

The Gestapo, under its fanatical leader, Himmler, was moulded into a highly efficient, ruthless, professional corps whose task was to penetrate every aspect of private and public life. Its aim was to seek out resistance to the Nazi regime.

The power of the Gestapo lay in its inhumanity to its victims, a cruelty unparalleled in the history of modern Europe.

NEW ENGLISH LIBRARY

NEL BESTSELLERS

T045 528	THE STAND	*Stephen King*	£1.75
T046 133	HOW GREEN WAS MY VALLEY	*Richard Llewellyn*	£1.00
T039 560	I BOUGHT A MOUNTAIN	*Thomas Firbank*	95p
T033 988	IN THE TEETH OF THE EVIDENCE	*Dorothy L. Sayers*	90p
T038 149	THE CARPETBAGGERS	*Harold Robbins*	£1.50
T041 719	HOW TO LIVE WITH A NEUROTIC DOG	*Stephen Baker*	75p
T040 925	THE PRIZE	*Irving Wallace*	£1.65
T034 755	THE CITADEL	*A. J. Cronin*	£1.10
T042 189	STRANGER IN A STRANGE LAND	*Robert Heinlein*	£1.25
T037 053	79 PARK AVENUE	*Harold Robbins*	£1.25
T042 308	DUNE	*Frank Herbert*	£1.50
T045 137	THE MOON IS A HARSH MISTRESS	*Robert Heinlein*	£1.25
T040 933	THE SEVEN MINUTES	*Irving Wallace*	£1.50
T038 130	THE INHERITORS	*Harold Robbins*	£1.25
T035 689	RICH MAN, POOR MAN	*Irwin Shaw*	£1.50
T043 991	EDGE 34: A RIDE IN THE SUN	*George G. Gilman*	75p
T037 541	DEVIL'S GUARD	*Robert Elford*	£1.25
T042 774	THE RATS	*James Herbert*	80p
T042 340	CARRIE	*Stephen King*	80p
T042 782	THE FOG	*James Herbert*	90p
T033 740	THE MIXED BLESSING	*Helen Van Slyke*	£1.25
T038 629	THIN AIR	*Simpson & Burger*	95p
T038 602	THE APOCALYPSE	*Jeffrey Konvitz*	95p
T046 850	WEB OF EVERYWHERE	*John Brunner*	85p

NEL P.O. BOX 11, FALMOUTH TR10 9EN, CORNWALL

Postage charge:

U.K. Customers. Please allow 30p for the first book plus 15p per copy for each additional book ordered to a maximum charge of £1.29 to cover the cost of postage and packing, in addition to cover price.

B.F.P.O. & Eire. Please allow 30p for the first book plus 15p per copy for the next 8 books, thereafter 6p per book, in addition to cover price.

Overseas Customers. Please allow 50p for the first book plus 15p per copy for each additional book, in addition to cover price.

Please send cheque or postal order (no currency).

Name..

Address ....

....

Title ....

While every effort is made to keep prices steady, it is sometimes necessary to increase prices at short notice. New English Library reserve the right to show on covers and charge new retail prices which may differ from those advertised in the text or elsewhere. (3)